TRIPOLI'S TARGET

ETHAN JONES

This book is a work of fiction. Names, characters, businesses, organizations, places, events, and incidents either are the product of the author's imagination or are used fictitiously. Any resemblance to actual persons, living or dead, events, or locales is entirely coincidental.

Cover design: Kim Killion

First edition: December 2012

ISBN: 1481198688

ISBN-13: 978-1481198684

PRAISE FOR TRIPOLI'S TARGET

"Tripoli's Target is a great read, but I kind of lost track of who was double-crossing who. Ethan makes it all come out straight in the end. And there are race cars . . ." -- Larry Bond, author of New York Times bestselling thrillers *Vortex*, *Cauldron*, and *The Enemy Within*, and co-author of *Red Storm Rising* with Tom Clancy.

"There's a lot to like in Tripoli's Target. It starts with a bang with action in Tripoli . . . The descriptions of the locale are good and give a nice feel to the action." -- Andrew Kaplan, author of the bestselling Scorpion spy thriller series.

"Taut, exciting and bang on the genre . . . very well done indeed." -- Thomas Mogford, author of *Shadow of the Rock*.

ALSO BY ETHAN JONES

Arctic Wargame (Justin Hall # 1)

Fog of War (Justin Hall # 3)

Double Agents (Justin Hall # 4) – coming out in January 2014

Burying the Truth

Carved in Memory: A Justin Hall Story

The Last Confession

To the brave women and men defending our country,
whose names we will never know

This work would have not been possible without the great support of my wife and son. I would like to thank Ty Hutchinson, Kenneth Teicher, Claude Dancourt, J.E. Seymour, Kevan O'Meara and April Plummer for their helpful suggestions.

"An army of sheep led by a lion would defeat
an army of lions led by a sheep."

"It is better to die in revenge than to live on in shame."

Arab proverbs

PROLOGUE

Tripoli, Libya
May 13, 6:15 p.m. local time

Satam, the driver of the suicide truck bomb, turned onto Ar Rashid Street, merging with the warm evening traffic. He rubbed his sweaty palms against his short khaki pants, his gaze glued to the silver BMW Suburban in front of him. He heaved a wheezing sigh and tapped on the brake pedal. A red traffic light halted the five-vehicle convoy.

A stream of cars rushed through the intersection leading to the business district of downtown Tripoli. Tall skyscrapers rose over most of the city's old colonial-style buildings. The green and gold banner of Jacobs Properties—one of the major British real estate developers in Libya—beamed from atop the glass-and-steel façade of the newly finished Continental Hotel. The same logo had been painted hastily on the left side of the BMW packed with Semtex explosives. Walid, its driver and a Jacobs subcontractor, had exchanged his blue coveralls for a business suit and the promise of martyrdom.

A glance at the dashboard clock told Satam the synchronized explosion would take place in ten minutes. The thought of the coming carnage drained the last drop of courage from his heart. He rolled down the window, but the humid air—blended with the aroma of fried falafel, onions, and lamb donairs from a nearby street vendor—made him nauseated. He gasped for air, sticking his head out of the window. He coughed and struggled to catch his breath. Drivers from other vehicles shot him curious glares. Behind the truck, the driver of an old Mercedes honked his horn twice. Satam swallowed hard and wiped the sweat off his narrow forehead. He waved at his audience to show them he was doing all right.

"Satam, what's the matter, brother?" the radio set on the dashboard crackled. He recognized Walid's gruff voice.

Satam looked at the BMW. His watery eyes met the reflection of the driver's face in the rearview mirror of the Suburban. The driver's usual wicked smirk stretched his lips, revealing his large buckteeth. Walid waved his hands wildly. Satam could not see behind Walid's black aviator shades but assumed his eyes were ablaze with rage.

"Nothing's wrong. Just needed some air," Satam replied over the radio.

He rolled up the window before Walid could scold him with another howl.

"Great. Now that you've closed the window, open your eyes!" Walid barked. "You're not a coward like the infidels, are you?"

Satam shook his head.

A third voice came on air before he could say anything.

"Cousin, I pledged my honor so you could be a part of this mission. Don't you back down now!" Satam's cousin said. He was driving the Toyota at the head of the convoy.

Satam sighed and paused for a couple of seconds. "I'm not backing down. You can trust me. I will not disappoint you or the brotherhood."

"That's my flesh and blood who is soon to be a martyr," said the cousin in a relaxed tone. "Our families will be proud of us, and our reward will be glorious."

"It's easy for you to say, since tonight you'll be welcomed to paradise," Satam said.

He noticed the traffic lights changing and stepped cautiously on the gas pedal. The truck jerked forward a few inches before the ride turned smooth again.

"Won't take long before you join us there," Walid said.

"Yes, but not before being dragged through the secret police hellish cells . . ." Satam's voice trailed off.

"Allah will give you strength, cousin, and soon he'll take you home."

"He will, brother, he will." Walid revved the BMW's twelve-cylinder engine. "For sure, I'm going to miss this ride."

"There will be plenty of rides up there to keep you and everyone else busy," the cousin said with a quiet laugh. "Now may Allah be with us all. Over and out."

Walid nodded and turned left toward the Continental Hotel.

Satam's destination, the Gold Market, was to the right. He steered in that direction. He zigzagged through a few crooked streets and slowed down when reaching the Old City. The blacktop disappeared, and the uneven gravel crackled under the tires. Old cars, horse carts, and pedestrians came into view, along with whitewashed stores selling gold and jewelry. The streets narrowed into barely a single lane.

Satam rolled down the window for sideways glances to avoid brushing against planters, chairs, and vendors selling all kinds of junk. A stomach-churning stench from days old fish, fried grease, and sweat overwhelmed him. Satam felt his head grow heavy and hit the brakes.

Street vendors lost no time peddling their wares. A crowd of young boys swarmed his truck. He yelled and shoved away a few of the bravest salesmen waving handfuls of souvenirs in his face. He kept pushing them away the hagglers, when suddenly a pointed metal object touched his forearm. Startled, Satam withdrew his arm inside the cabin. He glanced at one of the boys holding a string of scimitar replicas, the sword tribesmen in North Africa carried in ancient times. The curved blade was dull and had a rounded point to prevent accidental stabs. Still, the swift jab at his forearm summoned awful visions of the future.

He saw himself hanging upside down in a dark, grim dungeon, tied to the ceiling beams, while three secret police agents "interrogated" him. They would use various methods to "jog" his memory and break his psyche. Sleep deprivation and intimidation by police dogs were just the welcome package. Other techniques included breaking fingers, simulated suffocation with plastic wraps, and water boarding. *I will tell them everything right away before they even touch me.* He struggled to wipe the vivid images from his mind.

Satam slammed on the truck's horn to clear a path through the crowd. The blaring horn startled him more than the boys and the occasional onlookers. He glanced at the dashboard, realizing he had less than two minutes to reach the busy marketplace square five blocks away. *It will be impossible to make it on time.*

He blasted the horn again and stepped on the gas. The truck moved slowly, and Satam wrestled to make a left turn. The alley grew wider. The truck sped up, its wheels dipping and climbing in and out of the potholes. He rushed straight ahead, inches away from oncoming taxis, their honks protesting his unsafe speed. A few sidewalk vendors dove out of the way, their overflowing baskets of bananas and grapes spilling all over the place. Tires screeched as he turned right, jumping the curb and narrowly missing a large bronze planter outside a soap store.

The Mediterranean Sea was now visible to his right, through palm trees, coffee shops, and fruit vendor stands. Satam stared ahead at the square, one of the busiest markets in the Old City. The market rumbled with vendors squabbling over a few dinars with tight-fisted tourists. *I made it. Yes, I made it.* He turned his gaze to the left, toward Tripoli's skyline, and slowed down before parking the truck in front of a small restaurant. He took a deep breath and dabbed at his forehead with the back of his hand, wiping off a sea of sweat.

The dashboard radio crackled and he picked up the receiver.

"Allahu Akbar! Allahu Akbar!" The loud voice echoed over the radio.

Satam recognized Walid's shouts.

A second later, a loud explosion rocked the entire square. Satam's gaze spun toward the business district, where a cloud of grayish smoke billowed around the Continental Hotel. Chaos erupted among street vendors who scattered and forgot about their produce and the evening's clients. Patrons of coffee shops rushed to the streets, staring in disbelief at the sight. Cries of hysteria overtook the growing crowd. Elderly women beat their heads and chests with clenched fists. Young men pointed and shouted, their bodies restless. The sharp siren of an ambulance sliced through the cacophony of terror.

With a quick movement of his wrist, Satam consulted his watch. Just as the digits registered 6:31, another explosion shocked the crowd. This time, the bomb hit closer, much closer, a few blocks away. From inside his parked truck, Satam looked at the bright yellow glow of the blast. High flames leapt at a ten-story office building. A thick cloud of black smoke began to swallow up the tower. The crowd broke into smaller groups. People scurried in all directions. Some ran back to their shops and apartments. Others simply circled the area, perhaps unsure of the safe way out.

Satam knew his time had come. He revved the engine and stomped on the gas pedal. The truck arrowed toward the vendors' tables. The market was mostly empty, and the truck crashed into crates of fish, baskets of grapes, and barrels of olive oil. Produce scattered everywhere as the truck rampaged through plastic tables and chairs.

A police truck zipped toward him. Satam steered around, not to escape, but to meet the approaching vehicle. The two policemen in the truck ignored Satam. They were going to drive past him, but Satam swerved hard. The right fender of his truck smashed into the police truck. The police truck jerked to the other side. The driver pulled over and stopped less than thirty feet away. The other policeman rolled down the window. Satam stared at the muzzle of an AK-47 assault rifle.

"Don't shoot. Don't shoot," Satam shouted and opened his door.

A quick burst of bullets sent him ducking for cover in the front seat. A shower of glass shreds fell over his head.

They're going to kill me before I even have a chance to open my mouth. Or one of the bullets will blow up the truck. I can't let that happen.

He looked at the back of the truck. Thirty pounds of Semtex explosives wired into a homemade bomb were stored inside the seat compartments. He noticed the cellphone on the floor mat by his left hand. He reached for the phone. All it would take for him to set off the explosives—and pulverize himself and the policemen—was to tap three preset numbers. His fingers hovered over the phone, but he remembered his family's honor and the reward waiting for him in paradise. He dropped the phone to the floor, buried his head in the seat, and locked his fingers behind his head.

A minute or so passed before the shooting stopped, but the screaming continued. He heard the distinct thuds of combat boots marching up the street. The police were approaching his truck. He looked up slowly as a policeman pulled open the driver's door of his truck and aimed an AK-47 at his head

"Don't move!" the policeman ordered him.

Satam nodded.

Without a word, the policeman juggled the rifle in his hands and slammed its buttstock hard against Satam's head.

CHAPTER 1

Cairo, Egypt
May 13, 6:25 p.m. local time

Justin Hall did not want to fire his gun. Too many witnesses crowded the street.

I will kill those two men following me if I have to. Then, I'll clean up the mess.

His hand rested over the Browning 9mm riding inside the waistband holster at his thigh. He peered again at the reflections in the store window glass. He pretended to admire a black suit. In fact, he was checking every move of two young men behind him. Before he continued to his meeting, he wanted to make sure the pair, which had followed him for the last three blocks, were random strangers, rather than plainclothes police officers doing a poor surveillance job. Or worse. Assassins.

The two men did not stop by the store. They kept walking and, as they rounded the street corner, Justin followed them. He tailed the men for a couple of minutes. They wandered along the north side of Nile City Towers Mall, stopping at times for quick window-shopping but never looking over their shoulders. Still, he found their actions suspicious. He used the same counter-surveillance tactic. Justin wondered if a second backup team had replaced the first, after he had made the two men. *If this is mukhabarat, there has to be more than one.*

The sun had begun to set, its last golden rays bouncing off the reflective glass of nearby tall skyscrapers. A thin crowd was building up around the shopping district in downtown Cairo. Justin glanced around him on all sides. He tried to spot anyone who looked as if they belonged to a surveillance team. He scouted the area for operatives in dull or baggy clothing, wearing boring sunglasses, sporting earpieces, or simply standing out in the crowd. He listened for the slowing of footsteps, the shuffling of clothes, and any metallic click. No one fit the profile.

The men turned another corner and Justin continued to follow them. Twilight shadows and the flow of pedestrians out for the evening should have made it easier for him to track his prey, but the dry, sizzling air, scorched by a punishing sun for twelve hours, countered all his advantages. Drops of sweat formed on his broad forehead. The bulletproof vest underneath his loose-fitting polo shirt felt twice as heavy as when he had put it on earlier in the morning.

His BlackBerry chirped from his pocket, the sound breaking his concentration. Without slowing down, he pulled it out and glanced at the screen.

"Where are you?" the short e-mail asked.

It was from Carrie O'Connor, his partner. They worked for the Canadian Intelligence Service, and they should have checked in at the Fairmont Nile City Hotel an hour ago. They were scheduled to meet with Sheikh Yusuf Ayman, one of the masterminds of the terrorist organization Islamic Fighting Alliance, but the sheikh had scrapped the meeting at a moment's notice. Carrie was still surveilling the Fairmont, while Justin was returning from following two of the sheikh's associates to a previously unknown safe house.

I'll be there soon. He pocketed the BlackBerry. *A few more minutes.*

He followed the two men until they entered the Desert Rose, a hip bar favored by the young and rich. Justin kept a close eye on the main door, throwing casual glances at their table by the window. At the same time, he searched the streets for the elusive second surveillance team.

Ten minutes later, after the two men had finished their first drinks, Justin concluded they were not secret police, and he was not being watched by them or anyone else. But this was Cairo, and one could never be too careful. In a country still ruled by the General Intelligence Service, known simply as *mukhabarat*, one wrong turn could be the last, even for professionals like him. Controlled paranoia had saved his life more than once in the most dangerous back alleys of North Africa.

Justin headed toward the Castle, a small coffee shop where Carrie was waiting for him. The Castle was to the left of the Fairmont, with an unobstructed view of the hotel's VIP entrance. Rahim, the owner of the joint, was on the CIS Cairo Station payroll. The coffee shop provided a casual yet safe place for CIS agents to run covert operations.

Before pushing open the carved wood door of the Castle, Justin stopped and glanced at the alley in front of the coffee shop. He noticed a white sedan, an old model Ford, parked halfway between the entrance to a three-story apartment building across the alley and a grocery store. Justin squinted and noticed the silhouette of a small woman wearing a hijab crouched in the front passenger's seat. A tall man was talking to the shopkeeper by the fruit and vegetable stand in front of the grocery store. *Is that her husband? Her brother?* Justin scanned the windows of the apartments but noticed nothing suspicious. He threw another sweeping look at the other side of the street and stepped inside the coffee shop.

A thin cloud of tobacco smoke billowing from a handful of patrons engulfed him. Justin sneaked in, skirting around the tables and avoiding eye contact with anyone. He stood near the counter until Rahim, who was filling a couple of glasses with dark beer, took notice of his presence.

"Where have you been?" Rahim asked in a low voice. "You're late."

"Making sure I wasn't followed," Justin replied. "Is somebody waiting for a ride?" He gestured with his thumb back toward the door.

"I don't understand."

"There's an old Ford parked outside."

"That would be Leilah," Rahim said, his pot-like head bobbing with every word. "She's waiting for her husband, Farouk."

A few servings of *kofta,* minced lamb sprinkled with spices, sizzled on the grill behind Rahim.

"Did you send Nebibi for a closer look?" Justin asked.

"No. Why?"

A surveillance camera was installed above the archway entrance to the Castle, and it hidden inside one of the lighting sconces. It transmitted clear images to Rahim's computer screen, which doubled as a cash register. With a few clicks, he could keep a constant eye on what happened on the street. Justin preferred to be on the scene, the difference between being an observer and actually understanding an evolving situation.

Justin pointed to his left, toward the kitchen separated from the bar by a reddish curtain. "Have him check things out."

Rahim nodded and disappeared inside the kitchen.

The CIS trusted Nebibi, the cook, like they trusted his uncle Rahim. Justin, on the other hand, did not trust many people. He knew Rahim had great financial incentives to provide actionable intelligence to them, as the CIS paid him handsomely for his services. But he worried about another buyer tempting Rahim. The man was willing to trade in nearly all secrets for the right price. The Egyptian was not bound by the same code of honor streaming through the veins of CIS agents. Justin realized CIS had to rely on local sources to navigate the labyrinths of Cairo's streets and Egypt's foreign policies. Still, he kept his reliance on Rahim to the bare minimum.

Rahim returned.

"A man was talking to some guy from the grocery store when I walked in," Justin said.

"Yeah, that man is Farouk. He's a good friend of the store owner.

Nebibi is going out the back. Are you hungry?"

"No, not really. Still two hours until supper."

"Yes, for Egyptians."

"I am half-Egyptian."

"You're half everything." Rahim turned around to attend to his grill.

Justin grinned, rubbing his dimpled chin. His Mediterranean complexion—dark olive skin, raven wavy hair, big black eyes, and a large thick nose, inherited from his Italian mother—allowed him to blend in naturally among the countless nationalities living in the bustling city of eighteen million. Youthful stamina, a natural talent for languages, and an overdose of stubbornness had allowed him to master spoken Arabic like a native Egyptian.

"Can I bring you some *mezze* at least?" Rahim asked, referring to appetizers.

"Sure."

"Coffee?"

"Definitely."

Rahim turned around and poured coffee from a long-handled pot into a porcelain cup. Justin savored the strong aroma of the thick, concentrated drink and clenched the cup in his left hand. He climbed the concrete stairs, which took him to the second floor. A narrow hall led to two safe rooms, once part of Rahim's family apartment. Now they were reserved for the private use of CIS operatives. Justin knocked twice on the white door of the first room.

"Come in," a woman's soft voice called from inside.

"Hi," Justin greeted Carrie.

She sat cross-legged on a chair by one of the windows. A pair of powerful binoculars and two manila folders lay spread over a plastic table, next to a CIS-issued Browning 9mm and a tea mug. Poster-sized photographs of the Great Pyramid of Giza and the Sphinx covered the beige walls.

"Hey, you finally made it." Carrie tossed her reading glasses over one of the open folders. She tilted her head back, stretching her neck muscles. Her auburn shoulder-length hair, which she usually kept in a semi-ponytail, flowed down her slender neck. "What took you so long?"

"Trying to shake what I thought was a tail. A couple of guys who turned out to be nobody."

"Well, double-checking never hurt anyone."

"Sorry I'm late."

"Don't worry about it. Still hot out there, eh?" She pointed to the soggy shirt stuck to his chest. A trickle of sweat had made its way down his neck.

"Hell on Earth. Ninety degrees in the shade."

He placed his coffee cup on the table and stumbled onto an empty chair across from her. He took a deep breath, enjoying the cool breeze flowing down from the air conditioner mounted on the wall.

"Did you see a white Ford downstairs?" Justin asked.

"No. Nothing there when I came in."

"Rahim hadn't checked it out, but he's sending Nebibi now."

"OK, let's hope it's nothing."

Justin dabbed his face with a Kleenex. "Where did Team One lose Sheikh Ayman?"

"We didn't *lose* him. Johnson ordered us *not* to make contact, just track his movements, which we did. Sheikh Ayman arrived at Terminal 3 of Cairo International. Then he boarded a Sudan Airways flight bound for Khartoum."

Claire Johnson was the CIS Director General of Intelligence, the North Africa Division and their boss. Johnson's reputation within the CIS was that of a meticulously thorough individual. Terrified of committing a career-ending blunder, Johnson displayed a certain amount of sluggishness that crippled field agents. They joked that she was more efficient at witch hunting than terrorist hunting, as scapegoating often resulted from botched operations in her division.

Justin chewed on Carrie's words. The sheikh's departure aboard a regular commercial flight meant he was not hiding from Egyptian authorities.

"If mukhabarat is looking everywhere for the sheikh and his brotherhood, how come he can sneak right under their noses?" Carrie asked as if reading Justin's mind.

"I was thinking that too. The short answer: he's the sheikh and this is Cairo. The sheikh's men are everywhere, even inside mukhabarat. They may be looking for him, but that doesn't mean they're going to find him. And according to the Egyptians, the sheikh is only *allegedly* linked to the Alliance."

"*Allegedly? Allegedly?* What more do they want? A written and signed confession saying I am the second-in-command of Islamic Fighting Alliance?" Carrie clenched her fists.

Justin stood up. "It's more complicated than that. The government is fragile, unable to defeat the militants by force, at least at this time. Maybe after the elections."

"Oh, that's months away." Carrie sighed.

"That's why we usually don't accept *support* from the secret police. There's too much to lose by sharing intel with mukhabarat."

Justin unfastened his holster and placed it on the table. Then he unbuttoned his shirt and removed it, along with his bulletproof vest. He felt Carrie's admiring eyes. He thought he saw her cringe as he turned around, knowing she would never get used to the sight of three deep scars, almost eight inches long, carved along his shoulder blades. They were reminders of the time he was captured in Libya after a hostage rescue operation that went wrong.

Justin fetched a short-sleeve shirt from a white cabinet by the door. The shirt smelled of bleach. It seemed Rahim had forgotten to ask his wife, who often did their laundry, not to use chlorine. Justin sighed as he noticed a slight bleeding of his favorite navy blue shirt.

"Did any of the sheikh's men come back to the Fairmont?" He returned to his seat and took a big gulp of coffee.

"Yes, one of his bodyguards. He retrieved the armored Mercedes from the valet parking. I have the address of the house where he dropped it off." Carrie tapped one of the folders.

"The sheikh's abrupt, but not secret departure, is unusual. Why leave in such a hurry and without giving a reason? What's so urgent? Is he afraid of something? He's protected in Egypt. There's nothing to fear."

"Well, maybe there is *something* to fear."

"If so, it has to be something big. Something powerful for the sheikh to abandon our long-planned meeting."

Their meeting had been in the works for over a month. In late March, intermediaries of the Alliance contacted the CIS Cairo Station, seeking a meeting with them. Johnson initially had chosen another team of agents to handle this case, suspecting the militant was a low-level soldier. Once the identity of the senior leader requesting the meeting became known, Johnson insisted Justin organize all aspects of the operation. His presence became even more essential when they learned Sheikh Ayman held information about an assassination plot against a Western head of state.

"What do you think spooked him?" Carrie asked.

"I don't know. Very few things would scare someone like Sheikh Ayman."

"Will he reschedule our meeting?"

"I hope so."

While the location and the time of their meeting were determined two weeks ago, they knew nothing about the specifics of the assassination or the intended target.

"I just don't want it to take place in Sudan."

"Hey, why not? It's easier to bag him down there," Carrie replied with a wide grin.

Kidnapping or eliminating the sheikh had crossed his mind too, albeit as a fleeting thought. Sudan was a lawless land and the perfect place for such a hit. The zeal in Carrie's voice did not surprise him either. According to her, the most efficient solution to a problem was often also the most extreme. The one she always favored.

"That's not our mission," Justin said.

Carrie shook her head in resignation.

Justin walked over to one of the windows that overlooked the Fairmont VIP entrance and the Nile. Glowing lights from towering buildings shone from Giza, a suburb of the capital across the river. A constant stream of cars rushed through the top level of the Imbaba Bridge that connected the two parts of Cairo, their headlights flickering through the heavy smog. Justin hated the Imbaba Bridge. In fact, he hated all bridges. It was a bridge that shattered his life when he was only eleven years old.

Justin took the last sip of his coffee. He stepped closer to the other window, facing the apartment building across the alley. On a second floor apartment, two lights were on. They were almost in a clear line of sight to their room. Justin squinted and saw the silhouette of a man wandering around in the living room. A television set was flickering in one of the corners. A knock on the door startled him, and Justin turned around.

"It's me," Rahim said, "I brought the mezze."

"Come in," Justin said.

Rahim walked in, holding a round tray with pita and garlic bread, pickled olives, slices of cucumbers, and a few bread dips. Carrie began to make room on the table for their supper when a bullet pierced the window glass and slammed into Rahim's chest. The man tumbled to his knees. The small plates of food flew across the table.

"Get down, get down," Justin shouted. Carrie had already hit the floor, her hand clenching her pistol.

A short burst of gunfire exploded, breaking the other window. Sharp slivers of glass rained over the agents' shoulders.

"Two shooters!" Carrie shouted.

Justin nodded, reaching for his Browning pistol. He cocked it and held it tightly in front of his face.

"You can handle them?" Justin asked as he stared at Rahim. A dip dish still swirled next to Rahim's lifeless face.

"Yeah, I got them," Carrie replied.

"Cover me and watch your head."

He crawled to the door and ran outside.

* * *

As soon as the gunfire paused for a brief second, Carrie took a quick peek over the shredded windowsill. A gun muzzle flash betrayed one of the shooters' location. She squeezed her trigger. She ducked as bullets sailed past her head. A few long moments dragged on. She lay low, her chest heaving with each quick breath. The gunfire stopped for a second. She looked up just long enough to fire the rest of her magazine. Once she heard the dull clink of her empty gun, she slid in a fresh magazine. She leaned against the wall and listened. Chaotic screams and rushing footsteps came from the street, but no more gunshots.

Carrie looked out of the window. A car engine roared and tires screeched. Down on the street, Justin chased a white Ford, shooting even as he ran to keep up with the car. Despite his torrent of bullets that riddled the runaway target, the Ford rounded the corner and disappeared behind the grocery store. Justin, gun in hand, stood alone in the middle of the alley.

* * *

Carrie walked outside to meet Justin. She stepped cautiously around a body lying halfway through the entrance to the apartment building. She noticed an AK-47 by the man's hand and her eyes rested on the wound in his neck. Justin had fired kill shots. Most of their targets wore bulletproof vests, so they rarely aimed at their chests. After a couple of clashes with mercenaries in the Niger River Delta swamps two years ago, they almost gave up shooting at the heads of their enemies. Kevlar helmets were becoming increasingly resistant to small arms fire.

"There's another body upstairs in the hall," Justin said, drawing nearer to her.

Carrie nodded. "Is this the work of the Alliance?"

"If it is, it's lousy at best." Justin looked at the dead man.

"Did you get the men in the Ford?"

"Yes, I'm sure I got the woman passenger on the shoulder."

"A woman?"

"Yeah."

Carrie raised her hand and touched Justin's bristly face. A reddish stain appeared on her fingers trailing over his chin. "You're wounded?"

"Slivers. My favorite shirt is ruined though." He ran his hand over his chest. "That's Rahim's blood."

"If Rahim had checked the Ford, maybe this would have not happened."

"If *I* would have checked it, this would *not* have happened."

"It wasn't your responsibility. It was his. You can't do everyone's job."

"Maybe Rahim didn't want to check the Ford."

Carrie's gray-blue eyes narrowed. "He wanted this to happen?"

"Well, not the part where he died."

She glanced back at the Castle. Some of its patrons had run away. A few curious souls peered from behind the windows. She scanned the windows and balconies of the apartment building. Narrowed eyes of some of the residents glared in their direction. An old woman screamed at them in Arabic. A dog howl cut through the hot, heavy air.

Justin was staring at the dead man.

"What is it?" Carrie asked.

"I wonder if this is why the sheikh disappeared."

"You mean he lured us for a meeting and set up an ambush? That is, if Rahim gave us up."

"Yes, and before the ambush, the sheikh disappears."

"Uh-uh, the sheikh needs no alibi. It has to be something else."

Justin nodded and checked the magazine of his pistol. Four bullets left.

"You're right. But this was no coincidence either."

"Whatever it is, we'll find out."

"You're right about that too. Whoever it is, they made a grave mistake putting us in their crosshairs."

* * *

"Tell me what you see." The man passed his binoculars to the driver.

He took the Bushnell binoculars and peered through it. The powerful magnification produced a sharp close-up image even through the BMW's windshield. They had a clear view of the entrance to the Castle coffee shop from the Nile City Fairmont parking lot.

"He's standing outside the shop, talking to the woman," the driver said.

The man shook his gray-haired head.

"No, you see two brave soldiers ready for a fight."

His voice showed clear disappointment. After so many years in the Islamic Fighting Alliance, the driver still failed to see beyond what was in front of his eyes. "They still have their weapons drawn?"

"They do," the driver replied.

"Our men have become martyrs now." The man's voice held no regret. "Good thing they were our least talented shooters. They served their purpose."

"You don't think we went too far?" The driver raised the binoculars to his eyes. Justin and Carrie were now pacing in front of the Castle.

"No. We want to make this fight personal. Revenge is a powerful motivator. In this way, they'll be more eager. More dedicated. That's exactly what we want."

Faint police sirens sounded in the distance.

"I've seen enough. Let's go," the man ordered his driver while looking to his right for police cars. "It's time to brief Sheikh Ayman and play our next card."

CHAPTER 2

Canadian Intelligence Service Cairo Station, Egypt
May 13, 7:45 p.m. local time

George Patterson was struggling to establish a videoconference connection with the CIS headquarters in Ottawa. He kept pressing keyboard buttons and plugging and unplugging wires into the back of his laptop. Despite his efforts, no images appeared on the plasma screen of the Maple Leaf Conference Room.

George was the CIS Cairo Station Chief and Justin's direct supervisor, at least in terms of administration. For operations work, Justin and Carrie still reported to Claire Johnson. They had returned to their jobs with the Cairo Station last year, after a CIS internal inquiry had cleared them of any misconduct during a hostage rescue operation in Libya. The inquiry was completed right after the Arctic Wargame mission that almost claimed their lives.

Sitting across the square table from George, Justin mulled over the evening's events. As soon as Carrie had finished retrieving all their documents and gear from the Castle, the mukhabarat arrived at the scene. Of course they did not buy the agents' implausible cover story, according to which two employees of the Canadian Cultural Agency in Egypt had survived a shootout with barely a scratch. Justin and Carrie claimed they found the guns in the coffee shop where they were having dinner and used them in self-defense. Their explanation was unlikely, but that was their cover story and they were going to stick to it. The mukhabarat confiscated their guns and interrogated them for a few minutes. Once Justin produced two Canadian diplomatic passports, the mukhabarat had little choice but to escort them to their embassy.

The Canadian Embassy was in the lush neighborhood of Garden City, one of the safest neighborhoods in the capital. It was always crawling with Egyptian uniformed police, security contractors, and secret agents. The CIS station occupied several offices in the east wing of the embassy. It had its own entrance, parking lot, and security system. The station served the intelligence and operative needs of the entire North Africa. It was run in a quasi-independent manner from the rest of the embassy—mainly for "plausible deniability" purposes—but still under the umbrella of diplomatic immunity.

"Here, I think I got something," George said as a bright blue light flashed on the plasma screen.

"Great," Carrie replied with a sigh. Sitting next to Justin, she was impatiently drumming her fingers on the edge of the desk, swinging in her swivel chair. "That was only what, ten minutes?"

George ignored her and clicked a few more buttons. Then he proudly pressed the Enter key. The image on the screen changed. The three of them gazed at Johnson's long and narrow face, distorted because of how she hunched over the camera at her work station.

"Hello, Ms. Johnson, can you hear me?" George asked.

"Yes, yes, I can hear you. I've been waiting here for a while."

"Hmmm, we had some technical difficulties with the connection, but, we're, eh . . . we're good to go now."

"All right. I see you have Justin and Carrie there. How are you two holding up?"

"We're fine," Justin said.

"Everything's good," Carrie added with a nod.

"OK, now tell me what happened exactly? Your e-mail was quite short." Johnson spread her hands.

"We were at the Castle conducting surveillance when we were ambushed." Justin leaned over his folded hands with his elbows resting on the table.

"I know that much already," Johnson said.

"Those are all the facts we have so far. I suspect the shooters were from the Alliance, since Cairo has always been their home."

"The Alliance?" Johnson asked. "Why the ambush if their sheikh was meeting with us?" She frowned while pondering the answer.

"One possibility is that the ambush was the purpose of this so-called 'meeting,' to lure us into their trap," Justin said.

He glanced at Carrie and his eyes caught a slight jerk of her left hand. He nodded for her to speak her mind.

"One theory is that Rahim sold us out and helped stage the attack," Carrie said.

"Really? What evidence do you have for that?" Johnson asked.

Carrie shrugged. "None, it's a theory."

"I noticed a suspicious car parked by the Castle and asked Rahim to check it out," Justin added. "Two of the shooters escaped using the same car."

Johnson absorbed the information. "So Rahim never checked the car?"

"He sent his nephew, presumably."

Johnson did not ask why Justin was not sure if Rahim's nephew had searched the car. *She probably concluded he disappeared or died before I could talk to him*, Justin thought.

"Who is dead?" asked Johnson.

"Rahim, his nephew, and two shooters. I also wounded one of the passengers as the car sped away. She should die soon, if she's not already dead."

Johnson's eyes remained still despite the coldness in Justin's voice.

"I don't get it," Johnson said, "if Rahim, and maybe his nephew, sold us out, how come they're both dead?"

"I didn't kill them, if that's what you're asking." Justin said. "They both got popped during the shootout. I can't really tell whether if it was by error or on purpose."

Johnson nodded and a few strands of her gray hair came loose. "I want you to find out the identities of these shooters and their motives," she said softly, removing a pin from her hair and fixing her stubborn curls. "Then—"

A knock on her office door interrupted her.

"Yes, come in." Johnson turned to her left.

A man's voice could be heard, but he was outside the camera's angle, and his words were unintelligible. But Justin could read Johnson's facial expression. It went from shock to awe and then to doubt in a matter of seconds. Before he could ask anything, she said, "Justin, I've got to check something urgent here. I'll put you on hold for a few seconds, OK?"

"That's fine," Justin said. He had no other option.

"Yes, we'll be here waiting," George added but Johnson tapped a key and the screen turned black.

"Did you see that?" Justin asked.

"No, what was it?" George said.

Carrie nodded at Justin's question. "The news they just gave Johnson," she explained for George. "From the look on her face, it can't be good."

"Well, now she's gonna take forever to analyze it, so I'm out of here." Justin stood up and pushed back his chair. "If it's going to be a long night, I need some coffee."

George raised his hands. "Wait, what if she comes back on the line while you're gone?"

Justin shrugged. "You're the boss. Tell her I had to step out for a minute. But I'll be back before she does."

"Wait up," Carrie said, "I'll get some tea."

George sighed. "OK, let's all take a five minute break."

* * *

"Hi, boss." Justin pushed the door with his elbow, since he was carrying a coffee cup in each hand. "She's still not back?" His question pointed out the obvious as the plasma screen showed no image.

George replied with a headshake.

"This is yours. Black." Justin placed one of the cups next to George's laptop before returning to his seat.

"Oh, thanks." George lifted the cup and took a large sip.

"Hey," Carrie said as she entered in with a teacup in her hands. "How much longer you think?"

George opened his mouth to venture a guess, but the image of Johnson returned to the screen. Her face looked paler and her eyes had sunk deeper into their sockets. "Hello, can you hear me?"

"Yes, yes, we hear you," George said.

"I'm afraid I have bad news. There has been a series of explosions, car bombs in Tripoli, Libya, about twenty minutes ago."

"What?" Justin and Carrie asked almost at the same time and exchanged confused glances.

"Yes. The information we're receiving is still unconfirmed, but it seems four cars exploded close to major hotels in downtown Tripoli."

"Casualty count?" asked Carrie.

"In the tens, I guess. We don't have much intel yet, but we're trying to—"

Justin slammed his fist on the table. He startled not only Carrie and George, but also Johnson, who stopped talking. "That's why the sheikh left in such a hurry, to escape the Libyan mukhabarat."

The Libyan mukhabarat was as notorious as its Egyptian counterpart for its powerful revenge, which extended well beyond Libya's national borders. The looming backlash was more than a match for the Alliance and its leaders.

"Very good, Justin," Johnson said with a nod. "It is exactly so, confirmed by the sheikh himself. We just received word from him."

George let out a gasp, while Justin shook his head. Carrie kept her poker face on as she jotted down notes in her notebook.

"The sheikh denied the Tripoli bombing was the work of the Islamic Fighting Alliance," Johnson said.

"Really?" Justin asked, his voice dripping with sarcasm. "Did he also deny his men ambushed us tonight?"

"No, he took full responsibility for that attack. However, the intended targets were, let me find it . . ." Johnson shuffled papers on her desk and found her glasses. She began to read from one of the many documents covering her workspace. "Yes, the targets were 'despicable collaborators of the infidels.' I'm assuming that was Rahim and his nephew."

"Very convenient," Carrie said.

Johnson slid her glasses to the tip of her nose. "These words came through the sheikh's messenger. It doesn't mean I believe them. In any case, the sheikh still wants a meeting."

"No freaking way," George mumbled just loud enough for Justin and Carrie to hear him.

"This time he's offering the guarantee of his personal honor to protect his guests," Johnson continued.

"When and where?" Justin's eyes flared up.

"He insists the information about the assassination plot is time-sensitive, and he would like to meet tomorrow morning, in Sudan."

Justin frowned. "Sudan?"

"I'm assuming it's because of Tripoli," Johnson replied.

Justin bit his lip. Sheikh Ayman was luring them into the deadly no man's land. Sudan's deserts had been the breeding ground of rebellion, civil wars, kidnappings, human trafficking, and all kinds of smuggling for decades. Refusing the sheikh's invitation, especially after the ambush, would make the CIS appear weak. Justin had spent a long time building his own reputation, and that of the CIS, as brave and fearless. They were not going to start backing down now. He had been to Sudan three times. And had come back unharmed.

He looked to his left at a tense Carrie. Her hand was pulling on the handle of her teacup as if it were a gun trigger. *Let's do it,* her blazing eyes told him.

"Do you have the meeting coordinates?" Justin asked.

"Yes. I'll get them to you."

"Excuse my interruption," George said. His voice came out dry and staccato. He coughed then resumed his thought, "but sending a team to Sudan is the same as suicide."

A wrinkle the size of the Grand Canyon appeared on Johnson's forehead. She lifted her glasses and peered at George.

"George, let me tell you something." Johnson's frown melted and her voice turned soft, taking on a motherly tone. "Cairo is deadly. Sudan is deadly. All of North Africa is a death trap. The whole world is a dangerous place, George, especially for secret agents." Johnson sighed. Her left hand jerked in a dismissive gesture. "I appreciate your concern, though." Her voice returned to her normal tone. "Your objection to this mission is duly noted. And overruled." Johnson's past as a judge often returned in the form of legal jargon whenever she whipped her subordinates like she used to lash at contemptuous counselors in her courtroom.

"Justin and Carrie," she continued, "our contacts in the Egyptian Air Force should be able to provide you a safe passage across the border and a safe insertion into Sudan. I'll get in touch with them."

Justin nodded.

"The sheikh's message indicates the drop-off area is about sixty miles south of the Egyptian border. We need to find a neutral intermediary escort to take you to the meeting place."

Justin pondered the possibilities. The escort would have to be a local warlord with great authority in the area. But his authority could not be too strong, or the sheikh might consider it a threat to his own safety.

Justin nodded. "I know a few people, gunrunners in the area. The name of Ali Abd Alraheem comes to mind. If he's still alive."

"I don't recall him." Johnson rubbed her temples.

"I last worked with him three years ago."

"OK, see if he can serve as the go-between and let me know. The sheikh expects an answer in the next hour."

"He will get one."

"How do we know we can trust this man, Ali?" George asked.

Justin said, "We don't know and we can't trust. Unless a man has taken a bullet for you, never put your trust in them. You'll be disappointed and you could end up dead. I have worked with Ali but we're still going down there with eyes wide open."

A moment later, a stern frown covered his face.

"What is it, Justin?" Johnson asked.

"The change of plans and this detour."

"Take care of this matter and then you're off to your sailboat," Johnson said, faking a smile.

"Yeah, my deposit is nonrefundable," Justin replied with a smirk.

He could not care less about the three-thousand dollar deposit for the forty-two-foot cutter. Justin was worried about disappointing Anna, his fiancée, whom he had promised a ten-day sail in the Caribbean on the eve of her thirtieth birthday. Anna used to work for CIS Legal Services in Ottawa, and their bond was forged during the eventful Arctic Wargame operation. To avoid any conflicts of interest, Anna had moved on to become an in-house counsel for the Canadian bivision of Vigorsoul Pharmaceuticals. Two weeks away from her desk almost never happened.

"If you're quick, you can wrap this up by tomorrow at noon," Johnson said.

"I'm planning to," Justin said.

"When's your flight out of Cairo?"

"6:00 p.m."

"Yeah, you can make it."

Justin nodded. "Anything else?"

"No, I don't think so. Let me know when you've heard from Ali, or if not from him, your other contacts on the ground."

"By all means," Justin replied.

"Perfect."

Johnson turned off the satellite feed and the screen went black.

George signed them out of the connection with a big sigh. "What was that? You have a death wish?"

"Relax, George," Carrie said. "Nobody's going to die. Well, at least we're not."

"You're crazy, going all alone into the lion's den."

"Listen, the sheikh could have killed us today, if that's what he wanted," Justin said calmly. "I don't think we'll be of much use to him dead. He wants to talk. We want to listen."

"We'll fly down there and learn about this assassination plot," Carrie said.

George threw his arms up in the air. "Do as you wish," he said. Then he added with a sigh, "The two of you always do."

Justin stood up. "Thanks, boss. We'll bring back the intel. Now I've got to get in touch with Ali and finish making preps. Carrie, we'll leave ASAP."

"I'm ready," she said and gulped down the rest of her tea. She placed down the cup on the table. "I'm ready."

CHAPTER 3

Cairo, Egypt
May 13, 9:00 p.m. local time

Justin began to lose track of time as the hot shower splashed over his head and shoulders. He leaned against the white ceramic tiles, his fingers combing aimlessly through his wet hair. His scalp was smooth and soft, but he noticed some gray hairs stuck to his fingernails when he rinsed his hands. The water took them away and his eyes followed their swirl in the shower drain. A single hair became stuck to his left toe and it resisted the stream for a brief second. More water trickled down from his chest and the stubborn hair disappeared into the drainpipe.

Justin could not help but wonder about his swimming against the tide of death. He did not think much about dying, for death was an almost daily occurrence in his life. Few days went by without Justin shooting at or being shot at by someone. So far he had been wise and, in part, lucky. Flesh wounds, broken bones, stitches, but nothing he had not overcome. Despite that, his mind still raced at the moment when the current of violence facing him would grow strong, stronger than him, and it would drag him down the drain. Like the hair strand that had gone and could be seen no more.

"It hasn't happened in the last eleven years. It didn't happen today and it's not going to happen tomorrow either," Justin cried in a loud voice and slammed a clenched fist against the shower wall.

Speckles of grout burst out of the tile edges. Justin used his foot to push them toward the drain. He blinked to clear the last drops of water from his eyes and stepped out of the shower.

Fifteen minutes later, dressed in a short-sleeved white shirt and navy blue pants, Justin waited for Carrie in the hall of their apartment building, a short walk away from the Canadian Embassy. Both agents rented two-bedroom apartments paid for by the Service. At one time, Justin used to live in a small house, northeast of the Garden City, by the American University. But that was seven years ago when he first arrived in Cairo. At that time, field missions took him away once or twice a month. Now, he could not remember the last time he spent a full week in the city.

"Hey, you look sharp," Carrie said as she stepped out of the elevator.

"You, on the other hand, you look gorgeous."

Carrie's V-neck black dress flowed down to her knees. A gray cardigan added a casual touch to her look. Her shoes were the essential pumps, with a rounded toe and four-inch stiletto heels. She had applied very little makeup, just a light shadow of mascara and pink lip gloss. Her hair was pulled back and arranged in a small ponytail. A black leather purse hung loose around her left shoulder.

"A bit of overkill, you think?" Carrie pointed to her dress, noticing Justin's gaze moving up and down her body.

Justin hesitated for a second then nodded.

Carrie shrugged. "I thought so. Oh, well. How often do I get to wear a dress and heels in his job?"

"Not very often, but this is a simple dinner."

"If you knew how to cook, you'd know there's nothing simple when preparing a delicious meal."

Justin grinned. He remembered Carrie taking pride in cooking suppers when they were still dating. They had soon discovered they were better off being good friends. Once in a while, Carrie came over to his apartment and cooked supper for the two of them. Some of the best steaks he had ever enjoyed were grilled by her hands.

"I meant—"

She waved a hand. "I know what you meant. We'll go and enjoy our meal. Let's just hope nobody is planning to interrupt us like the last time."

"You never know." Justin swung open the doors for Carrie. "New York is two blocks away and that place has more Westerners than locals. Still, one crazy bastard wearing explosives can blow everything to pieces."

They walked out in the warm evening toward New York, an Italian restaurant around the corner. The narrow alley, cordoned off to vehicle traffic, was well-lit, with lampposts at every ten steps. The sidewalk was in a decent shape and a few security guards patrolled the area, offering a visible safety presence. But a dog yelp, followed by a short burst of gunfire, reminded them of the ever-present danger.

"Jim doesn't like it when you come in packing heat," Carrie said, pointing to Justin's right thigh.

The pistol in his waistband holster was not visible, but she knew it was there. And so did Jim, the restaurant's head of security. Three months ago, a brawl among a group of drunken Russian military contractors had ended in a free-for-all shootout. Justin had sent four Russians to the hospital, and New York's renovation bill had been over fifty thousand dollars.

"And I don't like it when they burn my steak." Justin nodded at two guards stationed in front of the Belgium Embassy. "Don't tell me you didn't bring yours."

"As a matter of fact, I did." She glanced at her purse. "But Jim doesn't seem to mind it."

Jim—the man Justin had nicknamed "Rhino," not only because of his body size, but also for his unexpected charge toward targets—was off duty this evening. Much to the delight of both agents, Wilson, Jim's underling, threw them a disinterested gaze when they came in. They had no reservations, but it was a slow night at New

York. The hostess escorted them to their table, next to a window overlooking the eastern shore of the Nile. They were the only people sitting in the dimly lit, non-smoking section of the restaurant.

While Carrie took her time flipping through the menu, Justin ordered his usual fare at New York: bruschetta, a 20-ounce ribeye steak, and sparkling lemon water. He tapped his fingers on the black tablecloth and fiddled with the pepper holder, a replica statuette of Lady Liberty. The waiter arrived with his drink as Justin's BlackBerry chirped.

"Is that Johnson?" Carrie asked, her eyes still glued to the menu.

Justin did not reply. He frowned as he glanced at the screen. He pressed the answer button then barked at the phone, "This is Justin. Who's dead?"

Carrie looked up, slowly shaking her head. Justin greeted only one person with that dreadful question: his father, Carter.

"Justin, I can't hear you very well." The weak voice of his old man came quietly over the waves.

"I'm not surprised. You never did. Now what do you want?"

"I just . . . I wanted to hear your voice."

"Are you dying?"

"No, no, I'm not dying. Not yet, anyway."

"Uh-huh."

Justin glanced at Carrie. She stood up and gestured to him she was headed to the washroom.

"How are things going?" Carter said.

"Fine."

An awkward silence followed for a few moments.

"You still there?" Carter asked.

"Sure."

"Yesterday was Seth's birthday, but he told me you didn't call him."

Yes, I was trying to forget all about it.

"It's always about Seth, isn't it? He's the son you always wanted."

"Not again, Justin. You know that's not true."

"It isn't? I never get a call from you or him on March 1. Or a card. Or a letter."

"You've said many times you couldn't care less about that stuff."

Justin sighed and shook his head. "I don't care about that stuff . . ." His voice trailed. *I care about the thought.*

"So, why are we fighting about this?"

Justin kept silent for a few seconds, clenching his teeth. Then he took a deep breath, cleared his throat and said, "Listen, I'm quite busy here, so I can't talk anymore."

He pressed the end button on his BlackBerry so hard he thought he broke it. Then he tossed the phone on the table, where it clanged against the glass of water. *Oh, he always gets to me. As much as I tell myself I'll stay calm the next time I talk to him, he always finds a way to drive me nuts.* Justin raised his left fist but saw Carrie out of the corner of his eye. He slowly dropped his hand to his lap, tried to regain his composure, and offered her a big fake smile.

"Don't use the washroom if you can help it," Carrie said while sitting down.

She took one of the napkins and scrubbed her hands. Justin detected the faint smell of smoke on her as the bathrooms were in the smoking section.

"Do you know what you want to eat?" Justin asked.

"Yes, I think so."

The waiter appeared to take her order: a salad of mix greens and a four-cheese ravioli alla napoletana. Carrie stuck to sparkling lemon water like Justin.

"So when do you think we'll hear from Johnson?" Carrie asked.

"If she's changing the plan, tomorrow morning. Five minutes before takeoff."

Carrie snorted. "Will she ever change?"

"Will we?"

"Oh, I don't know. Haven't we started yet?" She pointed to the BlackBerry on the table.

"Oh, no, that's not change," Justin replied with a headshake.

"Well, the more I try to change, the more he stays the same."

"But isn't Carter trying though, trying to reach out to you?"

Justin wondered if her encouragement was motivated by recent news her mom was having health problems and a desire for Justin to make peace with his father before something similar happened to him.

"His shadow is," Justin said. "I move to the other side of the world and he still finds me. I change my freaking phone number to classified, and the old man still pulls in favors to find it and harass me."

Justin's mother had gone off a bridge in her car when he was only eleven. The police had ruled out suicide, blaming instead the icy roads for the accident. But he knew better. And he hated the man he blamed for his mother's death. The man he never called "Dad" again.

Carrie's lips formed a thin line. "Yeah, big money buys pretty much everything these days. Even access to secret agent files."

"He still thinks he can run my life and tell me what to do. Like hell he can. I won't let him do that anymore."

Carrie reached over the table for Justin's trembling hand. "It's OK. It's OK," she said softly. "It's all over. Finished. He can no longer do anything. You, and I, we'll never allow it. Never."

His eyes found hers and she gave him a reassuring nod. Justin let out a sigh of relief.

"Talking of control freaks, me being one of them, Thomas is starting to worry me," Carrie said, changing the subject.

"You think your boyfriend may be chasing tail?"

"No, he's loyal, I know that. But lately he is kind of distant."

"Why do you say that?"

"I called him tonight and told him what happened. He didn't seem overly concerned."

"That's because he knows you're a big girl and you can handle things just fine."

"Yeah, thanks. His lack of interest was a bit unnerving, I should say."

"What was he like when you last saw him?"

"Last month in Malta? He was fine. Joyful, funny, relaxed. Everything was great."

"Could it be work wearing him down?"

"PR work? Give me a break."

"Well, Thomas is still CEO and I'm sure there's a lot on his mind."

"Not the same thing as on my mind." Carrie took a deep breath.

"Don't worry about it. He'll come through."

"I hope so. I really hope so."

"Thomas is a good guy. He's just looking for the perfect ring, for the perfect girl."

"Ha. Thanks. At this point, an onion ring would do."

She locked her fingers together, her elbows resting on the table. Then she said, "Oh, Thomas, Thomas, why does it have to be so difficult?"

"Love always is."

Carrie opened her mouth but saw the waiter bringing her drink. She waited until he left then asked, "Talking about love, did you call your sweetheart?"

"Yes. Anna's wasn't in her office and she wasn't picking up her cell. I left a message. She's probably in some merger meeting or something boring like that."

Carrie took a quick sip of the cold lemon water.

"Oh, that's good." She drew her lips together. "The lemon taste is so strong. Does she ever pick up when you call?"

"Anna's very busy and I always seem to call at the wrong time. It was better that way, 'cause I didn't feel like explaining that I'm going to miss my flight tomorrow."

"You don't think we will make it in time?"

"No. We haven't heard from Johnson yet and I doubt we'll leave before midnight. We're not meeting Ali until 8:00 tomorrow morning. If everything goes smooth, we'll not be back before nightfall."

Carrie shrugged and brought the water glass to her lips. Justin glanced out the window.

"They're taking their time with the appetizers." He turned his head toward the door leading to the kitchen and stared in that direction for a few seconds, hoping the waiter would appear with a tray of food. He did not.

"This place may be called New York, but their service runs on Egyptian time."

"Well, I'm starving here." Justin rubbed his stomach with his left hand.

Carrie grinned.

Moments later, the waiter waltzed in with a large tray of food in his hands. Justin instinctively looked out the window, his hand jerking toward the Browning pistol in his holster.

"Relax." Carrie said. "Twice in half a day?"

"It has happened before. It may happen again."

"Not here. Not now."

The aroma of the fresh baked focaccia bread, topped with tomato, garlic, and onions and seasoned in olive oil and herbs, loosened Justin up. He broke off a piece of the wedged-shaped bread and looked at the steam rising up in the air. Devouring the piece in a swift move, he looked over at Carrie. She was carefully sifting through her green salad, pushing to the edge of the plate every small slice of black olives.

"You know those things are good for your skin," he said and stuffed another large piece of focaccia in his mouth.

"And you know this is not a race."

"Hmmm, but it's so good."

Carrie rolled her eyes. She lifted a small portion of shredded carrots and peas to her mouth. She closed her eyes and savored her food.

* * *

By the time Carrie was halfway through her salad, Justin had cleaned up not only the last crumbs of the bruschetta, but also the sour cream and roasted garlic dips.

"Man, you were hungry," Carrie said.

"Starving." Justin wiped his lips with his blue napkin.

"Tell me, how did you convince Ali to help us?"

Justin smiled. "SCR 1267."

"UN's blacklist?"

Justin nodded.

"What promise we can't keep did you make him?"

"This one we *can* keep. Ali has a half-brother listed as a terrorist, an accomplice of Al-Qaeda. The man secured a car and drove a group of terrorists for a week or so around Baghdad about two years ago."

"So you told Ali that Canada will delist him?"

"I promised I'll write up a request, asking for his name to be removed from the list. It's up to our bosses to decide."

"You know your request is going nowhere."

"I can't control that. The man used to live in Canada and still has relatives in Ontario. Our government doesn't want him back, even though he hasn't been convicted of any crime."

"I see." Carrie sipped the last of her drink and looked over Justin's shoulder for the waiter. He was nowhere in sight.

Justin's BlackBerry chirped twice and he picked it up. "It's Johnson."

"Speakerphone."

"Hello," Justin said and placed the BlackBerry on the table between the two of them. "How are things going?"

"Great, great," Johnson said.

He thought her voice sounded with an echo as if she were in a tunnel. Then a familiar elevator ping solved the mystery.

"I don't have a lot of time as I'm running to a meeting. Just wanted to confirm the Egyptians reluctantly agreed to drop you into

Sudan tomorrow morning. Do you have a pen handy?"

"Yes."

Carrie pulled out a pen and a small notepad from her purse.

"This is the place where you'll meet the transport." She gave them the coordinates. "You'll take off at 1:00 a.m. The Egyptians have committed one of their helicopters to this operation."

Carrie shook her head.

"Is it a Mi-17?" Justin asked.

"Yes, it is."

Carrie swore under her breath. She hated Russia and everything Russian, even the Mi-17 helicopter. Ever since her father, a Canadian Army colonel, disappeared during a covert mission in the late eighties in the Soviet Union, she had begun to first fear, then hate everything related to the country that took away her father. She joined the Army with high hopes of learning about his fate, but she was no closer to the truth today than when she began scrapbooking her memories.

"OK," Justin said. "Anything else?"

"No, that's all. Good luck."

"Thanks." Justin ended the call.

Carrie looked out of the window staring at nothing in particular. Justin could see the fog of memories building up in her eyes.

"I'm sorry," he said.

Carrie shook her head. "It's OK, I guess. I should let go. I *will* let go."

Justin nodded. He had heard such pledges before and Carrie tried real hard. Some habits were extremely difficult to break. He knew that first hand.

CHAPTER 4

Sixty miles south of the Egyptian border
Great Sand Sea, Sudan
May 14, 8:15 a.m. local time

The gunman tightened the headscarf around his mouth and shut his eyes tight as he cocked his head to the left. It made no difference. The sudden wind gust swept a handful of red sand into his face. He coughed and spat. A spurt of obscenities burst out of his mouth. He cleaned his eyes, scrubbed the grit off his crooked teeth, and wiped his cracked lips and thick beard. Finally, Ali Abd Alraheem looked at the two men in the light brown Land Rover parked about fifty feet away at the base of a crescent-shaped dune.

"Where the hell is the helicopter?" he shouted at them.

"Should be here anytime," replied the driver. He was barely in his twenties, the younger of the pair. He coughed, more out of solidarity with his chief than necessity.

"Come take a seat," said the other man who was in his forties. "No point in eating sand and boiling under the sun."

"It's better than being blown to pieces by Zionist jets, Nassir," Ali replied. "That car is a deathtrap."

"Israeli F-16s strike convoys carrying big guns," Nassir replied, his right arm spearing out of the window. "We're only two cars." He pointed to an identical Land Rover about two hundred feet behind theirs. "And we only bring in light weapons."

"No fish is too small for Mossad." Ali took a deep breath through his nose. His right hand tightened around the AK-47 hanging on his left shoulder. "And they can hit anyone, anywhere."

"Suit yourself." Nassir mopped his brow with a crumpled white handkerchief.

Ali gazed intently toward the north. His eyes were glued to the horizon, right above the top of the dunes. The helicopter with two guests from Egypt was expected to arrive from that direction. They were thirty minutes late. In Ali's line of business delays meant trouble. He ran his black, calloused fingers over the pocket of his long robe, feeling for his cellphone, but he resisted the urge to dial the contact number and check the status of the drop.

It was still early morning, but the temperature had climbed to ninety-five degrees. The air was parched, without a single drop of humidity. Ali's body grew warmer with every breath he took. He felt his tongue dangling inside his mouth like a piece of dry meat and decided to return to the Land Rover for a sip of cold water.

He stepped down from the top of the sandbank, plowing through the steep slope. After a few seconds, he stopped and listened. His ears, trained to detect any kind of desert noise, sensed a light vibration in the sizzling air. Ali turned around and climbed fast, kicking up sand on both sides of his path. As he reached the peak, he blinked to clear his eyes and grinned at the anticipated sight.

A thick cloud of red dust was swiftly approaching the drop point, skirting over the tips of the sand ridges. It would have seemed like a dust devil to a mere observer. But Ali was not a mere observer. The thick cloud was the work of a man, piloting a helicopter at almost ground level. It was a crazy maneuver that had to be executed to perfection, so it would not turn deadly. *This pilot has brass balls, but he's still a man. A man who can be shot and killed.*

Ali dropped to the ground, cocked his AK-47 and pointed it to the ever-growing cloud. If the people who were going to rappel down from the helicopter were not the expected CIS agents, they would be welcomed with a hail of bullets.

* * *

Inside the Mi-17 helicopter cabin, Justin and Carrie wrestled the twirling curtain of dust sweeping in through the open door. The pilot had informed them only moments ago he was not going to land the helicopter. They would have to rappel down to the ground. *The Egyptians have taken the word "drop" quite literally,* Justin thought, but he had no time to argue. The helicopter wobbled, while the top layer of the sand began shifting at the dune seventy feet below.

"Olam!" Justin shouted at the pilot. "Steady the bloody thing!"

"I'm trying," Olam replied. "I'm trying."

The helicopter dipped about four feet then hovered almost perfectly still.

"Good job!" Carrie said between gasps.

"How does the anchor look?" Justin pointed to the rappel hardware affixed to the roof of the cabin right above the door.

"Slightly corroded," Carrie replied, checking the steel karabiner for damage and feeding the rope through the field clevis. "The hose jacket is missing."

"Will it hold?" Justin shouted, over the rumble of the two engines.

"I hope so." She pulled on the rope, testing its strength. "Yes, I think it will hold," she added without much confidence.

Justin stared at the untidy coil of black rope snaking around his feet then ran some of the rope through his gloved hands. The braided nylon cord felt solid, although some of its fibers were sliced, damaged by dirt, heat, and friction.

"Rope is good," said the second pilot. "Used it last week. Held five people. Trust me."

Justin shrugged.

Carrie snorted and tightened her gloves.

"Drop rope!" Justin gave the pilot the signal they were ready to descend.

He threw his camouflaged knapsack over his shoulders and swung his carbine to his right side. Then he stepped closer to the door. Carrie handed him the rope coil and he dropped it overboard.

"Good luck," Carrie said.

"You too. See you at the bottom."

Justin grabbed the rope with both hands and swayed his body outside the helicopter. He locked his feet around the rope and began to lower himself. He eased the grip of his hands, allowing for the rope to slide slowly through his fingers. He kept his boots fastened against the rope at all times, feeling the friction of the rope on his gloves.

The helicopter jerked a few inches upward. The rope scraped against his vest. Justin threw his head to the side to avoid bruising his face and held tight to the rope. As he reached the end, he let go and jumped down, rolling on the slope. He fell on his stomach and pointed his carbine toward the south, where Ali was expecting their arrival. *In case someone else shows up uninvited.*

Soon enough, Carrie dropped next to Justin.

"Everything OK?" Justin asked.

"Everything's OK." She nodded, her face tight in concentration and her eyes sharp.

The helicopter banked to the right, turning around at a fast pace, the pilot seemingly eager to return to Egypt. Justin and Carrie protected their faces from the whirlpool of dust and waited for the red haze to settle. Carrie readied her C7 rifle, while Justin glanced at his wristwatch. *Thirty seconds from hovering to securing a perimeter. Not bad, but it can be better.* He looked toward the south.

"Do you see Ali?" Carrie asked.

"No, not yet. Wait, I see someone at ten o'clock."

As the veil of dust began to clear, Carrie looked through her rifle's sight and spotted a man pointing a gun at her. She squinted but could not make his facial features.

"His eyes are the only thing visible," she said, "and I can't tell if he's our man. But I can tell you that he's got us in his crosshairs."

Justin's eyes narrowed. His carbine was still pointed at the gunman who was making no moves. After a few moments, the gunman raised his left hand and waved it in the air above his head.

"That's our signal," Justin whispered, but made no attempt to stand up.

"So the man's Ali?"

"I'm not sure."

The gunman kept gesturing for the agents to approach him. Finally, he rose to his feet, his AK still pointed at them, and slowly began to lower his headscarf. His face became visible.

"Yes, he's Ali." Justin eased his finger on the carbine's trigger. "We can go now." He began to get up.

"So trust no one, eh?"

"Yes, trust no one."

Justin shook the sand off his bulletproof vest but did not bother with his pants. The last two weeks spent between Mauritania, Nigeria, and Egypt had taught him sand crawling under your skin was a simple fact of life. And the same was true for deception and lies.

* * *

The agents waded through ankle-deep sand and crossed the distance separating them from Ali. Carrie followed in Justin's footsteps, her weapon in a cradle carry position in her hands. Justin's weapon was hanging muzzle down behind his back in a sling fastened to his vest.

"Welcome to Sudan." Ali put out his right hand.

Justin shook it as the gunman pulled him closer in a friendly embrace.

"It's great to see you again. You look fit." Justin observed Ali's tall, thin frame and his biceps flexing under his robe.

"So do you," Ali replied. "And tanned. I almost didn't recognize you there. I was looking for a white face."

Justin grinned. He threw a glance at the Land Rover at the bottom of the dune.

"You never trust anyone, do you?" Ali asked, nodding toward the Land Rover then pointing at Justin's body armor. But for a square, bulky patch on his chest, the bulletproof vest was invisible.

Justin shrugged. "A habit. Can't help it."

"Neither can I. But my men we *can* trust."

Justin looked at the two men positioned on each side of the car, holding rocket-propelled grenades over their shoulders. They were pointed in his direction.

"This is Carrie," Justin said.

Ali measured up the woman with his small eyes. *I can't believe he brought a woman here and didn't tell me about it. He just said "another agent." Nassir will hate me for this. Still, she looks like she belongs here. And she's with him, so she's OK.* In desert camouflage pants, similar to Justin's, Carrie wore a tan vest and a khaki shirt. Ali noticed her tactical knee pads and a thigh holster strapped around her left leg revealing the butt end of a pistol. She also carried a large knapsack on her shoulders.

"Nice to meet you," Ali said with a smile, placing his right hand above his heart.

"Likewise," Carrie replied.

"Let's go before Nassir gets nervous."

Justin nodded and they followed Ali to the Land Rover. Nassir waited until the group reached the vehicle before lowering his RPG-7 on the hood of the car.

"Nassir, this is Justin and Carrie. And this is Omar." Ali pointed at the young man whose RPG weapon was still over his right shoulder. Omar gave them a reluctant nod, his face still locked in a menacing grin.

"You said they were *Egyptians*," Nassir blurted in English with a slight British accent, his hands folded in front of his barrel chest. Then he switched to Arabic, pointing a finger toward Carrie, "And he brought a woman with him. *A woman?* Our deal with the local tribes doesn't include the transport of American—"

"We're not Americans," Justin said quickly in Arabic. His tone was calm yet firm.

Nassir peered into Justin's eyes and tried to read his face for any hints revealing his ethnicity. *He's definitely Caucasian, despite the suntan. The black hair and large nose are of no help. High cheek bones. Thick lips. Is he a Spaniard? Turk? Arab-born Brit?*

The woman is easier to read. And younger. Maybe early thirties. Her light copper hair made Nassir think of Ireland. *IRA?* Carrie had a small figure, a bit shorter than Justin, and he stood at five feet ten inches. *Pointed nose, thin lips and a stoic grin. She can't be Arab.* Israel came to Nassir's mind, more as an afterthought, since he knew well Ali's hatred for the Hebrew nation. He was sure Ali would never agree to provide a safe passage for two Israeli agents, but he also did not like having a woman around.

"They're not Americans," Ali said. "Local tribes don't care about anything else."

"But *I* do," Nassir said. "Americans, British, Spanish, Irish, they're all the same to me."

Justin stepped forward, moving closer to Nassir.

"It's funny that your disgust for Brits didn't stop you from studying at Oxford and *definitely* isn't stopping you from enjoying the best cars of the Kingdom." Justin pointed to the Land Rover.

Nassir was unfazed. "A+ on doing your homework and looking into my background. They taught you well at your secret service, whichever it is."

Justin craned his head toward Ali.

"He's not a fool." Ali spread his palms, grinning wildly. "A hothead maybe, but definitely not a fool."

Justin shook his head.

Nassir's nostrils expanded and his chest rose up as he drew in a long breath. "I don't hate the Brits, but I can't stand it when they bend over for the CIA. Europe is as guilty as the Americans, those bloody oil thieves, for the mess in the Middle East."

Justin stared into Nassir's eyes. "I don't like politics either," Justin said after a tense pause. "We're here to interrogate the high-value detainee."

Justin had given Ali a cover story about a man captured in Sudan, who could be in possession of important intelligence. If pressed for answers, anything Ali revealed would not put in danger their true operation.

"Listen to him. He even talks like a CIA op." Nassir snorted, handing his RPG-7 to Omar and opening the driver's door.

Omar took both weapons to the back of the Land Rover.

"Will you use 'enhanced interrogation techniques' to extract information from the detainee?" Nassir asked sarcastically.

"I was told the source is very eager to talk to us. Plus, we don't torture people," Justin replied.

Nassir groaned. "Yeah, yeah, I've heard all that before."

Justin and Ali took the second row of seats in the Land Rover, a newer model than what Justin was used to seeing navigating the Sahara Desert. He admired the tan trim of the doors and felt a bit of regret when resting his sandy boots on the new floor mats. He was able to breathe easier now since the air conditioner was going at full blast. Nassir got behind the wheel and Omar took the front passenger seat. Carrie sat in the third row behind Justin.

"I see business is going well," Justin said, his hands gesturing around the cabin.

"I'm not complaining," Ali replied. "The wars in Libya and Syria have created new markets."

Nassir released the hand brake and put the car in reverse.

"Cold water?" Ali offered Justin and Carrie two glass bottles Omar had fetched from a cooler in the car's trunk.

Carrie nodded politely and took a bottle but did not drink from it.

"Thanks," Justin said. He removed the cap and emptied the half-liter bottle in a long gulp. Then he began digging in his knapsack.

Ali noticed Justin's weapon resting on his lap. "C8 carbine?"

"C8 carbine," Justin replied. "Very reliable, yet compact. Short barrel, adjustable stock. I removed the carrying handle and attached an HK launcher." Justin slid his right hand over the Heckler & Koch 40mm grenade launcher.

Ali tried to hide his admiration for the shining carbine. "Eh, nothing beats my old Russian friend." He knocked on the wood stock of his AK-47. "Mud, sand, gravel. Still fires straight, right between the enemy's eyes."

"Yes, it does."

"How did you get your C8 to Egypt?"

"Diplomatic pouch."

The vehicle dipped into a shallow pit and Nasser bore down on the gas pedal. The Land Rover roared, jolted out of the hole and began rolling over a hard-packed trail.

"This is for you." Justin finally found what he was rummaging for in his knapsack. "You still smoke these, right?" He handed Ali an elegantly carved humidor with brass edges.

The gunman weighed the chest-shaped wooden box in his hand before lifting the hinged lid and discovering a row of thick cigars. "Man, you have a good memory." Ali's eyes sparkled with excitement as he picked up one of the CAO eXtreme cigars.

Omar, attentive to the flow of the conversation, produced a lighter.

Ali chewed off the end of one of the cigars, spit it out of the window and lit the cigar. He puffed a couple of times and groaned in pure pleasure. "Oh, I missed you baby."

"I have to warn you: smoking causes cancer," Justin said.

"Ha. Men like us don't live long enough so slow diseases can eat us up. We die fast, by taking a bullet right in our head." Ali tapped his forehead with his right index finger.

Justin nodded.

"How long has it been since we last met?" Ali asked

"Three years. Nigeria. Port Harcourt."

"Yes, yes, now I remember. The aid workers."

"Yeah, that crazy affair."

"It *was* a bloody mess. Sometimes I wonder what goes through those people's minds when they accept jobs in war zones. Kidnappers don't care if you're in their country to feed the poor and help the sick. To them, you're a goat waiting to be gutted. If not me, then someone else, they think. Plus, for the huge salaries these 'volunteers' collect, Africa can pay ten locals to do the same job and even better."

"I hear you," Justin said.

"You still race cars?"

"You still breathe air?"

Ali grinned. "When it's not a blazing hell like today. Did you ever make it to supercars?"

"Your memory is flawless too."

"That's because you never stopped blubbering about your dream cars: Mercedes-Benz this, Ferrari that. Even if I saw those cars in person when drivers fire up their engines, I don't think they'd be as loud as you were."

"Well, things have changed. I realized the only way I can ever afford to own a decent Merc would be to move here and work with you."

Ali nodded. "You'd fit in like a glove."

"I race occasionally at speed festivals or car shows. My girl doesn't really like it. She thinks it's too dangerous."

Ali's eyes met Carrie's in the rearview mirror.

"He's not talking about me," Carrie said. "And I don't think racing is dangerous. I've found it's always the driver, never the car."

"Do you think *this* is dangerous?" Ali pointed at her and Justin.

"As dangerous as you let it be." Carrie's eyes scanned Ali's and Nassir's faces. "Know who to deal with and to whom never to turn your back."

Ali nodded in silence.

Nassir's left eyebrow arched and the left corner of his lip twitched as if he were not expecting such a reply. His eyes lingered a few more seconds in the rearview mirror before he returned his gaze to the road.

Justin noticed the second Land Rover was following them at about three hundred feet so he asked, "Why are they staying so far behind?"

"Safety," Ali replied. "We've had a few Israeli air strikes on convoys smuggling long-range rockets, FROGs and such for Hamas. IAF comes down with F-16s, combat choppers, the works."

"Wasn't that in the east, by the Red Sea?" Carrie asked. "And those were larger convoys."

"Yes, but the Zionists' dirty fingers reach everywhere. We're just being careful, even though we don't deal in rockets."

"Small weapons only?" Justin asked.

"That's what rebels prefer these days. We're simply trying to satisfy the market and keep our customers happy," Ali replied with a grin.

While they're killing innocent women and children, Carrie wanted to scream. Instead, she locked her lips and looked away. A stretch of black jagged ridges was rising up on the horizon to their left. Rolling red sand dunes extended as far as her eye could see.

"How come Egyptians refuse to land their choppers in this area?" she asked without making eye contact with anyone.

"Landmines, mainly," Ali replied. "Some places are riddled with landmines left behind from old wars between Libya and Egypt and the Toyota War between Libya and Chad. We know where the dead zones are and we stay away. Then there's pride. Local tribes like to feel in control of their land even when they're not."

"Borders are simply straight lines in the desert, hacked in the Sahara by colonialists to divide their loot," Nassir said. "People cross them when they feel like it, and no one can do anything to stop them, neither Egypt nor Libya."

"Speaking of Libya, did you hear about the suicide bombs last night in Tripoli?" Carrie asked.

"We did," Ali replied.

Justin waited for a few seconds but no one seemed willing to talk about it.

"Who do you think did it?" he asked.

"Eh, that's hard to tell," Ali said. "Qaddafi's loyalists maybe. Unhappy Islamic groups since they lost in the last elections. In any case, it was a blow both to the West and to the new prime minister. After all, they were mostly American hotels."

Justin looked in the rearview mirror, catching a glance of Nassir's face. The man looked like he was deep in his thoughts, his wary eyes suggesting he had strong feelings about the matter.

"What do you think, Nassir?" Justin asked.

Nassir examined Justin's eyes before opening his mouth. "You really want my opinion?"

"Sure, if you have one."

"Those bombs are a warning to infidels in Libya that the country is not for sale." Nassir spoke slowly, with a hint of satisfaction in his voice. "America armed the rebels and bombed Colonel Qaddafi, kicking him out. Then they installed a new government in place, with this new prime minister, who is a little more than a puppet. After the civil war ended, Libya turned into a magnet for all American companies, at each other's throats over Libya's oil. Those bombs are a reminder that Libya is still a Muslim country, regardless of the sellout prime minister."

Justin nodded. "I see."

"We've set up camp about a hundred miles east," Ali said, eager to change the subject. "The prisoner is awaiting your arrival. Are you planning to take him with you back to Egypt?"

Justin held Ali's eyes for a moment. "It depends on what he knows."

"There are ten guards with him and they travelled in armored BMWs," Ali said. "He must know a lot."

"I hope so," Justin said, "otherwise, with all due respect, we came to this scorching hellhole for nothing."

"No offense taken. This may be hell, but it's *my* hell. And I love it all."

CHAPTER 5

Great Sand Sea, Sudan
May 14, 10:05 a.m. local time

After two hours of bouncing over the rough desert terrain, Carrie had had enough of the Sahara. She had seen more than her fair share of deserts during her two tours of duty in Afghanistan. She served with the Joint Task Force Two, the elite counter-terrorism unit of the Special Operations Forces, before joining the CIS. Carrie took to heart the motto of her unit: *Facta non verba.* Deeds, not words. Her hands were itching for some action, but they were still travelling to the meeting point.

A paranoid Nassir had insisted they steer away from the flat, sturdy trail, the common route for crossing the vast ocean of sand. The Land Rovers snaked around rocky cliffs and wandered around sandstone boulders, climbed over gravel dunes and descended into barren valleys. At some point, Carrie thought she could make out the tall ridges of Mountain Jebel Uweinat by the border with Egypt and Libya, but she was not certain whether it was real or simply a mirage.

Justin and Ali were absorbed in a deep discussion of the geopolitical state of affairs in North Africa after the Arab Spring. Nassir seldom threw in his two cents worth, mostly at the expense of "blood-thirsty infidels," "scumbag Westerners," and, of course, "the great Devil, America." According to Nassir, America influenced everything and shaped everyone's positions in politics. At times, Omar would jump in, usually with a rhetorical question or a not-so-subtle approval of Ali's opinions.

"Hey, Carrie, what are you thinking about?" Justin asked.

"Are we there yet?"

Justin threw her a sideway glance.

"Five, maybe ten minutes," Ali replied. "See that cliff there?" He pointed straight ahead to a tall black ridge jutting out of the sandy hills, about a hundred and fifty feet high. "There's a clearing and a cave right behind it. That's where we've camped."

Carrie began scanning the sharp rocks for signs of gunmen's positions. Machine gun muzzles, tips of RPGs, or even a glimpse of a turban flap would give away the men defending the sheikh's hideout. She felt a certain amount of satisfaction mixed with a hint of concern. The perfect camouflage of Islamic militants and Ali's men meant their trip to this God-forsaken land would prove to be worthwhile. A sheikh surrounding himself with well-trained fighters definitely held a high rank in the Islamic Fighting Alliance. So he was likely to have access to important and accurate information. But if things went haywire, fighting their way out of this place would be just about impossible.

"How many tribesmen do you have?" Carrie asked.

"Fifteen, including the three of us," Ali replied. "Everything's OK. You can trust us."

Why do they keep repeating we can trust them? she wondered. *It's like they think saying it over and over again will make us believe them.*

Nassir steered slowly through a narrow pathway chiseled through the ridge. Steep, serrated rocks rose up on both sides. The rugged trail dropped considerably and the Land Rover crawled almost to a standstill because of uneven stones in the pathway. *What a perfect place for an ambush.* Her fingers automatically tightened around her rifle. She shifted in her seat and raised the gun toward the left side window, her forehead resting against the vibrating glass. The grayish brown sandstone wall stood less than three feet away. She looked up at a stretch of blue sky framed between the jagged peaks stabbing at the heavens, about sixty feet above their heads.

The Land Rover bounced over a deep crack in the ground. The rear end of the car swerved, almost scraping a couple of overhanging rocks spiking out of the wall. Carrie was able to see a wider view of the surroundings. She spotted the glint of an assault rifle and the banana-shaped magazine of an AK as two gunmen gave away their positions.

"Is this the only way in and out?" Carrie asked.

Nassir nodded slowly.

"Unless you're a bird," Ali said.

The trail widened into an oval clearing. Two black BMW Suburban vehicles parked at a V-shape angle had formed a checkpoint. Four black-clad gunmen toting AK assault rifles and RPK machine guns and standing to the sides of the Suburbans focused their complete attention on the approaching Land Rover.

"Is the Rover bulletproof?" Carrie asked with a hint of nervousness in her voice as she looked at Justin. Her pulse was thrumming, her heart pounding in her chest.

"Relax." Ali turned around to face Carrie. "They're not going to shoot us. I've got my men on higher ground." His hand made a circular gesture in the air. "Plus, the prisoner wants to talk to you."

Justin nodded. At the same time, he flicked his carbine firing selector to automatic. He cocked the gun and held it firmly in his hands, the barrel slightly raised up, and pointed it to the windshield.

"I said relax." Ali's hand slid instinctively over his AK-47.

"I *am* relaxed," Justin replied. "Have you forgotten?"

"I must have," Ali mumbled. "Stop the car there," he barked at Nassir and pointed to the right, about fifty feet away from the checkpoint.

* * *

Two of the black-clad gunmen marched toward the Land Rover while everyone was getting out of the vehicle.

"Where are your men?" Justin asked Ali.

"The guests insisted their guards wait here for you." Ali stepped around a few rocks barricading any attempt to swerve around the checkpoint. "My men are at the back."

Justin peered straight ahead and noticed the entrance to a small cave behind the two BMWs. It was next to a couple of green tents. Ali and Nassir proceeded to meet the guards, with Justin, Carrie, and Omar following a few steps back.

"The guns," one of the guards said in Arabic, gesturing toward Justin and Carrie, "they have to give us their guns."

Ali turned toward Justin, who kept cradling his carbine in his hands in a semi-alert position.

"We were summoned here for this meeting, and we've satisfied your chief's request," Justin replied in Arabic, speaking in a firm voice. "Our guns are for our protection. They guarantee we can also protect anything your chief may give us."

The guard was a tall, broad-shouldered man with a short pointy beard. He peered at Justin and asked, "Are you Algerian?"

"No." Justin reinforced his denial with a strong headshake. "And I'm not American either."

Justin was told by more than one North African his language proficiency showed no traces of local dialects. *Maybe he is Algerian, or has friends who are Algerians. People typically explain what they don't know with what they do.*

The bearded guard kept staring at Justin.

"We don't have all day." Ali waved his hand impatiently.

The bearded guard flogged Ali with a vicious glare and clenched his teeth. The other guard muttered something in an Arabic dialect unknown to Justin. The bearded guard nodded.

"This way," he ordered them gruffly. He raised his hand and

gestured for Justin and Carrie to follow him.

Ali began to lead the way, but the second guard took two steps forward to block him.

"Your job's done," the bearded guard growled at Ali. "They're ours now."

Ali looked like he was pondering a reply for a brief moment but chose not to talk back to the guards. "We'll wait at the tents," he said to Justin and Carrie in English. "Don't worry. My men are looking out for you."

"Thanks. We'll see you there." Justin exchanged a quick glance with Carrie. Her tiny smirk at the left corner of her lips confirmed his suspicions. They were all alone to fend for themselves.

The bearded guard led Justin and Carrie between the two BMWs. Justin's eyes rapidly took in the details of the valley. Seven men in black and white robes huddled in front of the cave next to a Toyota truck. Two men were sitting by the tents to the right of the cave. A third BMW, identical to the first two forming the checkpoint, was parked about three hundred feet away from the cave and the tents. It was under the shade cast by the ridge and behind a tall dune, which separated it visually from the rest of the valley. They were led in that direction.

"Wait here," the bearded guard ordered Justin and Carrie when they were a few steps away from the BMW.

He knocked on the front passenger door. The window was rolled down and a few hushed words were exchanged.

"Come here," the bearded guard called the agents and opened the BMW's rear door. Justin and Carrie approached the car slowly.

"Welcome," a low, deep voice greeted them in English. "Take a seat."

Justin recognized the sheikh's voice. He was sitting in the front passenger's seat and was alone. Carrie's eyes checked the car for any signs of danger, wires sticking out, or anything else resembling a deathtrap.

"Care for a drink?" the sheikh asked politely after they got in and closed the doors.

Carrie shook her head.

"No, thanks," Justin said.

He inspected the sheikh's face. The high brow with deep carved wrinkles and the receding gray hairline made him appear older than his late forties. He had a long hooked nose and a thick black moustache. His eyes were staring at Justin from behind a pair of square-shaped glasses. Justin recognized the sheikh's scar at the left side of his protruding jaw, where an Israeli-fired bullet had grazed the skin of his face. Five years ago, Mossad had made an unsuccessful attempt on the sheikh's life in Jordan.

"How was the trip?" the sheikh asked with genuine interest, turning around in his seat.

"Hot, very hot," Justin replied. "I would have preferred we met at the Nile City Fairmont."

The sheikh nodded. "That would have been my preference as well. We might have been able to prevent that bombing attack in Tripoli."

Justin and Carrie exchanged a quick glance.

"You're telling us the Alliance is behind those car bombs?" Justin asked.

The sheikh shook his head. "No, those car bombs are not the work of the Alliance."

"But you know who did it?" Justin asked.

"Let me start at the beginning," the sheikh replied. "But, before I do, come up here in front. I don't like to twist my neck as I talk to you."

Justin sat in the driver's seat.

"First things first: the Islamic Fighting Alliance is *not* at war with and does not target Libya, its government, or any Muslim brothers in that country. We're waging a holy war against infidels, against America and its bastard child, Israel, along with their many slaves who serve their insatiable greed for our oil and our wealth."

That's new, Justin thought. He remembered reading scores of briefing notes and reports covering clashes between the Alliance and rebel groups in Sudan and factions of militants in Lebanon and in the Gaza Strip. The Alliance's support for various groups fighting among themselves depended on their expectations of the most likely winner and the greatest gains to their cause in the long run. *New approach or new bullshit,* Justin wondered, but nodded nonetheless.

"Recently, a breakaway faction within the Alliance has supported an increase of attacks against Westerners' interests in North Africa. America and Britain and their local dogs are crushing the bones of the people living in these lands. North Africa is soaked with billions of oil barrels, but the only ones enjoying the oil profits are the foreign companies. The poor go hungry and naked."

"How large is this breakaway faction?" Justin asked, repeating the exact words of the sheikh.

"A few dozen people, but they're well-funded and well-connected to certain organizations based in Afghanistan and Iraq. They have the resources and the willingness to turn North Africa into a bloodier and messier Middle East."

"The bombing of the First Union Bank in Tunisia was their work?" asked Carrie.

"Yes. This splinter unit began targeting foreign investment firms, oil companies, banks, and their interests in Tunisia, Algeria, and Morocco. Of course, they work together with local militia groups who hate the regimes in their countries."

Carrie shrugged. "So, what's the problem? Isn't that what jihad is all about?"

Sheikh Ayman smiled. "Yes, we want to spread our Muslim faith, fight back the occupiers and the oppressors of our people and bring the peace of Allah to the infidels. But the means of achieving these goals do not include the slaughter of innocents, people who share our same faith. Besides, we cannot allow things to get out of hand. Realistically speaking, the Alliance can fight only one war at a time."

"So the Alliance, the part still under your command, refused to engage in this expansion of jihad in North Africa?" Justin asked.

The sheikh's furrow at the bridge of his nose deepened. His eyes became narrow and his stern gaze fell on Justin. "The Alliance is under the command of Sheikh Issa Mahub Al-Arhabi, to whom I offer my humble support," he said in a cold voice. "Most of the Alliance's faithful members stand behind Sheikh Al-Arhabi's decision *not* to take part in these attacks. This will break up our resources, which in turn will weaken our efforts and affect our expected results."

Spoken like a true economist, Justin thought, wondering whether Sheikh Ayman had received a degree in economics or had worked as an economist in a previous life. If he did, it would have been before he embraced a more radical approach to the redistribution of the wealth of nations than the one suggested by Adam Smith. Justin tried to hide his grin and asked, "This splinter unit is responsible for last afternoon's attacks?"

"That's correct. Regretfully, we were not able to stop the carnage."

Justin peered at the sheikh, trying to read his face, taking advantage of a few seconds when he looked through the window's dark glass. *He's really regretting suicide bombings?*

"Did you know about the intended targets of these attacks?" Justin asked.

"We had a pretty good idea. A couple of trusted men inside this faction keep us informed about their plans. And we know exactly who's going to be the target of their assassination attempt."

The sheikh casually brushed the left corner of his nicely trimmed moustache.

Justin rested his back against the door and crossed his arms in front of his chest. "I suppose you'll present us your demands before giving us the name of the target."

The sheikh nodded slowly. "You're right. I will ask for something in return, yes, but the information you'll receive is more than worth it."

"I'm listening," Justin said.

Sheikh Ayman leaned forward. "Here is what the Alliance is asking from the Canadian government." After checking that his guards were not standing too close to the car, he lowered his voice to barely a whisper. "Tripoli's explosions have unleashed the wrath of Libya's mukhabarat upon the Alliance's network of connections, not only in that country, but also in Egypt, Sudan, and elsewhere. They can't tell between traitors and faithful members and don't care who they slaughter. We don't want our brothers to be gutted for crimes they didn't commit."

I'm sure your brothers are already guilty of a multitude of crimes even without these car bombings, Justin wanted to explode in the sheikh's face, but he just nodded in silence.

"Canada's mediation between the Alliance and the Libyan government officials, especially the prime minister, will ensure the punishment falls on the true instigators and executors of these attacks. At the same time, this will help bring an end to hostilities already started against families and relatives of the Alliance members in Libya."

Justin frowned. "Let me understand this: you want Canada to take the side of the Alliance in your war with Libya's government?"

"Absolutely not. Libya's government is not our enemy," the sheikh blurted out, unwittingly grinding his teeth. Realizing his blunder, he flashed them a reassuring smile and added in a much softer, lower voice, "Libya is not our enemy. We simply want its government to understand our true position. We have no involvement at all in these explosions in their country. In exchange, we're able to provide the Libyan mukhabarat with a list of names of those who are responsible for this bloodbath and where they can be found."

The sheikh paused and stared into the agents' eyes. Justin's face betrayed no emotion. He was looking at the sheikh's bodyguards standing about ten feet away from the car. Carrie seemed more concerned with wiping a stream of sweat from her forehead than giving any thought to the sheikh's proposal.

"This is a very tall order," Justin said. "Senior political figures will have to sign on to this deal. Concrete and valuable evidence will be necessary to convince them."

Sheikh Ayman closed his eyes and nodded slightly. "You're right, but we have a good chance of preventing further killings, *killings* that may lead to a new, bloody conflict."

"Why haven't you asked for help from the US?" Carrie asked. "They have much more clout than Canada in Libya now that their relationship is back on track."

The sheikh sighed. "America is our greatest enemy. Plus, once I tell you the identity of the faction's target, you'll understand our reasons for not contacting the US. But before we go that far, I need some assurances that Canada will facilitate the Alliance's negotiations with Libya."

"You have my personal commitment that we'll make our best efforts to clarify the Alliance's position and to seek a peaceful solution." Justin chose his words carefully, unwilling to make a promise he could not keep. "Still, I need the approval of my superiors, and they'll have to agree on the next steps."

Sheikh Ayman was nodding continuously, satisfied with Justin's reply.

"Now who's the next target?" Justin asked.

"The next target is the president of the United States of America."

"What?" Justin and Carrie asked in a single voice.

"You heard me correctly. The breakaway faction is planning the assassination of the American president in Tripoli next week, during her visit for the G-20 Summit."

"No freaking way," Carrie said, "how can you be sure of that?"

"We know about their plans and their preparations under way to execute a very sophisticated assassination. I have them in my briefcase, here with me." The sheikh pointed to a leather briefcase resting next to his feet.

"Is this intel true?" Justin asked.

"Absolutely. I trust these sources with my own life," the sheikh replied.

Here the T-word creeps up again. Justin pursed his lips. He always became tense whenever someone began to lean on the weak crutches of trust instead of the firm foundation of facts.

"I need to review these documents and verify this information," he said, "if, and when, we are certain about their—"

A rumble from the sky interrupted him. The familiar rattle of heavy helicopters grew louder.

"What the hell is that?" the sheikh asked, rolling down the window.

Before anyone could reply, the screeching sound of a missile cut through the air. A second later, a great explosion rocked the sheikh's car.

CHAPTER 6

Great Sand Sea, Sudan
May 14, 10:47 a.m. local time

The explosion sprayed metal shrapnel and rock fragments at the BMW. Its armored glass resisted the impact. Threads of cobwebs appeared in the cracked windshield. A long barrage of gunfire burst outside the car. The sheikh's guards were responding to the attack.

"Everyone OK?" Justin asked.

Carrie nodded. Ducked behind the front passenger's seat, her sweaty fingers wrapped around her rifle trembled slightly.

"You led those Egyptian dogs into my den," the sheikh howled at Justin in Arabic.

Justin met the sheikh's eyes. The air strike had enraged rather than scared the battle-hardened veteran.

"Of course not," Justin hissed.

The bearded guard threw open the driver's side door. He pointed his AK at Justin, who pressed his carbine into the guard's chest.

"I'm not the enemy," Justin shouted in Arabic.

The guard held his AK in place, inches away from Justin's face.

Sheikh Ayman barked an order and the bearded guard stepped back and lowered his gun.

The rumble, which had begun to fade, returned. This time, it was an almost ear-splitting thunder.

"The chopper's lower, much lower," Justin said.

The sheikh glanced out of a clear corner of the windshield. "Two of them." He pushed open the passenger's door. "First one, ten o'clock; second one, two o'clock. Seven hundred yards away at the most."

By the time Justin slithered outside the car, Carrie had assumed a firing position, kneeling by the rear wheels of the BMW. Her C7 rifle was pointed to the sky. She was waiting for the moment when the helicopters would appear in her sight. Justin pulled his carbine's retractable stock, adjusted its length, and set it firmly against his shoulder. Then he sat back on his right heel, two steps behind Carrie. His index finger rested on the grenade launcher trigger.

"Who knew about our meeting?" Justin shouted at the sheikh.

"Your gun dealing friends," he replied.

The sheikh had fetched himself an RPK machine gun. He was stretched over the sandy ground, holding his fire until the helicopters drew nearer.

"My gun dealing friends are getting hammered just like us," Justin said

A missile exploded about fifty feet away from one of the Land Rovers. A few men scurried away from the tents in all directions. Two or three of Ali's gunmen were spraying volleys of bullets against the helicopters dropping over the valley. Two rocket-propelled grenades screamed through the sky. Their smoke exhaust tinted the sky with a grayish hue, but both projectiles missed their swift moving targets.

"Sudanese?" Justin asked.

"No clue," the sheikh replied.

The helicopters swooped over their heads. Carrie took a deep breath and swung her rifle, following the movements of the helicopters. She squeezed a rapid burst, emptying the entire 30-round magazine. She fed the rifle a fresh clip and before the empty magazine hit the ground, she resumed blasting at the first helicopter.

Justin took a little longer before firing his single shot. He aimed about half an inch higher than the second helicopter then pulled the trigger of his grenade launcher. The high-explosive warhead whooshed toward the target. It struck the helicopter at its tail shaft, under the three-bladed rotor hub. Black smoke swallowed up the helicopter, then bright yellow flames began licking at its long brown tail.

The helicopter dropped a few feet but was able to complete a one hundred and eighty degree turn. It rushed back for a second sweep over the valley, following the other helicopter.

"Hide, hide, hide," Carrie shouted, sliding underneath the sheikh's car.

The sheikh kept drumming his machine gun. A torrent of bullets poured forth from the weapon against the incoming helicopters.

"Hurry up! Come here! Quick," Justin shouted.

The helicopter rattle rose above his cries. Another missile flew out. Then came the shrill of the explosion. The warhead blew up at the base of a tall sandstone boulder. It smashed it into two large blocks ten feet away from the sheikh's position. A downpour of rocks and sand covered him. Bullets from helicopters' gunners began scraping away bedrock fragments around his position.

"Sheikh, Sheikh Ayman," Justin shouted. *Is he wounded? Dead?*

No reply. The sheikh's machine gun was silent.

"Is he dead?" Carrie asked.

"I don't know."

Justin turned around underneath the BMW, careful to avoid bumping his head against its rear axle. Bullets thumped against the doors.

"What's Ali doing?" Justin's eyes followed the helicopters. They had ascended over the cliffs and resembled two black dots against the background of a cotton-ball cloud. Justin had no illusions the attack was over.

"There's three, no, four guys still fighting." Carrie looked at the gunmen around the tents. "One Rover's hit; a tent's on fire. A dust cloud is around the cave . . . Looks like a missile landed there."

"We need a heavy gun, an RPG will do." Justin searched the clearing for the best vantage point. "There." He pointed to his left toward the narrow opening leading into the valley.

Carrie followed his hand gesture. She saw a bullet-ridden Land Rover with two doors ajar. The front tires had caught fire. "Negative. Too far and too hot," she said. "Rover by the cave is a better option."

Justin shook his head. "We don't know if there's a mole in Ali's band. Cover me."

He began sprinting toward the Land Rover. Carrie turned her attention back to the cave. None of the gunmen scrambling by the tents were paying attention to Justin running bent at the waist. But the helicopters were taking notice. A long barrage of machine gun fire burst from the air. Bullets kicked up dirt as they struck a few feet away from him.

"Cover fire, cover fire," Carrie shouted at Ali's gunmen.

She blasted her rifle in rapid succession. Two gunmen followed her calls.

Justin was crisscrossing between clusters of small dunes. He rolled down a gentle slope while one of the helicopters circled over the clearing. Justin pointed his carbine toward the flying target, firing quick bursts before resuming his sprint. Seconds later, he reached the burning Land Rover.

Two gunmen lay sprawled beside it. There was nothing he could do for them. But they could still do something for him. An RPG-7 launcher was lying at the feet of one of the dead gunmen. He made sure the weapon was intact and the grenade was loaded properly at the launcher's muzzle. Then he shouldered the grenade launcher with a swift gesture. Justin estimated the distance from the helicopter at about a thousand feet. The rotor blades and the dolphin nose shape of the fuselage were visible as his sight locked onto the closest target.

He pulled the trigger.

The grenade screamed, leaving the launcher at over three

hundred feet per second. Justin's eyes followed the diagonal flight of the warhead through the gray smoke curtain mushrooming around him from the weapon's breech. The helicopter swung abruptly to the left. Justin bit his lip, thinking the grenade would miss its target. But the warhead hit the tail boom close to the engine mount.

The helicopter lost altitude, nose-diving into the valley. It dashed at full speed, straight for a head-on collision with the mountain ridge. A trail of black smoke followed its unstable course.

The helicopter struggled to soar up before reaching the sheer rocky walls. It seemed to succeed in scaling the two hundred feet high climb and almost cleared the entire face of the ridge. At the last moment, the two rear wheels banged against an overhanging cliff. The helicopter crashed over the peak. Black smoke clouded Justin's view, just before an overwhelming explosion. Scorched debris from the wreckage rained over a wide area down in the valley.

Justin turned his attention to the second helicopter. Carrie and Ali's gunmen had concentrated all their firepower on bringing it down. The helicopter began its retreat, gray smoke pouring out of its tail shaft. Its getaway flight was erratic, with constant dips and dives. He wondered if the pilot had little control over the helicopter or he was dodging rocket-propelled grenades exploding around the helicopter's tail.

It was the latter. The helicopter rocketed high above the ridge and disappeared over the narrow pathway connecting the valley to the rest of the desert.

"The bastard escaped." Justin let the grenade launcher fall to the ground, looking up at the empty sky.

A car engine cough startled him. He turned on his heels, drawing his Browning pistol from his ankle holster. A Land Rover stopped next to him.

"Get in," Carrie called from the driver's seat. A gunman was sitting in the front with her.

Justin noticed a bruise on the left corner of her lips and scratch marks on the right side of her chin.

"You're wounded." Justin walked to the car. "You OK?"

"I'm fine. You got clipped too." She pointed to his left knee.

A trickle of blood was trailing over his torn pants.

"A sharp rock." Justin shrugged.

"Get in. We can still catch the pricks."

"You think so?"

"Positive. I poured two mags into the chopper. Khalid here believes an RPG tore through its tail. That's on top of your grenade. They can't go too far."

Khalid nodded, his white teeth flashing against his dark skin.

Justin sat behind him and Carrie gunned the Land Rover. They passed by the checkpoint and Carrie slowed down. She avoided the debris and the dead bodies littering the area. The two BMWs were burning slowly, bright orange flames chewing through the front tires and the rear doors. A column of dark smoke was rising up. It followed sudden gusts of a soft breeze changing direction almost every second.

"No survivors," Justin said.

Khalid spat out the window. "Good. Those Arabs brought death here, like they always do. They deserved to die."

Carrie entered the narrow pathway. She drove fast through the broken terrain. The Land Rover bounced over natural speed bumps, its wheels turning dangerously with every swinging curve. The left side of the hood scraped against the wall.

"Maybe you want to slow down," Justin suggested as the Land Rover jumped over a pile of rocks.

Carrie eased on the gas pedal but only for a few seconds.

"What's the status of your team?" Justin asked Khalid.

The gunman took a moment to process the question. "Some men dead. Seven, maybe eight. Two or three still alive," he replied in broken English.

"Ali, how's Ali?" Justin asked.

Khalid shook his head. "He got shot in chest by shrap . . . rocket pieces."

Justin frowned.

"How did they find us?" Carrie asked.

"The Arabs. They gave enemy our location," Khalid replied.

OK, but who is this enemy? Justin wondered while they passed through the last turns of the pathway.

They had not reached the open desert when an ear-splitting explosion caught them by surprise.

Carrie steered around a sand dune, and the helicopter crash site appeared in front of them. Reddish dust had begun to rise over the wreckage about five miles away from the ridge.

"Unlucky bastard," Justin said in a low voice. "Escaping the battleground only to fall to his death."

They drove toward the crash site. Justin took in the scene, imagining how the crash might have taken place. The tail boom of the helicopter was split in half and the cabin was turned to its starboard side. The fuselage was buried halfway into the sand, evidence of a violent but fireless crash. The rotor blades were twisted and tangled.

"Watch out for survivors," Carrie said.

They surveyed the area from a distance of a few dozen feet without leaving their vehicle.

"I don't see anything moving but let's push in carefully," Justin said.

They stepped out of the car and began to advance very slowly. Guns drawn, they carefully covered every direction and every angle.

"Pilot and co-pilot dead." Justin peeked at the flight deck through the crushed windshield. He sidestepped around a mound of sand and fragments of rotor blades to reach the port side of the helicopter.

"Gunner's toast." Carrie pointed to the body of a young, dark-skinned man.

Justin looked around.

"What's that?" He gestured toward a brown square-shaped object tossed about fifty feet away from the helicopter's mangled doors.

"I don't know," Carrie replied.

She walked over to the object. "It's a military pack."

"How did it get there?"

"Thrown by the crash, I assume."

A deep sigh, almost a rasp, followed by a muted cough startled them.

Justin pointed his gun to the left, in the direction of the sound, which came from behind a small dune.

"Did you hear that?" he asked Carrie in a hushed voice

Carrie nodded. "A survivor."

They fell down, their noses inches away from the sand.

Carrie said, "He's wounded but probably armed."

A short burst of automatic gunfire confirmed her words.

"I'll go left. You cover me." Justin pointed to the small dune.

"Let's do it."

Carrie cocked her rifle and gestured to Justin to move forward. He began crawling, his pistol in his right hand and ready for fire. After Justin had covered about twenty feet up the gentle slope, Carrie got up to her feet and began pounding the dune. She fired short bursts, two or three rounds each time, advancing a few steps between the shots. The return fire was weak, sporadic, and not on target.

After reloading, Carrie switched her rifle to automatic. She fired a long barrage, about half of her 30- round magazine. Her bullets pierced through the crest and the slopes of the dune. Their purpose was to force the shooter to stay down and seek cover. She glanced at Justin, but he had already edged around the dune and out of sight.

A couple of seconds later, she heard a loud shout. "Drop it," Justin barked in Arabic. "Drop it now! I said put down your gun!"

There was no reply.

Carrie rushed to the top of the dune. She saw Justin pressing his pistol against the head of a young man. He was wavering on his knees, struggling to balance his weak body. The young man had raised his right arm over his head in sign of surrender. His left arm dangled along his side like a withered branch. He was no older than thirty, clean-shaven and was wearing a beige shirt and matching pants. They resembled some kind of uniform, the same as the clothes worn by the dead helicopter crew. A camouflage pattern bulletproof vest and a rig with ammunitions and supplies covered his chest and his waist.

"Justin, you're OK?" Carrie asked, moving behind the captive.

"Yes, I'm OK."

"Is he Sudanese militia?"

"Haven't questioned him yet."

The young man gasped, his head falling over his chest. Khalid ran toward Carrie.

"Oh, good, one of them alive," Khalid said in English while catching his breath. He switched to Arabic and asked the captive, "What's the name of your unit?"

The young man shook his head. When Khalid repeated the question, the young man barked his reply in two short, broken sentences.

"What did he say?" Carrie asked impatiently, her eyes bouncing between Justin and Khalid.

Justin's gaze was fixed on the captive's chest. Khalid shook his head and spat on the ground.

"What the hell did he say?" Carrie asked.

"Not the words but how he speak," Khalid replied. "This man, this fighter, he's no Sudanese. He's no Egyptian."

"So, where did he come from?" Carrie glared at the man's dark face. Justin could tell what she was thinking: *he looks Arab to me.*

Justin locked eyes with Carrie. "Come here," he said.

He was paying more attention to Khalid, who was headed toward the helicopter, than to the captive's hands. When she got really close, he whispered in her ear, "I think he's Israeli."

"What? Impossible!"

"He's wearing a necklace and the pendant is the Star of David. See for yourself."

Carrie pushed down the young man's shirt collar with the muzzle of her rifle. A thin gold chain held a small pendant in the hexagon shape, the well-known symbol of the Hebrew nation.

"Shit! Shit! Shit!" Carrie blurted out. "Who the hell are you? IDF? Mil Intel? Mossad? Tell us!"

The captive offered them a tired but stoic grin.

Justin sighed. "Whoever this man is, our mess just got ten times harder than we thought."

CHAPTER 7

Dubai, United Arab Emirates
May 14, 1:55 p.m. local time

Zakir clutched the BlackBerry in his small hand as if the tight grip would make Monsieur Burgoyne at the other end of the call change his mind. He took a deep breath to gain a few precious seconds, then selected another word instead of the string of obscenities served by his enraged mind. "The prince will be extremely displeased and very, very disappointed."

His tone of voice conveyed a terse edginess. Like Saudi Prince Husayn bin Al-Farhan, Zakir, the prince's personal aide, was not accustomed to people saying "no" to his demands.

"My sincerest apologies to you and to the prince. I apologize on behalf of our staff and of our company." The Frenchman's apology came with his trademark politeness and nasal accent. "It is impossible, simply impossible to satisfy the prince's request. Bugatti Veyron Super Sport creations, like all our editions, have to fulfill very strict international standards of safety. We cannot, simply cannot, boost the engine horsepower in order to increase the speed. You see, the other parts of the automobile, the tires, headlights, mirrors, they cannot withstand such radical changes."

"I'm not interested in a crash course in car mechanics. I'm

interested in making sure the prince owns the fastest and the most powerful car in the world," Zakir said. "You will hear from me again, once the prince is informed about your refusal. I promise you, it will not be pleasant."

He ended the call and began cursing at Chief Engineer Burgoyne and his design team at the Bugatti manufacturing plant in France. *How dare they refuse the prince's request? Don't they know who he is and that he can buy the entire plant, if he wants?* The prince was not considered extremely rich by sheikhs' standards. Still, with a net worth of five billion dollars, he frequently made the Forbes list of the richest people of the world.

A range of options appeared in Zakir's mind. He could present those options to the prince, to ease the sting of the French rejection and to save himself a great amount of humiliation. Prince Al-Farhan was notorious for literally shooting the messenger, especially when they bore bad news. Zakir had learned many tricks over the years to ensure his survival. The prince wanted the 100th car of his collection to be a Bugatti Veyron Super Sport, but customized with a larger engine and a higher speed to fit his billion-dollar ego. *I can set up a meeting with the Board of Directors of Bugatti and convince them to accept the prince's proposal. Perhaps the prince can make a considerable donation to one of their stupid museums or universities. Or perhaps I can convince the prince to accept a German or Italian aftermarket customization of a standard Veyron.*

He stood up from his desk and glanced through floor-to-ceiling windows down at the city's fascinating skyline. From the prince's apartment on the 72nd floor of the newly finished Burj Khalifa, Zakir admired the city unfolding underneath his feet. His eyes followed the traffic racing through the six lanes of Sheikh Zayed Road. The thirty-for-mile stretch led to the border with Abu Dhabi, the capital of the United Arab Emirates, where Prince Al-Farhan was sealing an oil exploration business deal with powerful French investors.

His BlackBerry chirped with the arrival of another call. Zakir checked the caller ID and grinned. He spoke with clear anticipation in his voice, "Nassir, what is the good news?"

"We were ambushed," Nassir rasped, loud clatter echoing in the background. "Almost everyone is dead. We're pulling bodies out of the cars as we speak."

"The sheikh?" Zakir asked. "Is the sheikh alive?"

"No, sir. The sheikh is dead."

"Did he finish his job?"

"I think he did. He was talking to the Canadian agents when two choppers attacked our camp."

"What rebel group was it?"

"Unconfirmed. We brought down both choppers, old Mi-17s. Everyone aboard is dead. The Sudanese Air Force often uses such choppers to attack rebel strongholds. The Liberty Front and Unionists also have such models. Egypt too is full of them."

"What are the Canadian agents doing?"

"The man, Justin, is on a satphone. Talking to his chiefs, I assume. The woman, Carrie, is examining the briefcase. She's going through a stack of documents in a large black folder."

"The sheikh's briefcase? Tell me it's the sheikh's briefcase." Zakir placed the BlackBerry in front of his mouth so that Nassir would not miss a word.

"Yes, it is," Nassir confirmed.

"Allahu Akbar! This is the good news that should have started your call," Zakir shouted. "The prince will be extremely pleased to know you have delivered on your promise." *And maybe, just maybe, the news about the Bugatti Veyron will not sound that bad after all.*

Nassir barked a few orders to someone and Zakir quickly turned down the volume on his phone. "Nassir, you're still there?" he asked after a few seconds.

"Yes, just having trouble with one of our Rovers. A bullet has pierced the radiator, so I'm telling my men how to patch it up."

"Do you know if the agents are going to intermediate for the Alliance?"

"I'm not sure. All the sheikh's men are dead."

"That's not a problem. They're all replaceable," Zakir said. "Stay close to the agents and learn their intentions. Then call me with an update."

"Sir, they've already picked one of Ali's men as their guide. It will be difficult to follow their moves."

Zakir began to pace around the room. "Nassir, do I have to explain everything to you? *Become* the replacement for the guide at any cost. In this way, you'll always be with them. We need to know what they're going to do and where they're headed."

"I understand. My tasks are clear now," Nassir replied in a humble tone.

"Great, I'm glad you finally got it. Sometimes I wonder why the prince wastes his money on you."

Nassir did not mouth off an angry reply. "I'll call you back to inform you of new developments," he said.

"Do so in good time," Zakir said before pressing the End Call button on his BlackBerry.

Great Sand Sea, Sudan
May 14, 11:55 a.m. local time

"No, we have no way of confirming his identity with a hundred percent certainty." Justin curbed his anger to a mere raise in his voice.

"I understand you're in a difficult situation, Justin, but keep your cool," Johnson said over the satellite phone connection. "How do we know this man is not simply a supporter of the Israeli cause?"

"One of the local Tuaregs swears the man's accent is not North African. And I mentioned earlier the man is wearing the Star of David around his neck." Justin clenched the phone handset.

"Any helpful evidence found on him or at the crash site?"

"No, none. Ali's men indentified some of the bodies of the helicopters' crews as Sudanese militants. They belonged to a group called Freedom for North Sudan."

There was a tense pause for a few moments.

"So you believe your captive is a Mossad field agent?" Johnson asked.

"Yes, I do. And I don't want to be his watcher or get in the way of a Mossad rescue mission."

Another pause followed. Justin could hear the mental gears turning inside Johnson's head.

"What are you suggesting, Justin?" she asked finally.

"An intel exchange. Israelis tell us the nature of their operation here in Sudan and how it ties to the attack against the sheikh. In turn, we give them the location of their agent."

"Is this man in your custody?"

"No, but we know where he is," Justin replied, looking at the black smoke from the burning helicopter ballooning above the ridge. They had lit up the fuel, leaving no evidence for the surviving gunmen to dig up when rummaging through the wreckage. Their attempts at looting the other helicopter had produced nothing of significance. "I don't want Mossad to come after us, thinking we have their man. I want to avoid a war with Tel Aviv at all costs."

"Is he safe at least?"

"Yes, for the moment. But deserts of Sudan are not the safest place on the planet even for well-trained Mossad agents. The man has a shoulder wound, which we treated, and which will not cause his death. Dehydration, on the other hand . . ."

"All right, ensure his safety until I get a reply from the Israelis."

"I will, but my first priority is to ensure the safety of my team as we complete our mission."

"I expect nothing less," Johnson said dryly. "Now back to the late sheikh's demands. You told me about the promise you made him. I'll talk to our minister about that. How certain are we the intelligence obtained from the sheikh is reliable?"

Carrie coughed and Justin moved the satellite phone handset closer to her. She said, "At first glance, the documents seem legit. The photos look undoctored, the signatures authentic. The assassination plan against the US president is very real."

"OK, I'll talk to the CIA and the Secret Service. They have

advance ground teams already in Libya, since their president's visit to Tripoli takes place in three days."

"Great, so they can handle this situation and return us the favor later," Justin said.

"Not so quick," Johnson said, "I want you to deliver this intelligence to the Americans and assist them in investigating this plot."

Justin took a deep breath before replying to his boss, "This is not part of our mission and was not—"

"Now it *is* part of your mission, Justin. I expect your fully cooperation with the Americans. You will get to Tripoli tonight."

Justin's right hand tightened into a fist. His fingers crackled and his jaws clamped shut as he began grinding his teeth. Two years ago, a botched rescue operation in Libya had landed Justin and Abdul—one of the CIS local contacts—in one of Libya's worst torture chambers. Their nightmare ended with a prison escape as they fought their way out of hell, leaving behind a long trail of dead demons. The torture slashes on Justin's back healed well in a matter of months; the grave marks carved in his memory took much longer. Some never healed.

Carrie leaned closer to the phone. "Ms. Johnson, with all due respect, our relationship with the Secret Service has not been the greatest. After yesterday's explosions Tripoli will be extremely hostile. Our presence will only complicate the situation."

"I understand your concerns, Carrie, and I'm fully aware of recent developments in Tripoli. Our Cairo station is providing us hourly updates and they'll give you any support you need, serving as your backup."

Justin cleared his throat. "Can't the rest of the Cairo station handle this?" he asked with caution, avoiding a direct confrontation with his boss.

"Yes, they can, but not as efficiently as you and Carrie. You've already been briefed and are familiar with all details. Besides, you have experience working in Libya and a considerable network of contacts. And this is a matter of national security for Canada too. Our prime minister will attend the G-20 Summit in Tripoli along with the US president and dignitaries of other countries."

"Oh, really?" Justin asked.

"Well, schedule permitting." Johnson seemed to take a step back from her previous assertion. "In any case," she added hastily, "an assassination attempt would throw Libya and the entire North Africa back into chaos. After the civil wars, the car bombings and the events in Tunisia and Egypt, we need to do everything to maintain stability in this region."

Justin mulled over Johnson's last words. She was right, in part. It was a very sensitive situation and he was already at the center of the storm. *Anna will never forgive me for missing both her birthday and our anniversary.* More than the revenge of his sworn enemies in Libya's mukhabarat, Justin feared shattering Anna's hopes of a peaceful and memorable getaway.

"I'll arrange for a chopper to meet you at the Egyptian border. It's too hot to have them fly into Sudan as originally planned because of this attack," Johnson said. "I'll ask them, but I'm sure they'll not do it. Once you're back in Cairo, secure the intel from the sheikh and the alleged Israeli agent at two separate, safe locations. I'll update you on Mossad and US Secret Service responses. Then, make plans to get to Tripoli and meet with the Secret Service advance team."

"We've taken pictures of the Israeli agent and of some of the documents from the sheikh's briefcase," Carrie said. "I'll send them to you right away."

"Perfect."

"The sooner we return the agent to Mossad, the more time we'll have to unravel this plot," Justin said without much conviction. He was not sure if he preferred staying in Cairo while chained to an Israeli agent, waiting for a Mossad rescue team to shoot him in the face, or sneaking into Tripoli and risk being chained to a torture pole, waiting for Libyan henchmen to cut his throat.

"Cairo is not their most preferred place to do business. Although, if this man is really theirs, they'll send a team in no time," Johnson said.

"This man is not my responsibility," Justin said, "I hope the Israelis don't delay. And I hope they come in peace."

"Saving the life of their field agent is sufficient reason to come in peace. *Mazel tov,* Justin."

Justin sighed, not appreciating Johnson's attempt at humor. He mumbled, "Let's wait for congratulations until the exchange is over."

"Call me in an hour. I should have some instructions by then about your transport and this man."

"We'll do."

"Good luck to both of you."

"Thanks," Justin and Carrie replied almost in a single voice.

They stared at each other in deep silence for a few long moments.

"What are the chances we'll still be alive at the end of this?" Carrie asked.

"Do you have a will?" Justin replied.

Before she could say anything, loud noises erupted in the gunmen camp. Two men were exchanging blows. Justin recognized Nassir and Khalid as the fighters while two other men were cheering them on. At one point, Nassir produced a pistol. He pressed it against Khalid's chest, who threw his arms up in complete surrender.

"Hey, knock it off! Stop! Stop!" Justin charged toward the grim spectacle. "What's the reason for—"

His words were cut off by a loud gunshot. Justin's hands instinctively went to his carbine. Khalid collapsed to the ground two steps away from Nassir's feet.

"What the hell did he do to you?" Justin shouted at Nassir as he leaned over Khalid's body. Blood was gushing from a large wound and the man had no pulse. At point blank, Nassir's shot had proven fatal. Carrie held up her rifle inches away from Nassir's head.

"He . . . he was a traitor," Nassir replied, a small GSh-18 Russian-made pistol still in his left hand. "And, you saw, it was an accident . . . I mean self-defense."

Justin gazed at Nassir. There was a glow of self-contentment on the man's grin. The killer's face showed no hint of guilt or remorse. *Not even the slightest concern about the young man, whose life he ended with a single, cold-blooded gesture. A natural killer. But I've got more important issues on my plate.*

"Time to go," he said to Carrie, who was still holding her rifle pointed at Nassir.

"What about Khalid?" she asked.

Justin gave the dead body another glance. Then his eyes rested on the two gunmen. They were standing at the side of the Land Rover, dazzled by the deadly turn of events.

"You," Justin called at the younger of the two, barely in his twenties, who had no weapons in his hands or on his body. "You speak English?"

The man gave no reply while the other one opened his mouth and said, "I speak English."

"I will take you safely to the Egyptian border—" Nassir said.

Justin interrupted him with a stern glance and a strong headshake.

"Carrie, kill this man." Justin pointed with his hand to the silent young man.

She nodded and swung her rifle away from Nassir, who blinked rapidly in shock. The young man kept staring at Justin, then asked in Arabic the other man, who was slowly backing away from the Land Rover, "What is he saying? What are they doing?"

"Don't talk to him," Justin shouted. "Carrie, kill this man," he repeated his order.

She moved closer to the young man with her gun pointing down. The young man, still oblivious to the threat against his life, eyed her curiously. It seemed he was wondering about the agents' sudden interest in him.

Justin was using a CIS trick to find out if the man really understood their language. If he remained calm in the face of mounting danger, the man either knew no English or knew no fear. In both cases, these were qualities Justin was looking for at this moment.

"What do you want?" the man asked finally, again in Arabic, as Carrie stood right in front of him.

"Do you know the roads to northern Chad?" Justin asked him in Arabic.

The man nodded. "I can get you to Agoza by sunset," he replied with confidence.

"That's in the Ennedi region, right?" Justin asked, to check if the man was telling the truth and knew how to get them to Sudan's western neighbor.

"Right," the man replied. "Very secluded and remote."

Justin smiled. *He is telling the truth.* "Yes, it's a great hiding place."

He could not care less whether Agoza was secluded or whether it was a safe place. They were not going west to Agoza. Cairo, their destination, was northeast. But if Mossad, the Alliance or anyone else asked about the agents, Justin wanted to lead them after false trails in the deserts of northern Chad.

"Fantastic," Justin said. "We've got a deal. What's your name?"

"Mus'ad"

"Well, Mus'ad, today's your lucky day," Justin said, emphasizing the young man's name, which in Arabic meant favored by fortune. He pulled out a wad of American dollars from his knapsack. "Five thousand." He waved the money in the air. "If we're in Agoza by sunset."

Mus'ad's eyebrows jumped up at the lucrative proposal. The amount was a remarkable payoff even among gunrunners. Justin could see the man was already thinking how he was going to spend the promised cash.

"I'll get you there in plenty of time for dinner and drinks," Mus'ad said.

Nassir was observing their exchange in silence.

"We part ways here," Justin said, turning toward Nassir and stretching out his hand.

Nassir hesitated for a moment. He holstered his pistol inside his belt and gave Justin's hand a firm grip.

"Watch out for rebels," he whispered, "the road to Chad is full of traps. Starving refugees, militia, bandits, kidnappers . . . Without proper protection, you're in grave danger."

"I appreciate your concern, but we're going to be just fine," Justin replied. "So long."

Carrie followed him as Justin approached the other gunman. He was still standing at a distance from Nassir and the Land Rover.

"We need a favor," Justin whispered and shoved a few hundred dollar bills in the man's left hand, "give Ali and Khalid a proper burial. They died fighting and they deserve to leave his world in an honorable way."

The gunman nodded and quickly hid his money underneath his robe.

"Thank you and so long," Justin said, loud enough for Nassir to hear, if he was eavesdropping. "Mus'ad, it's time to go."

CHAPTER 8

Forty-five miles south of the Egyptian border
Great Sand Sea, Sudan
May 14, 12:35 p.m. local time

Ten minutes later, Justin ordered Mus'ad, the driver, to stop the sheikh's BMW by the burning helicopter's wreckage. Carrie stood guard to ensure Mus'ad did not steal a glance at their precious package. The four-seater had only two rows, and Justin and Carrie debated whether their package should be stowed away in the trunk or should stay in the backseat.

At the end, they decided the first option provided more discretion. Justin led the suspected Israeli agent inside the BMW's trunk. He made sure the captive had sufficient oxygen and the air circulation inside the car kept a reasonably cool temperature in the trunk. Justin left the lid of the trunk inside the BMW slightly open, to provide for a greater visibility when checking the package's conditions. Wounded, tied, and gagged, the Israeli agent presented no real threat of escape. At least in theory. But Justin had witnessed numerous cases of incredible disappearances. He was leaving nothing to chance, convinced that everything was possible for a man of Mossad.

Half an hour into the drive, Justin took out his satellite phone from his knapsack.

"You ready for this call?" Carrie asked.

"Not really. But I've got to do it."

"She's not gonna like it."

"I know," Justin replied with a deep sigh.

The satellite phone grew heavy in his hand as Justin considered his options. Realizing he had none, he forced his fingers to dial Anna's number.

"Hi, sweetie," he said softly after hearing Anna's voice, "how are things there?"

"Great. You're OK?"

"Yes, yes. I'm fine."

"You didn't call me yesterday. I waited by the phone for an hour."

"I know, I'm sorry," Justin replied with a wince as Carrie shook her head. "I just didn't have a chance."

"I understand. Now tell me you're calling from the airport."

"Hmmm . . . No, I'm not at the airport. There has been a change of plans."

Dead silence followed. Justin thought the connection was interrupted, but a second later he heard Anna's weak breath.

"So you're not flying home tonight?" she asked.

"No, not tonight."

"Tomorrow night?"

"Sweetie, I don't know when I'll come home."

Another few dead moments.

"Should I cancel our trip?"

"Yes, please."

"Will you at least make it for my birthday, and . . . and our anniversary?"

It was now Justin's turn to hold his tongue.

"I take that as a no, Justin."

"Sorry, it doesn't always depend on me."

"Where is Johnson sending you now?"

Justin hesitated before answering. "I can't . . . can't really explain that . . . I'm not alone at the moment."

Although they had sealed the Israeli's ears with rough and ready earplugs, and Mus'ad understood no English, Justin was not willing to take any unnecessary risks. Besides, agents were expected not to reveal the nature or the location of their missions. Justin preferred to give Anna any another explanation than the standard reference to the agency's operatives manual.

"So what can you tell me?" Anna asked.

"That I love you," Justin replied.

"Are you going to be safe? Promise me you're going to be safe."

"You know I don't like making promises I can't keep."

"Exactly. So make it and keep it."

"I'll do my best to be safe. And I want you to take care of yourself as well."

"Oh, what will happen to me? A legal briefing will fall on my lap?"

"You know what I mean."

"I know what you mean. I just don't like it when we're apart. Actually, I hate it."

"I don't like being away either, but . . ." His voice trailed off as he glanced at the trunk, catching the gaze of the Israeli's bloodshot eyes. Justin's eyes inspected the double overhand knots in the rope securing the man's wrists and ankles. The knots were tight and in their original place. *Maybe he won't even attempt an escape.*

"Justin? You're still there?" Anna's voice echoed in his ear.

"Yes, yes, I'm here. I was just checking something. Listen, I'll explain everything when I get home," he said quickly. "OK?"

Anna sighed. "I just want to be with you," she whispered, her voice trembling. "Come home safe, will you?"

"I'll try."

"OK. When will you call me?"

"I don't know. Soon, I hope."

"Tomorrow?"

"Maybe."

"OK. I'll let you go now."

"I love you," Justin said under breath.

"I love you, too," Anna replied.

"Well, that wasn't too bad," Carrie said as soon as Justin dropped the satellite phone back into his knapsack. "She took it very well."

"Thanks for the privacy."

"Hey, we could have stopped the car."

"No, I don't want to waste any time. The terrorists already have a head start."

Justin had instructed Mus'ad to change the direction of their course from west to north and drive toward the Egyptian border. The driver's face had suddenly lost its color, turning white, as if they had given him a death sentence. He made every effort to change their minds, at one point threatening to quit altogether. Justin did not know if Mus'ad reluctance was intended to be an extortion tactic, in order to press the agents into increasing his payment, or the man was truly afraid of crossing into the land of the Pharaohs.

"Remember to stay off the common routes, Mus'ad," Justin said to the driver.

"Yes. We are. We're driving parallel to the trails set by the Tuaregs but making our own path. Unless the terrain is too difficult for that."

Justin glanced at the sand dunes. They were taller and wider than when they were closer to the valley of the ambush. The landscape resembled a stormy sea with angry waves ripping and peeling in an endless struggle. Lone acacia trees appeared occasionally among hill slopes. Their umbrella-shaped branches were a constant reminder that life was possible even in the deepest, driest parts of the Sahara. Further north, a brownish mountain range was slowly beginning to take shape on the horizon. Its purple round ridges arched from behind a glowing curtain of simmering air.

"That's Jebel Uweinat." Mus'ad pointed to where Justin had fixed his gaze.

Justin nodded, still staring at the high mountain rising up right at the border between Egypt, Libya, and Sudan. Jebel Uweinat was the most famous attraction in this part of the desert.

"Yes, and let's stay away from trails leading there," Justin said. "The place is crawling with tourists."

Mus'ad nodded. "And bandits," he said. "Last week, bandits kidnapped ten Germans while they were touring Gilf al-Kebir in Egypt to visit its prehistoric cave paintings. They were taken across the Libyan border." Mus'ad gestured to his left toward a shallow valley cutting through the sea of dunes. "Bandits released them only after their families paid a fat ransom."

"Watch out that *we* don't end up in Libya," Justin said. "I don't want trouble with their rebels or police, secret or not."

"Not yet," Carrie added in English.

Justin nodded at her.

"The borders are not very clear," Mus'ad complained. "Most of the time, there are no checkpoints, no border guards, no signs at all."

"Just keep your eyes open and avoid everything that moves," Justin said in an abrupt tone intended to end the discussion.

Mus'ad got the hint and kept silent, driving upward as they climbed around a steep dune. Black rocky humps the size of camels dotted the surface of the slope.

"You will not have to worry about Libya's mukhabarat," Justin whispered as he leaned closer to Carrie. "In Cairo, we part ways."

"Uh-uh," Carrie replied in a low voice. "I'm going with you to Tripoli."

"No, you're not. One of us has to handle the agent's transfer. Just be careful with Mossad."

"I can take care of myself and it can't be worse than this. At least in Libya we know who the enemy is."

"Eh, I thought so and see where we are. We sit down for talks with Islamic terrorists and we fight alongside with them and Sudanese gunrunners. And who are we up against? Our greatest friend and ally in the Middle East."

"We didn't know some of the attackers were . . . from that country," Carrie said. She avoided mentioning the name "Israel," fearing the driver may pick up the word.

"I'm sure Johnson will come up with a more elaborate official explanation," Justin said. "Are you confident in handling the transfer?"

"Alone?" Her eyebrows arched and a frown formed on her face.

"With assistance from the Cairo station." Justin pointed to the north.

"It will depend on who George will give me."

"Johnson will make him give you whoever you want." His voice was strong, decisive.

"So this deal, this will be *quid pro quo*?"

"Yes, something for something. If this man is a field agent, which I'm absolutely sure he is, then they'll send a team to retrieve him. After they give you the intel about their mission in Sudan, you give them his location."

"Simple enough," Carrie said sarcastically.

"Manageable," Justin replied. "We'll set it up together as fail-safe as we can. Then you'll take over."

"I'm already thinking of places where we can have this exchange meeting."

"We'll have to wait for Johnson and for that country's reply."

"I'm sure that country won't like it. We kidnapped and threw their agent in the trunk," Carrie said in a warning tone.

"Well, I didn't like it when this man was firing missiles at my head. Everything is fair in war. And what we did saved his life."

"I just hope they come in peace."

"So do I," Justin muttered thoughtfully, "so do I."

CHAPTER 9

Tripoli International Airport, Libya
May 14, 6:00 p.m. local time

Aboard EgyptAir Flight 831 landing at Tripoli International Airport that evening was one Australian citizen. At least, that is how the dark-haired man was identified by his biometric passport, an authentic document issued by the Department of Foreign Affairs and Trade of Australia. The CIS did not risk any unnecessary exposure by counterfeiting travel documents for their agents. Instead, they secured foreign passports by applying for them through entirely legal ways. Interventions by senior political officials ensured a smooth process through the government offices dealing with such applications.

Jack Schmitt passed his first obstacle, Justin thought as he dropped his Australian passport with that name inside the front pocket of his black jeans. A few hours earlier, an Egyptian Air Force Mi-17 had picked them up at the border with Sudan. They flew to Aswan, a city in the south of Egypt, then took a military plane to Cairo International Airport. George picked up Carrie and the Israeli man while Justin boarded a flight to Tripoli.

He nodded a quick goodbye to the customs officials at the arrivals counter of the International Terminal and began strolling toward the gates, following a large crowd of North Africans. Besides his two Kodak Pro digital cameras hanging around his left shoulder—part of his cover as a travel journalist—Justin had brought a single carry-on suitcase, which he rolled slowly behind him. The luggage was lighter than he pretended it to be, but a slow, relaxed walk allowed him a few extra seconds to observe his surroundings.

I admit it, he thought, *it's not the safest way to enter this hostile country, strutting through the front door.* But time was of the essence and most of Libya's secret police watched its land and coastal borders. Tripoli International Airport was the last place a foreign secret service operative would choose as his entry point. At least, that was Justin's reasoning and he prayed his reasoning was right.

Man, this place has changed so much. He passed through a set of automatic glass doors and stopped to admire the marble floors, the glass windows and the steel structures. Justin turned left and passed by a prayer room, a duty-free shopping area with not much selection, and a first-class passengers' lounge. *I think they expanded this hall. Or does it feel roomier because I haven't seen the mukhabarat yet? Oh, there they are.*

He kept his gaze fixed straight ahead as he reached a couple of tall skinny men in gray suits, who seemed to be doing nothing but chatting at one of the empty corners of the hall. They were standing to the right of the escalators. To the untrained eye, the men looked like stranded travelers killing time during layovers. But Justin's eyes were trained to identify exactly what was there, and most importantly, what was not.

With a quick, casual glance in their general direction, as if wondering whether he was going in the right way, Justin noticed the men had no hand luggage. This was not the arrivals area, so they were not waiting for relatives or friends. The men from the Internal Security Service, Libya's mukhabarat, were standing beyond the terminal's security perimeter. Only authorized personnel were allowed in this area, but the men wore no identification badges and no uniforms.

They sported dress pants, dress shirts, and loose fitting jackets—

perfect for hiding a small arsenal of firearms—and no ties. It was too casual for businessmen and overkill for common bodyguards. But what gave them away, what usually gives away most secret agents, was the look. The piercing look, aimed at understanding the intentions of an individual simply by looking at his eyes, his face, his hands, his body gestures.

Justin dropped his gaze to the floor as he approached the escalator. He did not shuffle his feet, cough, comb his hair with his hands, rummage through his pockets, or make any gestures that would attract the Libyan agents' attention. There was no visible reason for his behavior to be out of the ordinary. Justin was unarmed and was not carrying any illegal or prohibited substances. Any frisking by the mukhabarat would reveal nothing incriminating, but Justin knew the mukhabarat did not need any evidence to hold a foreigner in their cells for weeks if not months.

"Sir, your shoe is undone," one of the Libyan agents called at him in Arabic.

Justin resisted the urge to turn his head toward the voice or to stop and look at his black runners. A foreigner arriving alone and not as part of an organized tour, was still less suspicious than a foreigner who spoke the language of the country. *Nice trick, but I'm not falling for it.*

"Hey, you should tie your shoe," the other agent said in English with a heavy Arabic accent.

Justin looked at the man and then at his feet. The shoelace of his left runner was slightly loose, not quite undone, and almost certainly it would not untie during Justin's short walk to the taxi stand. But the small, almost undetectable detail, had not escaped their watchful eyes. *Extremely observant these two.*

"Thank you, mate," Justin replied. He knelt and tightened the shoe lace.

He took the escalator down to the first floor. He never looked back, knowing the men of the mukhabarat would not stop staring until he was out of sight. *They may even radio their buddies downstairs to keep an eye on me.*

Justin strode past a long row of airline desks and customer service counters, their logos flashing over colored glass and fluorescent lights. Since the lifting of the UN sanctions in 2003 and the US sanctions in 2004 against the country responsible for the Pan Am Flight 103 bombing in 1988—a bombing that claimed the lives of 270 people, 180 of them Americans—a stream of foreign companies had flocked to Libya, a place flooded with oil cash.

Most of them had left during the months of the civil war and rebellion that toppled Colonel Moammar Qaddafi and his forty-one-year, iron-fisted rule in 2011. They had returned soon after a new government was installed in the country with the help of the US and its European allies. The new leaders, especially the new prime minister, had promised democracy and an end to Libya's long support for terrorist and rogue regimes all over the world. Still, four decades of tyranny could not be undone overnight. Change was slow, especially for the mukhabarat.

As soon as Justin reached the main entrance to the terminal, he felt the heat wave slap him across the face. A boiling, dusty wind gust embraced him as soon as he stepped outside. A crowd of taxi drivers swarmed him. They were all men, mostly in their thirties and forties, but he spotted a few age-wrinkled faces. They groped at his luggage, vying to pick him up, while shouting at him in Arabic, English, and French. He politely declined their offers and kept walking beside the long row of black and white taxi sedans. A couple of half-torn posters of Qaddafi caught his attention. Qaddafi was shown in a long black and green tunic, against a background of the map of Africa, saluting the nation with a clenched right fist. Someone had written a few insults over the deposed dictator's face.

Justin started searching for a taxi driver. He was looking for someone less zealous and brazen and definitely younger, perhaps too young to be recruited by the mukhabarat. After a few sideway glances at the parked cars, he stopped next to a young man leaning against the hood of an old, rusty Fiat, reading a folded newspaper. Under the shade of a tall palm tree, the young man was enduring the ninety-five degree temperature, ignoring the sweat soaking his forehead and the collar of his short-sleeved shirt. The young man's skin was dark brown, but his thick, broad nose, and short curly hair testified to his central African origin.

"Hey, is your taxi for hire?" Justin asked the young man who could not be older than seventeen.

"What? Oh, taxi, yes, yes, sir," he replied in English, the language in which Justin had asked the question. "Yes, taxi."

He tossed his newspaper in the backseat and opened the front passenger's door. Before Justin had a chance to slide into the seat, a large number of taxi drivers crowded around the Fiat. They began to exchange harsh words with the young man who was stowing away Justin's luggage. Amidst the commotion, Justin heard words like "pig" and "thief" and "evil." The young man and Justin managed to get inside the car and drove off, the driver using uninterrupted honks to force away the people standing in front of his taxi.

"What was that all about?" Justin asked, feigning ignorance, after the Fiat rounded the curve. They headed toward Tripoli, twenty-one miles north of the airport.

"Huh? Oh, they… they says not my turn. You came to me. I did wrong nothing," the driver explained in broken English.

Justin nodded. He was telling the truth, albeit sugar-coating it for him.

"Where are we going?" the driver asked.

Justin said one word, "Corinthia."

Corinthia Hotel Tripoli was perhaps the most luxurious hotel in Tripoli. Even the US Embassy temporarily used its fifth floor when it first opened after the renewal of the diplomatic relation between the two countries. Now the embassy had its own building on Al Jrabah Street in the heart of Tripoli.

"Yes, I take you there," said the driver.

Justin was not staying at the Corinthia. He had reserved a room at the Four Seasons Hotel, more than ten city blocks south of the

Corinthia. If the driver moonlighted for the mukhabarat or was pressed to reveal his client's destination, the diversion could buy Justin precious time. In Libya, a few seconds of advantage made all the difference between life and death.

"And I don't want to share the taxi with anyone else," Justin said.

Sharing taxis was a common practice and taxi drivers stopped regularly along the road to pick up more passengers. A general understanding existed among taxi drivers that foreigners disliked this practice, but Justin wanted to make sure there were going to be no uninvited guests and no unscheduled stops.

"Of course, not," the driver replied. "My taxi black and white. We don't stop for no one. Yellow cabs, they do that."

"Great. If you make it a good trip, I'll give you forty dinars."

The driver's eyes lit up. The usual fare from the airport to downtown Tripoli varied between twenty to twenty-five dinars, about twenty dollars. "You must be a rich man."

"Not really. But I appreciate good service when I can find it."

"It will be very good trip. If you want, I don't talk."

"A little talk doesn't hurt."

Justin leaned back in his seat.

"First time in Tripoli?"

"Yes."

"Where you from?"

"Australia."

"Oh, Australia. Sydney?"

"No, Perth."

"Perth?"

"Yes. It's in west Australia. Sydney is on the other side."

"My cousin Ishmael live in Sydney. He drive taxi there."

"Sorry, I don't know him."

"Ishmael very good man. He doing good in Australia. He ask me to go and work there."

"Well, you're still here. How are things in Libya?"

The driver hesitated before giving an answer. "It's OK. After civil war over, more foreigners came, more companies, more clients, so more money."

"How safe is Tripoli?"

The reply came after another moment of hesitation. "Well, so-so. Many people disappointed with the new government. Some say Qaddafi was better. Violence continue." As an afterthought, the driver added, "The suicide bombers, they stupid. The ones who sent them, the men of the Alliance, they will be caught and hung. All of them."

"Where are you from?"

"My mother Libyan, my father from Burkina Faso. But I want my country safe."

Justin nodded.

They drove in silence over the next few minutes. Justin observed the ever-changing landscape. Rows of palm trees and olive orchards were cultivated meticulously on parcels on both sides of the three-lane divided Airport Highway. Now and then, they were separated by strips of bronze-colored sand, sprinkled with scraggly looking weeds. Two- and three-story houses dotted the hills.

The houses grew larger and closer to one another as the Fiat approached Tripoli's outskirts. Large mosques with green domes and white minarets pierced the sky at regular intervals. The driver would point out a warehouse, a hotel, or a restaurant and give Justin a word of advice about its owner, services, or meals offered at those establishments.

Justin mostly tuned out his driver and ignored the grits of sand entering through the open windows, the only air conditioning available in the taxi. His mind was planning the evening's meeting at the US Embassy. Johnson had arranged for a briefing with Matthew Garnett, the Assistant Director of the Office of Protective Operations in the US Secret Service. Garnett was the man in charge of the US president's security and safety in Libya. A twenty-year veteran with the Secret Service, Garnett had watched over the trip of the US vice president to neighboring Egypt less than six weeks ago.

He was now running the Secret Service's interim station in Tripoli. Justin was sure Garnett would welcome any help in accomplishing his mission successfully.

"Mister, mister, sir."

The driver's voice pierced Justin's ears like the annoying buzz of an alarm clock at 4:00 a.m., pulling him away from his daydreaming.

"Huh . . . hmm . . . what?"

"You no talking to me. How you doing?"

"I'm fine, just trying to relax. Is that too much to ask?"

"Sorry, boss."

Justin noticed they were at the edge of Tripoli. A complex of ten-story apartment towers rose up to the right of the Airport Highway. The towers were surrounded by cranes, backhoes, dump trucks, and an army of other heavy machineries and construction workers. The driver explained the government was building housing projects and he grumbled it took knowing people in "important positions" to get an apartment in the government complex.

"What's that factory there?" Justin asked, pointing to this right as they approached an overpass. A Nissan dealership stretched out on that side, with a line-up of used cars and vans for sale. He had never seen some of the models and assumed they were produced specifically for Nissan's African market.

"That's the Pepsi-Cola factory," the driver replied.

Justin glanced over the driver's shoulders and saw another used vehicle dealership almost identical to the one they had left behind. At a distance, the tall Tripoli's skyscrapers made their first appearance. Roadside buildings became more colorful, although green still remained the dominating color of facades, domes, and walls. The driver took a few turns, and the Fiat entered a maze of narrow alleys as they cut through the heart of Tripoli. Curbside vendors displayed their merchandise, while crowds of people lingered in squares, parks, and sidewalk cafes, sipping coffee and tea and passing their time.

Finally, the taxi reached Al Kurnish Road, which ran parallel to Tripoli's northwest coastline. The splendor of the Mediterranean Sea

unfolded in front of Justin's eyes. The fiery disk was setting over the dark blue surface of the still waters, beyond the golden strips of sandy beaches. A cool sea breeze carried a fresh scent, inviting them to stop and enjoy a relaxing break.

The thought of strolling underneath the palm trees crossed Justin's mind, but he quickly dismissed it with a flick of his hand, in the same way he had swatted away the flies pestering him throughout the ride from the airport. He gazed ahead and found himself under the impressive shadow of the Corinthia Hotel Tripoli. Two curving towers situated at the top of a man-made hill dominated the entire Tripoli's skyline. Built in a unique, slanted S-shape, the 28-story and 14-story towers provided their guests with unobstructed views of the Mediterranean Sea from every one of their three hundred rooms. The hotel's vast garden, filled with tidy, green lawns, fountains, and palm trees of all sizes, created a haven of serenity and peace, away from the chaos and the racket of the city.

Justin asked the driver to stop at the corner of Al Rashid Street and Via Antonio Stoppani, a few blocks south of the Corinthia. The driver offered to pick him up the next day at any time, but Justin declined his offer. He paid the driver, got out of the taxi, and headed toward the hotel.

As he walked through the hotel grounds, his runners tapping on the cobblestone paths, Justin could not help but marvel at the hotel's magnificence. Its gold and cream façade was brightly lit, yet a soft and inviting glow reflected from the windows' glass. No expense was spared when marble, glass, and steel were used to create the gigantic structure. Justin climbed a wide staircase and found himself in front of the tall, arching doors leading to the reception area. In another life, *I could have come here and actually enjoy my stay in Tripoli. Maybe another time. Not tonight for sure. And not tomorrow either.*

CHAPTER 10

Corinthia Tripoli Hotel, Tripoli, Libya
May 14, 6:50 p.m. local time

The front desk clerk, a young woman with smooth mocha skin and large hazel eyes, quoted Justin the cheapest room at five hundred dollars per night. And that was for a standard room with a queen-size bed. Justin paid no attention to the details: the satellite TV, the high speed Internet access, the mini-bar, and, of course, the panoramic view of the Mediterranean Sea. His room served simply to cement the cover of his business trip to Tripoli: photographing Libya's natural and historical landmarks.

After coughing up enough cash for three nights' accommodation, Justin turned down the bellboy's services. He lingered in the hotel lobby and the lounge area for about ten minutes, to make sure he had not been followed by any suspicious character. No one fitting the general profile of a government minder or a mukhabarat officer entered the hotel during that time. Only then he felt comfortable to proceed to his room on the tenth floor.

He had no reason to search the room for electronic bugs since no conversations were going to take place in there. He disarranged the sheets and the bed covers and tossed one of the pillows on the floor, then spread out his toiletries on the bathroom counter. The room now had the feel of being used by a careless man, just in case the mukhabarat paid him a visit.

After a quick shower, Justin changed into khaki pants and a beige shirt. He rode the elevator down to the mezzanine floor and found the Venezia Restaurant. He wanted to enjoy a good meal and wanted to like Libya, but everywhere he set his eyes, he found a source of irritation and a reason to feed his growing hate for everything in this country. The waiter serving him spoke bad English. The lights flooding from the ceiling were too bright. The restaurant was too crowded, with noisy patrons and slow service. The food was bland and there was no wine or alcoholic drinks on the menu, since Libya was a dry country.

In silence, Justin ploughed his way through a lukewarm minestrone soup and a dull frutti di mare risotto. He tasted nothing, but a feeling of premonition sizzling down in his gut. Bad things happened every time he visited this country. People died or were badly hurt, sometimes innocent people, and, more often than not, he was the one pulling the trigger. Hating the place and its people, in theory, should make his job easier. But Justin knew psychology experts who wrote those theories had never completed a covert mission on the ground. He had. On days like today, he wished he really worked as a travel journalist and relied on cameras and voice recorders, instead of pistols and carbines.

"And here is your bill, signore," the waiter said, faking a big smile.

The waiter's lame attempt at Italian pulled Justin back to the restaurant and away from his bad omens. He was actually pleased to see the waiter and left him a generous tip.

The front desk clerk called him a taxi. While waiting for its arrival, Justin complained to the clerk about knee pain in his left leg. Carrie had neatly cleaned the wound he suffered during the gunfight in Sudan and had wrapped it in surgical gauze. It hurt, but not enough to complain about it. But Justin needed to give the clerk a reason why he needed to visit a medical center or a hospital. As if coached, the clerk recommended the Libya British Diagnostic Center, which, in her exact words, was "the best in the entire country." The clinic was open until 10:00 p.m. and it was exactly in Justin's direction, a short walk to the US Embassy.

Corinthia Tripoli Hotel, Tripoli, Libya
May 14, 7:35 p.m. local time

The heavyset man pacing up and down the reception hall of the Corinthia grew more frustrated and impatient with every passing moment. The target he was supposed to be watching had disappeared. He was last seen climbing aboard a taxi, whose driver was picking up neither his employer's radio, nor his personal cellphone. The front desk clerk insisted "the Australian" was limping and had gone to the Libya British Diagnostic Center. A sweep of the Australian's room had revealed nothing out of ordinary. However, his instructions were clear. Every move of the foreigner should be carefully monitored and reported.

Unknown to the heavyset man, earlier that day Prince's Al-Farhan personal aide had placed a call to Colonel Farid Haydar, who commanded Tripoli's Counter Terrorism Branch in the Internal Security Service. Colonel Haydar had immediately agreed to offer the prince, his longtime benefactor, the unconditional assistance of the Agency. A team of six men was dispatched without delay, in anticipation of Justin's arrival. Two of them had subtly welcomed him at Tripoli's International Airport. Another pair had followed his taxi, which dropped him off at the Corinthia. However, the last two men, one of which was nervously pacing the hotel's reception, had lost track of their target on their way to the medical center.

The man's cellphone rang inside his jacket pocket, but he ignored it. It buzzed again, this time a bit louder, yet he still did not answer it, hoping the caller would realize the man was busy and would hang up. The annoying sound buzzed a third time, attracting stares from a group of people huddled around one of the coffee tables. The man dashed up the white marble staircase leading to the second floor and flipped open his cellphone.

"Hello, Colonel," he said quickly.

"Tell me you've found him," Colonel Haydar demanded.

"Hmm…it's… hmm…" the man stumbled, "we're waiting for his return to the hotel."

"I can't believe you're so stupid. You can't even follow an old man in a taxi."

"The driver was going like a crazy maniac. We didn't want to give away our position and our mission."

"Our mission? There's no mission anymore because of your fault. Our target has disappeared and we've no idea of where he is or what he's doing."

"His luggage is in his room, and the receptionist says he took nothing with him," the man whispered on the receiver, as a bellboy in a black uniform walked by, slowly wheeling a luggage cart. "He'll come back eventually."

"I wanted to know what he was doing at all times. He may or may not return to the hotel. This man is a trained pro; he speaks Arabic fluently and has many contacts in Tripoli. I wanted to know whom he's meeting with, but thanks to you now I can't."

The man listened patiently to the colonel venting, while staring below at the ring-shaped fountain in the center of the lobby and at the two small palm trees to its sides. The atmosphere was supposed to relax the hotel guests, but the only thing the man was experiencing was fear about his mistake.

"What are my orders?" he asked.

"There's no point in giving you orders if you can't follow them. I'll find someone else who can actually do what he's told to do."

The line went dead.

* * *

"Do you see all these idiots working for me?" Colonel Haydar slammed the phone onto the receiver. "They can't even follow a basic order."

"You should never send an amateur to do a pro's job," Nassir replied.

The colonel looked up at the man standing next to the tall bookcase. Ever since Nassir had refused to take a seat, the colonel had begun to resent the man. He was too proud, too full of himself. The colonel was going to tolerate Nassir, since he was the prince's envoy, but that did not mean he had to like him.

"I don't think the prince sent you here for your great sense of sarcasm," the colonel said. "Let's see what you can do."

Nassir cracked his knuckles. "We can do this the hard way or the easy way." He slid his hand over a large combat knife hanging in its sheath at his thigh.

"Just do it the efficient way," the colonel said. "As much as I want Mr. Hall dead, it's not the right time. Find out whom did he meet or is meeting, what help did he get or will get."

Nassir frowned. "I thought you wanted me to do something. I'm not much for asking questions, unless Justin refuses to answer them."

The colonel sighed. This is why I didn't want to involve you in this. I don't need a sledgehammer for a small nail.

"Let me make myself clear, Nassir. We need Mr. Hall alive, so that he can brief the Americans. I just want to know what happened during the time we didn't have our eyes on him. Do you understand that?"

"I do."

"And can you do that?"

Nassir stared at the colonel.

"You're asking me?"

"Yes. I want to make sure you get it."

"Yes, I can talk to Justin, if he wants to talk. In Sudan, he didn't strike me as a man of many words."

"Oh, now you know everything about him?"

Nassir shook his head.

"Let me tell you something about Mr. Hall. He was here two years ago, on a rescue mission. We dragged his wounded body to a cell and threw away the key. But he fought back and slipped out of our hands, destroying a mosque, and killing fourteen people in the process. An entire unit of elite operatives. Very good men."

"Why are you telling me this?"

"So that you don't underestimate him. Tarek will go with you to ensure you don't."

Nassir looked at the other man in the colonel's office. Tarek had not said a word ever since Nassir had arrived, about an hour ago. He was just staring at the colonel, his small body leaning forward in the chair. His hands rested on his knees and he looked ready to spring to action at any time.

Nassir began, "Look, I don't need any—"

The colonel interrupted him with, "You're a simple mercenary. Tarek is mukhabarat. He knows the city and he knows Mr. Hall."

"I know—"

"You're wasting time, Nassir."

Before the colonel finished his sentence, Tarek was already on his feet.

* * *

The taxi driver, a thin-framed, elderly man who looked like he should have retired about ten years earlier, drove fast and hard. The Nissan rattled in loud mechanical protests every time the driver negotiated swift turns around narrow curbs. The brakes screeched as the wheels barely missed garbage heaps, stray cats, and all types of waste thrown almost everywhere. The driver chose the emptiest alleys as he raced for the fastest shortcut to the Libya British Diagnostic Center. As the taxi came to an abrupt halt in front of the four-story grayish building, Justin's wristwatch indicated he still had ten minutes to spare.

* * *

The US Embassy's compound stretched over an area of two city blocks. Justin walked by its white and beige walls, two feet thick and eight feet tall. They were topped with an additional two feet of cast iron staggered fence. The Old Glory flew atop a tall flagpole, under the bright glow of white floodlights.

The entire area was well-lit and a few uniformed police officers were patrolling the streets leading to the diplomatic residence. Two police trucks were parked on a sidewalk. Justin assumed police backup was in there.

* * *

"There he is." Nassir stared through the windshield of the second police truck at Justin across the street. "Let's go."

Tarek, in the driver's seat, shook his head. Both were dressed in police uniforms.

"We have only five minutes before he gets inside," Nassir insisted.

"Wrong. He'll circle the complex, to familiarize himself with the surroundings." Tarek started the truck and put it in reverse. "We'll wait for him on the other side."

* * *

Marines manned an observation station set up to the left of the main entrance gate to the embassy. Justin could not see their faces, but he was sure the Marines were monitoring his moves from behind the small, bulletproof windows. He walked down the street that was the farthermost from the embassy walls and rounded the corner, coming face to face with a police truck parked about thirty yards away. Its length blocked most of the sidewalk. Two police officers were inside the idling vehicle.

Justin's body tensed involuntarily. *Are they here for me?* No reports mentioned police patrols along the east side of the compound. *Perhaps they beefed up security because of the bombings.*

He looked beyond the police truck. A small convenience store was a hundred yards away, at the end of the backstreet. Someone from the embassy was supposed to be waiting there for Justin.

Turning around will raise more suspicion than if I just keep going. One last obstacle.

Justin slowed down but kept moving toward the truck.

* * *

"Now," Nassir said, leaning on the door handle.

Before he could move, he felt a sharp pain stabbing through his ribcage. He opened his mouth to scream, but Tarek's low voice stopped him.

"That's for being full of shit."

Tarek twisted the knife he had snatched from Nassir's side. The sharp, serrated blade slashed through Nassir's lungs, and a muffled cry escaped his bleeding mouth.

"And this is for disrespecting the colonel."

Nassir left hand twitched, in a lame attempt to grab Tarek's arm. Tarek blocked the effort with ease and held it there for three more seconds, the time it took for Nassir to stop breathing.

He pulled the knife and opened the truck's door.

* * *

Justin stopped as one of the police officers, the one in the driver's seat, stepped out of the truck. The other remained in the front passenger's seat, his head slightly turned to the right, as if staring out the window.

"Good evening, officer," Justin said in English, while looking to the left at the apartment complex and then at the officer approaching him. He was holding something in his right hand, something that seemed to continue up his sleeve. Is that a baton?

"What are you doing here?" the officer's voice came out rough and accusatory.

"I was out for a walk. Is that a crime?" Justin took a step back, his mind calculating his options. The second officer was still inside the truck. Maybe I can outrun him. No need to start a fight.

"Show me your ID," the officer demanded, closing in on him.

"Sure."

Justin's left hand went for a front pocket, but his eyes never left the officer's frowning face. Where have I seen this man? A flash of headlights from a turning car lit up the area and Justin recognized the man. He was one of the prison guards.

Before Justin could act on his realization, the officer stretched his right arm. A long blade glinted briefly under the diming light. Justin had a split second to throw his head back. The tip of the blade sliced through the air, an inch away from his throat.

"Remember me?" the officer asked, stepping forward, while Justin fell back.

"Yeah, Tarek. You're the one I left for dead."

"Mistake. Should have finished your job."

"I won't waste this second chance."

Tarek lifted the blade again. This time Justin had a defense plan. As Tarek thrust his arm forward, going for Justin's chest, Justin took a step back. He deflected Tarek's attack with his right forearm and grabbed Tarek's wrist with both hands. His fingers sank into the attacker's hand and he twisted the man's wrist, his body moving away from the knife. Tarek began to scream, but Justin stifled him with a forceful punch to the throat. Choking, Tarek stopped fighting.

"How did you find me?" Justin asked.

"Eat my—"

Justin interrupted Tarek with a sidekick to his left knee, disabling his foot. Tarek began to fall. Justin shoved Tarek's hand, which was still holding his knife, toward the man's neck. Tarek's head came down hard on the sharp blade. Blood flowed freely from a large gash as Tarek's body writhed on the ground. Justin's eyes rested on the attacker until he drew in his last breath.

"See, Tarek. I corrected my error."

* * *

Justin approached the convenience store at a slow pace. He was double-checking every corner and every shadow. The knife attack less than two minutes earlier had pitched him into an extreme level of alertness.

A young man in a black suit was standing just inside the store's entrance.

"Mr. Schmitt?" the black suit asked Justin.

Justin nodded, glancing at the store's clerk, a middle-aged man who continued to watch the news on a small TV by the newspaper rack. Undoubtedly, he was on the embassy's payroll, one of their many eyes inside the Libyan society.

"How are you feeling?"

"What?" Justin said.

"I asked how are you feeling?" the black suit repeated his question, this time pointing at Justin's heaving chest.

"I'm fine, just a bit rushed."

"Ready to go?"

"Yes, ready to go."

The black suit whispered something unintelligible into a microphone stitched inside his left sleeve, and a black Cadillac sedan glided out of the night's darkness. Its windows were tinted black, its headlights were turned off, and the car coasted without making a sound. Seconds later, it was parked on the sidewalk, two steps away from the convenience store's entrance.

"Come with me," the black suit said, "They're expecting you."

Aided by the night's blackness, the two men slid inside the

Cadillac, Justin in the backseat, his escort in the front. The driver, a heavyset man with a large head and a small ear piece, gave him a quick glance, as if to confirm Justin's identity to the photograph he had seen earlier that evening. He nodded to the black suit and stepped on the gas pedal.

"We're going through the service door, right?" Justin asked.

"Correct," the driver replied. "Mr. Garnett is waiting for you."

CHAPTER 11

United States Embassy, Tripoli, Libya
May 14, 8:00 p.m. local time

Matthew Garnett was not the only person awaiting Justin's arrival in the George Washington Conference Room on the third floor of the embassy's east wing. A woman with a strawberry blonde ponytail and big emerald eyes—in her late thirties or early forties, Justin could not be certain—was sitting to Mr. Garnett's left, around an oval-shaped mahogany table. A small laptop lay closed on the table in front of her. A dark-skinned man, who reminded Justin of the late Ali, but shorter and stubbier, sat across from them. He was busy fumbling with a gold-plated pen and a yellow notebook.

"Welcome, Justin," Matthew said in a casual tone, as everyone stood up. "Let me introduce you to my team. This is Jordan Mahoney, the embassy's political chief." He gestured toward the woman and Justin shook her extended hand. "And this is Noureddine Milad, chief of security. He goes by Nour." The man's handshake resembled a clamp, as he firmly squeezed Justin's fingers.

"How was your trip?" Matthew asked after they returned to their chairs, with Justin sitting to Nour's left.

"It was good. Uneventful."

"Custom officials treated you all right?"

"Yeah, I guess. I'm here, all in one piece."

Matthew grinned. "How are things in Cairo?"

"Less flashy than Tripoli for sure."

"I heard you had a brushfire last night too."

Justin nodded. Obviously, Matthew has reliable sources in Cairo's mukhabarat. Do they have anyone in the mukhabarat in Tripoli? "There's always a brushfire I need to snuff out."

"This one was really close though."

"Yes, it was."

Matthew laughed out loud. Then, he spread out his palms over the table.

"All right," he said. "Let's get to the point of this briefing. Ms. Johnson informed us that your team came in possession of highly sensitive information about the visit of my president."

"This conversation is not being recorded, right?" Justin asked while twirling his right index finger in the air, as if to point at security cameras hidden in the gray ceiling.

"No, of course not," Matthew replied, "you requested that there be no evidence of this meeting ever taking place, and we share that view."

"I'll need a laptop to show you the evidence."

Matthew nodded toward Jordan and she slid her laptop across to Justin. He raised the cover and pressed the power button. The machine quickly woke up, the screen ablaze with a bright, blue sky over Yosemite National Park.

"Is there a password for the Internet connection?" Justin asked.

"Yes, but you're already logged in," Jordan replied.

With a few quick keystrokes, Justin was on the Internet. He typed in a secure server address in the browser's search toolbar. Half a second later, a window prompted him for an access code. Justin entered it and accessed a temporary database. Carrie had scanned most documents retrieved from the sheikh's briefcase and they were already uploaded to the secret servers.

"I'll need a printer for some of the documents and the pictures,"

Justin said.

"Simply hit print and they'll come out at that machine." Jordan pointed at the end of the room, where a printer was set up on a small office desk.

Justin tapped a few keys and dozens of pages began spilling out of the printer's mouth. He went and gathered them and set the stack of papers, as well as a stapler, next to the laptop.

"Before we review this information, give me a quick debrief of what you already know about the Islamic Fighting Alliance, so I avoid any repetition," he said.

"Sure," Matthew said. "On any given day, we receive tens of threats against the life of the president and her family. This number, of course, multiplies when it comes to an announced, scheduled visit, like this one, to a hot area like North Africa. So, we're aware of the threats and we have measures in place, to ensure the highest around-the-clock protection. By the time she lands in Tripoli, dozens of agents, in addition to local security personnel, will guarantee her safety throughout the forty-eight hours she'll be here."

Justin nodded. "Were you aware of specific death threats from the Islamic Fighting Alliance?"

"Yes, we know about the Alliance, how they operate, who funds them and the extent of their network of sleeping cells. They have been waging jihad against America and our interests in North Africa for many years."

"True, however, the recent bombings are unprecedented, even by the Alliance's standards," Justin said.

Matthew shrugged. "Unprecedented yes, but not unexpected. Violence always spikes prior to the president visiting a rogue country. Last month, the vice president visited Jordan and three suicide attacks rocked Amman, as late as the day of his arrival. These are simply pathetic attempts to force dignitaries to cancel their visit. As you know fully well, that's not the habit of our chiefs. And, we're not in the mood to start cowering at this time."

"We thought these car bombings were random acts of violence, until we received this information." Justin passed around two documents. "The first one is a detailed schedule of the president's visit to Tripoli. Times, places, locations, size of escort, length of time to reach and duration of stay at a specific place, the works."

Matthew nodded thoughtfully, while scanning the report. After he finished, he removed his black horn-rimmed glasses and tossed them over the report. Then, he combed what was left of his thin, gray hair, as the receding hairline had taken away more than half.

"All right," he said, with a sigh, "it seems we have a mole, most likely somewhere in White House's admin. There are many temps and press secretaries and interns who can get their hands into an early draft of the president's schedule. I can tell you some of these details have already changed. So, this draft is probably two, three weeks old. I'll inform DC right away and they can start smoking out the mole. What else do you have there?"

With a flick of his wrist, Justin flipped the other document to his right, first to Nour, and then to Matthew.

"Here's a short extract of English transcripts of intercepted communications between members of the Alliance. They're discussing the assassination plan, the means, the guns, the location, the participants. We have the complete Arabic recording, which we'll make available to your team very soon."

"This is serious," Jordan said. "How did you obtain this information?"

"Unlike you Americans, we keep the option of negotiating with terrorists on the table," Justin replied in a matter-of-fact tone.

Jordan's face turned a reddish hue. Nour and Mathew simply stared at Justin.

"I meant no offence," Justin offered, more as an explanation, rather than an apology. His voice was steady, as he was used to making no excuse for his over-the-top bluntness. "I mean, look where we're meeting. Tripoli, Libya. Twenty years ago, President Reagan, called the leader of this country at that time, Colonel Qaddafi, 'the mad dog of the Middle East.' Libya supported terrorists of all flags for over thirty years. But the US built hotels and explored for oil in the same country that once was your archenemy."

"Libya agreed to hand over those responsible for the Lockerbie airplane bombing and renounced its programs of developing weapons of mass destructions," Jordan said in a clear, solemn tone, as if addressing a crowd of supporters in a political rally. "It has always been the policy of the United States to lend a helping hand to its old friends, to welcome them in the international community, and to guide them in the long and difficult road toward democracy and progress. This is a time of change in the relationship between America and Libya. Especially now that Qaddafi is history and Libya is on a path to becoming a democratic country, our politicians are working hard to usher in a new era of cooperation."

Justin shrugged. "In defense and oil contracts, I assume," he mumbled.

Matthew dismissed Justin's words with a hand gesture. Justin interpreted it as a signal to continue, but Matthew was not finished. "We shouldn't forget that Libya is where it is today because we, Americans, showed him our wrath with Baghdad bombings in 2003. Qaddafi feared he was going to meet the same fate as Saddam, with a noose around his neck. So, he stopped supporting terrorists and rebel groups and stopped being a constant threat to global security. Then, he turned on his people when they began demanding change, and we, Americans, helped in getting rid of him. We're here to support the new democratic regime and to make sure Libya doesn't turn into a rogue nation or a safe haven for Islamic terrorists."

Justin leaned back in his chair. "I thought Qaddafi had a change of heart because Al-Qaida issued a fatwa on his head. Islamic militants wanted to overthrow his regime and replace it with a Sharia law state, like Saudi Arabia. That's the true reason he decided to draw nearer to the Western world."

Matthew sighed. "Let's get back to the intel, shall we?" he said.

"Sure. We were talking to people inside the Alliance and that allowed us to dig deeper into this plot. Our contacts with top-level militants produced this intel."

Matthew gave his half-bald head a good scratch.

"And this information is reliable?" he asked finally.

"Absolutely. It came into my possession directly from one of the sheikhs of the Alliance. Needless to say, I can't give you his name, but the intel is true. These conversations really took place. These schemes are really unfolding as we speak."

Matthew heaved a deep, resigning sigh.

"I need those recordings, so our experts can pick them apart and match the terrorists' voices to our database samples. Then, they'll have to determine the authenticity of the transcripts as well. It's not that we don't trust your Service, but, if an assassination attempt is in the works, we need to analyze every piece of information ourselves."

Justin nodded. "Do you want me to download the files to this laptop?"

Matthew replied "Please do."

Jordan offered a slight nod as well.

"What intel do you have on the explosions?" Justin asked, while typing on the laptop's keyboard.

Nour shifted in his chair and Justin knew it was the security chief's turn.

"Terrorists launched a coordinated strike, targeting four hotels in the heart of Tripoli," Nour said. "They hit the JW Marriot, Continental, Grand Hotel, and Radisson. These are all places frequented mostly by foreigners. Businessmen, contractors, tourists, mainly Westerners, which makes them legitimate targets for Islamic militants. The toll, as expected, is catastrophic. Eighty-five dead, more than a hundred and fifty wounded. We've confirmed twenty-five victims are Americans. An additional ten are reported as missing. The target of the fifth car bomb was the Gold Market, in the Old Town."

A fifth car bomb? Johnson said nothing about a fifth car. How come we don't know about it?

"The Old Town is also a preferred destination for Tripoli

visitors," Nour said. "Fortunately, the police neutralized the suicide bomber of that truck before he could detonate the explosives. He was a young man who obviously didn't know how to set them off."

Was? I guess he's not anymore. "Did you talk to him?"

Nour shook his head.

"Libyans interrogated him already. He gave them some general information about an Alliance plan to kill the president, the Alliance's war against the infidels, and other general threats. Then, he committed 'suicide,' as most prisoners do in Libya's jails. Libyans kept this story out of the press, but they shared some information with us. We dismissed that man's claims as irrelevant, until we received your intel."

That's why Johnson and our Cairo office didn't learn about the fifth man. Still, I hate when Americans are one step ahead in the game.

"Anything else from the local investigation?" Justin asked.

"No, nothing else."

"Have you examined the evidence? The car truck? The bomb? Interrogated any eyewitnesses?"

"This is not our investigation, Justin," Matthew said. "The Internal Security Service is running the show. We have some contacts within the Agency, and we're collecting pieces of information here and there, and completing this puzzle, one piece at a time."

"In light of recent events, you may want to reconsider," Justin said. "You don't want another Benghazi."

Matthew frowned. An angry mob had stormed the US Consulate in Benghazi, east of Tripoli, and had murdered the US Ambassador to Libya and three other Americans. Order and stability in Libya was still fragile.

"You're not telling us how to do our job, are you?" Nour asked.

"Oh, no, of course not," Justin replied, "after all it's your president's life under threat. Terrorists have made their move and it's up to you to leave no stone unturned in protecting her. I'm not the one who'll have to explain to her family and to the nation the president was blown to chunks, as a crucial piece of evidence was overlooked because of a technicality." Justin finished by folding his arms across his chest.

"All right, Justin, I hear what you're saying," Matthew said. "And, since you're insisting on an investigation, you'll have it. Your boss offered us the CIS's full cooperation, and I understand you're here to provide us with more than a simple briefing. You claim to know all the ins and outs of this case, so I'm requesting your assistance in leading this joint investigation."

Justin's face remained calm. He had made no such claims, but he was expecting to be a major player in this operation ever since Johnson had dispatched him to Tripoli. He knew his task consisted of more than simply delivering a message.

Nour frowned and his displeasure did not go unnoticed by Matthew.

"Nour, you'll work together with Justin, representing our interests in gathering this information. This will be an unofficial investigation; however, the embassy will provide all necessary support. I expect the CIS will put its contingent of operatives in the country at the disposal of this investigation."

"Johnson will have to authorize that and the CIS's role in this operation," Justin said.

"Of course. In principle, she has already given her seal of approval, but I'll let you and her figure out the details."

Justin drew in a deep breath. "Since we'll be working closely, do you mind sharing your intel on the current situation of terrorism in Libya and in the region?"

He could not ask directly if the US was aware of Mossad's agents conducting assassination missions against senior terrorist leaders in Sudan. Therefore, he tried to frame his question as broadly as possible, without raising any suspicions.

Matthew gestured with his left hand toward Nour.

"Libya is relatively stable. After the civil war ended, acts of terrorism have been rare. The recent improvement of Libya's relationship with the West has brought in investments, money, higher standards of living. A few people are upset by these developments and some Qaddafi's supporters are trying to spread fear among the people. Then there are people settling old scores and creating new feuds. Libya is awash in weapons and many young men are using them to resolve their arguments."

Justin nodded.

"There are some weak factions of former rebel groups that fought Qaddafi who seem to be reconsidering their objectives," Nour said. "Now, they're targeting Westerners and foreign interests in Libya, and filling up the terrorists' ranks. The Islamic Fighting Alliance recently began a wave of attacks throughout North Africa. First Algeria, then Morocco, and Tunisia. They're penetrating every country in the region, vowing to burn the entire continent, until the last of the 'white colonialists' are thrown into the ocean."

"How strong is the Alliance and who finances it?" Justin asked.

"We believe they have a couple of hundred men, armed and ready at all times. There are many other supporters, mainly outside Libya. They have strong links to militants in Algeria and, to a lesser extent, in Egypt. Money pours in from wealthy Saudis, in the form of 'private donations' or through different types of 'charitable foundations.' Other financing comes from smuggling weapons or immigrants across the borders of Libya and Egypt."

"What kind of support is the US providing to these countries to fight the Alliance and terrorism in general?"

"Technical and training assistance."

Justin was not expecting such a dull and short reply from Nour. Earlier that year the US had targeted objectives described as "terrorist training camps" and "weapons facilities" in Sudan. They also launched air strikes against Islamic militant "strongholds" in eastern Syria, and "selective targets" in various locations in southern Somalia, against Islamic rebel factions.

"Anything else you want to know?" Nour asked.

"No, it's enough for now."

In fact, Justin wanted to ask whether the security chief had any intelligence about other foreign countries involved in military operations in the region. He decided not to trigger the Americans' intuition about the real motive of his question.

"I've finished downloading everything on your laptop," Justin said. "There are a few pictures of some of the Alliance's known suspects, which will help you in identifying them, as well as a couple of amateur videos of the bombings in the city. As you can see from the clips, there were many witnesses who can provide us with information about these bombings."

"Tomorrow you'll get a chance to hit the streets of Tripoli, looking for these witnesses," Matthew said. "If that's everything, we thank you for your assistance."

Justin nodded, as he stood up.

They shook hands.

"Do you need a ride to your hotel?" Matthew asked.

"No, thanks, I'll get a cab."

"Whatever you need, let me know."

"Thanks. At the moment, I can't think of anything."

"Stay safe."

"You too."

Justin shook Jordan's slender hand and braced himself for Nour's bone-crushing grip. Fortunately, this time Nour spared Justin the knuckle-crunching experience.

"Where do you want to meet tomorrow?" Nour asked.

"If you can pick me up at my hotel, Corinthia, at 8:15 a.m. That would be great."

"Sure, I'll see you there."

"Perfect."

CHAPTER 12

Tripoli, Libya
May 14, 8:45 p.m. local time

Justin left through one of the embassy's back doors. He walked for a few minutes, then found a taxi at a large intersection. In simple English, he instructed the driver to take him to the Martyrs' Square and sat in the backseat. The thirty-something driver voiced a small objection, claiming the famous landmark of the capital deserved a daytime visit. Justin simply repeated his order. A few minutes later, he stepped into the cool evening, among cars zooming through the streets and pedestrians milling around the sidewalks surrounding the Martyrs' Square.

He took in the sights of the buildings around him, mostly three-story, colonial-style architecture—a legacy of the Italian occupation before World War II—with gray and green the dominating color schemes. He stared at the Red Castle, the Roman fortress dating from 200 A.D. Its well-preserved towering walls glistened under the yellow glow of street lamps.

"Taxi, do you need a taxi, sir?" the strong voice of a cab driver startled him.

Justin shook his head and turned on his heels. His feet took him toward his hideout, at least for tonight. The Four Seasons Hotel was twelve blocks west, a distance Justin decided to cover on foot. He passed by more colonial-style buildings, including a beautiful Catholic church and many mosques. As he reached an almost empty and dim parking lot, two blocks away from his hotel, he noticed the familiar shape of a Nissan Maxima sedan. He squinted while gazing at the vehicle, and slowed down his steps. The Nissan was definitely a police car; its body painted white with black wings, the opposite color scheme of taxis, which were black with white wings. He never understood the reasons for such a confusing similarity between vehicles fulfilling completely different tasks. Taxis drove you to your desired destination, a resort hotel or the airport. Police cars dragged you to places you had no intention of going, a detention center or a prison camp.

Justin sidestepped around the Nissan. He could make out a man sitting behind the steering wheel. He recognized the silhouette of the driver, the pointed tip of the goatee beard and the trademark aviator shades he always wore, even in the darkest of the nights. Justin scanned the parking lot and the sidewalk. The only people he saw were across the street, heading in the opposite direction. Once he was convinced no one was surveilling him, he knocked twice on the driver's window, the agreed upon signal.

The glass rolled down. Justin glared at the barrel of a small pistol, a Glock 19 glistening in the soft streetlight.

"Welcome to Libya," the man said grimly.

A second later, he broke into a quiet laughter.

"You really know how to welcome a friend, Abdul, you son of a…" Justin walked around to the passenger's side.

"Well, what do you expect?" Abdul handed Justin the pistol, once he was inside the car. "You slip in the country under an assumed identity. You give me a pretty tall order with little advance notice. I'm sorry, pal, I can't exactly roll out the red carpet for you."

Justin weighed the 9mm Glock in his hands, turned it over, inspected its trigger, and pulled back the slide with his left hand. The slide sprang forward. The weapon was cocked and ready for action.

"Glad to see you, Abdul. I would have liked our meeting to be under different circumstances, but I don't get to decide much these days."

"Oh, neither do I, so don't worry about it. Now, seriously, welcome back to my home."

"Thanks. You have everything I need?"

"Of course. The gun is clean. US army issue, smuggled from Iraq. Police recruits in Baghdad have this bad habit of forgetting to register and then 'losing' things. A box of pistols here, a load of RPGs there, the occasional truck stolen and never recovered. The silencer is in the glove compartment."

Justin fetched the black, tall suppressor, slightly longer than the Glock's length, about seven inches. He screwed the suppressor at the end of the gun's threaded barrel.

"Thanks, man."

"Yeah, no problem. Four extra mags are behind that book there."

Justin dug out a dusty Tom Clancy paperback with a dog-eared cover. He retrieved the Glock's magazines.

"OK, that's about a hundred and fifty rounds." Abdul observed Justin's skilled hands checking the high-capacity magazines. He slid one in place, inside the gun's handle, noticing the bottom of the magazine sticking out a couple of inches. "What do you intend to do?"

Justin gave Abdul a sideways glance. "You're good at math. Four mags times thirty-three rounds each, plus fifteen in the standard one, yeah, that's about one fifty."

Abdul shook his head. "You're gonna start a war, like the last time, aren't you?"

"Me? I'm a peaceful guy, you know that. I only return fire."

"As peaceful as a camel in heat. If you didn't carry such an arsenal, we wouldn't have to return fire."

"We? Who said anything about we?"

"Oh, come on! I always end up caught in the crossfire. This time around I want to know up front what I'm getting into."

Justin gazed at Abdul's face. He could not see the man's eyes, but he noted his jaws were clenched like a tight vice.

"OK, here's the deal. Americans are doing their own investigation into the car bombings, since some casualties were Yankees. I'm just helping out, 'cause I know the city and I have a few contacts."

Abdul chewed on this information. "That's it?" he asked after a few seconds.

"Yeah, that's it. A small job. In and out the country in a few days."

"Eh, I have heard that before. I have a feeling things will not go according to plan."

"You know things never go according to plan."

"That's what I'm afraid of. Listen, Justin, my life becomes much more complicated when you're in town." Abdul's voice turned into a whisper and he wiggled closer to Justin. "Giving you and your agency the occasional files and reports is one thing; providing weapons, ammo and logistics, especially in the heart of Tripoli, at this crazy time, that's a suicide mission, pal."

Justin nodded, but Abdul cut him off before he could start speaking.

"No, let me finish. Look, Tripoli is not Cairo. I've moved up the ranks of the mukhabarat, and I'd like to see my son's graduation next summer."

Justin hesitated a second before replying. "Of course you will, Abdul. I appreciate your help, and I'll limit your involvement with this case to a minimum."

"You're never satisfied with the minimum. And neither am I," he replied with a sigh. A few moments went by before Abdul spoke again, "I've got to tell you about the colonel."

"What colonel?"

"Colonel Farid Haydar. He's the chief of the Agency's counter-terrorism section for the city. And he's heard about your antics."

"What do you mean?"

"He knows you're in town. His men followed you to the Corinthia. They have already swept your penthouse."

"It was a standard room, thank you very much. And, you don't have to worry, because the room is clean."

"Where have I heard that before? The 'don't worry' part, huh?"

"C'mon, Abdul, you know our business is unpredictable."

"Exactly. So, let's try to make it less impulsive, shall we?"

Justin groaned.

"Yes, we shall," he replied.

Abdul shook his head in disappointment but kept talking. "You came here on a very short notice, alone, and without a clear purpose. That always gets the attention of the mukhabarat."

"Yes, I saw two goons eyeing me in the terminal."

Abdul nodded. "Yeah. Those guys radioed their partners, who, lucky for you, lost you as you left the Corinthia."

"Yes, my cabbie was driving like a rally pro."

"I made a couple of calls and found out so much. I wanted to make sure no one was following you as you came to meet me."

"Nobody did. I…" Justin hesitated.

"What?" Abdul said with a frown.

"I eliminated them."

"You did what?"

"Shhhh, you're too loud."

"No, no, no. You've been here only two hours and you're already killing men."

"Man. One man." Justin raised a finger.

"Oh, that makes a big difference."

"It was self-defense." Justin shrugged.

Abdul cursed out loud.

"Now, I've got to clean this mess."

"Unfortunately."

More loud swearing followed, while Justin looked out the window, worried someone may hear Abdul's choice words.

"What happened?" Abdul asked after he was more or less calmed down.

"I was attacked by the Embassy's east wall. A man in a police uniform, who turned out to be Tarek."

"Tarek? From jail?"

"Yes. He came at me out of nowhere, knife-wielding and wanting blood."

"I thought Tarek was dead."

"He is now. How did he find me?"

"Well, you walked through the main door to Tripoli. What were you expecting?"

"I was expecting to have some room to breathe, not people coming back from the dead to hunt me down."

"Shouldn't you be used to this by now?"

Justin sighed. "Maybe I should. Tell me, what does this colonel want?"

"You have to ask?"

"I mean is he interested in me personally or in my operation?"

"I don't know for sure. I'll do some digging. After I clean up the crime scene."

"OK. In any case, I'm sure I'll cross paths with the colonel as the Americans move forward with their investigation."

"And how exactly is a travel journalist caught in a terrorist investigation, Mr. Schmitt?"

"Hmmm… that's a good question. How about, as a freelancer, I write about issues that pay good money, and traveling is very much affected by suicide bombings?"

"You may sell it if you put more heart into it."

Justin snickered.

"Who's your wingman from the embassy?"

"A certain Noureddine Milad, chief of security. You know him?"

"I've heard of him. Never met him though. Jordanian by birth, a naturalized American. Tough as a rusty screw. A take no bull type of guy." Abdul's four years of study in the US in the late nineties came back in the form of typical American expressions.

"I noticed that much when I talked to him."

Abdul's hands fiddled with the steering wheel.

"What's the CIS got to do with these car bombings if there were no Canadian casualties? Americans have their own resources and they're not shy about flexing their muscles to get what they want."

"I don't want to lie to you Abdul, but I can't tell you the entire truth."

"What a shocking surprise." Abdul grinned, his left lip curling up.

"Trust me. I wish I could let you into all I know."

"I thought you never said that word."

"I do trust you, Abdul, but you also have to trust me. Some of these things are state secrets. All I can tell you is that Americans want to get to the bottom of this matter. They want Libya to be as stable and as safe as possible."

"Of course, so they can suck out our oil and gas."

"Yes, that and other things, which are not relevant to our mission. I'll help the Americans for a few days, we'll wrap this thing up, and I'll be out of your hair."

Abdul sighed.

"I wish I could believe it was that simple."

"Simpletown is just a mirage, Abdul. Life is complicated."

"Yes, sometimes more than ever."

Abdul pushed on a button, popping up the Nissan's trunk.

"I forgot the bulletproof vest, but there's a bag with some clothes and a satphone in the back. Unregistered number, extremely difficult to find. As with the Glock, take it apart and get rid of the pieces when you're done."

"Thanks, Abdul. I appreciate your help."

"Don't mention it. Hopefully, you won't need anything else, but knowing you, I'm sure you will."

"Again, thank you."

"Good luck."

Justin shook Abdul's hand before getting out of the police car and retrieving the black duffel bag. He watched his contact speed out of the parking lot. As soon as he turned the right corner, in front of a small mosque, he disappeared into the dark of the night.

Justin walked to the edge of street and looked around. A few young men were standing in front of a grocery store about a hundred feet away. He could hear their loud shouts. Soccer fans replaying recent victories of British clubs.

He proceeded in the opposite direction. When he was sure no one was within eavesdropping distance, he took out the Thuraya satellite phone and placed a call to Anna. The cold electronic voice of the answering machine startled him and he stuttered while leaving a short message. Anna was probably running errands or perhaps had gone out for supper with her girlfriends.

The next call he placed went unanswered as well. This time he heard only the continuous beep of the phone ringing, but no one picked it up. Did the operation go wrong? Justin paced back and forth in the parking lot. Carrie, answer the freaking phone. He began having second thoughts about leaving her behind in Cairo to face the men of Mossad without him. There was not much he could do now. He dismissed the option of checking with the CIS station in Cairo. Carrie would frown at what she would certainly interpret as a lack of trust in her. I don't need a babysitter to remind me of bedtime, she would blurt out. I'll try her again in half an hour or so. He turned around and headed toward the Four Seasons Hotel. He would not fall asleep until he had talked to Carrie.

CHAPTER 13

Museum of Egyptian Antiquities, Cairo, Egypt
May 14, 10:15 p.m. local time

Carrie knew Mossad's agents were never late. Without a reason, that is. It was a different matter if they were playing a cruel game of patience with Carrie's nerves. When employed efficiently, the famous tactic of "lying in wait" produced surprising results. As time trickled away, agents grew nervous and began making rookie mistakes. The extended state of alert wore out even the most weathered marksmen. Inaction and fatigue killed even the most skillfully planned mission.

She could not allow her operation to meet the same fate. Her meeting with Eliakim Ben-David, the liaison sent by the Israeli Embassy in Cairo, was set for 9:30 p.m. Forty-five minutes later, Carrie still held hopes the liaison would arrive sooner or later. "Something is holding him up," she repeated more than once to agitated CIS agents. "This meeting is too important for him to be a no-show."

However, she harbored her own doubts. Were the Israelis willing to negotiate the return of their man, if he was indeed one of their own? Were they planning an ambush as she withdrew? Carrie knew her team was most vulnerable while leaving or arriving at a location. Cairo's crooked alleys and clogged roads offered endless opportunities for executing a hostage-taking mission. "An eye for an eye" was the Golden Rule of the Hebrew nation. Their long wars with neighboring Arab countries had proven this beyond any doubt.

The reason Carrie had chosen the Museum of Egyptian Antiquities as the meeting place was security. The museum exhibited and stored over 100,000 priceless relics—world treasures from Pharaohs' tombs, such as the Statue of Khafre and the solid gold mask of Pharaoh Tutankhamen, the Boy King—therefore, the security cocooning the complex was comparable to that of the White House or Fort Knox.

The security measures consisted of metal detector checkpoints at entrances to the fenced area surrounding the museum buildings. A second perimeter of protection was provided by security booths inside the main entrance, manned by local guards brandishing AK-47s. The crowds of history junkies were an added protective measure. The evening was the busiest time for the museum, as tourists squeezed a few hours of sightseeing before leaving Egypt earlier the next day. The doors of the museum stayed open until 10:30 p.m.

Carrie chose a quiet room on the ground level. Away from most of the flow of visitors, it still had sufficient tourist presence to deter any violent outburst of the Israeli team. Fire exit doors, leading to the back of the museum, were at hand, in case a quick exit became necessary.

Carrie glanced at her wristwatch. Five more minutes and the bell would toll the signal for the closing, giving visitors ten minutes to clear the halls. Still no sign of Eliakim or anyone else looking for her. She held the eyes of an agent stationed by the entrance to the room. He responded with a swift headshake. Carrie sighed and stood up from the small, uncomfortable leather chair. She began pacing around the room, looking at a showcase of poison dart blowpipes. The air was cool, thanks to powerful air conditioning systems, in place mostly for the preservation of relics, rather than the benefit of visitors, and it carried a musty smell that reminded Carrie of thrifty bookstores.

"Carrie, we got something." The strong voice of one of the agents positioned at the end of the hall pierced her left ear.

"What is it?" She adjusted her earpiece volume and walked to the entrance of the room.

"Tall, muscular man. Blue blazer, khaki pants. Late thirties. Coming to you from the left, at nine o'clock. He's staring at you, Mike."

"Yeah, I see him," replied Mike, the agent by the entrance to the room. He had spotted the man among the thinning tourist crowd.

Carrie could see him as well. The man had sharp facial features, a chiseled nose, dark penetrating eyes, and a well-trimmed anchor beard.

"I got him." Mike took a few steps forward, blocking most of the narrow hall with his three hundred pounds body.

Unfazed, the man kept walking toward the CIS agent.

"Here to see someone?" Mike asked when the man was two steps away.

The man nodded. Carrie thought she heard a slight growl of annoyance, but she could not be sure because of the background noise.

"Face the wall." Mike gestured with his left hand.

"This is not necessary," the man replied in a slow, dry voice.

Carrie tried to place his accent, but it was nearly impossible. The man sounded like he could be an Egyptian, Jordanian, or from anywhere else in the Middle East.

"Standard procedure," Mike said. "You know the drill."

The man spread his legs and arms, as he stood inches away from the beige wall.

"He's clean," Mike said after the pat down.

The man jerked his head back."Happy?" he asked Mike, his palms spread in front of his face.

"Delighted. This way." Mike motioned with his head for the man to walk in front of him.

Three seconds later, Carrie shook the man's hand.

"Thank you," she said, as Mike retreated outside the room. "Mr. Ben-David?"

The man nodded. "Call me Eliakim," he said.

"OK. Eliakim, take a seat."

They sat in chairs facing each other, underneath a showcase displaying ancient pottery.

"My name is Carrie O'Connor. My operational chief arranged for this meeting, which was supposed to take place almost an hour ago."

"We're handling another crisis at the moment, and the traffic was a mess," Eliakim replied with a slight grin. "I see you don't have much trust, do you?" The man pointed at the entrance to the room. Mike's shadow was still visible on the wall.

"You're an Israeli in Egypt; do you trust anyone in this country?"

The man grinned again.

"Let's not waste more time. You have the intel I need?" Carrie asked.

"I have to make sure the man in question is alive and well."

"That will be impossible. This is not a ransom drop; it's an intel exchange. You give me what was promised to my boss, details about your agent's mission to Sudan. I'll give you his location."

Eliakim shook his head. "I need to talk to the hostage before I tell you anything."

Carrie frowned. "Your man is not a hostage. He was rescued after his chopper crashed, after he and his team tried to kill me and my team. Your man was wounded in the fight. If we had left him in the desert, you would have found his sun-baked corpse. If we had turned him over to the gunmen who survived his attack, you would have found his gasoline-scorched bones."

She stared at Eliakim, who was taken aback by her sudden eruption.

"So, we saved his life, taking him with us. He was never and still is not a hostage. We are keeping him safe until Mossad is willing to take him back."

"I understand, but I still need to establish that he's alive. Like your agent said, it's standard procedure."

"We sent you a photo, which shows his current state. Your man is alive and well. We have no reason to kill him now, after saving him, informing you that we have him, and arranging for this meeting."

Eliakim shook his head. "Once you learned he was an Israeli, you crafted this plan to squeeze out information, rather than hand him over to us, like the good tradition requires between friends."

Carrie leaned forward, pointing at Eliakim with her left hand index finger. "Friends? How many times do I have to tell you? This man attacked us with missiles and .50 cal machine guns. See this bruise?" She pointed at the left corner of her lip, just underneath her dimple. "And these scratches?" Her hand brushed against her right cheek. A purple streak was carved about an inch away from her eye.

Eliakim nodded and opened his mouth, but Carrie was quick to stop him.

"No, you listen to me. Your man was captured right after a gun battle, which almost cost me my life. So, I'm not going to take any bullshit about friendly relations."

Eliakim leaned forward. "This conflict, this shootout, was unintentional. It was what they call 'friendly fire.' We didn't know you were running an op at the same time and in the same area where the terrorists were hiding…"

"OK, let's assume for a moment that's true. How did you know about the sheikh being at that exact location?"

Eliakim hesitated for a second. "Do you know that these people, with whom you're involved, smuggle rockets and missiles to Arab terrorists, who use them to kill innocent people, women and children, in Israel?"

"I'm the one asking questions here and don't use that tone with me," Carrie replied. She noticed Mike's shadow getting closer to the entrance as her voice rose to a shout. After taking in a deep breath, she said, "Cooking means getting messy, and we work in a very dirty kitchen." Her voice returned to a calm tone.

"Uh-huh, go on."

"And yes, unfortunately, there are casualties, but we were there to negotiate a peace deal, which means less bloodshed."

"Now, you listen to me." Eliakim stood up, his muscles bursting underneath his blazer, and his chest rising up in anger. "There can be no peace in the Middle East without Israel at the table. The bloodshed will continue as long as terrorist rockets fall on our cities. And, for your information, sometimes the cooks get burned while they're fixing these secret recipes for disaster."

"Sit down," Carrie said. "And answer my question. How did you learn the sheikh was there?"

Eliakim took his time pacing around the room. Then, he stumbled to his chair, clenching his fists.

"Of course, we knew Sheikh Ayman was somewhere in the desert. Our operatives have been following every move of the Alliance ever since they started their bombing campaign. As the violence spread across the region, a decision was make to execute, what do you, Americans, call it—"

"I wouldn't know about that," Carrie interrupted him, "I'm Canadian."

Eliakim gave her a smirk. "Yes, now it came to me, 'targeted killing.' A decision was made to eliminate the operational head of the Alliance, Sheikh Yusuf Ayman."

"Who made this decision?"

"High government officials."

"Any names?"

"Uh, that's classified."

"Declassify it for me, please."

"The prime minister gave his approval," Eliakim said.

"Was anyone aware that a breakaway faction of the Alliance was in fact responsible for the suicide bombings?"

"We were. But splinter units are nothing new. There's always someone who considers this or that sheikh as 'weak' or 'inefficient,' and decides to start up their own killing business."

"So, the purpose of the choppers' mission was to assassinate

Sheikh Yusuf Ayman?"

"Yes. We received a tip that he was travelling in North Africa. Most of the time, he stayed in densely populated areas, where a precise air strike was almost impossible. He never ventured too far out in the desert, and for that I guess I have to thank you."

"Us?"

"Well, maybe not you personally, but definitely your boss."

"Johnson?"

"Yes."

"Why? She gave you his location?"

Eliakim nodded reluctantly.

"She gave you his location. That's how you knew exactly where the sheikh was," Carrie said slowly. "Did Johnson tell you we were meeting with the sheikh?"

Eliakim shook his head.

"I think you should discuss that with Johnson."

"Tell me, did she tell you we were there?" Carrie demanded.

Eliakim grinned. "I've already said too much."

Carrie gave him a cold stare. His voice was convincing, but his grin told her he was not really sorry this information had "slipped" his lips.

"Of course she told you. She gave you the location and the time of our meeting. That's why you said you didn't know we were in the area at the same time and in the same place as the terrorists," Carrie said. "But we were late getting to the valley, and your people assumed we were already gone. Or your people arrived earlier."

Carrie stopped talking, but her thoughts raced on. That's why Johnson was so skeptical, unwilling to accept we had a Mossad agent with us. But she knew what we were claiming was true because she gave the Israelis this intel. And, of course, she knew they were going to eliminate the sheikh. Now, is it a coincidence, we were caught in the middle, or the sheikh was not the only one set up for elimination? But, why would Johnson want to kill me and Justin?

The last thought darkened her face. She tried to clear her mind and focus on the task at hand. This will have to wait until I talk to Justin.

Eliakim shrugged, feigning indifference about Carrie's confused state. "All I can say is that we have this intel sharing agreement, under which—"

"I know about that. We, well Johnson, gave you the intel and this is how you repay us, by almost killing us."

"I told you earlier, it was unintentional, and I offer you my apologies. I'm truly glad you're not seriously wounded." Eliakim offered a seemingly sincere smile.

Carrie did a double take at Eliakim's sudden change of tactic. He's after something.

"OK, I accept your apology. Now, what you do want?"

Eliakim's smile disappeared at once.

"Can you confirm our target was eliminated?"

Carrie grinned. "You're forgetting the rules, Eliakim. Do I need to remind you?"

"No, they're very clear. You're the one asking questions here."

Carrie nodded. "You'll find your man at this address."

She handed him a piece of paper she took out of her shirt pocket. "Thank you for your assistance." Carrie stood up. "If there is nothing else…"

"Actually, there is. May I ask a question?"

"Sure. But I may not answer it."

"I'll ask it anyway. You said earlier you were talking to the Sheikh about a peace deal. What was he offering you?"

"I'm not at liberty to give you that information."

"Can you, at least, tell me if the sheikh is dead?"

"I thought you said one question."

"This is the last one."

"I can neither confirm, nor deny—"

"What if I gave you the name of our next target?" Eliakim took a step forward, getting closer to Carrie.

"The target of another Mossad assassination?"

Eliakim nodded.

Carrie hesitated for a brief second. Sooner or later, they'll find out the sheikh's dead. I'll take the deal. "OK. Sheikh Ayman is dead."

"Thank you. Our next target is Prince Husayn bin Al-Farhan."

"What? Is Mossad trying to start the World War III?"

"I think you're overreacting." Eliakim shrugged.

"You call this overreacting? How do you think the Muslim world will overreact to the assassination of a Saudi prince by Israelis squads?"

"The prince has made many enemies over the years, many of which have vowed publicly to seek revenge. He started feuds with Chechnya's separatists, Nigerian warlords and, more recently, with Chadian rebels. His death will be celebrated by many people."

"Why does Mossad want to settle the score with the prince?"

Eliakim's face showed his surprise at Carrie's question.

"Al-Farhan has supported terrorism for years, channeling funds to charities in the West Bank, Gaza, and Lebanon. This money is used to purchase grenade launchers and Kalashnikovs. Over the last few months, he has shown a greater interest in North Africa. Two months ago, he was in Algeria. Then, he was seen in Egypt, where we lost him. Then, we picked up his trail in Sudan, but we lost him again. There is a strong connection between his travels and the spike in violence after he leaves these countries. Suicide bombs go off, people die, countries sink into chaos."

"Did the prince visit Tripoli before the hotel bombings there?"

"We don't have any information on such trips, but I wouldn't exclude the possibility."

"Do you think he has a hand in these explosions?"

"We have no evidence, but given his old and new track record, it is a safe assumption."

Carrie drew nearer to Eliakim.

"I don't understand one thing. Isn't the prince a close friend of Libya's prime minister? Why would he organize such an attack in Tripoli?"

Eliakim shook his head with a shrug. "Al-Farhan fell out of favor with the prime minister last year over disagreements about an oil deal. Apparently, they couldn't agree on some exploration investment. We're talking about tens of billions of dollars. Things got really ugly, with the prince cursing the prime minister and wishing his death."

"Interesting," Carrie said. "This gives me a new perspective about many things."

"Explain that to me, would you?" Eliakim asked.

"Oh, no, I can't." Carrie tapped on her earpiece, turning on its microphone. "Mike," she whispered, "our guest is ready to leave."

Mike appeared at the doorway and Eliakim took a couple of steps toward him. As he was almost stepping out the room, Eliakim turned around. "You know, O'Connor, when they first told me Canadians had a young woman running this operation, I thought someone had royally screwed up. But, then, they gave me your name, and I knew you would turn out to be a tough bone to crack, even for me. That doesn't happen too often."

"If you're complimenting me because you're gonna ask me out, I have to say 'no.' I no longer date people in my profession."

"I know. I've heard what happened in Afghanistan and what you did to that Northern Alliance warlord."

Carrie shrugged. "People tend to exaggerate when they tell stories. I simply neutralized the pervert's threat."

Eliakim grinned. "More like 'neutered' the pervert. People say you blew his balls off and that got you an honorable discharge."

Carrie shook her head. "See, I told you people exaggerate. He lost only one of his family jewels."

"Well, for all purposes, one of the US allies in Afghanistan is now fixed."

"He should have listened when I told him I wasn't interested in becoming one of his concubines. And the honorable discharge came because I refused to apologize. I'll make no apologies for defending my honor and my life. Not then. Not ever. Now, you'll have to excuse me."

Eliakim nodded. He raised his right hand in the air, waving his goodbye.

"Mike, escort the agent to the fence gate," Carrie spoke on her microphone. "Then, have a team follow him. I want to make sure they pick up their man right away."

"Yes, ma'am," Mike replied.

"James, the SUV," Carrie ordered another agent, as she left the room and headed to the right, toward the exit. "And get me Justin on a secure line. I need to talk to him right away."

CHAPTER 14

Tripoli, Libya
May 15, 4:00 a.m. local time

Justin woke up covered in hot sweat. The air conditioner did not work well. The Four Seasons Hotel still used old, bulky models from the nineties, and Justin felt like he was riding a rickety train. Lying in his twin bed and staring at the gray ceiling, Justin's mind wandered from his fiancée Anna, to his father Carter, to his phone call last night with Carrie, to her meeting with Mossad, and to Abdul and the Glock under his pillow.

"What will happen today?" He found himself asking the question aloud, albeit in a little more than a whisper. Then, he frowned at the sound of his voice, and at the realization he was talking to himself.

It's interesting. We say it's OK to think, but if you start talking to yourself, people think you're crazy. Am I crazy? Am I going crazy? Well, here I am, risking my life, Abdul's life, and now I'm bringing Carrie into this dump. What am I doing here? Why can't I let the Americans handle this? After all, it's their president. And if Israelis want to kill Prince Al-Farhan, why should I care? Am I getting so blind by my urge for action that I'm willing to overdose myself with a danger rush? When will this urge stop? Will it ever stop? Have I not given my country enough already? Have I not given myself enough?

He rolled over to his side, staring at the window. The curtains were parted in the middle and a sliver of light from an office tower across the street fell on his bare chest.

Is Johnson trying to kill us? Why? Or was it just a fuck up, with us being in the wrong place at the wrong time. Johnson should have told us about Mossad's mission. But if she's trying to kill us, then it makes sense to send us to Libya, so the mukhabarat can finish her job. I've had it with being stabbed in the back by the people who are supposed to watch my back and whom I'm taught to trust.

Maybe I should take Anna's advice and request a transfer. A transfer to a place closer to her. A place safe, for both of us. Maybe after this mission. Maybe this one will be my last. After all, it's extremely important to stop this plot against the US president. The life of our prime minister is at stake as well. The world doesn't need another war in North Africa.

Justin rolled to the other side and glanced at the alarm clock. 4:05 a.m. He argued with himself whether he should head to the gym but dismissed the idea. He needed to keep a low profile. He wasn't really sleepy, so he chose to spend a few more minutes relaxing in his soft bed. The day was going to be extremely busy.

* * *

Justin dozed off until the alarm clock woke him up at 6:00 a.m. He placed a short call to Anna on the satellite phone Abdul had given him, ensuring her answering machine he was doing well and promising to call again, perhaps in the evening. Then he ordered breakfast, while surfing through TV news channels, mostly from the Arab world. They all reported on Tripoli's bombings, but none gave any new details.

Still wrapped in a housecoat, he worked through his French toast, scrambled eggs, and bacon, washing everything down with a generous portion of orange juice. He showered, shaved and changed into a pair of blue jeans and gray polo shirt, courtesy of Abdul.

However, he felt unprotected without his bulletproof vest. He could not have brought one inside Libya and Abdul had forgotten to bring one. Let's hope we'll go a day without shooting. He buttoned his shirt in front of the mirror and placed his Glock inside the waistband holster to his right side.

At 7:25 a.m. Justin walked through the hotel lobby, nodding at the young clerk behind the reception desk. He declined the clerk's offer to fetch him a taxi and walked outside through the main doors. A couple of blocks south of the hotel, he climbed into one of the unlicensed taxis parked in an alley and ordered the driver to take him to Bab El Bahr Hotel. His true destination was four blocks south, the Corinthia, where he was meeting Nour.

After making sure no one had followed him, Justin sat on one of the benches of the pristine lawns surrounding the Corinthia. He glanced at the glittering of the occasional sunray over the Mediterranean's stormy waters. A few gray clouds fluttered in the distance, hovering over two oil tankers awaiting their turn to dock at the port. The sea breeze kept toying with the bank of clouds, tossing them toward north, and then, sweeping them in the opposite direction.

Ten minutes later, a white GMC Envoy with US diplomatic license plates stopped a few yards away from Justin. He gazed over his sunglasses. Nour waved at him.

"Hello," Justin said. "How are you doing this fine morning?"

"Great, what about you?"

"Wonderful. I'm glad its cooler and maybe it will rain. At least, that's what the forecast said."

"I doubt it. Those clouds have been hanging around for a week, but we haven't seen a drop. Get in."

Justin buckled his seatbelt before Nour stepped on the gas.

"Where do you live?" Justin asked.

"Palm City, Janzour. That's about ten miles southeast."

"How do you like it?"

"OK. Beachfront homes in a fenced complex. The embassy rents apartments and houses for its staff. Most expats live there."

"You're an expat?"

Justin wanted to confirm if Abdul's intelligence was accurate and see if Nour was going to lie to him.

"I was born in Jordan, and I lived all over Africa before moving to the States in the early nineties. I came here when the embassy reopened. You?"

"Born and raised in Canada, although my relatives came from Scotland and Italy."

"That explains the hair and the temper."

"Eh… thanks?" Justin replied with an arched eyebrow.

"You're welcome."

Nour honked his horn, to tell the other drivers he was going to make a lane change, illegal as it was, in the middle of an intersection. Justin noticed traffic had become heavier as they were getting closer to Tripoli's downtown business district.

"What family do you have?" Nour asked.

"I'm not married," Justin replied. "With our job, there's never time."

"I found time not only to tie the knot, but also to have a couple of sons."

"Congratulations," Justin said. He added as an afterthought, "At the moment, I'm dating this gal from back home."

"I hope things work out."

"I hope so, too. It's difficult to keep it going when I'm away for weeks at a time."

Nour nodded. His eyes became warmer, and a smile began to form in his face.

"I know what you mean. My wife didn't want us to move to Libya. Too dangerous, too hot, too far away from home. Any excuse you may think, she had it on her list."

"She agreed at the end, didn't she?"

"There was no other option. I follow orders and so does she."

Nour's smile disappeared and Justin realized that was the end of their small talk.

"Speaking of orders," Nour said, "Mr. Garnett has arranged for a meeting with a senior official at the Internal Security Service. At 9:00 a.m. we're to exchange our intel with Colonel Farid Haydar."

Justin's face remained still as Nour mentioned the name of the man Abdul had warned him about last night.

"Who is Farad?" Justin mispronounced the colonel's name on purpose.

"Not Farad, it's Farid. And he prefers 'Colonel' or 'Mr. Haydar.' He's the chief of the Agency's Counter Terrorism Branch for Tripoli, and he's also in charge of the car bombings investigation."

"Is he keen on cooperating with us?"

"Would you? If some guy from the Libyan embassy in Ottawa knocked on your door and demanded to take over your investigation because he thinks you're not doing a good enough job, would you want to be on their beck and call?"

"We're not taking over anything; we're simply doing our own investigation, in order to show to our, I mean American, citizens that we've done due diligence."

"Libyans don't see it that way. They interpret this as the US meddling in their internal affairs, and as a lack of appreciation for their efforts. Remember, most of the victims are Libyans, and they're within their rights to carry out this investigation."

Justin nodded. "I understand."

"However, the colonel seemed unusually accommodating of Mr. Garnett's request. He agreed to meet us in person. That's very strange, considering two days ago he wasn't even taking our calls."

"Yes, that is strange." Justin looked away from Nour's inquisitive eyes.

"Now, when we get to the colonel's office, let me do the talking. I've met him before, and I know what makes him tick. Besides, you are very unofficially in this case, Mr. Jack Schmitt, and a time bomb, may I add."

I don't remember your boss putting it that way, Justin wanted to reply. Instead he returned a confident smile. Also, your boss said something about me leading this inquiry, not you.

"Of course," Justin replied. "I'll wait for your signal before saying anything."

"Great. Our experts took apart the data you brought in and concluded the voices are those of identified terrorists. There's a slim margin of error in these voice matching exercises, but the probabilities they offered were in the higher 90s."

"So, Mr. Garnett is convinced there's a plot in the works to assassinate the American president?"

Nour held Justin's eyes for a long moment.

"Yes," he replied finally. "We've increased the security level surrounding every detail of the president's visit. Everyone's on high alert." He stared back at the road, adding, "None of this should find its way to the Libyans. At least, not at this time."

"You don't have to say it."

"It doesn't hurt to make sure we understand each other."

"We do."

They drove without exchanging a word for the next two minutes. Nour made a left turn on Al Jamhuriyah Street and they kept going south.

"Where's the colonel's office?" Justin asked.

"In Fashloum Street."

Justin glanced at his watch.

Nour took notice. "We'll be there in ten minutes."

"I'm not worried about that. Just expecting an important call."

"Your girlfriend?"

"Oh, no. My partner."

"He's coming here?"

"Yes, she is."

"She has new intel on the bombings?"

"Well, not exactly, but we need to follow a few leads."

"I hope that doesn't distract you from this investigation."

"It won't. If anything, it will help me… us."

"OK. Now, the colonel should have some reports for us, police interrogations of Satam al-Raziq, the man whose truck bomb did not explode. We'll go through them, and, depending on how useful that information is, decide on our next steps."

"I think it's a good idea to visit the explosion sites and see what the police may have missed. Any witnesses they couldn't find or hotel guests reluctant to talk to the mukhabarat."

"And what makes you think they'll open up to us?" Nour asked.

"Because we're not locals. Foreigners tend to keep their mouths shut when it comes to talking to local authorities, especially here."

"Good for them."

"Yeah, but they may feel different about talking to Americans."

"Let's hope so. We know a few names of Alliance members and my men are staking out their known hideouts in the city. Once they nab someone, they'll call me, and we'll pay them a visit."

Nour changed lanes and slowed down, while driving to the right, turning into Fashloum Street. They passed by mostly two- and three-story buildings hosting a variety of shops, restaurants, office complexes and business centers. Further away, Justin noticed the grayish towers of a hospital.

"The Agency's offices are there," Nour pointed at a narrow alley, beyond a tall row of palm trees.

Justin squinted and noted a black iron gate. Its guards, a pair of tall men in blue fatigues, were wrangling submachine guns.

"Here is your embassy ID."

Justin took the plastic badge Nour handed him, and looked at it. The Great Seal of the United States was engraved on the badge. He touched the raised surface of the American flag and the bald eagle with its wings displayed. Justin's cover name and his title were written below in silver accented letters.

"Senior Security Consultant?" Justin asked.

"Sorry, Chief of Security was taken," Nour replied with a grin as the GMC inched forward toward the checkpoint.

* * *

One of the guards escorted both men through the shaded, squared courtyard. A dozen or so unmarked Nissan Patrols and Mitsubishi Pajeros were lined up by the fence. The three-story, beige-colored building, in a large L shape, had no identifying signs, not even an address number. Its colonial façade was in a dire need of repair; the faded paint and the chipped plaster of its columns were clear signs of neglect.

As they crossed the doorstep of the main entrance, Justin was greeted by a very different interior. Plush, green carpets covered most of the floor. The uncovered surfaces showed shiny, white marble tiles. The furniture in the oval hall was scarce, but practical: two sets of leather armchairs, with matching coffee tables. A row of three silver chandeliers hung from the ceiling. Ample sunlight entered through arched windows.

"Colonel Haydar's office is on the second floor." The guard directed them to a set of marble stairs.

Nour and Justin followed the guard until he slowed down his marching pace and knocked on one of the doors to his left.

"Come in," a deep, throaty voice called from inside in Arabic.

The guard ushered the two men inside and disappeared without a word. Nour and Justin stood by the door.

"Welcome, welcome," Colonel Haydar said, standing behind his large dark table.

He was a thin, small man, perhaps in the early fifties. His hair had silvered completely, without even a sign of receding. His small, gray eyes peered at the two men from behind black-framed glasses. The colonel had a squared face, suntanned and wrinkled, and framed by large ears. A thin moustache line matched perfectly his hair color. He walked to meet them and first shook Nour's stretched hand.

"You must be Mr. Schmitt?" the colonel turned to Justin.

"Yes, Colonel Haydar, this is our Senior Security Consultant, Mr. Jack Schmitt."

The colonel gave no hint of recognizing Justin's face or his alias. Justin was not expecting any.

"Pleased to meet you, sir." Justin offered his hand.

The colonel's handshake was firm for a man of his built. He tapped Justin on his shoulder with his left hand in a friendly gesture. "Schmitt, is that German?"

"Yes, sir. My great-grandfather was a silversmith in Bavaria," Justin recited a part of his cover.

"Well, my friends, take a seat." The colonel pointed at a couple of straight-back chairs across from his paper-littered table. Nour sat in the chair to the left; Justin took the other one. His eyes moved from the square ceiling light, to the air conditioner panel, to the bookshelves leaning against the wall, and rested at the portrait of the Libya's prime minister staring at the men in the room.

"Thank you for meeting with us," Nour said. "We really appreciate this opportunity to exchange information for the purpose of increasing the security in the country."

"Of course, no problem. Cooperation with the United States is very important to us. The safety of our citizens and of our country is number one priority. Especially, in this unfortunate case when there are so many innocent victims, some of which, are Americans, Germans, and other nationalities, who were enjoying the hospitality of my hometown."

Justin could sense no trace of a foreign accent in the colonel's English, besides, obviously, a hint of his native tongue. He tended to divide his sentences in small phrases, and shoot them out of his mouth in one quick burst.

"Our resources are focused on arresting all members of the Alliance responsible for this massacre," the colonel said. "In cooperation with other departments, we'll hunt them down and throw them all in jail."

"We're pleased to hear that, Colonel," Nour said.

"Now, Mr. Garnett said the embassy was interested in the details of our investigation. What exactly do you want to know?"

"We would like an update. Suspects arrested, interrogated, progress made. Given that our head of state is the target of the terrorists."

The colonel made a quick dismissive gesture with his right hand. "Oh, you are talking about the dead prisoner and his claims? These terrorists have always threatened our leaders and foreign officials visiting our country. But we will not be scared by a group of cowards that blow up innocent people."

The colonel took a brief pause. He licked his lips, waiting for Nour's and Justin's reactions. They nodded in agreement.

"We'll increase security at the airport and of the convoy as your president comes to the city. I will personally make sure that my men are everywhere. Your president will have the same security, if not greater, than even my prime minister," the colonel said and nodded toward the portrait of the Libya's prime minister, as if he were truly present in the room.

"We appreciate that," Nour said. "We are taking these threats very seriously and we need to take all measures to eliminate any danger."

"Well, of course, of course. We're searching for members of the Alliance in Benghazi and al-Akhdar, two of their main bases. Several arrests have been made already. People are being interrogated and, like you Americans say, we'll leave no stone unturned until we learn everything."

Nour nodded. "We're here to help. Anything you need, simply let us know."

"We have everything under control. My men can and will handle this operation. If we need assistance from your embassy, which I don't believe will be necessary, I know who to call."

"OK," Nour said.

The colonel shuffled through the papers on his desk. He picked up a black folder, about half an inch thick. He reached forward and handed it to Nour.

"Now, out of respect for Mr. Garnett, I've put together some reports from operatives who interrogated one of the men responsible for these car bombings, Satam al-Raziq. Since he was only a low-ranking member of the Alliance, he knew only crumbs of information. He had heard they were planning an attack against the American president, but he gave us no helpful details. Then he hung himself."

Nour began flipping through the pages of the folder. Most of them were photocopied in a poor quality. Some were handwritten. Everything was in Arabic.

"It's all in there, but I don't think there's much else that's crucial. In any case, we're going after the Alliance with all we've got. It's time to wipe out this evil from our land, once for all."

"Has any other witness given any useful information?" Nour closed the folder and passed it to Justin, who began to review it.

"No, otherwise it would be in the reports." The colonel pointed at the folder. A frown began to form in his thick brow.

Nour understood the clue. "Thank you, Colonel. We'll review the reports and if we have any questions or if we need any clarifications—"

"You can call me at any time," the colonel interrupted him. "It's my pleasure to offer you my complete cooperation. Now, what exactly are your plans?"

Nour leaned back in his chair. "We'll examine the valuable information you've given us. We'll assess the situation and strengthen our security measures regarding our president's visit. On the other hand, we'll continue to work with our partners, to ensure we react strongly to the Alliance."

The colonel raised a cautionary finger. "Not in Libya, I assume," he said in a nervous tone.

"Of course, not." Nour was quick to reply, spreading his palms. His face feigned surprise the colonel was bringing up this issue.

"What are you thinking, Mr. Schmitt?" the colonel asked Justin, still skimming through the folder.

Justin looked up, first at Nour, and then at the colonel, who waved his hand in the air, indicating his impatience. Nour nodded for Justin to answer the question.

"Hmm… nothing really," Justin replied.

"No, please, if you have a concern, I'd like to hear it."

If you are being sarcastic, you're a very good actor, Justin thought.

"All right," he said, "since you're insisting. I couldn't help but notice the absence of any findings about the undetonated explosives." He flipped through the pages of one of the reports. "After Mr. al-Raziq was detained, I'm sure his vehicle was searched and his car bomb was deactivated and taken apart."

The colonel replied with a startled face. "Mr. Schmitt, you… you can read Arabic?" The colonel's enthusiasm was clear, although he was slurring his words. "I'm… I'm so surprised."

Justin's eyes dropped from the colonel's grin to the folder on his lap. He was still expecting an answer.

"Yes, the findings that you can't find…" The colonel's face turned serious, and an aura of mistrust seemed to loom over his head. "Al-Raziq's truck was ripped apart, meticulously and thoroughly." The colonel had overcome the first moments of surprise and the hammering of words had returned. "We dusted for fingerprints and our experts did all the cute tricks you Americans promote so fancily on your CSI shows. I tell you, there's nothing that deserved further attention. Nothing."

The colonel paused for a second to swallow and to catch his breath.

"You don't mind if we have a look at the truck bomb?" Justin asked quickly before the colonel resumed his tirade.

Nour opened his mouth, but the colonel silenced him with a quick hand gesture.

"You doubt my word?" he asked in an accusatory tone.

"Absolutely not, sir." Justin closed the folder and placed his hand over it. "I simply suggested that, instead of wasting your valuable time, we go ahead with our own due diligence. The families of these innocent victims, Libyans, Americans and others who lost their lives in this massacre, as you called it, would want us to find out everything we can. In this way, we can work together to prevent future attacks like this."

"There will be no other attacks like this. We'll make sure this will never happen again. Ever!" the colonel exclaimed. "But, you don't trust me, and you want to check for yourself; well, go ahead."

Justin wanted to jump in and sugar-coat his position, but the colonel was right. Justin did not trust him.

"I'll have one of my best operatives take you to the evidence lab, where you can examine the explosives for yourself. I assume you have sufficient forensic expertise to analyze this car bomb?"

Justin nodded with a slight hesitation. "Yes, I've seen more than my fair share in the field," he said slowly.

"Eh, I knew it," the colonel snapped back. "There's much more to you, Mr. Schmitt than one's made to believe. And nothing surprises me anymore about you."

Justin remained silent. It was not a compliment; it sounded more like a threat.

The colonel reached for his phone at the edge of his desk. He barked a few orders then slammed the handset back in place.

"Everything's ready." He took a deep breath. "Abdul will be here right away."

Abdul? My Abdul? Justin stayed calm and did not betray his stomach-twirling feeling. The colonel was eyeing him like a viper ready to swallow a rabbit, which had just happened to fall inside his cage.

A few second later, there was a knock on the door.

"Oh, here he is," the colonel said. "Abdul, come in," he added in a strong voice.

"You asked to see me, sir?"

Justin did not have to turn his head. He recognized Abdul's voice.

"Yes, I'd like you to meet Mr. Nour Milad, chief of security, and

Mr. Jack Schmitt, senior security advisor at the American Embassy."

"Pleased to meet you," Abdul shook Nour's hand and, after a split second of hesitation, reached for Justin's limb frozen in mid-air. Their eyes did not meet, even though they saw face to face.

"They're here to provide their assistance with our car bombings investigation. I'm assigning you to take these two men to our warehouse, I mean the evidence lab, where they are to inspect the vehicle of the failed suicide bomber. You'll also take them to the hotels where these bombings took place, so they can poke around. I'm sure that's what you were planning on doing. Correct me if I'm wrong," the colonel said, looking more at Justin than at Nour.

Nour and Justin exchanged a quick undecided glance.

"We accept your offer to work together," Nour said slowly. "In no way do we intend to put down the efforts of your team, only to build on their results."

The colonel stared at Nour and Justin over his glasses. "I expect nothing less, Chief. Keep me informed."

"By all means, sir," Nour replied.

"Well, then, I'll let you go. You've lots on your plate and so do I." The colonel pointed at his desk.

CHAPTER 15

Tripoli, Libya
May 15, 9:20 a.m. local time

Colonel Haydar wiped a drop of sweat from his forehead as he dialed Zakir's number on his cellphone. For reasons he could not explain, he became nervous just before calling Prince Al-Farhan's aide. It happened every time, even when things were going precisely according to plan, like now.

"Yes, what is it?" Zakir barked in his snappy voice, impatient as always.

"They just left my office," the colonel whispered quietly, even though he was alone. "I gave them the reports as instructed."

"Good. What did they say?"

"They said they'll review them, draw their own conclusions, and tighten the security around their president."

"Did you promise increased Libyan security around the convoy?"

"Yes, of course, I did. I said their president will be as protected, if not more protected than our prime minister."

Zakir let out a small snicker. "Good one. Yes, their president will be extremely well protected."

"There's something else," Colonel Haydar said with some hesitation. "They're running their own investigation into this matter."

A few seconds of pause followed and, this time, the colonel wiped a stream of sweat off his brow.

"You fool!" Zakir finally blurted. "Why did you allow that?"

"Well, we're supposed to work together with them and… hmm… and they were going to go ahead with it anyway. I thought, in this way, we know exactly what they're doing and whom they're talking to."

"Really? Like we knew where Justin's spent last night, right?"

"It's different this time."

"How is that?"

"I sent one of my best men with them, to escort them at all times. He'll report to me on their actions."

"And you trust this man?"

"Yes, absolutely."

The colonel swallowed hard as another tense pause followed. He could hear a few whispers over the phone and wondered whether Zakir was conveying his words right away to Prince Al-Farhan.

"OK, so where are they now?" Zakir asked.

"They've gone to inspect the fifth truck bomb, at one of our labs."

"Have you made sure all traces of our involvement have been erased?"

"Yes, my men have double-checked, and there's nothing there to make them start wondering."

"You need to make sure they don't find anything. We need them to believe the story we've told them and not grow suspicious. You understand that?"

"Yes, yes, I get it."

"Good. They shouldn't be allowed to discover anything. I can't stress enough the importance that they have no doubts about the target of the Alliance."

"I'll do whatever it takes to make sure that doesn't happen."

"Good. Anything else?"

"No, that's it."

"Keep me informed," Zakir hung up.

* * *

"What the hell was that?" Nour shouted at Justin as soon as he slammed shut the GMC's door. They were alone in the privacy of the SUV's cabin. "What part of 'keep you big mouth shut' was unclear?"

"The colonel asked me what I was thinking, and I simply told him," Justin replied calmly, buckling his seat belt.

"No, you didn't simply tell him. You accused his men of being sloppy because of a missing report. And you told the colonel we are better than them, and that we can prove it."

"I made no such claims."

"Really? Well, what did you mean when you asked to 'have a look at the truck,' huh?" Nour turned toward Justin, his brow furrowing and his eyes squinting.

"I got us permission to go over the evidence collected so far, and a chance to find new evidence. Something the mukhabarat may have missed, overlooked, or outright buried. Isn't this what we're supposed to do?"

"Yes, but we're also supposed to be discreet about it. You almost blew your cover in there. And now, we have a babysitter monitoring our every move."

Justin shrugged. He wished he could tell Nour that Abdul was, in fact, working for the CIS. Instead, he said, "Libyans were going to follow us no matter what. You really think we can get into the evidence lab and interrogate witnesses without the mukhabarat knowing about it?"

Nour heaved an expletive.

"Let's get the hell out of here." He shifted the SUV into gear. "And when were you going to tell me you can read Arabic?"

"When were you going to tell me you have a bad temper?"

Before Nour could utter a reply, Abdul knocked on the driver's window. He was wearing his aviator shades.

"Don't say a single word," Nour warned Justin and rolled down the glass.

"The colonel wants to see you." Abdul pointed his thin finger at Justin. "Alone," he added, when he saw Nour unfasten his seatbelt.

Nour shook his head. "He can't see anyone without me."

"You want me to tell that to the colonel?" Abdul asked.

Nour ground his teeth. "Go," he ordered Justin. "Just listen this time, OK?"

"OK," Justin replied.

He followed Abdul inside the Agency's main hall. Abdul pointed to the right, on the main floor, instead of upstairs. Justin realized that Abdul, not the colonel, wanted a word in private with him.

"You want us both dead?" Abdul said in a hushed voice after they entered a secured interrogation room at the end of the hall. "The colonel told me about you insulting him with your doubts. What's wrong with you?"

"You really have iron balls pulling this stunt." Justin leaned against the dark wall of the small room. "What if Nour marches back into the colonel's office?"

"He won't. And you're the one with the iron balls defying the colonel. Did you already forget what I told you last night? Let me repeat it: The colonel is after your sorry ass, and now the two of you are crossing not only paths, but also swords."

"What can I do? He challenged me to a duel."

Abdul leaned so close Justin could feel the man's tobacco breath on his face.

"It's not funny. The colonel will not think twice about hanging us for treason."

"Then we need to be really careful."

"How can we do that when we're in plain sight of him and his men?"

Justin shrugged. "We'll figure it out. In due time."

Abdul let out a loud groan and stepped back. "Ah, in due time, yes, everything, in due time."

"Did you find out why the colonel is so interested in me?"

"Yes. And it's not good."

"It never is."

"The colonel's cause is personal. He happened to be in the same Unit 78 of the prison."

"Unit 78? The same unit you and I decimated during our prison break."

"We killed his brothers in arms…"

"And he's out for revenge," Abdul finished Justin's thought.

Justin sighed. "He acts so gentle, so polite. What great self-control." After a moment, he added, "That explains Tarek last night. The colonel sent him to settle the account."

"Yes, about that," Abdul said, "I spent two hours at the crime scene last night."

"You found him?"

"No, I didn't."

"What?"

"There was no Tarek there."

"Impossible. His body fell right in front of my feet. I saw him stop breathing with my own eyes. Did you find the pool of blood?"

"Yes. And we also found the body of a dead policeman. But it wasn't Tarek."

"Who was it?"

"A new guy."

"Somebody took Tarek's body away before you got there."

"Why would someone do that and leave the other body behind?" Abdul asked.

"Or maybe, just maybe he made it. Maybe my wound wasn't deadly. Did you check hospitals? Medical clinics?"

"Or maybe Tarek wasn't there," Abdul said quietly.

"What are you saying, Abdul, that I'm making things up? That I'm crazy?"

"I'm saying that people who used to be dead are now suddenly alive, and you are killing them again. But, we can't find the body."

Justin realized he had no time to argue about this with Abdul. *I'll have to figure this out later. On my own.* "We have to go now, otherwise Nour will become wary."

"When he asks, tell him the colonel wants you not to be too nosey and not to cause any scandals."

"Why would the colonel say something like that to me?"

"Because you're a pain in the ass. He told me so, after you left his office. He also warned me to keep you two on a tight leash. Nour will believe this. He knows you're a loose cannon."

"Huh?"

"I saw him shouting at you earlier in the car. Tell me it had nothing to do with your meeting with the colonel."

Justin grinned and turned around. "That would be lying."

"I thought so."

They walked back to the GMC. Nour was fidgeting with the steering wheel.

"OK," Abdul said, "I'll lead the way to the lab, which is half an hour away, down south. Stay close, so you can follow me."

"Can you give us the address, in case we lose you in traffic?" Nour asked.

Abdul shook his head. "There is no address. And you won't be able to find it on your own. Just keep up with me."

"OK," Nour agreed.

As soon as Justin climbed in his seat, Nour asked, "Tell me you didn't screw things up even worse with the colonel."

"Thanks for your confidence."

"Don't be a smart-ass. What did he want?"

"Making sure I don't cause trouble."

"Kind of late for that. Did he threaten you?"

"No, no, he didn't."

Nour nodded and turned the steering wheel, after Abdul passed them in a white Nissan Patrol. They drove in silence for a few minutes, until Justin's BlackBerry chirped.

"I have to take this," he said after glancing at the caller ID.

"Sure, but I ain't pulling over."

"Hi, what's up?" Justin said in a low voice, and with certain uneasiness, since Nour could hear every word.

Nour kept his eyes on the road, seemingly uninterested in Justin's conversation.

"Hello, Justin," Anna said. "How are you?"

"Good, good. How 'bout you?"

"OK, I guess. Sorry I missed your calls. We're in meetings all the time. The merger, you know. The client's so secretive, and they don't allow us to bring our BlackBerries into the conference room."

"No problem. How's everything?"

"Oh, crazy. I miss you so much. When are you coming home?"

Justin hesitated for a moment.

"You're not coming home any time soon, are you?"

"No, I'm afraid not."

"Will you call me tomorrow?"

"Yes, I will. For sure. I'm not going to forget your birthday."

"And our anniversary. But nothing we plan seems to work out any more." Her voice shook with a tinge of despair

"Once this is over, it won't be this crazy. Then, we can make plans."

"Plans to sail the Caribbean? Again?"

"Hey, that's not fair," Justin replied to her sarcasm.

"It's not? We cancelled our Caribbean trip because of your tour of duty. I'm not up for another rejection, so why bother to pick a place?"

"You know I'm not the one making decisions."

"Yes, Justin, I know. That's the nature of your business and you're just following orders. I've heard this all before."

"So, why are we even having this conversation?"

"Because I don't want to be alone, without you. And that's why I get mad when you're away."

Justin looked over at Nour. He was focused on the congested traffic in all four lanes of the road.

"Move it you jerk, c'mon, move it." Nour slammed his left fist on the horn.

"What's going on?" Anna asked.

"Oh, nothing. We're stuck in traffic."

"Where are you? Some place warm?"

"Bloody hot and sweaty, but we've got air conditioning." Justin adjusted the dashboard's air vents, so the cold air would blow toward his damp face.

"Tell me you're gonna take good care of yourself," Anna said.

Justin shifted in his seat and felt a needle-like pain on his left knee. The shrapnel wound was healing fast, but it still gave him sharp jolts of pain.

"I'll try," he replied warily.

"Is Carrie there?"

"No, she's not here."

Justin did not tell her Carrie was going to land in Tripoli in a few minutes.

"When will you call me?"

"No idea. Later, perhaps in the evening. If not, tomorrow for sure."

Anna sighed and fell silent. Justin waited, his eyes following Abdul's car changing lanes, in order to escape the crawling traffic.

"OK. Hopefully, we'll talk then."

"I hope so. I love you."

"Ditto."

Justin saw Nour's smirk forming at the corner of his lips. "Women," was all he said.

How much did he hear? Before Justin could put away his BlackBerry, it vibrated in his hand.

"More women." Justin glanced at the screen, displaying the word 'Carrie.' "Hey, you're early."

"Yeah, we made good time."

"What's rattling in the background?"

"Oh, I'm in a taxi, we're on our way to the city. How far till we're there?" she asked. "The driver tells me about thirty minutes," she added after a couple of seconds.

"Was the flight good?"

"Excellent. Where are you?"

"Good question. Let me see." Justin peered through the window and began searching for a landmark or a road sign. "Hmmm… I think we're on Tariq Zanatah Road, right?" he said, as he looked at Nour, who nodded. "Yes, we're on TZ Road and we're going south, toward a large traffic circle, and now, now we're stuck in traffic."

A few seconds of silence followed.

"Carrie?"

"Yes, I just told my driver to take us to this TZ Road. He seems to know where that circle is. Where are you going?"

"Some kind of a warehouse where the police took the unexploded car bomb. Believe it or not, there was nothing in their report about the explosives, their type, amount, the way in which they were packed and wired, nothing."

"Really?"

"Yes, do you find that strange too?"

"Oh, yeah, that's strange. Did they do forensics?"

"They say they did, but there's not a single word about it in the report. At least, on the one the colonel gave us. Anyway, I'll tell you more when we meet."

"All right. Give me a shout when you get to the place."

"OK. See you later."

"Be safe."

"You too."

The traffic light changed. The GMC rounded the corner and entered the traffic circle.

"That was your partner, I imagine?" Nour asked.

Justin nodded. "She just landed at the airport, and she's going to meet us at the warehouse, this evidence lab of sorts."

"Is your partner an expert on explosives forensics?"

"She knows more than I do. She studied it for a year or so,

before deciding it wasn't for her."

"What exactly do you expect to find?"

"Anything there's to be found. Right now, I'm very suspicious why the police left out any information about the car bomb and its explosives. We don't even know their type, composition, blast range, nothing."

Nour shrugged. "Maybe you're overanalyzing it."

"Why do you say that?"

"Well, look at it from the Libyans' point of view. The bomb didn't go off. The police detained the wannabe suicide bomber and deactivated the bomb. OK, so they didn't include a few details."

"These may be important, which can lead us somewhere else."

"Yeah, maybe," he said without conviction. "You don't trust the colonel at all?"

"Do you?"

"It depends."

"Depends on what?"

"His interests. Here, he wants to close this case. It's clear who sent the suicide bombers. The Alliance claimed responsibility for it. Their targets and their motives are also clear. The colonel thinks it's time to move forward. They'll start moving against the Alliance and increase security for my president. Everyone's happy. Other than the terrorists, but the colonel wasn't trying to please them."

Justin shifted in this seat. "What do you think about that?"

"Pretty good plan. Personally, I'd like to know the details of their operations against the Alliance and how many troops they're planning to commit to our convoy. Hopefully, we'll get some of those details later. But, I do agree, the ultimate goal is to protect my president and the G-20 Summit, which is only three days away."

Justin nodded. "Well, let's dig up some facts and see what we can piece together."

"What leads does your partner have?"

"Huh?"

"You said earlier your partner had some leads you were planning to examine. Care to share?"

Justin hesitated. "Yeah, sure, after I receive a complete briefing."

Nour squinted. A slight frown appeared on his face. "I have a feeling you're not leveling with me."

"You're right," Justin replied, "I'm not at liberty."

"Oh, don't give me that. We're on the same team."

"We are? Do you give me everything you have?"

"I tell you what you need to know."

"Yeah, and so do I."

An awkward silence followed for about a minute. Nour's eyes were glued to Abdul's car. Justin fiddled with his BlackBerry.

"Look," Nour said at some point, "we both want the same thing. It will be easier to get it if we worked together, rather than each following our own leads."

"Agreed."

"So?" Nour invited Justin to speak with a gesture of his hand.

"There may be more at stake here than meets the eye. Carrie, she's my partner, has learned that another player has a horse in the Alliance's dirty game."

"Who?"

"That's classified. CIS agents only."

"Fair enough. What does this player want?"

"We're not sure, but anything we may discover in the explosives and during this investigation may be crucial to uncovering his plans."

"It may be the Israelis," Nour wondered, "they often seem to be pulling the proverbial strings."

"So I've heard," Justin replied with a straight face, "sometimes it's true, and then, sometimes it isn't."

CHAPTER 16

Tripoli, Libya
May 15, 10:00 a.m. local time

"You're sure this is it?" Justin asked, as Nour pulled into an almost empty lot, the size of a city block, surrounded by a large space of wasteland. A grayish, two-story warehouse stood to the north, the only building probably within a mile radius. Two apartment buildings towered in the south.

"Of course," Nour replied. "See where Abdul parked?"

Justin glanced to his left. Abdul opened the driver's door and stepped outside, talking on his cellphone.

"This used to be a training facility for police recruits before they moved to their new complex, about ten blocks that way." Nour pointed to the south, beyond the apartment towers. "I wish Abdul would have said we were coming here," he added, reaching for the black folder in the backseat. "Let's go."

"Give me a second to phone Carrie our location."

"OK."

Nour browsed through the report's pages, while Justin placed his call. A minute later, as Justin was pocketing his smartphone, Nour produced an embassy personnel badge, similar to the one he had slipped Justin earlier. "For your partner."

Justin picked up the badge. Underneath the bald eagle, the engraved name spelled Carrie O'Connor.

"Since we've started to level with each other." Nour stared at the cloud of disbelief veiling Justin's face. "I thought she may need this."

"How did you know she was coming here when you had this made?"

"Sorry, buddy, but that's classified. Embassy personnel only."

Justin rolled his eyes and shook his head. A smart guess, he thought. "Just Security Consultant?" he pointed at the badge.

"She doesn't have the same rank as you in the CIS, does she?"

"No, but it's almost the same."

"Let's go now."

They jumped outside into the morning heat, the dry, hot air assaulting their exposed faces.

"You were struggling to keep up there at one point," Abdul said to Nour after flipping shut his cellphone. A curtain of sweat draped his forehead.

Justin wondered if Abdul's car had no air conditioning but refrained from embarrassing him by asking the question. The outside temperature had risen to eighty-seven degrees, according to the GMC's thermometer; however, the asphalt mirrored the simmering sunbeams bombarding the parking lot.

"Didn't want to run a red light or flatten any pedestrians," Nour replied.

"I just got our clearance from the lab security." Abdul headed toward a small side door of the warehouse. "Ismail, the ballistics expert, will assist us."

"I don't think that would be necessary," Nour replied.

"Colonel's orders." Abdul shrugged at Nour's objection and gave Justin a sneaky wink. "Ismail is very good at his job and will be very helpful to you."

Justin understood Abdul's cue. Ismail was someone Abdul trusted.

"We have a new man, I mean woman, joining our team," Justin

said.

"Has the colonel authorized her presence here?" Abdul asked.

Justin noticed an ounce of mischief in his voice. Abdul's sweaty face showed plain annoyance, rather than a true concern about procedures.

"Yes, he has," Nour replied quickly.

"Fine then," Abdul conceded.

He knocked twice on the steel panel door of the thick wall. Justin noticed a white electronic keypad to the left of the door knob and a black dome-shaped camera overhead. They waited in silence until the door opened with a loud rattle. A bespectacled young man, with a chin strap beard, looked bemused at them, as if they had the wrong place.

"Ismail, this is Nour and Jack. And this is Ismail." Abdul used Justin's cover name, Jack Schmitt.

The ballistic expert let them inside the police laboratory. With cement floors and steel panel walls, the place looked more suitable for servicing cars than serving as a forensic unit. A large IVECO truck, partially disassembled, took almost a third of the space of the large entrance hall. Two men were examining its engine and its cabin; a third was jotting down notes on a clipboard. Two Nissan SUV bodies, stripped of their tires and wheels, stood on the other side, along the walls. All kinds of tools and instruments filled a few tables at the end of the hall.

"Our offices are in the back. This area is for analysis of large objects, trucks and the like." Ismail gestured toward the IVECO.

They followed him through another door, which led to a narrow hall. It was painted gray and smelled of a strong chemical stench that stirred up in Justin the uncomfortable feeling of walking into a hospital. Doors were assigned sequential numbers and names of employees, but no titles.

"Here, this way," Ismail said, pointing at one of the doors.

He tapped a series of numbers in a keypad by the door's handle and pushed open the door. They stepped inside an oval-shaped office. Gray metallic tables, covered with all types of laboratory gadgets stood along the red brick walls.

"This is my office," Ismail explained. "Well, I share it with three other guys, my colleagues, but they're out today, working in the field."

He took them toward his work station. Next to a computer monitor, Justin noticed a picture of Ismail and another older man taken at the Martyrs' Square. Is that his dad? An uncle?

"Show them the bomb that didn't go off," Abdul said.

"Oh, yeah, sure. That one, oh, that one was quite an interesting device," Ismail began enthusiastically, but then held his tongue. "I don't mean to offend any of the victims," he added somberly, "even though this one did not explode."

Justin's BlackBerry chirped. "My partner just arrived," he said, after glancing at the phone.

"I'll let her in." Abdul turned around, heading for the door.

"Wait a second. Here's her badge." Justin handed Abdul the embassy badge.

"So, what's so special about this bomb?" Nour followed Ismail to one of the tables.

"Nothing, it's nothing special, apart from the fact that it didn't explode," Ismail replied. "The Alliance never makes mistakes. They've placed over fifty bombs, suicide bomber belts or car and truck bombs over the last year and no mistakes. Not even one."

Justin stared at the table. It was covered with trays of wires, cables, fragments of electronic circuits and a few tools. A large porcelain sink stood to the left. In the middle of the table, there was a square-shaped package the size of a backpack, wrapped in black tarpaulin. The three men huddled around the centerpiece.

"These are the explosives." Ismail pointed at the package. "Thirty pounds of military-grade, high-order Semtex. From what we can tell, they're from the pre-nineties stock, the odorless type. Extremely difficult to detect."

Justin frowned. "Like the bomb that tore apart Pan Am 103?"

"I can't confirm they came from the same box, but they were manufactured about the same time, probably at the same place. Czechoslovakia. Shaped like bricks, the explosives were concealed inside the backseat of the truck, right behind the driver."

Ismail took a pair of rubber gloves from a desk nearby. He lifted one of the sliced corners of the tarpaulin with a pair of pliers. They saw the orange colored blocks of explosives, stacked and wired.

"Was Semtex used in the other four car bombs?" Nour asked.

"Yes. We're not sure whether the loads were placed in the trunks or under the seats, like in this case, because those explosives actually did explode. However, from the blast wave, around two hundred yards, there was probably between twenty and forty pounds of explosives in each vehicle."

"How was the bomb rigged?" Justin asked.

"Standard Alliance style. A cellphone was attached to the package, connected to the detonating caps by copper wires. All the suicide bomber had to do to trigger it was to dial the cellphone's number."

"Why didn't he dial the number?"

Ismail shrugged. "No idea. I heard the police got to him before he could do that."

"Do you have the cellphone?"

"It's in the electronics section. I can have someone bring it."

"Please do," Nour said.

Ismail withdrew to another table to use a phone.

"What are you thinking?" Nour whispered to Justin.

"I am thinking of the 'why.'"

"The suicide-bomber? Why didn't he set off the bomb?"

"Yes."

"Well, the report says the police got to him first and neutralized him."

"I read that, but why didn't this man press the buttons when he saw the police coming toward him?"

"Maybe he didn't see them. Or maybe he was waiting for them to come closer, so he could kill them too. Maybe he forgot the phone number. His hand trembled. This man was hardly a terrorist; the report notes this was his first mission. Maybe he received little training. There are endless possibilities here."

"Yes, but what's the most likely?" Justin saw Ismail walking back to them. Ismail said, "We'll have the cellphone in a couple of minutes."

"Thanks," Nour said.

"Was the package damaged when they brought it here?" Justin asked.

"What do you mean?"

"Police reports said the suicide bomber crashed into a police truck."

"OK, and…"

"I'm trying to figure out whether the bomber could have still detonated the package after he crashed."

"Well… I guess he could have," Ismail replied. "I didn't notice any problems with the bomb. It wasn't damaged in the crash."

"But you sound unsure," Nour said.

"I am unsure because I just can't see this man, part of a suicide mission team, failing to carry out a simple act of punching a few keys. I mean, I'm glad he didn't do it, but I was scratching my head as to how it happened this way."

Justin gave Nour a meaningful glance and Nour nodded, both at Justin's glance and at Ismail's words. A second later, they heard footsteps and saw Abdul and Carrie.

"Hey, Carrie, good to see you," Justin said. "This is Nour and Ismail."

She shook their hands and Ismail brought her up to speed on the explosive device. "I was asked earlier if the bomb was damaged during the crash," Ismail said. "Now that I think about it, I remember seeing that one of the wires connected to the blasting caps was sliced off. I paid no attention to it, assuming one of the police officers had cut it, to avoid the bomb from blowing up. The cellphone was also detached and turned off, its SIM card and batteries removed, so that another terrorist could not dial in the code and detonate the bomb."

"Do you still have the sliced wire?" Carrie asked.

Nour gave her a disapproving frown, but she ignored him, pretending to be consumed by Ismail's explanation.

"Yes, the wires are here somewhere," Ismail sifted through the pile of debris with his pliers. He rummaged through a dozen or so cables and wires, packed in two small boxes. Finding what he was looking for, he held up a six inch wire. The evidence was in a sealed plastic bag.

"I need to take a closer look," Carrie said.

"There's a box of gloves in the first drawer to the left." Ismail pointed at a desk to his right.

Carrie tossed a pair of gloves to Justin, another pair to Nour, and wore a pair herself. She opened the evidence bag, took out the wire and analyzed the cut.

"Magnifying glass," she said.

Ismail, not used to taking orders from a female, hesitated for a second, before handing it to her. Carrie noticed the wire had a precise cut, which had stripped the thin insulation clear from the copper conductor.

"Check this out." She lifted up the piece of evidence. "It's a perfect cut. No ripped insulation, no pressured ends and no incision to the conductor."

"What does this mean?" Abdul asked.

"When you slice a cable or a wire, in a rush, with a knife, there's no way you can get a perfect cut like this. The police didn't do this. It was done by a professional blade, die blade most likely. An auto repair shop would have some machine that can do this. Maybe that's where they cooked the bomb."

"Wait a second," Nour said. "You're telling us the terrorists screwed up when they prepared this IED?"

"No, I'm telling you this," Carrie placed the wire back in the evidence bag, "this was done intentionally. I don't know if an Alliance member was working for the police or he felt some kind of remorse and wanted at least this part of the bombing to fail. But I know this cut was done on purpose."

"Makes sense and would explain the 'why,'" Justin said.

"What 'why'?" Abdul blinked in confusion.

"The reason why the suicide bomber didn't detonate his bomb before the police got to him. He couldn't. If this wire was damaged on purpose, sabotaged that is, there was no way for the suicide bomber, or anyone else for that matter, to cause the blast. Right?" Justin said, looking at Ismail.

"Well, yes, that's possible," Ismail replied, but without much conviction. "The Semtex is intact and so are the blasting caps, the detonator, and the cellphone."

A door cracking behind them brought the conversation to an abrupt pause.

"Sorry, so sorry," a young woman said, as she hurried toward them, carrying a white evidence box on her hands. "This is the cellphone of the bomber, Ismail."

"Thanks, Aisha," Ismail said.

The woman left without saying another word.

"Let me see that," Justin said. He dipped his hand into the box and pulled out a flip model LG cellphone. "This is it?" He waved the cellphone.

Ismail nodded. "The only fingerprints we recovered were those of the truck driver."

Justin drew out a small evidence bag containing the cellphone's lithium-ion battery. A small note was taped to the back.

"What does this say?" Justin pointed at the note.

"It says 'drained,' meaning the battery was drained when it reached our lab. That's a technician's handwriting."

"When did the police bring the bomb here?"

"Around midnight."

"Were you here when it happened?"

"Yes, it was my night shift."

"So, how come the battery was dead within six hours from the time of the blasts? Did anyone use the cellphone?"

"Of course no one used the phone. It's evidence. And I have no idea why the battery was dead." Ismail shrugged.

"Where are you going with this?" Nour asked.

"If the bomber was expected to use the cellphone, this cellphone, to trigger the explosion, don't you think the terrorists would have made sure they charged the battery, before giving the cellphone to the driver?"

"Yeah, I guess they should have."

"The phone was new, right?" Justin asked Ismail.

"Yes, brand new. Never used. No numbers found in its directories."

"So, three weird coincidences: A suicide bomber who's practically an amateur, a bomb wire sabotaged, and dead batteries on the explosives' remote control. Someone was trying really hard not to make this bomb go off."

"What are you saying?" Abdul asked. "Are you saying the Alliance didn't want this car bomb to explode?" Abdul asked.

"I'm not saying that, but everything seems to point toward that conclusion," Justin replied. "I still don't have an answer to their objective. However, the target of the Alliance has to be something bigger than a massacre in the Old Town market. Terrorists must have in mind a plan much greater than these explosions."

Nour gave Justin a stern glance and bit his lip. Shut up, his glance said, you've already said too much.

"We're working to figure out what that may be," Nour said, "but, at the moment, we have no clues and no ideas."

No, Nour, I'm not talking about your president. I mean the purpose of this driver was more than to deliver the unexploded bomb.

"Thank you for your great help," Justin said and shook Ismail's hand.

"I think we're done here," Nour said. "We appreciate your valuable assistance."

"Yes, no problem. It was my pleasure," Ismail replied.

Abdul said. "I'll take it from here."

Ismail returned to his desk.

"You didn't tell us what this target is, the one bigger than a car bombing in Tripoli's busiest market?" Abdul whispered, as they walked through the narrow hall.

"I'm going to let my boss do that." Justin glanced at Nour. "Carrie and I need to catch up on a few things."

Nour rolled his eyes. "We have no time to waste," he grumbled. "We still have to investigate the scene at the market and find witnesses."

"Is it OK if we follow you in the Nissan?" Justin asked both Nour and Abdul.

Nour replied with a frown, while Abdul spread his palms.

"If you can stand the heat…" he replied and tossed his car keys to Justin, "the air conditioning is gone."

"Nour?"

"Fine," he replied in a flat tone, "but I need a complete briefing as soon as we return to the embassy."

"Sure thing," Justin replied.

"Ignore the radio," Abdul said. "And follow us closely."

Justin nodded. "I know where we're going. We won't get lost."

CHAPTER 17

Tripoli, Libya
May 15, 10:35 a.m. local time

Ismail reached for his phone, after glancing around and making sure he was alone in his office. "They just left," he said quietly, after the colonel answered his call.

"And?" Colonel Haydar said.

"They figured out the sabotaged wire and the drained battery."

"What? What? How could… Why did you let them?"

"I had no choice." Ismail moved the phone away, to save his eardrums from bursting. The colonel's was shouting at the top of his lungs. "They asked to see the evidence, and I showed it to them."

"What do they think?" the colonel's voice was a bit calmer, though still very loud.

"They think the Alliance is preparing another attack, more important than these car bombs."

"Did they say what other attack?"

"No, I don't think they know. I don't even know what we're doing."

"You trust in me and you trust in Allah. That's all you must know."

"Yes, of course."

Tripoli, Libya
May 15, 10:40 a.m. local time

"This wasn't a very good idea," Justin said, after they headed toward downtown Tripoli.

"Which one: me coming here or melting inside this rusty tin can?" Carrie replied, attempting to cool off by undoing the top button of her brown shirt. A pair of light blue jeans had replaced her usual khakis.

"Well, both, but I'm talking about the first. Did I forget to mention how crazy this place is?"

Carrie gave him a long measuring gaze. "You seem to be doing pretty well."

"I'm not kidding."

"Where's your vest?"

"Abdul forgot it." He fumbled with the seatbelt, and the edge of his shirt rose up. Carrie caught a glimpse of his Glock.

"Hey, where is mine?" she asked with a pout.

"Abdul brought only one. At the time, we had no plans of you coming here."

"Seems like your American partner has greater foresight." She played with her Security Consultant badge.

"Yes, he thinks he knows everything."

"I see the match of wits has started."

"Oh, the match is over. He never stood a chance," Justin said with a smile.

"I take it you've told him very little."

"I've told him what he needs to know."

"That's why I said very little."

"The Americans don't need to know about the prince. They're in bed with the Saudis."

"So are we."

"Yes, but we haven't been stabbed in the back. Not yet, anyway."

"Lighten up, would you? The US is our ally and we're to work together in this op."

"We are working together."

Carrie sighed, while Justin grinned. He honked at a taxi that cut in front of him, and switched to the other, faster lane. Cars slowed down as they came to an intersection, and the traffic light turned red. Justin pressed hard on the brake pedal. The Nissan took a while to respond and the car stopped inches away from a white van in front of them.

"Have you received any news from your sister about your mother?" Justin asked.

"Yes, I got a hold of her this morning, before flying out." Carrie let out a deep sigh and stared out the window at a large mosque coming into view. They heard the prayer chant from the mosques' minarets.

"And?" Justin pressed on.

"Oh, I've had better conversations with Susan."

"How did your mom's tests come out?"

"Inconclusive. Doctors are scheduling more liver and thyroid tests next week to determine her Alzheimer's stage and the care she needs. They'll do a head CT as well."

"Sorry to hear there's no good news."

"It's not bad news either."

Justin stepped on the gas pedal as the traffic light changed. The car growled and jerked forward, the engine rattling.

"Before you ask, I did get in touch with Thomas too," Carrie offered.

Justin smiled. "I wasn't going to—" he began.

"Yeah, yeah," Carrie interrupted him. "Thomas was worried about me, since I hadn't called him."

"Why didn't you call him?"

"So he would worry about me."

Justin blinked. "I don't get it. You're trying to be unpredictable?"

Carrie nodded.

"But, that's a given, because of our profession."

"Oh, but it doesn't hurt to point out at times that I can be as detached as he is."

"Beating him at his own game, aren't we?"

"Not yet, but trying hard to."

"If you keep this up, you may be overplaying your hand."

He adjusted the rear-view mirror and checked a couple of cars tailgating them. His eyes searched the faces of the drivers, who were both old men.

"You think grandpas are mukhabarat?" Carrie noticed his actions.

"In this place, everyone's mukhabarat. What do you think is Prince Al-Farhan's game?"

"I'm not sure. According to Mossad, he's interested in burning up all of North Africa. That's for short-term, clear objectives. In the long run, he may have many goals. Establish a Sharia law state in the region, without country borders. Create safe havens for terrorist training camps. Maybe he's after safe routes for large-scale weapons contraband to the Middle East. He's not doing that well financially and he's not the favorite grandson of the Saudi King."

"We need to find out what he wants."

"I've already talked to Johnson, and she has the entire section digging up intel on the prince. But, she warned me not much is known about him."

"A man shrouded in mystery?"

"As much as his women are veiled in burqas."

Justin grinned. "Anything from our post in Dubai?"

"They're scrapping together what they can."

Justin sped up, trying to keep up with Nour, whose GMC was already two cars ahead. "So, if the prince had a feud with the Libyan prime minister, could that mean he's striking back?"

"It could be. The bombs have definitely rocked the prime minister's regime."

"True. And the mukhabarat has begun its backlash against the Alliance. Jails will be overflowing any time now."

"Then, what about this American president plot?" asked Carrie.

"I don't know what to make of it. It serves the overall purpose of attacking the government, for sure. Any attempt at harming the American president, a guest of the Libyan leader, is a slap across his face. As long as she's in the country, she's under his protection, according to Arab customs of honor."

"But the evidence we're finding seems planted, don't you think?"

"Definitely. I have the impression the Alliance is trying too hard to convince us they're going after the US president. First, the suicide bomber botches up his operation, confesses without hesitation and winds up at the end of a noose. Then, Sheikh Ayman wants a 'deal' in exchange for 'sensitive' information. Now, we discover one of the bombs was sabotaged."

"But?" Carrie noticed Justin's hesitation at finishing his thoughts.

"But none of this evidence is conclusive. Like Nour said earlier, there are many ways to explain these events, these circumstances. I don't want to rush into drawing wrong conclusions."

"What are the Americans doing?"

"They're tightening the security around their president and changing her schedule and her route. I haven't heard anything about cancelling her visit."

Carrie wiped sweat drops from her lips with a Kleenex and rolled down the window about an inch. Dusty air swept around the cabin, and she hurried to close the window before Justin could voice his objection.

"Sorry, I thought it would help with the heat."

Justin shrugged and rubbed his forehead with the back of his hand. Carrie leaned over and sponged off a sweat trickle drizzling along the edge of his cheekbone. "Speaking of cancellations, I have some bad news, but don't get angry," she whispered.

"I never shoot the messenger," Justin said with a grin.

"Our prime minister will not be at the G-20 Summit."

"Well, one less thing to worry about. Why is that bad news?"

"Because he never planned to come here."

"What? Johnson said he was attending the meeting."

"Possibly. I remember Johnson saying 'schedule permitting.' I made a few calls and I learned that he never made such plans. Instead, he'll be in China, on a trip planned six months ago."

Justin eyes turned dark, a glint of disappointment lurking underneath. "I want to believe Johnson didn't know about it, and she truly believed the prime minister was coming to Tripoli."

Carrie closed her eyes and pursed her lips. "Unfortunately, she had full knowledge of his travel plans. And she's not the kind of person who forgets crucial details like that."

"So, you're saying she tricked me, tricked us, into coming down to this snake pit?"

Carrie hesitated a second before replying, "I'm afraid so."

Justin slammed his fist into the center of the steering wheel, the blaring horn covering the barrage of expletives pouring forth his mouth. "First she told Mossad about our meeting with the sheikh, but hid that from us, putting us into harm's way. Or worse, she wanted to kill us. When that failed, she dispatches us into this hellhole for nothing, by selling us a straight face lie."

"I don't think she wants to kill us. There's no bad blood running between us. She lied because she felt you would have not taken this assignment."

Justin looked deeply into her eyes. "I might have, and rightfully so. This is a very low blow, even for Johnson. In-fucking-credible."

"Have you talked to Anna?"

"Yes."

"And?"

"She's still upset about the cancelled trip. And now I find out it was all for nothing. This is making me livid. Johnson is not getting away with it."

Carrie looked at the traffic ahead. Nour's GMC was three vehicles ahead, in the other lane to their left. They were getting closer to an overpass.

"Why the hell are we slowing down?" Justin asked.

Carrie rolled down the window and stuck her head outside, as the car came to a complete stop.

"There's some kind of road construction ahead, just as we begin to climb up the ramp. This lane is cut off about a hundred and fifty feet ahead."

The cars were chaotically merging into the left lane. The brown truck ahead jerked forward and Justin stepped slowly on the gas pedal. Their Nissan gained about a foot. He peered through the windshield and saw a long line of barrier boards cordoning off a part of their lane. The brown truck moved again and, without signaling, forced his way into the other lane. Justin waited until there was a gap in the traffic, signaled and drove in front of a blue van. They were now almost ten vehicles behind Nour's GMC.

"I don't see any cranes or dump trucks anywhere," Carrie observed.

"No construction workers either." Justin checked both his right side and the rear-view mirror, as they crawled up the ramp, along barrier boards and pylons.

A rattling motorcycle caught his attention, as it zigzagged through the cars behind them. Then, it sped up to their right, using the ramp's shoulder. The motorcycle's passenger was holding a Kalashnikov.

"It's an ambush," Justin shouted, his foot instinctively pressing on the gas pedal. The Nissan came dangerously close to the van.

The motorcycle cut through a gap between the pylons and drove into the cordoned off lane, gaining quickly on them.

"It's getting closer," Carrie said.

Justin pulled out his Glock and handed it to Carrie. "Shoot the bastards."

Carrie cocked the gun and turned around.

"Hang onto something." Justin ploughed through the traffic barriers.

Debris went flying over the car. Pylons and wooden fragments were thrown at other vehicles and the chasing motorcycle. Justin slammed his foot on the gas and the Nissan drifted around the curb. The bike swerved around the scattering debris. Its passenger aimed his stretched hand toward them.

"Incoming fire." Carrie dropped against her seat.

Justin veered to the left and then to the right, as bullets riddled the car. Fragments of broken glass showered his head and neck. A bullet grazed the edge of his left shoulder. He swore then clenched his teeth. He glanced at Carrie, wondering why she was not returning fire, just as she began shooting through the shattered windows. "There you go, blast them!"

Carrie kept firing, but their car was still being hammered by automatic gun fire. The vroom of the motorcycle grew louder and the incoming barrage intensified. The car sank, its tires exploding with a loud bang. The wheels scraped the asphalt and Justin struggled to keep the swerving car under control.

"Carrie," he cried, while the car banged against the metal rail of the climbing ramp, "take them out."

Carrie shuffled to the backseat and the Glock was heard again. Two quick bursts and a long barrage. Justin heard a great explosion coming from somewhere underneath and saw huge flames leaping at the overpass. Another explosion erupted from the highway below. Black and gray smoke clouded the sun, mushrooming over the scene.

"Justin, you can stop now."

He listened to her and pulled to the side. The engine puffed as he turned off the car.

"You OK?" Justin asked

Carrie was panting heavily in the backseat. The Glock lay next to her.

"Uh, uh, yes, I'm fine."

"Let's get out of here."

He helped her climb out of the car. Carrie handed him back the Glock. She ran her hands through her hair, staring in disbelief at their car and at the cloud of smoke.

"Did any bullet get you?" she asked after a long moment, stepping closer to Justin, searching his face and his arms.

"A bullet clipped my shoulder."

She helped him clear some glass fragments off his body. Then, she inspected his shoulder wound. Justin's shirt and skin were ripped open. The bullet had made an inch-long superficial cut, and some blood had trickled down Justin's chest.

"We'll get you cleaned up soon."

"Yeah, it's nothing."

They looked at the scene underneath their feet. The twisted wreck of the motorcycle had landed on a gray sedan. A plume of smoke was soaring upward from the burning rubble. Another car was turned upside down. The hood of another truck was badly damaged at the driver's side. The traffic had pretty much stopped, with the occasional car pushing its way around the burning barricade. A couple of dozen people were walking around, yelling and screaming, staring and pointing at the top of the overpass. Justin saw Nour and Abdul standing next to their car on the other side of the overpass and began waving to get their attention.

"Hey, Justin, look at this." Carrie pointed to her left, about twenty yards away, at a man lying on his back.

"Was he one of the bike guys?" Justin asked, as they ran toward the man.

Carrie nodded. "I guess he jumped off in time."

They saw a Kalashnikov a few steps away from the man.

"He's still alive." Carrie leaned over him.

The man's face and ears were severely bruised. He was bleeding from a large bullet wound on his right side.

"You know, you should have worn a helmet," Carrie said.

"And a vest." Justin knelt next to the man. "Who sent you?" he asked in Arabic.

The man spat out a bloody cough. As he tried to talk, a wheezing rasp came out of his mouth. His eyes flickered irregularly, like broken windshield wipers. The dim light left in them was going to fade out very soon.

"Who sent you to kill us?" Justin asked again, this time in Arabic and in English. He wiped a trickle of blood oozing from the man's left eyebrow, which had made its way down to his thick, black beard.

"Go… go to hell," the man groaned in English.

"You first, you prick," Carrie spat out.

"We'll take you to a hospital right away, and you'll make it," Justin said, his mouth very close to the man's ear. "Tell us, who wants us dead?"

"The… the Alliance," the man let out a faint whisper, almost too quiet. In truth, Justin read the man's bleeding lips rather than heard his words.

"Why? Why the Alliance?"

The man's eyes grew dimmer, and he jerked his head to the left. Justin gently lifted the man's head with his cupped hands.

"Don't die. Don't you die. Why did you try to kill us?"

"You… you can't…"

The man's breathing became shallow.

"We can't what? Go on."

"You can't save…"

"Who? Who can't we save? Who?"

"No one… no one can save the… akh," the man hacked out his reply along with his last breath.

"What!?" Justin cried. "What was that?"

"What did he say?" Carrie asked.

Justin looked at the man's lifeless eyes. He checked the man's pulse at the left side of his neck.

"He's dead. And we learned nothing."

"What was he mumbling?"

"The Alliance sent them to stop us from saving somebody."

"Who?"

Justin shook his head and wiped his hands. "He didn't say. He just faded away."

"What the hell? What the bloody hell?" Abdul bellowed as he and

Nour reached the top of the ramp. "You stupid coward," he yelled at the dead man. Nour stood to the side, punching a few numbers on his BlackBerry.

"Calm down." Justin stopped Abdul from getting closer to the dead man. "We're all fine. Nobody's hurt."

"Nobody's hurt? Nobody's hurt?" Abdul paced around Justin. "Shit, I'm hurt. My car's wrecked. This mission is ruined. Dead people and burned cars are everywhere. It's like another bomb ripped through the highway. The colonel will have my balls on a platter."

Justin put a reassuring hand on Abdul's shoulders. "Abdul, it's OK. These people ambushed us. We had to defend ourselves. It's easy to explain."

"No, no, no, nothing is easy to explain. Not to the colonel. Nothing is easy with the colonel."

"Listen, this is your Nissan and you were supposed to be in there." Justin stared deep into Abdul's frantic eyes. "This attack was against you. These men, they wanted you dead."

Abdul blinked rapidly at the revelation of Justin's words. He was silent for a few seconds. Then, he found his tongue. "Bloody cowards," he hollered, this time even louder, "I will show them." He pushed Justin aside and marched toward the dead body.

"No." Justin clenched Abdul's right arm. "He's dead. Gone. We need to figure out why these two targeted you."

"Before the police show up, we need an explanation why we were driving your car instead of you," Carrie said.

Abdul drew in a deep breath. He had stopped struggling to free his arm from Justin's firm grip.

"I'm calm now," Abdul said.

"OK." Justin released him.

Abdul began to walk toward the overpass. At some point, he turned around, stomped the ground with his foot and punched the air with his left fist.

"He said he was calm," Carrie whispered to Justin.

"Wait till you see him angry," he replied.

"I got it," Abdul shouted.

"What is it?" Justin asked.

"You needed to make a few private calls and we didn't want to waste time, so you took my car, that's it, yes, that's it." Abdul moved his arms around like a wind mill in a strong storm. Then, he stopped and dropped his arms to his sides. His face sank. "This is the least of my worries. The colonel will hang me."

"Don't worry." Justin stepped closer to him. "You're not alone in this." He gave Abdul a comforting wink.

Nour was still on his cellphone, with his back to them, oblivious to their gestures, but not their words.

Abdul feigned a smile, just as Nour hung up and turned around. "Well, I've informed the embassy. A liaison team is on their way. We'll use every diplomatic means to keep this incident tight."

Abdul nodded, but a mask of despair was slowly covering his face. Police sirens could be heard in the distance. They were getting louder by the second.

CHAPTER 18

One hundred miles off the coast of Nice, France
May 15, 10:50 a.m. local time

Prince Husayn bin Al-Farhan glanced at the cellphone on the office desk. The phone call he was expecting was late, and he hated delays. The Frenchman was supposed to arrive at his yacht in fifteen minutes, and while waiting for his arrival, the Prince was wagging a battle of wits against his eight-year-old son Sameer.

"Checkmate!" With his small hand, the boy moved the solid gold white bishop next to his father's emerald black king.

The Prince had seen Sameer's strategy when the boy first advanced his troops to the center of the board, cutting off any movement of the black king. The boy's skills were improving, but he still needed work on timing. Waiting for the right moment to strike was crucial in chess, as in real life, a lesson the Prince wasted no time drilling into his son's mind on a daily basis. Today, though, he decided to give his son a well-deserved break.

"You win." The Prince toppled his cornered king on the platinum chessboard.

"Yes!" Sameer threw a victory punch in the air. "My best score ever."

"You fought well. Now, come here."

Sameer jumped into his father's chest and the Prince wrapped his arms tightly around his son's shoulders and leaned back against the soft leather couch. As he played with Sameer's dark, curly hair, he remembered the boy's mother, Aamina, his first wife, and his firstborn son Hakim. The last time he saw them was five years ago, when they boarded one of his private jets in Riyadh to visit relatives in Yemen. Notice of the plane crash over northern Yemen came amidst accusations between rebel and government forces fighting in the area, blaming each other for the incident. However, reliable sources on the ground confirmed the plane had been shot down by a unit of the US Special Operation Forces in the area, which mistook the Prince's plane for a weapons delivery to the rebels. The US neither confirmed, nor denied such reports, and delivered no official apology to the Prince or the royal family.

Nevertheless, the House of Saud did not allow for such a trivial matter to affect their strong friendship, commercial ties, and oil joint ventures with the US. The King and senior princes had never accepted Aamina in the royal family, since she was the daughter of a small businessman, without any blue blood in her veins. They had shunned Prince Al-Farhan and had stifled his initial calls for an inquiry into the plane crash and then his repeated demands for revenge. After the US had promised such an incident would not happen again, the House of Saud had decided to close the case.

The House of Saud may have let the matter drop, but Prince Al-Farhan could not let it go. Soon after, eight members of Team Bravo 2, rumored to have carried out the attack against Prince Al-Farhan's family, fell into a trap during a routine reconnaissance operation in northern Yemen. Houthis, Shia rebel fighters battling the Yemeni government in the area, ambushed the Special Operations team a few miles away from the site of the plane crash. His thirst for revenge quenched, Prince Al-Farhan replayed the snuff video of the ambush in slow motion in the privacy of his Riyadh suburb mansion. The best ten million dollars he had ever spent sparked an insightful realization. These "freedom fighters" could give him something even his own family was unwilling or unable to hand over: power. True power. Without the shadow of an authoritative king looming over head. The Prince had completed his initiation into jihadist warfare.

Prince Al-Farhan began supporting ragtag militias and rogue armies fighting in the name of jihad across the Middle East and North Africa. He kept his mansion in the capital of the Kingdom but began travelling extensively throughout these troubled lands, meeting with rebel leaders and radical clerics. He embraced most of the ideology of these men, sharing in the common goal of establishing a true Islamic law state without borders.

A few years back, the House of Saud strongly rejected any and all claims of Prince Al-Farhan to the Saudi throne. A grandson of the King, Prince Al-Farhan was not seen as a favorite for the position of absolute authority in the Kingdom. He was considerably outranked by other princes, siblings and sons of the King higher up in the line of succession. Only sudden death or incapacitation of both the King and the appointed Crown Prince would advance Prince Al-Farhan's ambition. But the bitter feud following in case of such a grim scenario would result in a fierce clash between rival branches within the royal family, whose outcome was very uncertain.

"Excuse my interruption, Your Highness," Zakir said in a low voice, "the Frenchman has arrived."

The Prince nodded. "I'll meet him in the lounge in ten minutes."

"Yes, Your Highness."

* * *

Prince bin Al-Farhan sipped his 1998 vintage Dom Pérignon Rosé from a tulip-shaped glass with a gold-plated foot. His thick fingers held the stem gently while he rocked the glass, looking at the slight movements of the golden grape juice. Smacking his lips in complete satisfaction, the Prince offered a smile at his guest, Pierre Bouitillier, the CEO of FranceOil, one of the largest petroleum companies in Europe.

"You, the French, are masters of creating the best wines in the world," the Prince spoke softly, referring to Bouitillier's present.

"I'm extremely satisfied it pleases Your Highness," the Frenchman replied with a wide grin of gratitude and a great bow of servitude.

Bouitillier nursed his own glass, to quench his thirst and to drown his urge to tell the Prince the French were also masters at squeezing another type of liquid from the earth. This time, not in the northeast province of Champagne, the land of the prestige French wine, but far away, in the home of the Prince. The area of Jubail, Saudi Arabia, was a top priority in the FranceOil's expansion in the Persian Gulf. Bouitillier's task was to convince the Prince to whisper a good word on behalf of FranceOil to the House of Saud royals.

The Prince nodded and finished his drink with a swift gesture of his hand and a quick gulp. He raised the glass up, as his 10-carat diamond ring brushed against it. Immediately, a sommelier, another present of the Frenchman, appeared and refilled the Prince's glass. He glanced at the wine but did not drink from it. He placed the glass aside, over a small side table. Then, he leaned back on the white velvet couch, his arms resting on the black pillows around him. The Prince and his guest were in their private meeting on the top deck of the "Arabia"—the Prince's two hundred and seventy feet sailing yacht—a hundred miles away from everything and everyone.

"I'm a man of the desert. I like to be alone, by myself. Undisturbed." The Prince rubbed the corners of his gray thin moustache. He arranged a flap of his red-and-white checkered headdress after a gust of wind blew it into his face. Flattening the front of his white robe, he continued, "This is why I like to sail. It's the closest I can get to solitude when I'm travelling around Europe. I come out here to think, analyze, decide. I come here to make important business decisions."

I wish you would decide on our business, Bouitiller thought. A long time ago, he had mastered a great command of his tongue. He was an experienced business negotiator, carrying the weight of many years of fighting with energy tycoons throughout Eastern Europe and the Middle East. Bouitiller had haggled over exploration and refinery contracts with democratic governments and dictators, tribal chiefs and warlords. He believed he knew how to handle the Prince, but he was not going to allow his natural arrogance to get in the way of achieving his goal. The Prince very rarely met potential business partners in his floating office quarters. Bouitillier was not going to waste this once-in-a-lifetime opportunity.

"I'm flattered and very thankful for your generous invitation, especially to meet here, aboard your majestic yacht," he said, his gaze taking in the expanse of the luxury vessel.

Bouitillier had heard that the Arabia was once owned by a now bankrupt billionaire, and another time it was the set for one of the James Bond thrillers. That was before Prince Al-Farhan purchased the yacht at an auction, completely renovated it and turned it into one of his offices. The Arabia was very spacious and very fast. The Prince loved it.

"I'm confident I'll be of good advice as you make your wise business decisions," the Frenchman said.

The Prince nodded, his headdress wavering in the wind. The morning had started perfect: a gorgeous, cloudless sky, with a cool breeze forming foamy wavelets around the yacht. However, about an hour ago clouds had begun to gather in the east. White crests of tall waves now were crashing against the bow.

"Yes, I will decide, in good time," the Prince replied dryly. Accustomed to flattery and obedience throughout the entire fifty years of his life, he had come to hate false praise from his business partners. He knew that underneath their veneer of reverence they masked their hegemony-sharpened claws and hid their dollar-injected muscles. Still, he found amusement in this type of vain worship and had come to expect nothing less.

"Tell me, what is the experience of FranceOil in oilfield explorations?" The Prince leaned forward and held his hands together.

Bouitillier smiled and contained a frown that began to form on his sloped, moist forehead. He had given detailed reports of FranceOil exploration activities to one of the Prince's aides a week ago, and he was sure Prince Al-Farhan had received the information. The Prince was a shrewd businessman, known for his familiarity with business operations of his partners, potential partners, and, above all, his business rivals. *He's testing me, to see if I can live up to my reputation.* Bouitillier kept his smile ironed on his face and reached for a company's portfolio, inside one of the folders on the glass table standing between him and the Prince. He glanced at it, as if double-checking some information, although most details of the company's explorations were stored in his memory.

"FranceOil has considerable experience in managing the downstream oil industry, from Algeria to Uzbekistan, since 1969. Over the last five years, we've made substantial investments in the North Sea, in the Gyda oilfield, as well as in the Gulf of Mexico. Our experience with oil explorations in the Persian Gulf region is in its development stage. We're present in the area with several upstream deals in the Tasour Field in Yemen and the Burgan Field in Kuwait."

"What's FranceOil's stake in Libya's oil fields, particularly in the Sirte Basin?"

Bouitillier peered into the Prince's eyes concealed behind oval-shaped sunglasses. The Frenchman opened his mouth but waved his left hand in front of his face, as if to dismiss the thought.

"Libya remains on our radar screens, but for the time being, the country represents a difficult market. The new government is still hostile toward foreign investment in that area. Along with Libya's National Oil Corporation, they have made the entry of new firms in the exploration market practically impossible."

"Still, would you invest in Libya if the political environment was, let's say… more favorable?"

Bouitillier hesitated, pondering his options. In truth, he did not have any. He knew the Prince did not like to hear "no" as an answer. On the other hand, Bouitillier was aware that the relationship between Prince Al-Farhan and the Prime Minister of Libya was not stellar, to say the least. The Frenchman could not see how the Prince would shift the balance of interests of Libya's government officials and top oil executives to give FranceOil a fair chance.

"Of course, Your Highness. Our Board of Directors will give serious consideration to all offers for exploration or development of new blocks in the Sirte Basin and elsewhere in Libya."

The Prince nodded. "A round of new leases for the Murzuq and Ghadames basins is in the works. The new chairman of NOC and the new Minister of Oil will be reviewing FranceOil's bids with special attention, once they have been submitted to my aides."

Bouitillier noticed the Prince used "once" and not "if" when describing the FranceOil bids for explorations in Libya. The Frenchman nodded, and his broad smile stretched from ear to ear. His eyes could already see the enthusiasm of the Board of Directors and their eagerness to sign his bonus as per his performance contract. Sealing a deal for exploration rights in the highly coveted Ghadames fields in Libya was equivalent to a refinery building contract in Saudi Arabia.

One of the Prince's three BlackBerry phones lined up on the table began to vibrate. He threw a curious glance at the phone, his eyes the only part of his body that moved. His right hand jutted up, almost instinctively, as if he were brandishing a sword ready to storm into battle. Zakir, the Prince's personal aide, appeared in an instant, and bowed down with profound respect.

"I have some urgent business matters to attend to," the Prince said, pointing at the phone vibrating on the table. "Zakir, escort Mr. Bouitillier ashore at once."

"Thank you so… so much for this honor…" the Frenchman began to express his final gratitude, as Zakir gave him a gentle but firm pat on the shoulders. Mr. Bouitillier gathered his folders and his briefcase and left the deck. Only then, did the Prince punch the answer key on his phone.

"Tell me my problem is gone."

"Well, it is, kind of…" Colonel Farid Haydar replied in a low voice.

"Wrong answer, Colonel," the Prince cut him off. "How did you screw this up?"

"It's… the two of them are… the Americans are now involved in our affairs."

"Of course, they are. What were you expecting? We tell them there's a plot against their President and you think they're going to do nothing?"

Colonel Haydar let out a deep breath, but no words.

"Are they gone?" the Prince asked.

"Negative, Your…"

"What happened?"

"The men I sent to do the job… they failed."

"You told me that already. Give me details," the Prince hissed the last word.

"They… my men tried to eliminate the targets while they were driving away from the police lab. There was gunfire and some vehicles were damaged in the shooting. We can easily blame this on the Alliance as another terrorist attack."

"I asked you to handle this discreetly and I wanted them gone. They know about the bomb and they're becoming very dangerous."

"My apologies, Your Majesty, I assumed they were going to do a clean job. They told me their plan was…"

"Whatever it was, it failed. Are these lowlifes you hired dead?"

"Yes, they are."

"And you're sure there's no way they can be connected to you, and then to me? I don't want any headaches."

"Yes, there's no connection, as far as I know."

"That's not good enough, 'as far as you know,' Colonel." The Prince imitated Farid's voice with a nasal accent. "Make sure all ties between you and them are severed. Erase all traces."

"Yes, I have my men investigating the shooting."

"Where are the targets now?"

"Holed up in the US Embassy, but I can still get to them."

"Are you that stupid?" the Prince's voice echoed on the empty deck. "One attempt on their lives may be explained, but not two. And absolutely not on American soil."

"I understand," Farid said. "My apologies."

"This is what you'll do, and listen carefully, so that you'll not screw this up too. Arrange for a deportation order and put the agents on the first plane out of Tripoli. I don't want them nosing around in my business and discovering the truth. They already know too much. The Americans have received their warning, and the agents have served their purpose in full."

"It will be done as you wish."

"I hope so, for your own sake. Call me once they're in the air."

The Prince tossed the BlackBerry over board. Before the phone plunged into the dark blue waters, the Prince snapped his fingers. Two aides materialized from thin air and stood behind the Prince's couch, out of sight, but within earshot.

"The colonel's services are no longer needed," the Prince spoke slowly as if the aides were taking notes. He did not want them to miss a word or misunderstand his order. "Make sure his body is never found. And send the Americans a gentle reminder that their President's life is only a sniper's bullet away."

US Embassy, Tripoli, Libya
May 15, 11:55 a.m. local time

"The colonel's furious. He's mad and I'm in deep shit." Abdul folded his cellphone. He collapsed on the leather couch and dipped his head in his shaky hands.

"Abdul, look at me," Justin said from across the room. He was pacing by the window of a small office on the second floor of the US Embassy. Matthew had reluctantly whisked them off in an armored vehicle from the highway shootout after the arrival of local police. *It's is only because you're investigating for us,* Matthew had repeated more than once. *Otherwise, I would have not lifted even the smallest finger.* Within the safety of the diplomatic residence, they were awaiting their looming fate.

The Libyan stared at Justin with his bloodshot eyes.

"Did he fire you?" Justin asked.

Abdul shook his head. "No, but this will never leave my record. I'm done, finished. I'll never make captain, let alone higher ranks. I'll be lucky if I don't get transferred to direct traffic."

"We'll do our best, so that nothing happens to you, and that your career remains unaffected."

Abdul replied with a barely noticeable nod, and a fake smile.

"Did he say anything about us?" Carrie asked.

She was sitting behind a desk, toying with a black stapler and a few sheets of blank paper. She had already stitched a couple of smiley faces.

"No, but I'm sure your investigation is over."

Carrie sighed. "We were just getting started and then…" She stopped in mid-sentence as the office door swung open.

Matthew marched in. He was carrying a folder in his hands and a somber mood on his face. "Could you excuse us for a few minutes?" he asked Abdul.

The Libyan dragged his feet out of the room.

"Colonel Haydar has faxed me your deportation orders, based on disturbance of public order and threatening civilian lives. Neat trick." Matthew waved a printout from the folder.

"That's bullshit." Carrie stood up and spread her arms, as if she were going to snatch the deportation orders from Matthew's hands and tear them to shreds. "Both Abdul and Nour and many other witnesses can testify our reaction was in self-defense."

Matthew shook his head. "That may be the case, but the facts remain that you fired weapons, illegally obtained, I assume, and killed two civilians."

"Two assassins who were shooting at us," Justin clarified.

"Still, this order ties my hands." Matthew sat in a chair and gave his temples a deep rub. "Oh, why did I believe your involvement would make things easier for me?"

"Because it did," Justin replied. "Look, we understand Farid is pissed off and he wants us out of here. But we're not finished. We still have to interrogate witnesses and check the crime scene."

"Uh-uh." Matthew shook his head. "I can't have you out there. All I can do is delay your deportation until tomorrow morning, at the most. I'll make up some excuse that you need to brief me and then process some paperwork."

"That means our conclusions are incomplete," Justin objected.

"As far as I'm concerned, they'll do. We've changed the times and the routes of the President's convoy during her visit, reviewed our emergency options, redoubled our manpower, and requested extra support from the local police and the Internal Security."

"You're making a grave mistake," Carrie said, "our findings at the lab, along with this attack may point at something else."

"What else?"

"We're not sure, but we've reason to believe there's more to this plot than what we've discovered so far."

"Yes, yes, you explained it to me once, half an hour ago, when you talked about another target. The suicide bomber's confession on the platter, the Sheikh's strange request, and inconsistencies with the unexploded bomb. But these are all circumstantial evidence. Inconclusive at best."

"True enough," Justin said, "and this is exactly why we can't abort our mission now. Not before we have all pieces of the puzzle."

Matthew shook his head. "You really believe this is all smoke and mirrors?"

Carrie and Justin exchanged a thoughtful glance.

"Give me everything you've got if you want another stab at this," Matthew demanded. "After all, it's my ass on the line, since I'm lying about you being American diplomats."

"All right." Justin showed Matthew his BlackBerry phone. "Our post in Dubai has intercepted a wire transfer from Saudi Prince

Husayn bin Al-Farhan to Sheikh Yusuf Ayman, the Islamic Fighting—"

"Yes, I know who he is, and we know of Prince Al-Farhan alleged financing of terrorism. However, there has never been any hard evidence of his—"

"Hold on a second, Matthew." Justin raised his left hand. "No one is accusing the US of having a cozy relationship with the Saudis. I'm just stating the fact that Prince Al-Farhan transferred twenty million dollars from one of his offshore holdings to the main terrorist group active in Libya."

"OK, let's assume this intel is true. Maybe this money was transferred to finance the attack against my President. There's no reason to believe in the existence of another target."

"Still, no reason to exclude other possibilities," Justin insisted. "That's why it's crucial we continue our investigation."

"By all means." Matthew pointed at Justin's BlackBerry and at the phone set on the desk. "Work at your heart's content. But neither of you is leaving this building. Don't even go out for a cigarette break."

"You're crippling us," Carrie protested.

"Just making sure you stay alive, at least until you board a plane, first thing tomorrow morning. Anything else?"

Before Justin or Carrie could answer, there was a quick knock on the door. Nour barged in without waiting for anyone to call him.

"Sir, you should have a look at this." He handed his boss a single sheet of folded paper. "A communication we just received from our source in the Alliance."

Nour glanced at the two Canadian agents, their faces pale with surprise. "Yes, we've covered all angles," he said.

Matthew read the short printout. He blinked and glanced at Justin and Carrie. He looked again at the sheet of paper in his hand and shook his head.

"I can't believe I'm saying this, but I think you're right." Matthew stared at Justin. "This intel confirms that the US President *is not* the target of this plot."

CHAPTER 19

United States Embassy, Tripoli, Libya
May 15, 12:15 p.m. local time

"So, who is the target?" Justin pointed at the document. "May I see that?"

"We still don't know." Matthew gestured for Justin to pick up the folded sheet lying on the desk.

Justin scanned the half page transcript of a phone call. Two short paragraphs from someone identified as "Seif" indicated the US President was not the intended target of the assassination attempt. Furthermore, the transcript noted that Sheikh Issa Mahub Al-Arhabi, the head of the Islamic Fighting Alliance, was planning to travel to Yemen the next day.

"Who's Seif?" Justin handed the transcript to Carrie.

"Our man within Sheikh's intimate circle," Matthew replied.

"Can you trust him?"

"So far his intel has never failed."

"Why didn't you tell us about this Seif?" Carrie handed the document back to Justin, who gave it a second look.

Matthew shrugged. "Homeland Security protocol. Plus, I wasn't sure what Seif was going to find out."

Justin finished reading the transcript a third time and placed it back on the desk. He rubbed his palms together and took a step forward, getting closer to Matthew. "What's next?" he asked.

Matthew spread his arms. "Business as usual," he said with a chuckle, "as long as my President is not the target, I don't really care. Terrorists can blow up whoever they want."

"You can't be serious," Carrie said. "We have solid evidence that something big is under way, and you're simply going to stand and watch from the sidelines?"

A stern gaze froze Matthew's face. "No." He shook his head. "I'm going to be right in the middle of the shitstorm, right in front of the presidential limo, on the lookout for any son of a bitch who dares to smile funny at the convoy. So, don't you dare tell me how to do my job!"

Carrie raised a protective hand. "Hey, no need to be pissed off at me. We both want the same thing."

Matthew's left side of the face twitched as he produced a fake grin. "We do, but the two of you have a reckless way of getting results. I want my President's visit to go as smooth as possible: in and out the country without firing a shot. The two of you, you want to get to the bottom of this story, which is beyond my interests."

The phone on the desk rang.

"What is it?" Matthew barked at the caller. He listened for a minute then shook his head. "Ehe, ehe," he said. Then he hung up.

"Guess who that was?" Matthew pointed at Justin. "Your minder from Internal Security, Abdul. One of the extremists they've been torturing since last night finally spilled his guts. And you've got your answer. The target of the Alliance is the Prime Minister of Libya."

"What?" Justin shouted. "You must be joking."

"What? The islamists want to kill the Prime Minister?" Carrie asked.

Matthew nodded. "If you believe this poor man's confession."

Justin's lips pursed. "A man under torture would admit to anything."

"Well, your initial suspicions came because of information

obtained through torture. Whether you like it or not, this is how things are done in Libya," Matthew said.

Justin decided it was not worth correcting him. The agents had received the details of the assassination plot from Sheikh Ayman, in exchange for Canada's mediation between the Islamic Fighting Alliance and the Libyan authorities. The confession of the wannabe suicide bomber had served as collaborating evidence to support their theory. However, this latest piece of information came as a fierce blow, knocking down the idea about a conspiracy to assassinate the American President. Justin realized Sheikh Ayman had lied to them about the true target of the plot.

"Well, I'm out of here," Matthew said. "If you'd like to tell the Libyans more about the extremists' plot, be my guests. But since this intel came from them in the first place, I'm sure they have a handle on things. This isn't the first time an attempt has been made on their Prime Minister's life."

"But—" Carrie began, as Matthew walked to the door, but Nour interrupted her with a promising wink and a flick of his wrist.

"As I said earlier, this is no longer my business." Matthew turned around and raised his left hand to his eyes, making a quick I am keeping an eye on you gesture. "And it's none of your business either. Nour will arrange for your transportation tomorrow at zero six hundred. Is everything clear?"

"Yes, sir, it is clear," Justin replied.

Carrie just nodded.

"And no tricks, Justin. There will be no other shoot 'em up under my watch." Matthew raised a finger in the air and waived it in front of their faces.

"We get it. We'll do our job from inside this trap hole," Carrie said.

Matthew forced out a snort. "You'll thank me later."

Then, he walked out the room.

"What a jerk," Carrie mumbled. She walked over to Nour, who had a slight grin on his face. "So, you're going to help us escape?"

"No freaking way. Do you think I'm crazy?"

"No? So, what's with the wink?" Justin asked.

"This." Nour produced a satellite phone from his pants pocket. "It's my personal phone, untapped by the embassy. All phones here are monitored, and all calls are recorded. If you use my phone to call Johnson, maybe she'll twist Matthew's balls until he agrees to let you go."

Justin eyes shone.

"Thanks, we appreciate this." He glanced at the satellite phone. "But, what's in it for you?"

"For starters, the pleasure of seeing Matthew squirm," Nour replied with a quiet chuckle. "He can be a real jerk at times, although I understand his hands-off approach. In a few days, he'll be out of this place, and I'll still be in charge of the security for American diplomats. I don't want this place to become more hostile than it already is."

"Do you really think the Alliance has a chance?" Carrie asked.

"In Libya, everything's possible," Nour replied. "The Prime Minister came to power after a civil war that toppled a forty-one-year rule of a strongman, and he may go out in a car bomb."

Justin weighted the satellite phone in his hand. "You call Johnson." He handed the phone over to Carrie. "I'm gonna talk to Abdul."

"I'm starving." Nour followed Justin to the door. "There's this place around the corner that makes the best falafels in Tripoli. I can bring you some lunch, since you shouldn't leave the building."

"No, but thanks," Carrie said, "I can't stomach anything until after I've finished reporting to my boss."

"Is she giving you guys a hard time?"

"Not more than usually," Justin replied. "After you." He waited for the American to go through the door. Then, he said to Carrie, "I'll be back in fifteen or so."

"I'll be here, on the phone," she dragged her words.

"You're welcome any time," Justin said. Then, he dropped his voice to a low whisper, "at least she's not dropping *you* somewhere you can get killed."

"Oh, no, not yet," Carrie replied with a sigh, "but ask me again when you come back. She may have something else in mind."

CHAPTER 20

United States Embassy, Tripoli, Libya
May 15, 12:30 p.m. local time

"Tell me this once again. The Americans have a spy in the Alliance?" asked Abdul.

"Keep your voice down." Justin gestured toward a couple of women walking through the embassy halls. He nodded at them as they turned the corner by two L-shaped leather couches, where Justin and Abdul were sipping bitter coffee from small paper cups. The young redhead returned a pretty smile; the older woman whipped them with a stern frown.

"I still can't believe it," Abdul dropped his voice to a silent hush, "that is so bold."

"Yeah, that's true, but I'm not supposed to share this intel with you." Justin took a sip of his drink.

He reached back, pushed the window curtains aside, and glanced outside. From the second floor of the embassy he could see the whitewashed walls and a small stretch of the street leading to a row of coffee shops and falafel restaurants across the intersection. Nour had yet to return from picking up his lunch. It had already been fifteen minutes. *Did he find a long line or he is eating there? He said he was going for takeout.*

"Oh, so we're expected to bend over backwards, but Americans aren't giving away a thing?" Abdul asked.

"You'll go a long way, Abdul, because *now* you're getting it."

"Thanks?"

"You're welcome. Now, can we believe this guy you're torturing?"

"My agency does not torture and personally, I haven't beaten anyone." Abdul went on the defensive. "Well, not in the last two years, at least."

"So, yes or no?"

"Well, that's tricky to say. Torture confessions are useful only if we find other evidence or at least have these claims confirmed by other sources."

"Well, the US source knows only that the US President is not the target, but he can't confirm the identity of the new one."

"And our raids haven't produced any evidence. We're back to square one."

"Has your agency infiltrated the Alliance?"

"If it has, I'm not aware of it."

"Would the colonel know?"

Abdul shrugged and leaned back on the couch. Its springs squealed under his weight.

"Maybe, but don't count on him telling you."

Justin sighed. He conceded, "So, really, we don't have much."

"No, we don't. And if you're locked within these walls for the rest of the day, and then get on the first plane tomorrow morning, we'll find nothing else."

"Unless the colonel scraps his deportation order."

"He might, if the Americans ask for a favor. But you told me Matthew doesn't want to do that."

"Yeah. Apparently he's washed his hands of this case."

"And your boss?" Abdul asked.

A dark shadow fell on Justin's face. He delayed his reply, allowing for the spark of anger to die down, to avoid mouthing off any swear words about Johnson.

"She's… I don't think she's willing to intervene either," he said after a few seconds, his fingers clenching the paper cup so hard that coffee almost spilled over the top. "She'll get us outside the embassy, but most likely Carrie and I would have to leave tomorrow."

Abdul leaned forward and picked up his own cup. After a quick sip, he asked, "What if you simply disappeared?"

"I thought about it, but running will worsen our chances. How can we investigate and gather evidence if we're wanted by the mukhabarat?"

"You're right about that," Abdul said. "Nothing good will come from running."

Justin glanced again outside the window. A taxi was parked in front of one of the restaurants. A group of people huddled in front of the next door coffee shop. His gaze soared, and he noticed two men sitting in one of the balconies of the apartment complex across the intersection. They were on the fourth floor, about three hundred yards away.

"Still nothing," Justin said, consulting his wristwatch.

"Relax." Abdul leaned back, his right hand stroking his chin. "He's probably enjoying some decent coffee. Unlike this one."

"You bought it."

"Big mistake, but it was the only thing half decent at the machine."

"If we're running and hiding, sooner or later we'll get caught, not to mention that you'll land in hot water, all over again."

Abdul shook his head. "That's if I help you."

"Huh? What?"

"I'm kidding. Of course, I'll help you. Now, the risk is great, but if we can undo the plot to kill the Prime Minister, that will mean great rewards, great rewards, for all of us." Abdul's voice echoed with envy.

"Chief of the mukhabarat?" Justin noticed Abdul's drooling.

"Oh, yes, yes. Even army's chief of staff."

"No way! Isn't that position reserved for a general? I don't see any stars on you."

"If we save his life, the Prime Minister can make me a general with a snap of his fingers."

"That's an extremely long shot."

"Not impossible."

Justin stood up and paced impatiently along the wall. He stole a glance at his wristwatch and pulled the window curtains aside again. His gaze found Nour crossing the street by the eastern wall of the embassy. Nour was carrying two plastic bags on his left hand and holding his cellphone pressed against his ear with the other hand.

"Nour's coming back. He's just… wait, what the hell?"

"What's going on?"

Justin squinted and raised his hands to his forehead, to ward off the reflection of his face in the window's glass. A rifle's barrel jutting out from the fourth floor balcony tolled his alarm bells.

"Sniper, there's a sniper, fourth floor, two o'clock."

"What?"

"Nour's their target. Go, go, go!" Justin shouted.

He sprang over the couch like a leopard chasing an antelope. His left foot banged against the table, sending Abdul's coffee spilling on the couch and the carpeted floor. Abdul jumped to his feet and hurried behind Justin. They ran down the hall, turned the corner and began jumping the stairs three and four at a time. As they reached the first floor, one of the guards by the reception desk, a tall, bald man, stepped forward, spreading his arms to stop their approach.

"Where d'you think you're goin'?"

"Nour's in danger. Outside—"

The guard shoved his large palm into Justin's chest.

"You ain't leaving this—"

Justin cut him off with a right fist slamming against his square jaws. A left knee to the stomach dropped the man to the floor. Abdul went for the other guard, but before they had exchanged any blows, Justin leveled the pistol he took from the guard sprawled on the floor at the head of the second guard.

"Don't move."

Abdul disarmed the second guard and followed Justin, who opened the door leading to the courtyard.

"Open the gate, open the freaking gate," Justin screamed at the guards manning the main entrance of the embassy, threatening them with his gun. Abdul raised his pistol as well, but the heavy steel plate gate was already rolling. Squeezing through the narrow opening, Justin raced down the street.

"Nour, Nour," he yelled at the top of his lungs. "Nour!"

The American was about a hundred yards away, strolling at leisure and focusing solely on his cellphone conversation. Dashing forward, Justin fired a warning shot in the air. The gunshot sent a few people scattering for the safety of nearby stores. The chaos caught Nour's attention. He stared at Justin barreling toward him, gun drawn and shouting in panic. Nour raised up his hands, asking about the unbelievable scene unfolding in front of his eyes, when a second gunshot erupted, echoing in the empty street. It did not come from Justin's gun. The bullet struck Nour in the back. His phone flew out of his hand. A second later, his lunch spilled on the ground. Nour's feet gave in and he dropped face first into the concrete sidewalk.

"No, no, no," Justin cried, aiming his pistol at the sniper's balcony, and squeezing off one round after the other. He kept running toward the fallen American. Other gunfire came from behind him. Justin figured it was Abdul firing his weapon. A bullet wheezed past his head and Justin realized now he had become the sniper's moving target. He jumped to the side and rolled over the ground. Then, he climbed to his left knee and fired a quick burst. The bullets shattered the glass door behind the sniper. Justin fired his last rounds and then tossed the empty pistol aside, as he hid behind one of the embassy SUVs parked on the side of the road.

"Abdul, I'm out."

Abdul replied by firing two more times, before diving for cover inside one of the stores to his left. The sniper shot back, hammering the SUV's widows. Justin peeked out from underneath the car at

Nour. The man was motionless. A pool of blood was forming around his head. More rounds poured toward Abdul's position.

"Fire back," Justin shouted.

"I'm empty. Are you OK?"

"Yeah, I'm fine. Nour's down."

A loud rumble came from his right and Justin turned his head. Two white GMC Envoys rolled out of the embassy, accompanied by armed guards in dark blue fatigues. As they edged closer to him, weapons at the ready, Justin glanced at the fourth floor balcony. The shooter was gone.

"Medic, he needs a medic," Justin shouted at the guards.

Two of them began to check Nour's body for signs of life. Justin stood up, shifting the weight of his body to his right leg. He had reopened his left leg wound and blood was tricking down his foot. Carrie was running toward him and he gave her a smile. Seconds later, she fell into his arms for a tight embrace.

"I'll have that treated," Carrie said in a worried voice, her eyes noticing the bloodstain around Justin's foot.

"Thanks."

"I tell you not to go shooting without me, but you never listen." Carrie raised a stern finger and shook her head very dramatically.

"You were busy having a girly talk with Johnson." Justin searched the street for Abdul. "By the way, how did that go?"

"Slightly better than this." Carrie pointed at the guards hovering over Nour. An ambulance pulled into the intersection and screeched to a halt next to the wounded American. The Libya British Diagnostic Center logo was painted on the left side of the ambulance.

"You took one for the team." Abdul jogged toward them.

"No, old wound." Justin replied. "Oh, no," he added, looking over Carrie's shoulder.

"What is it?" she asked.

Carrie turned around, just as Matthew appeared at the embassy's gate. His dark gaze first fell on his chief of security, whose body was being lifted into a gurney and wheeled into the back of the ambulance. Matthew ran to the ambulance and exchanged a few words with a guard and one of the paramedics. Justin read Matthew's rage through his body gestures: sinking shoulders, clenched fists, a kick to the ambulance rear tire. Then, the man's blazing eyes found Justin and the rest of his group. He braced for the verbal storm that was about to hail upon their ears. However, Matthew's blue eyes cooled off as he measured up the agents. He walked over to them.

"Nour is barely alive. Thank you for helping him. After you patch up your wound, meet me in my office," he said. "The two of you." He pointed at Justin and Carrie. "In fifteen minutes."

CHAPTER 21

United States Embassy, Tripoli, Libya
May 15, 1:30 p.m. local time

Matthew's office was on the second floor, in the eastern corner of the embassy. The walls were adorned with portraits of American presidents. Washington, Lincoln, Roosevelt, Gerber. Justin slowed down his pace as they reached the last portrait. Stacy Gerber, who was to arrive in Tripoli in two days, was looking at him through her still green eyes. A true politician gaze, inspiring and comforting, secure and confidant. *She may be off the terrorists' hit list, but this is far from over.* A moment later, he noticed Carrie and the guard had stopped and were staring at him.

"I'm coming," he said, before they had a chance to say anything.

"What is it?" Carrie asked.

"Nothing. I was just looking at the President's picture."

The Secret Service Assistant Director's office door was open, but the guard still tapped it lightly out of courtesy. Matthew, standing by a small window, glanced at them. He gestured for Justin and Carrie to take a seat next to a stainless steel table with a round glass top. A few piles of manila folders were scattered over the table. Justin noticed a few aerial photographs and mug shots, as well as a few reports. Some were stamped TOP SECRET.

"I guess I owe you an apology," Matthew began in a flat voice, his back toward them, his gaze still floating outside the window. He allowed a few seconds to pass and then, after the agents' respectful silence, he added, "I hope you still want to get to the bottom of your investigation."

"We do, sir," Justin replied.

"Absolutely," Carrie added.

"OK, then." Matthew turned around, resting his back against the window and pointed at the table. "I *want* this bastard and I don't care if his uncle is the King or the Crown Prince. If Al-Farhan is behind Nour's shooting, I want him to pay."

Justin threw a quick glance at one of the pictures. *Is that the Prince?* he wondered. Instead, he asked, "How's Nour doing?"

"The British doctors are working on removing the bullet. If it has pierced his lungs, his chances of coming out of the coma drop significantly. At this point, they're still assessing the internal damage. Let's just hope his spinal cord is intact. Those damn bullets are so unpredictable. You never know what has been pierced and slashed along its path, and…"

Matthew's voice trailed off, and Justin did not ask for further details. He knew that even surface gunshot wounds could deteriorate into life-threatening situations. Nour had taken a bullet inches away from his vital organs. His prognosis did not look good.

"Anyway." Matthew attempted to clear the glooming cloud shadowing his mood, "I was saying, if this jerk had anything to do with sending Nour's shooter, he has no idea what's coming to him." He walked to the table and sat across from them. "My men searched the apartment on the fourth floor, but the shooter vanished. The place is now teeming with secret and not-so-secret police."

"I saw two people on the balcony minutes before the attack," Justin said, "but only one person firing the rifle."

"It doesn't really matter, since the mukhabarat will find nothing. They'll arrest some poor schmuck, who'll confess to the shooting under torture. We have no jurisdiction outside our embassy. My hands are tied."

Matthew pointed both his index fingers at the agents. "But yours are not. You're willing and you're able."

"Wait a minute," Justin said. "What about the deportation order? Colonel Farid wants us out of Libya by tomorrow morning."

"That's taken care off. The colonel has been MIA since noon."

"What? Where did he go?"

"His blue Fiat was found abandoned just south of the city. Farid's not answering his cellphones and no one has any idea of his whereabouts."

"You're thinking what I'm thinking?" Carrie asked Matthew.

Matthew nodded. "Yes, Prince Al-Farhan seems to be the only known link between these incidents. First, you're attacked after discovering something's amiss in the plot against my President, which we know was a decoy. Then, after the attack failed, Colonel Farid disappears without a trace, and one of my men is shot assassination-style. There's only one man we know who can pull this off in a matter of hours. Prince Al-Farhan."

"Oh, now you're connecting the dots," Carrie said.

Her voice came out a bit accusatory, although Justin knew she did not mean to be brazen. Matthew was already on their side.

"No, I made the connection when I first heard you, but things were different at the time. Two hours ago, I didn't have my right-hand man lying half dead on a surgeon's table, and I was missing the last two pieces of evidence that support this theory: the disappearance of Colonel Farid and the two shootings. If Al-Farhan brought his dirty war to us, making Americans his target, we'll pay him back. The Prince is now our target."

"Wasn't Al-Farhan targeting America all along? After all, the initial plot was to assassinate the American President during her visit here," Carrie said.

"He was, but see, that plot was a hoax, a decoy. And good thing we found out. The President gets about three hundred threats a day, most of which completely outlandish. I admit, this plot seemed to have teeth, and we did investigate and take all necessary measures. When a US President visits a foreign country, especially one with which we haven't had the greatest relationship in more than forty years, a lot of henchmen start coming out of the woodwork. And these henchmen drew blood. The blood of my man." Matthew rapped his knuckle over the manila folders on the table. "Now, more evidence has piled up on my desk during the last two days. The Secret Service has been trailing Prince Al-Farhan's movements over the last month, as soon as we learned about my President's visit for the G-20 Summit. But the Saudis' are so rich we struggle to keep up our surveillance. When they vacation for weeks in private islands, we can't always send our men incognito. They have their own banking system, cloaked in secrecy. They fly in their private jets and pay off everyone to seal their lips.

"So, our cases on their alleged support for terrorism are always full of holes. Often we need to make great leaps of faith in drawing our conclusions. On top of everything else, even when the evidence points straight at the villain, the Saudis are always protected by this, this aura of exclusivity, because of their close relationships with our political and business masters."

"What's the evidence you have on the Prince?" Justin asked.

Matthew opened one of the folders, shuffled through its papers, and handed Justin a stack of about a dozen documents. "These are bank transactions. Companies controlled by associates of the Prince have been wiring thousands of dollars to Islamic charities and foundations throughout North Africa. Some of the recipients allegedly have loose ties to the Islamic Fighting Alliance," Matthew said, using a pencil to point at the documents.

"Oh, so you *are* in the know about these wire transfers?" Carrie asked.

"Yes, we are, but I'm not going to repeat myself about the protection surrounding the Saudis. I said *allegedly* and *loose ties*. We can fill in the blanks and that's what we're doing, albeit quite late. Trust me, I wish I would have done this earlier, before my man was shot down."

Matthew's fingers clenched around the pencil and it broke in half. Slivers flew across the table.

"Who are these other people?" Justin gestured with his head toward the photographs.

Matthew pushed aside the pencil halves. A sliver had slipped into the skin of his left palm. He headed to his desk for a Kleenex to wipe away a trickle of blood.

"The gentleman in the tuxedo is Prince's personal aide, Mr. Zakir Al-Dakhil. Zakir is his right hand, a real son of a bitch. These photos were taken at a wedding reception late last year, so he's not expected to have changed much."

Justin stared at the photo. The man staring back was clean shaven, with a dimpled chin and shiny, bleached blonde hair cut to ear length. His nose had a fleshy drooping tip, and the man carried large fat sacks underneath his gray-blue eyes. A couple of thin wrinkles had formed in his broad forehead.

"How old is Zakir?" Justin passed the photo along to Carrie.

"There should be a file on him in there, with all personal details." Matthew returned to his seat. "Here it is." He found it after riffling through the papers.

Justin analyzed the document. It listed Zakir's birthdate as January 10, 1970. His birthplace was Dhahran, Saudi Arabia.

"And this is Prince Husayn bin Al-Farhan." Matthew dug up another photograph and gave it to Justin. "This was taken last month, in his yacht, off the southern coast of France."

The man smiling from the photo was dressed in a white robe and a red-and-white checkered *ghutrah,* the headdress worn traditionally by Saudi royals. Justin stared at the man's expressive face, ambition and power displayed clearly in his black eyes, which also carried a dark glint of malice. He had a straight forehead without the hint of a wrinkle, at least as far as the ghutrah left uncovered, and healthy ruby red cheeks. The Prince had a thick nose, perfect teeth, a gray thin moustache and a protruding chin.

"He's carrying his fifty years really well." Justin flipped through a few documents Matthew had pushed toward him. They contained the Prince's personal information, which read like a long resume.

"Good health is just one of the privileges of a few billion dollars," Matthew replied.

"What's this?" Carrie pointed at one of the aerial photos.

She could tell it was a large complex of buildings, made up of three interconnected wings that formed a large Y-shaped structure. It was most likely a house, since Carrie could make out a large swimming pool and what seemed like a huge garage and a stable at a distance from the main building. Her question was about the location of the complex.

"That's Prince's sixty-five thousand square feet mansion in the outskirts of Riyadh." Matthew paused for a brief second and added quickly, "But that's not our point of attack."

"Attack?" Justin and Carrie gasped.

Matthew offered a justifying head tilt and a resigning hand gesture.

"Well, maybe 'attack' is a strong word. I meant to say a 'raid.' Hmmm, a 'search.' Hopefully, we can find some irrefutable evidence about his involvement in Nour's shooting and the plot against Libya's Prime Minister. But this search can't take place at his mansion. It's extremely well-protected."

"His main office?" Justin asked.

"Well, his main office is in his yacht, this humongous floating fortress that never docks in the same port more than twenty-four hours. It's named 'Arabia' and it's a two hundred and seventy-feet long beauty. Like his mansion, it's heavily guarded at all times. And we can't deploy a large team. Well, basically, this is the team." He motioned toward the two agents sitting across the table.

Carrie frowned. "Let me get this straight. You want the two of us to raid the Prince's fortress and get killed while trying?"

Matthew grinned. "Of course not. I said his usual strongholds are unassailable. We'll try to breach the Prince's security where he's most vulnerable, given our limited resources."

"Pathetic, not limited, was the first term that came to mind," Carrie blurted.

Matthew frowned. Carrie just shrugged.

"I guess you have some kind of a plan?" Justin asked.

"No. Not yet anyway." Matthew rubbed his chin.

"What else do you have on the Prince?" Carrie asked.

"This is just the tip of the iceberg." Matthew placed his right hand over the folders. "I've requested the rest of the files from the Secret Service and the CIA. We should get them soon. We know the Prince always travels in his own private jet, a Boeing 707, which is virtually a flying palace. He has been seen taking choppers for shorter rides, but he's always surrounded by an entourage of aides and protected by a company of bodyguards."

"So, his palace in the air is better guarded than his palace on the ground," Carrie quipped.

Matthew ignored her dry wit remark. "If you gain entry to Prince's private jet and search it, maybe you'll find some evidence of his involvement in this plot."

"And how exactly do we do that?" Justin asked.

"I haven't thought it that far. As I said earlier, I wasn't going to say anything to you if it were not for Nour getting shot. A few minutes ago, we received this piece of intel." Matthew held up a single sheet of paper.

Justin held out his hand and Matthew gave him the document.

"A CIA source learned the Prince is visiting a hot area in the Gulf Region. Yemen."

"Yemen?" Carrie's eyes narrowed in suspicion. "Isn't some sheikh, yes, Sheikh Al-Arhabi going there too?"

"Yes, the leader of the Alliance is going to Yemen too," Matthew said. "This isn't a coincidence. I dug a bit deeper and found out they're both visiting Northern Yemen. Not clear exactly on the location, but I bet the ranch the Prince is meeting the Sheikh. And we know what kind of deals they're cutting in that terrorist haven."

"Yemen has been an Al-Qaeda base for many years. Iran and

Saudi Arabia flex their muscles in this no man's land." Justin pondered over the new piece of information. He was staring at the Xeroxed note as if it could reveal the location of the secret meeting.

"Yes, and I'm advising against following Al-Farhan into that hellhole," Matthew said with a deep sigh. He brought his hands behind his neck and slowly leaned back in his swiveling chair. "Here's all I've got on Al-Farhan so far. Analyze it and let me know your plans, keeping in mind we don't have much time. I can provide some logistics, but that's pretty much it. I wish I could do more, but since a Saudi prince is involved, I don't have much leverage." He sighed again, this time bitterness and rage spreading across his face like dark tornado clouds.

Justin gathered the paperwork, stacking it in two thick piles. Carrie picked up the one closer to her.

"We'll use the Washington conference room," Justin said, referring to the room where he first briefed Matthew less than twenty-four hours ago.

"I'll send someone to bring you some lunch. But first, I'll check on Nour."

CHAPTER 22

United States Embassy, Tripoli, Libya
May 15, 2:05 p.m. local time

"This has turned into an unbelievable nightmare." Justin closed the opaque glass door of the George Washington Conference Room, and dropped his stack of briefing notes on the table. "Two days ago, we were only messengers. Now, we're chasing ghosts of princes and terrorists, while bodies stack up as if hacked down by the Plague."

"None of this is our fault." Carrie sat next to Justin and spread her folders in front of her, "but now, we must unravel this plot."

"Oh Johnson." Justin threw his head back and stared up at the ceiling, as if Johnson were a goddess up in the skies. "Why do *we* have to clean up this mess?"

"Because you're a great janitor, my dear," Carrie imitated Johnson's high-pitched voice and mimicked her tight facial expression. She puckered her lips and narrowed her eyes, lowering her reading glasses to the tip of her nose. "And I know you can fix any screw-up."

Justin rolled his eyes and shook her head. "This is not a screw-up; this is a clusterfuck of galactic proportions."

Carrie grinned.

"What did Johnson tell you on the phone?" Justin asked.

"She's unhappy with the way our mission has turned out, especially the highway shootout. I tried to explain it was self-defense and if we hadn't responded she would have had to ask for two Canadian flags to wrap our coffins. Still, she scolded us, well, me, since you weren't there, saying something along the lines of us not showing 'sufficient restraint.'"

"Typical of Johnson. The cleanup process is dirty and they don't like it. But when we reach the goal, then, the mission is described in superlatives."

"Yeah. She said she'll talk to Matthew about letting you collect your belongings from the hotel and move freely in the city. Although, she warned us against it. How did she put it? Oh yeah, 'the US Embassy is *definitely* the safest place for you at this moment.' That's what she said. She wants us to file a report, close the case, and get the hell out of Libya by tomorrow morning."

"Perhaps she's worried about more Libyans dying if we roam the streets of Tripoli."

Carrie shrugged. "Could be. Or worried about having to give longer explanations and more apologies to our ministers."

"What do you think she'll make of this turn of events?"

"What, us going after the Prince? I can't see Johnson backing you on this now. She will order us to stand down. That's if we tell her about it, after we decide whether we're going ahead with this plan."

"What plan? We don't have one." Justin spread his palms, as if Carrie was expecting the plan to be resting on his hands. "And so much for Matthew talking about 'we' and 'ours' when it is only you and I actually doing something."

"We'll come up with a plan. If Al-Farhan is involved in this assassination plot, I'm sure he's left behind plenty of traces. We only need to find one."

"What makes you so sure?"

"Al-Farhan is rich, filthy rich. Rich people like him don't expect to be caught. They believe they *can't* be caught. So, they're careless. If there's any evidence, we'll find it."

"I wouldn't be so sure. I mean, at the moment, we have nothing. How do we get close to the Prince? How do we get inside his private jet or his yacht?"

"We'll figure it out." Carrie reached for a notebook in her papers. Then, she pointed at the stacks of documents in front of them. "Shall we?"

"Before we do that, I've got to tell you something."

"What is it?"

"Last night, before meeting with Abdul, I ran into an old enemy. Tarek."

"His name doesn't ring a bell."

"He was a prison guard here in Tripoli… four years ago."

"Oh, so he's out for revenge."

"Was… I cut his throat."

Carrie blinked then stared at Justin's face. There was no emotion in his voice, no glow in his eyes. He was lost somewhere in space.

"Well, it was self-defense," Carrie said.

"Yes, the first time too."

"I don't understand."

"I shot Tarek when Abdul and I escaped from prison. I thought he died at that time, but apparently I was wrong. Last night, I thought I killed him, but Abdul tells me they can't find the body."

"So? There can be plenty of explanations for that."

"Carrie?"

"Yes, Justin?"

"Am I… Am I losing my mind?"

"No! Of course, not."

"Am I seeing enemies even when there's no one there? Ghosts from the past?"

Carrie reached for Justin's hand. "We all have ghosts from our pasts, and time after time, they come to pay us a visit. But if you're saying you saw Tarek and finished him, I believe you. Perhaps someone took him to a hospital. Or just got rid of the body."

"Abdul said they couldn't find it."

"Have him check again. This is Libya and things tend to get a bit cloudy, especially when dealing with the mukhabarat."

Justin swallowed hard and sighed.

"I'll ask him, but only after we've figured out this other, bigger mess in our hands. And we need Abdul's help. We need all the help we can get, and he's proven himself a trusted ally."

"What?" Carrie curved her voice for a dramatic effect. "You're saying the T-word? What happened to 'We're in North Africa; we can't *trust* anyone,' eh?"

"That was before Johnson stabbed us in the back. And I trusted Abdul even before that. He was tortured when we were captured but gave up nothing."

"He's still mukhabarat!"

"Yes, but he has strong incentives to foil this plot, like we do."

"Do we?"

"Carrie, if that's sarcasm, you need to work on your tone."

"No, Justin, it's not sarcasm. I'm getting tired of this cat-and-mouse game."

"You can't be serious."

"I am."

Justin leaned back in his chair and gave Carrie a strange gaze, as if he were looking at her for the first time.

"You just said we can do this. We can find the evidence that Al-Farhan is involved in this plot. Suddenly, you're tired?"

"I'm not tired of this mission. I'm so overwhelmed with everything in my life right now."

"You're not thinking of changing careers, are you?" Justin asked in a low voice, afraid of her answer.

"Time's working against me, Justin. Next year, I'll be thirty-two. I want to have a family, a husband, children. I can't have all that if I don't know when or if I'll go home at the end of the day."

Justin stared silently at Carrie's overcast face.

"I've done this for eleven years now and it takes a toll on you, your body, your mind, your soul. It's one thing to teach students, train recruits, even work undercover. But these daily travelling, endless shootings; it's just getting to be too much."

"C'mon, you know it doesn't happen all the time. Once you're back in Ottawa, you'll get so bored you'll be craving field duty."

"That may be true, but right now I feel so worn down."

Justin locked eyes with Carrie, noticing her sad glare. "How much of this is because of Thomas?"

Carrie shrugged. "He hasn't asked me to leave the Service."

"No, but he has hinted at the possibility."

"Look, just because we don't talk twice a day like you and Anna that doesn't mean Thomas hates my choice." Carrie crossed her arms in front of her chest.

"Fine, no need to snap at me. I was just thinking with him being loaded, he may not want you to work at all."

"No, it's not like that. Everybody thinks Thomas is flush with money. But he's not rich."

"He drives a Mercedes CLK convertible. I beg to differ."

"He bought that car in a … Oh, why are we even talking about this?"

"Because we care about each other. And I don't want to see you leave."

"I'm not going anywhere." Carrie made a dismissive hand gesture, though her facial expression seemed less convincing. "I'm just considering my options. Nothing wrong with that, right?"

"Yes, nothing wrong with that," Justin replied with a light sigh. "I'll go and get Abdul and see if Matthew actually did order our lunch. Then, we can get back to work."

"Great idea. I'll get a head start." She went for one of the manila folders.

* * *

Matthew had ordered their lunch, choosing Chinese takeout. He had no news about Nour, which everyone interpreted as good news.

Nour was in stable condition, and doctors were running more tests.

Over the next three hours, Justin, Carrie, and Abdul poured over the files, looking for a way to get their hands on specific details about the plot against Libya's Prime Minister.

The first option they examined was the one Carrie suggested: organizing a raid on Prince Al-Farhan while he was in Yemen, overpowering his bodyguards and forcing a confession out of him. After that, the House of Saud could twist the Prince's arm into aborting his plans for the Prime Minister's assassination. Justin pointed out that Americans were unwilling to commit any ground troops or air drones to such an operation. Abdul argued they could draw on tribal militias backed by the Yemeni government, which operated in the Saada region of northern Yemen, the destination of Prince Al-Farhan. These militias hated any Saudi involvement in their internal affairs. Still, there was not enough time to organize these ragtag troops for such a sensitive mission, since the Prince was visiting the region in three days. Besides, neither Justin, nor Abdul knew anyone they could trust amongst the Yemenis. Too many things could go wrong even if they got all planning details right. Justin did not like the odds.

With Yemen out of the picture, they switched their focus to getting close to the Prince while he was travelling. It was possible to pull a few strings, intercept the itinerary of the Prince's Boeing 707, and learn its times of arrival, layovers, and departure. However, it was another thing to plan and carry out a successful covert operation in foreign, mostly hostile countries. Syria. Jordan. Oman. Saudi Arabia. All possible stops on Prince's trip to Yemen. Their meager resources and short time frame excluded such a mission altogether.

Hitting a dead end, they decided to return to the Prince's current known location. He was vacationing in the Mediterranean Sea, somewhere south of France. Carrie suggested they raid the Prince's yacht while in international waters. Her suggestion raised more questions than answers, since Al-Farhan's Arabia was practically, as Matthew had put it eloquently, "a floating fortress."

They explored the possibility of hijacking the Prince's Boeing 707. According to the information provided by Matthew, at the moment, the airplane was at one of the private hangers of London's Heathrow Airport. Justin had to admit that taking over the Prince's Boeing 707 was going to be very difficult, especially with no back up from Britain's intelligence agencies, MI5 and MI6. Johnson had made it clear she wanted no further involvement of the CIS in this matter, now that the American President was no longer the target of the Islamic terrorists. Justin, Carrie, and Abdul were on their own, the odds stacked high against them. So far, every scenario ended up with them being killed, or tortured and then killed.

At some point during the afternoon, Matthew popped his head into the conference room to check on their progress. His interruption was met with frustration at the American refusal to provide any further support for the team. Then, Justin decided to go out for a short walk and some fresh air, promising to Matthew that, barring any shootout, he would stay within the embassy's protective walls. Carrie went back to reviewing the files, in hopes of finding anything she may have overlooked. Abdul stepped out for a few personal phone calls.

Out in the backyard, Justin sat on a bench by a small water fountain. The shade from a cluster of small palm trees provided some relief from the scorching sun. A gentle breeze gave him a breath of fresh air. Justin's mind unavoidably went to the task at hand: finding a way to get to Prince Al-Farhan. He began reconsidering all options, moving the pieces of the puzzle around in his head. While he was still wondering, the cooing of a pigeon startled him. He looked up, just as the grayish bird fluttered at the edge of the fountain. Its claws scratched the fiberglass for a firm footing. Oblivious to Justin's gaze, the bird dipped its orange beak for a quick drink, sucking the water. Then, it slid into the fountain, flapping its wings and tail, and puffing out its plumage. A second later, the pigeon spotted Justin, meeting his observant eyes. The bird cocked its head to the left and Justin thought he saw the pigeon blink. Then, the bird spread its wings and took off, flying over the embassy walls.

Justin shook his head, but before he could start to feel bad about scaring the pigeon, he heard a woman's laughter coming from above his head. The cigarette smoke reached his nose before he heard footsteps on the second-floor balcony. Someone was out on their cigarette break. As Justin stood up and began to walk, to avoid the killer smoke, he heard a quiet whisper, "Of course, he'll accept, Jenny. Hey, Jenny, can you hear me? All I hear is static."

She's on the phone, Justin thought, with a sense of uneasiness about spying on the woman's conversation.

"Oh, yeah, I can hear you now," the woman spoke again, this time louder, "I was saying, I don't have to ask for a transfer. Lee will have to come to me, 'cause I have what he wants, if you know what I mean. Yes, yes, he'll agree to come here."

That's it, Justin almost shouted, as he jumped to his feet. *If we can't go to the Prince, we'll have the Prince come to us.*

* * *

"That's your great idea?" Abdul asked, "We just pick up the phone and say, 'Hey, Prince Al-Farhan, why don't you drop by?' Just like that?"

"Actually, this may work, Abdul," Carrie said, "after all, if we can't go to the mountain, the mountain will come to us."

"Yeah, you think so? But why, what do we have to make the Prince come to us?"

"I haven't thought that far yet." Justin reached for one of the photos of the Prince. He stared at the man in the headdress, tapping the photo with his hand. "What could you want, eh? What could you want?"

"Nothing. The man has everything," Abdul replied.

"I wasn't really looking for an answer. And I know everyone wants something. What does Prince Al-Farhan want?"

Abdul opened his mouth, but Justin stopped him with a swift

headshake.

"Peace on earth?" Carrie said with a grin.

"No, something more concrete and doable." Justin rolled his eyes.

"Well, I don't know what he wants, but let's see what he has." Carrie sifted through the piles of documents. "I saw a few reports here listing his assets. We can start there and see what's missing, although like Abdul said, if the Prince doesn't have something, it's not because he can't afford it."

"This is futile," Abdul said, leaning back in his chair. "Say Prince Al-Farhan doesn't have a solid gold diamond-encrusted Rolex. Do we have one to offer him?"

Justin sighed and scratched his chin. "No, but let's worry about our offer after we find something he may want. We'll start with what we have here. I'm also going to get some help from our analysts. Our desk in Dubai has a few dozen files on Saudi princes."

"Fine," Abdul said, "but I don't have high hopes."

"It's worth a try, and we're out of options," Justin replied.

While Carrie and Abdul started to navigate through the paper maze, Justin requested the support of the CIS bureau in Dubai. Its task was to comb through the Prince's activities, travels, finances, and purchases over the last three months. They were looking particularly for unusual purchases, any item that jumped out of the extraordinary life of a Saudi billionaire.

Thirty minutes later, as Justin's patience was wearing thin at Abdul's whining about the "useless, menial chore" assigned to him, the first results began to come in from the team in Dubai. Over secure Internet servers, encrypted files were downloaded into Carrie's laptop. With a few clicks, she revealed the expected craze of the filthy rich. Prince Al-Farhan loved spending money. By the truckloads. He truly lived the lavish life of the billionaire. A jet, a yacht, vacations in luxurious mansions in the French Riviera, a palace he called "home" in Riyadh, diamond rings, paintings, and a huge collection of automobiles.

Prince Al-Farhan owned ninety-nine cars, mostly modern sport cars, but also the occasional restored gem of the sixties and the seventies. His collection included not only the latest models of Jaguar, Ferrari and Aston Martin, but also a 1965 Shelby Cobra Roadster and two 1959 Alfa Romeo Giulietta Spider coupes. Apart from the extravagance of the collection, Justin noted the absence of the latest thoroughbred of speed: the Bugatti Veyron. The Prince did not own any Bugattis. Justin began to wonder about the reason why one of the most powerful supercars in history did not make the cut for the Sheikh's priceless collection. The reason could not be its price, since to Prince Al-Farhan a few million dollars was spare change.

"So, how come the Prince owns no Bugattis?" Justin asked, rubbing his tired eyes with the palms of his hands, before taking the last sip from his coffee cup. He got up and went for a refill from the coffee machine brewing a fresh pot on one of the side desks.

"The Prince hates Germans?" Carrie got up from her chair and stretched her arms and legs, pacing by the windows.

"No, he doesn't," Abdul said, after taking a sip of his now cold coffee. "He has five Mercedes and two BMWs in his garages. Can you bring me some coffee, too?"

"Sure."

Justin poured Abdul a tall paper cup.

"Here you go. Now, the Prince having no Bugattis is like a Catholic church without a cross. It can't be, and we need to find out why."

"Is the reason really that important?" Carrie asked.

"It could be." Justin pointed at the laptop's screen. "I mean, Al-Farhan has ninety-nine cars. Maybe he's waiting for a special limited edition Bugatti to top up his collection."

"Didn't they make a special edition for their hundredth anniversary?" Abdul said, "What was its name?"

"Bleu Centenaire," Justin replied.

"Yes, that one."

"Oh, they make new editions all the time. Same car, if you ask me," Carrie said.

"Maybe he just doesn't like Bugattis," Abdul suggested, "I mean, there are other supercars missing here." Abdul picked up one of the documents listing the Prince's automobile collection. "I see no Porches, no Lamborghinis, no Bentleys."

"One can do without those," Justin replied, "trust me, Abdul, I know cars. And I know car collectors. You can't have a one hundred racecar collection without a Bugatti. You just can't."

Abdul shrugged.

"Fine," Carrie said.

"I'm gonna have Chris find out if the Prince is still in the market for a Bugatti," Justin said, referring to one of the analysts with the CIS Dubai office.

"Why? You've got one for sale?" Carrie asked.

"No, but it may give us the hook we need. We'll figure out our next step if the Prince is still game."

"I'm not going to argue with you." Carrie turned her chair around and sat in it with a loud thump. "At this point, everything is worth a shot. I'll trace back the Prince's last few days in the French Riviera. *Again.*"

* * *

It took Chris and his team in Dubai less than an hour to come back with an answer. Indeed, Prince Al-Farhan was still looking for a Bugatti, but not any Bugatti. Justin could hardly believe his eyes when reading the note Chris has drafted. The Prince was not satisfied with more than a thousand brake horsepower of the 8.0 liter W16 engine in the Bugatti Veyron, which reached a top speed of more than 235 miles per hour. He had also shrugged aside the more exclusive, limited production of Bleu Centenaire, or even the most recent and the fastest model of the supercar, the Super Sport. Instead, the Prince had insisted the Bugatti manufacturing plant roll out a tuned-up car to his own liking, boasting around 2000 brake horsepower. The

Prince wanted his car to beat all other souped-up supercars of the uber-rich. He had to own the ultimate machine in power, speed and, of course, price. Still, he had not succeeded in convincing the Bugatti plant executives. Lately, the Prince had begun looking for a modified Bugatti, one with a considerable aftermarket upgrade.

"I think we've got our hook," Justin said, his eyes squinting. The left corner of his lips formed a sly grin.

"Uh-oh," Carrie said with a headshake. "I know that grin and it usually means trouble, big trouble."

"Here's my idea: we find a Bugatti Veyron the Prince wants and offer it to him. He'll agree to come out and meet—"

"It's never going to work," Abdul cried.

"Hear me through."

"OK, first of all, where are we going to find a Bugatti?"

"I know a friend."

"Which one?" Carrie peered at Justin over her reading glasses.

"Romanov."

"I can't believe you're calling that Russian son of a bitch a 'friend.'" She threw her arms in the air.

"He owes me one, Carrie, and I was describing him to Abdul, who doesn't know him," Justin said. He continued to Abdul, "He's not really my friend."

"So, who is this Romanov?"

"He's a Russian oil thug who owns half of Moscow." Carrie snorted. "And who has bribed and killed his way to the top."

"And this billionaire owes you one because…" Abdul's bushy eyebrows arched and his forehead wrinkles doubled.

"Regretfully, he saved the thug's life," Carrie replied. Noticing Abdul's awestruck face, she explained, "We were staking out this bar in Nice, a couple of years back, looking for a CIS agent gone rogue. At some point, Romanov pulls in with his bodyguards and that's when we realize our agent turned sniper was planning the oil thug's death. Our guy pops two of the bodyguards and wounds Romanov on the shoulder, before Justin could get close enough to our agent.

The thug's alive because of Justin."

"The whole story it's a bit more complicated, but, yeah, that's the gist of it," Justin said.

Abdul kept shaking his head.

"Even if Romanov agrees to lend you his Bugatti Veyron, which he would be crazy to do, how are we going to tune it up and show it to the Prince, all in less two 48 hours?" Carrie asked.

"Valerie," Justin replied.

Carrie looked sideways at Justin.

"Let me guess," Abdul jumped in, "she owes you her life as well?"

"Ha, ha, not funny," Justin said. "When I used to race, she worked for Joy's, this hotrod garage in north Montreal."

"And you dated her for some time," Carrie added. "Now, I doubt she learned at Joy's how to fine-tune Bugattis."

"You're right. She got out of there about the same time I did, oh, fifteen years ago. Now she works for Monsati, a small Italian car tuner, out of Milan. And she's already souped-up two Bugatti Veyrons."

"How come you know so much about this woman?" Abdul asked, his voice implying more than simple curiosity.

"Facebook."

"Does Anna know you're tweeting her?" Carrie asked with a wink.

Justin sneered. "I'm not tweeting her; we exchange an e-mail or two now and then. And yes, Anna knows I have friends, like she does, and that occasionally they happen to be of the opposite sex."

"So, just to clarify, your plan is to borrow Romanov's Veyron, have Valerie pimp his ride, and then we'll use it as bait for Al-Farhan?" Carrie asked.

"In a nutshell. Anyone has any better idea?"

Carrie shook her head. Abdul spread his palms.

Justin fell silent for a few seconds.

"Now, what's wrong?" Carrie asked.

"This… this plan. This crazy plan. I can't make you follow me into this hell I'm creating." Justin's eyes moved from Carrie's face to the table and then rested on Abdul.

"You're not making me do anything," Carrie said. "This is my job, stopping terrorists and their evil plots. This seems the only way to do it."

"I just feel this time we're getting very close to the fire, to a large hellish fire."

"Eh, we play with fire all the time. It's a professional hazard." Carrie tried to lighten up the mood.

Justin looked at Abdul, who was staring at them in silence. "What do you say, Abdul?"

"Let's assume everything goes without a flaw, and we do get to see the Prince face to face," Abdul said in a dry voice. He coughed a couple of times, before adding, "Then what? We tie him up? Force him to confess? What do we do?"

Justin nodded. "We'll talk to him. We'll tell the Prince we know about his plot and demand he calls off his dogs."

"And point out the obvious, that we're not the only ones who know," Carrie said. "It wouldn't hurt to add that the Prime Minister has a few dozen mukhabarat agents ready to storm the Prince's mansion if something happens in Tripoli. People dear to his heart, like his son, could get hurt."

"But there's no such a thing—"

"Of course not, Abdul," Carrie said, "but the Prince should believe an assassination attempt against the Libyan Prime Minister will cost him dearly, and he'll have to pay for it, if not in blood, then in tears."

Abdul shrugged. "When I joined the Internal Security Service, well, at the time it was called the Internal Security Agency, I vowed to protect my country. Here's a chance for me to make good on my promise." His voice, quiet at first, grew stronger and steadier. "If the government is toppled and terrorists come to power, first, they'll go after mukhabarat members, since we've been fighting them for years."

"Oh, and don't forget the reward from the Prime Minister," Justin pointed out.

"Yes, the reward, how can I forget that… If I'm still alive to enjoy it." Abdul's voice wavered and he looked out the window. "I don't want my son to receive a medal of honor for his fallen father."

Justin nodded. "I'll understand if you stay behind."

Abdul shook his head and took in a deep breath. "No, no, no," he said quickly, "worse than leaving my son as an orphan is to shame him with a coward father."

Justin laid a reassuring hand on Abdul's shoulders. "We'll try to ride this out, my friend, but it won't be easy."

"Nothing's easy. A simple ride through Tripoli can get one killed," Abdul said. "Let's get him," he added strongly. "The Prince tried to kill me." The thought of revenge had renewed Abdul's spirit.

Justin nodded. "Well then, I'll get on the phone with Romanov and convince him to hand us the car keys. If that doesn't work, then we're out of luck. If Romanov agrees, I'll call Valerie and arrange for the Veyron to be flown to Milan. Carrie, if you can find us accommodation in Nice, that would be great. Prince Al-Farhan's yacht is close by, so it shouldn't take him long to get there. And we have to look like billionaires if I'm pretending to be a rich Russian who we can afford a Veyron."

"Russian? Why do you have to be a bloody Russian?" Carrie asked, her voice filled with venom.

"Because besides Saudis, only Russians are snob enough to buy a Bugatti Veyron, and then decide it's not good enough for them and demand the car be modified to suit their whims. Plus, I speak Russian. The Prince doesn't. You'll easily pass for my trophy wife."

"I hate this part," Carrie said, "I hate it."

"I know and I'm sorry, but there's no other way."

Carrie clenched her left hand into a fist, and slammed it into her right palm. "We're running through a minefield here."

"Yeah, blindfolded," Justin said.

"What a way to inspire confidence," Abdul said with a sigh.

"Sorry, never been good at pep talk."

"We can say we're selling the Veyron since we lost a fortune in the recession."

"If Carrie's going to be your wife, who will I be?" Abdul raised his left hand to rub his chin.

"You'll be one the bodyguard," Carrie replied. "We'll come up with a cover story and stick to it."

"If God wills," Abdul whispered with a deep, loud sigh, "if God wills."

CHAPTER 23

United States Embassy, Tripoli, Libya
May 15, 9:05 p.m. local time

Romanov, the stories went, never made decisions on the spot, even when he had already made up his mind. The appearance of thorough consideration to every business deal was very important to him, and that is exactly how he was regarding this transaction. A business deal. Borrowing his Veyron may have seemed like repaying an old favor to Justin, but Romanov saw it as an opportunity to get inside the CIS. For men like Romanov, striking a deal with a CIS agent was a precious investment, which would yield a high return. At some point in the future, Romanov would be in need of assistance from Justin.

While waiting for Romanov's reply, Justin called Valerie. She sounded extremely enthusiastic at the prospect of working on another Veyron, adding her personal touch to a motoring masterpiece. That was, of course, if Romanov agreed for his two-tone, red and orange, two million dollar supercar to be flown from Moscow to Milan.

Romanov's consent came while Justin was still on the phone with Valerie. Justin placed her on hold and hammered out with Romanov all the details for the Bugatti Veyron to make it to Valerie's garage in the outskirts of Milan. Underlining the urgency of the favor, arrangements were made for the vehicle to be flown by overnight express delivery. Valerie would pick it up by 7:00 a.m. the next day.

While Justin made no mention of any tune-ups to Romanov, he discussed the proposed modifications to the Bugatti Veyron in great detail with Valerie. He left it to her, the expert, to figure out the exact makeover of the vehicle, provided that all modifications were reversible, and that the overall exterior look of the Veyron remained unchanged. After all, it was a loaner and he would have to return it to the Russian tycoon. Valerie agreed to have all work completed within twenty-four hours of receipt. It meant that Justin could show the car to the Prince two days from now, on the day of the American President visit to Tripoli.

With the largest hassles out of the way, Justin and Carrie focused on sorting out the other elements of the plan. Abdul was charged with processing the necessary paperwork for them to leave Libya without being held at the border. Carrie updated Matthew about their plan and checked on Nour. He was still in a coma, but doctors had greater hopes now that all results had returned negative. The bullet had shattered a couple of ribs but had missed Nour's lungs. There was no damage to Nour's spinal cord, and, despite the fact that he had lost a lot of blood, doctors were still hopeful of a speedy recovery. But Nour was still fighting for his life, and he was going to be under round the clock care over the next seventy-two hours.

Justin undertook the most grueling task of requesting the authorization for the operation. He was determined to go ahead with the plan regardless of Johnson's decision. Still, he preferred the advantages that came with the official approval of his chief.

Johnson approved the operation, but only for reconnaissance purposes. Justin's report had been quite brief. He informed her that a tip had come in about Prince Al-Farhan possibly stopping in France, looking into purchasing a car for his collection. Justin suggested that surveillance may result in information about the Prince's associates, without giving Johnson any exact details. *No need to find ourselves in the crosshairs of the Mossad or the CIA,* Justin decided.

After breaking for supper, the team continued thrashing out the remaining parts of their operation. Carrie pulled a few strings with the CIS post in Paris and secured access to a small apartment in Nice. The owner was an old agency contact on business out of town. The apartment was going to be their safe house while in France.

The meeting with the Prince, if it were to happen, was going to take place at Le Bataillon, a belle époque palace, converted into an exquisite hotel shortly after World War II. Le Bataillon's selective clientele and its secluded location had favored this hotel as the perfect place to meet Prince Al-Farhan. The hotel was situated just half a mile from Route Nationale 98 skirting along the coastline and overlooked the Mediterranean Sea. It was the kind of place where one would meet oil tycoons and media moguls, Hollywood celebrities and Internet entrepreneurs. Besides, it just happened to be one of Prince's favorite spots in Nice.

Over the next hour, Abdul and Justin spread the word to all the Prince's associates and their contacts that a modified Bugatti Veyron, almost in mint condition, was being sold by a Russian millionaire. It was a great deal not to be missed. They knew it was a very long shot, and they could only hope and pray it would work.

A providential hand was pulling the invisible strings because an aide of the Prince called Justin's number at exactly 11:07 p.m. The aide wanted to confirm the rumors he had heard about the sale. Justin fed the aide the information he wanted to hear. The meeting was arranged for two days later in Nice, at 11:00 a.m., at Le Bataillon. Prince Al-Farhan was going to show up in person, in order to inspect the vehicle.

Justin, Carrie, and Abdul simply could not believe this part of the plan had actually worked, at least so far. However, the hardest part, convincing the Prince to abort his assassination attempt, was just about to begin.

Matthew insisted it was too dangerous for the agents and Abdul to venture outside the embassy and offered them three of its guest suites. He sent his men to collect Justin's belongings from the Four

Seasons Hotel and the Corinthia. Around midnight, after placing a call to Anna, Justin laid his head on the soft pillow of his bed.

CHAPTER 24

Somewhere over the Mediterranean Sea
May 16, 7:30 a.m. local time

Aboard flight Alitalia 871, Justin gazed through the small window at the ash clouds engulfing the airplane. He wondered whether Anna would receive the bouquet of flowers and the chocolates he sent last night to her apartment, before leaving for her office. He knew he could not buy his way out of the guilt for not being with her on their special day. Still, it would sweeten Anna's day, even if for only a few moments. His eyes rested on Carrie, dosing on the seat next to him. A second later, she opened her left eye and gave him a curious, sideway glance. "What?"

"Nothing."

"So, why are you staring at me?"

Justin snorted. "I wasn't."

Carrie shifted in her tiny seat, her knees pressing against the back of the seat in front of her. The old Airbus A320 plane was a model of the early nineties. Small seats, no TVs, no power plugs, and now, thanks to the economic downturn, not even a tiny breakfast. Justin flicked the useless food tray in front of him.

"Now that you woke me up, are you gonna tell me what's the matter?"

Justin leaned closer to her. Since the airplane was half empty, they had sat next to each other on the second last row, with no one in front or behind them. Abdul was two rows to their right, sound asleep.

"I dreamt of Marcel last night," Justin whispered after a brief pause. "Same dream as before."

Carrie gave him a slight frown, gripped the armrests and sat up straight. Marcel was the first person Justin had ever killed.

"How come?" Her hand gently rubbed Justin's arm. Her eyes offered him a place of comfort.

He sighed. "No idea. Maybe… maybe it's because this is all a mistake, like that time, when I went alone to the warehouse."

Almost eleven years ago, in his first stint in France, Justin had arranged to meet with a source at an abandoned warehouse in Marseille. Marcel, a homeless man, had jumped from behind a garbage bin, spooking Justin. Instinctively, he had planted three bullets in Marcel's chest. Upon a closer inspection, Justin had realized that Marcel, in his drunken state, presented little more than a nuisance. The CIS station in France had cleaned up the mess, erasing whatever little trace of Marcel may have ever existed. Justin had locked away memories of Marcel. Still, now and then, the grim face of the homeless man returned to torment him.

"This is not a mistake." Carrie held Justin's hand between hers. "We're going to France. That's why you're reminded of him. And that episode in Marseille wasn't a mistake either. Overreaction, perhaps, but definitely not a mistake."

"What if I'm miscalculating the Prince? If he is really planning to kill Libya's Prime Minister, who am I to try to stop him?"

"You're the best agent I've ever worked with." Carrie's voice was full of conviction. "You're smart, brave and capable, and together, the three of us," she nodded toward Abdul, "we're going to put an end to the Prince's plans."

"I hope so, I really hope so."

"I know so and we will do it. We will."

Carrie dropped her voice and smiled at a middle-aged woman waddling through the aisle toward the washroom.

"Our plan is failsafe," Carrie added, once the washroom's door was closed, "at first sign of foul play, we pull the plug."

"That's great if we notice the foul play. This isn't a game for the Prince."

"It isn't a game for us either. We've done this before and we'll do it again. This time, we're just a few men short."

"About seventeen men short."

"Eh, details."

Justin smiled.

"Well, the good news is that Pierre is already assembling our gear," Carrie said. "We'll have cars, Russian and French passports, money, guns, the works."

Pierre Lamont was the only support Johnson had authorized for the team. After all, this was supposed to be only a reconnaissance mission.

"Pierre's a genius," Justin said.

"Yeah, he is."

"I don't have any good news," Justin said, as one of the flight attendants, a tall Italian man, walked through the aisle.

"Will you call Anna today?"

"Definitely. I'll call her from Nice."

"Well, happy birthday to her." After a brief pause, Carrie added, "And happy anniversary."

"Thanks."

"I might give Thomas a call too. He's supposed to be in Vienna today, for some kind of shareholders' meeting."

"You're still playing games with him?"

"Always." A mischievous grin formed in her face.

Fiumicino Airport, Rome, Italy
May 16, 9:15 a.m. local time

The team cleared customs in Rome without a hitch. During the thirty-minute layover, Justin placed a call to Valerie. Romanov's Veyron had arrived at the Monsati's garage at 7:00 a.m. Valerie's team was already at work on their makeover. In rapid Italian, Valerie explained the procedures, which sounded extremely complicated even for a racecar enthusiast like Justin. He decided to trust her completely, realizing it was something he was doing more and more over the last few days. He was trusting people.

Nice, France
May 16, 11:30 a.m. local time

Soon after their arrival in Nice, they stopped for brunch at Petit Café, a cozy restaurant a few blocks away from Rue St. Pierre. Carrie hid behind a large cup of cappuccino after ordering pain au chocolat. Abdul took only an espresso. Before sitting down, Justin decided to walk around the block and check if anyone was following or surveilling them.

When he returned to their table on the sidewalk, he noticed a large plate of food on the table in front of his seat.

"I got you strawberry pancakes and black coffee," said Carrie, sitting cross-legged in her chair and taking a small bite of her croissant.

"What are you getting?" Justin asked Abdul.

"Nothing."

"Eat now, 'cause I don't know when we'll do lunch."

"Why, what's wrong?" asked Carrie.

"Nothing, but our day is full and there's food here and now. So dig in."

Abdul called the waitress and ordered French toast.

"I want to survey Le Bataillon and its surroundings," Justin said between bites of pancakes. "We'll find a couple of places where we can meet the Prince and decide on how to approach him, where to park the Veyron and where to close the deal."

Carrie nodded. "I'm still waiting for some files from the office, but we know the Prince travels with an escort of twelve bodyguards. Since he's coming to us, getting past the bodyguards isn't an issue. At least for a few minutes."

"He would want to take the Veyron for a ride," Abdul said, "are you going to let him?"

"Of course," Justin replied, "but I'm going with him. That way, I have a few minutes to talk to him in private."

"The Prince may already have his men in place at and around Le Bataillon," Carrie noted. "We shouldn't stay too long at the hotel."

Justin nodded. "I agree. We'll go separately at three different times. Pierre should have our cars ready, along with the cameras, at the apartment. Take pictures of everything, so we'll become familiar with the layout."

"I've asked for the blueprints of the complex, parking lot and nearby buildings, as well as aerial photographs," Carrie said. "In case of a quick getaway."

"I don't think that will be necessary," Abdul said.

They both glanced at him, eyes wide open.

"Of course," Justin said, "it will be necessary, extremely necessary, Abdul. Do you think the Prince will just let us walk after we corner him?"

Abdul looked at the white tablecloth and scratched his head. "No, I guess not."

Carrie explained, "Unlike a recon op, we'll be in plain view. The Prince will know what we want soon before we get out. We've worked out the entry; now, we've got to figure out the exit."

"OK, I get it." Abdul took a sip of his coffee.

"Our exit will depend on the Prince's reply, which we can guess isn't going to be pretty," Justin said. "He's not accustomed to be told what to do, so our tactic will be to allow him to come to his own conclusion. We'll simply inform him of the big mistake he's about to make and warm him against it, pointing out the end result."

"And you think that's going to work?" Abdul asked.

Justin shrugged. "That's our plan. The Prince will have to make up his own mind, but we'll offer him some incentives."

Carrie placed both her elbows on the table, while Justin brought a fork full of pancakes to his mouth. "Oh, how I wish we could drill him about the assassination plot." She stirred the bottom of her cappuccino mug.

"Yes, me too," Justin added, "but that's not the plan. If we play our cards right, nothing unusual will happen in Tripoli tomorrow."

"And if he calls our bluff?" Abdul asked.

Justin hesitated before answering, "In that case may your God protect your Prime Minister, because no one else can."

Nice, France
May 16, 5:00 p.m. local time

Justin was the first to drive to Le Bataillon for his reconnaissance mission, which lasted sixty minutes. Back at their safe house on Rue St. Pierre, the team analyzed the photographs he took, comparing them to the aerial shots provided by the Agency.

After Abdul returned from his stint, around 2:00 p.m., and after more analyses of his handiwork, it was Carrie's turn to stakeout the hotel, the traffic in and out, the security, in short all aspects of the operation on the ground.

Carrie returned to the apartment at 3:10 p.m. Everything had gone well. She had not been made and no one had followed her. They printed more photographs, made more drawings on whiteboards, and drafted and redrafted more scenarios.

"I feel really good about this, now that I've been at Le Bataillon," Justin said, tapping a poster-sized aerial photograph of the hotel complex. He walked to the dining table covered with papers and made room for the photograph. "We'll use the VIP parking area to show the Veyron to the Prince, right here by the left side door." He pointed at a spot in the photograph.

"These are the last of my pictures." Carrie handed Justin a stack of about thirty 8" x 10" color photographs. She sat by the window overlooking the Promenade des Anglais and the Mediterranean Sea. A few waves slapped against an old, wooden pier, and a swift breeze raised white grains of sand. The weather had turned cold and windy, and Carrie thought it may rain, considering the gray streaks of clouds to the south.

"Where are you first meeting the Prince?" Abdul asked, hiding a yawn. Without waiting for a reply, he got up from his seat next to Justin and walked to the kitchen. "Anyone want coffee?"

"Sure, I'll have some," Justin replied.

"Make that two," Carrie said.

"I'm thinking of meeting the Prince or his aides or bodyguards at the Royal Lounge, just off the main reception area." Justin sifted through the photographs, while Abdul was still in the kitchen. "It's for the exclusive use of hotel guests. Very private."

"By the way, when are we checking in?" Carrie asked.

Justin did not answer her. He was staring at one of the photographs in his hands.

"Justin? What is it?" Carrie asked.

"When did you take this picture?"

Carrie moved closer to him. The photograph showed three men talking to each other, sitting on couches by the hotel's entrance.

"It was one of the last ones, I believe. I parked, talked to the receptionist, walked around pretending I was making a phone call. Then, I came back to use the washroom. On the way out, I snapped three last shots. Why?"

"I think I've seen one of these men before." Justin's voice was dry and cold. "Can you show me the photo on your laptop?"

"Sure."

Carrie typed a few keys and a folder with the picture files appeared on the screen. She switched to the thumbnail view.

"It's this one." She clicked on the right one.

"Zoom in the face of the man to the left."

Carrie tapped the keyboard and the face of the man filled the entire screen. The image became grainier but still sufficiently clear for Justin to reach his conclusion.

"I think he's one of the Prince's men. Let me check the files Matthew gave us." Justin looked through a couple of folders, until he found it. "Yes, look at this." He showed Carrie a picture of a man in his early thirties, with a thick black moustache. "It's the same man."

"Yes, you're right."

"What does this mean?" Abdul walked in the dining room with two large coffee mugs. "I only heard part of the story."

"This means the Prince's men are already in place. We can't risk being seen around Le Bataillon any more, if they haven't spotted us already."

"Even venturing around the city is too risky," Carrie said. "We could blow our cover."

"But what about tomorrow?" Abdul asked. "What if they recognize us tomorrow as we drive in and start shooting? Or if they recognize us as we meet the Prince?"

"They won't shoot with all hotel guests and staff around. This is Nice, not Tripoli," Carrie replied.

Justin nodded. "And tomorrow, we'll be prepared. We'll have the advantage of surprise. Even if the Prince or his bodyguards recognize us, we'll be closer to the Prince than we are at the moment. I just don't want us to run into these people today, while we're still making plans."

"What if the Prince is a no-show and this is an ambush?" Abdul asked.

Justin took a few seconds to think of an answer. "That's a possibility and a risk we take every day. Everywhere we go, everyone we meet may not be what they seem."

Abdul sighed. "OK. Let's hope this isn't an ambush. I was so looking forward to spending a night in that palace."

CHAPTER 25

Nice, France
May 17, 9:45 a.m. local time

The team left their apartment in a black Mercedes-Benz CLS 550. *If we're going to act like millionaires, we need to look like millionaires,* Justin had told Pierre, who had also found designer clothes and fashion accessories for the team. Justin had never heard of the brand names, evidence of their exclusivity. He was wearing cream-colored pants, a gray short-sleeved shirt, and a sports jacket. Carrie had put on faded blue jeans and a pink tie-back blouse with a purple cardigan. They wore dark sunglasses, and Justin had a Rolex and a thick gold chain around his left wrist. Carrie's jewelry included a white gold necklace, matching earrings, and a couple of diamond rings. Abdul, their driver and bodyguard, was dressed in a more conservative fashion: a black three-button blazer, dark blue shirt, and black pants.

Although Le Bataillon was only fifteen minutes away, Justin did not want to get bogged down in traffic, in case of an accident or a detour. According to Valerie, Romanov's Bugatti Veyron, polished and ready, was going to be delivered at the hotel at 10:30 a.m. Justin wanted to be there when it arrived, to make sure everything was in place for the meeting with the Prince.

"Relax, Justin. We got it all under control." Carrie held his right arm as Abdul stopped in front of a discrete, low, iron gate. A video intercom box with a black buzzer was attached to the white wall on the left. On the right side of the gate, small blue letters announced the visitors had arrived at Le Bataillon.

Justin nodded, as Abdul rolled down the window and pressed the buzzer. He smiled at the tiny camera mounted on top of the intercom box monitoring the entrance gate. Two seconds later, the gate swung open without a sound. Abdul pressed on the gas pedal and the Mercedes slid forward, beginning the uphill climb along the private driveway leading to the hotel.

"Let's see if the welcome team is still at two o'clock," Abdul said.

Yesterday, he had spotted two security guards hiding behind the perfectly trimmed hedges and tall cedars along the narrow road. They were stationed about a hundred feet from the gate.

Justin glanced casually at the expected guard post but did not see anyone.

"Maybe they change positions daily," Carrie said.

"I guess so," Abdul said.

Justin slid his hand over his right thigh, at the placc where usually rested his Browning 9mm.

"I feel naked without my gun," he whispered in Carrie's ear.

Abdul, their bodyguard, was the only one carrying a pistol.

"Hopefully, this will be peaceful," Carrie said.

Justin snorted. "You wish. Abdul, stay close to us."

"Of course, boss. I'm your bodyguard, remember?"

The car rounded a corner and a wide vista of the Mediterranean Sea opened up in front of them. Justin caught a glimpse of the turquoise waters and the red-roofed houses along the coast, before the lush shrubs closed the view. Then, he looked straight ahead and saw a black Rolls Royce Ghost coming from the other direction.

"Don't stare," Carrie said, "You're a Russian oil thug. You can have any car in the world. In fact, you're dumping the most powerful car ever built."

"I know, I know, but the Ghost is just… it's a work of art."

The road curved downward and Abdul slowed to take the sharp turn.

"Watch the tree." Justin glanced at an overhanging branch of an old mulberry tree. "Don't scratch the car."

"Boss, you need to relax." Abdul gazed at Justin in the rear-view mirror.

"My darling, you should try to loosen up, seriously," Carrie said in a flirty voice with a fake Russian accent.

"You know you can do better than that," Justin replied, unamused by Carrie's half-hearted effort.

Carrie shrugged and offered no reply.

Abdul turned another corner and the splendor of Le Bataillon appeared in front of their eyes. Built in a style blending late Gothic, early Renaissance and Belle Époque architectures, the palace was a miniature castle. Grayish-white stone walls with small balconies and arched windows were arranged in perfect symmetry. Green-roofed turrets and a great dome rose above the main entrance. No signs advertised the purpose of the building. One could easily mistake the palace for the residence of a French tycoon or a celebrity.

"Hey, check this out." Abdul pointed to his right.

His remark was unnecessary, for Justin had already seen the blue transport truck. Prestige Transport was written in large white letters on its side. A man dressed in a blue uniform was resting against the truck door, a clipboard in his hand. Behind the truck, Justin saw the taillights of Romanov's supercar.

"The Veyron's here," Justin said, trying to suppress the alarm in his voice.

"Our Prince is here too." Carrie nodded toward one of the hotel windows. "First floor, fourth window. Three o'clock."

Justin first glanced to the other side and slowly moved his eyes to the fourth window. A man in a red-and-white checkered headdress and a white robe, sitting on a couch, was looking at them behind dark sunglasses. He was flanked by two tall, thick men, in black suits. A second later, the man stood up, turned around and disappeared inside the room.

"Park there, at the corner," Justin said.

Abdul followed the driveway, which encircled a tall, marble fountain depicting a woman taking a bath from a jar on her shoulder.

"Let's do this." Justin opened the door.

He marched in long, hasty strides toward the truck. Abdul hunched his back and followed him closely, wearing a menacing look on his face. Carrie stood by the Mercedes, deciding to apply some lipstick and fix a few hairs that had escaped her pinned up bun. She lifted up her sunglasses and used her mirror to check the treed area along the parking lot and across the driveway.

"You're early, very early," Justin shouted at the delivery man in Russian, waving his arms wildly in the air, pointing at the Bugatti Veyron and making a phoning gesture. "You should have called, you useless man."

Justin's outburst caught the attention of a couple entering the hotel. The man, perhaps in his late forties, was dressed in a gray, pinstriped suit. The blonde-haired, long-legged model in a white and blue dress hooked onto his arm was twenty years his senior. She gave Justin a smile, which was cut short by Carrie's arrival. The man simply nodded at the two of them.

"*Dobry den,*" Justin greeted the couple. Then, he returned his attention to the delivery man, who was staring blankly into Justin's fuming face. "You should have called in advance," Justin barked at the man in heavily accented English.

"Eh, yes, we should have," the bearded redhead replied. "I couldn't find your phone number."

The calmness in his voice surprised Justin. *He must be used to rich pricks yelling at him all the time.*

"I assume you're Mr. Arkady Alexandrov," the delivery man said.

"Yes, of course, I am." Justin kept up the arrogance in his voice. A moment later, he resented it and decided to cool off his pretense. "Abdul, take care of the paperwork."

Abdul showed the delivery man Justin's Russian passport and

signed the necessary documents for the delivery, while Justin walked to the Bugatti Veyron Super Sport. Carrie was ignoring the supercar and was typing on her BlackBerry, standing at a distance of a few feet. Justin caught himself gawking at the supercar. He slid his hand over the sleek carbon fiber body and rested it over the driver's door handle.

"Can we get in now?" Carrie asked in a boring tone, playing her part.

"Hey," Justin called to his bodyguard in a snappy voice, "the keys. Now."

Before Abdul could fetch him the keys, Justin noticed two tall, thick men, in black suits coming out of the wide doors of Le Bataillon's entrance. Two feet behind, the man in the headdress walked with purpose, followed by another two bodyguards, a perfect copy of the first pair.

"They're headed this way." Justin whispered to Carrie.

"We're unprepared," she replied.

"We'll improvise."

Abdul stepped in front of Justin, as the group crossed the fifty feet distance between them and the team. Carrie stood to the side, blinking nervously.

"Arms up," one of the bodyguards ordered Abdul.

Justin nodded to Abdul and he raised his arms for the obligatory search. One of the bodyguards removed Abdul's Glock 19, unloaded it, and gave both the empty gun and the magazine to the second bodyguard. Then, he found Justin's passport in one of Abdul's pockets, inspected it for a few seconds and then handed it back to Abdul.

"I don't carry a gun. Neither does she," Justin said.

The bodyguard was unimpressed and proceeded to search him anyway. Before it came Carrie's turn, the man in the headdress spoke in Arabic, "That's good enough."

Justin straightened the collar of his shirt and the buckle of his belt. He removed his sunglasses.

"I am Prince Husayn bin Al-Farhan," the man in the headdress said in English, extending his hand toward Justin.

"A pleasure to make your acquaintance, Your Highness." Justin shook the Prince's hand. "My name's Arkady Alexandrov. I see you have arrived early."

"Yes, I have to attend to some urgent business, so let us close our deal right away."

"Eh, yes, by all means."

Justin turned on his heel and pointed at the Bugatti Veyron. "This is the merchandise, Your Highness."

Prince Al-Farhan shot a glance at the supercar, unimpressed by its glamour. Justin swallowed before proceeding with his spiel.

"Zero to sixty in 2.5 seconds. An unbelievable 1500 brake horsepower, for a top speed of 267 miles an hour, the world record of land speed. This is number three of only five World Record Editions of the Super Sport ever built. I've had it modified, adding 300 brake horsepower to the original 1200. I've raised the chassis and reinforced the shock absorbers for rough roads." Justin was repeating the words Valerie had written in a text message.

He observed the unexpressive face of the Prince, before continuing with, "Top speed is unlocked, since the racetrack tires are virtually indestructible. Other modifications are too complicated for me to understand, but this I know: This is not only the fastest Bugatti Veyron out there, but also the fastest and the most powerful car in the whole world."

The Prince's face remained calm, but Justin thought he saw a barely noticeable nod. A second later, he said, "Let's take it for a test drive," and began walking toward the Veyron.

Justin glanced at Abdul, who swiftly handed him the keys. Justin gave them to Prince Al-Farhan with a polite nod. The Prince opened the door but stopped before getting inside the supercar.

"There's a scratch mark here," he said.

Justin hastened around the Veyron and looked at the Prince's pointed finger. He squinted and barely noticed a hairline mark by the door handle. Then, Justin's eyes met the Prince's curious glare.

"Hmm, oh, yeah, my fiancée scratched it with her diamond ring," Justin said, improvising.

Prince Al-Farhan stared at Carrie, who shrugged and raised her left hand. A solitaire diamond ring sparkled on her fourth finger.

The Prince nodded and got inside the supercar. Justin glanced at Carrie and Abdul, giving them a reassuring nod. Carrie blinked at him twice, their signal that she and Abdul were going to follow them in the Mercedes. Abdul stood motionless. Justin threw a quick gaze at Prince Al-Farhan bodyguards, walked behind the Veyron, and slid into the passenger's seat.

He caught himself gawking again, this time at the exquisite details of the cockpit. Black leather and aluminum finish surrounded him on all sides. The sport seats, the steering wheel, the dashboard, the armrest, the gearbox, everything was created with pure perfection in mind. *Focus, Justin,* he said to himself, *you own this Veyron, you've been inside it many, many times.*

The Prince did not seem to notice Justin's lack of concentration, as he was starting up the Veyron. Justin had done this so many times in his mind and had seen it in so many videos. Still, it was fascinating to experience it in person. The Prince folded the edges of his robe, so it would not interfere with his driving, and pressed the start button, located below the speed stick shift. The gadgets on the dashboard lit up with bright red and orange colors. Once the Prince turned the key, the engine roared and the rear spoiler began to retract. This was the standard driving mode of the Veyron for up to 130 miles per hour, and Justin had no plans of getting anywhere close to that speed. He pulled the seatbelt over his shoulder and felt like a rocket man, with sixteen cylinders and four turbochargers of the monstrous engine strapped to his back.

"Are you ready, Mr. Alexandrov?" the Prince asked, pronouncing Justin's fake name in a slightly different tone.

Is he suspecting something? Does he know who we are?

It was too late to back out now, even if the Prince was aware of their ploy.

"I'm ready," Justin replied.

The Prince steered to the left and the Veyron rolled down the driveway. Justin threw a quick glance to Carrie and Abdul but was able to spot only their silhouettes as they headed back toward the Mercedes.

"There's a side road behind the hotel," the Prince said, as they took a downhill turn. Le Bataillon disappeared from their view, hidden behind a tall hedge of pine trees. "It's almost a closed course and there we can test this Veyron beauty."

The Prince's voice rang with excitement, and his Arab accent became thicker. Justin's mind raced to the aerial photos of the hotel and its surrounding area. He remembered a thin line of a road, but none of its details, since he had never considered it as part of their getaway. *Where is the Prince taking me?*

"How's your business doing?" the Prince asked, driving with both hands on the steering wheel.

"Has gotten worse over the last year. Too much competition in the oil business, as you know very well. Now that prices have returned to their usual levels, there's less money to go around."

"Is that why you're selling *your* Veyron?"

Justin noticed again the change in the Prince's voice.

"Yes. I don't need it anymore."

The Prince slowed down as they turned a sharp corner. The side road snaked downhill through a valley carved out between rows of twin hills. To the left, Justin saw the glimmering reflection of the sun on the Mediterranean still waters. To the right, a series of mansions with stonewall fences were nestled among small olive and orange groves.

"Let's see how it handles the curves." The Prince stepped on the gas pedal.

The Veyron raced downhill with a loud vroom. The punch of the swift acceleration threw Justin against the seat. He clenched his fingers on the door armrest, praying the sides of the supercar did not scrape against any of the orange branches. The Prince steered sharply to the left and the Veyron responded with a drift, tires squealing on the asphalt.

"Quite balanced. I'm impressed," the Prince said.

Justin glanced at him then at a speed sign as it flashed passed them. It was too blurry for Justin to read it, but he thought he saw a five in there. *Fifty kilometers an hour?* His eyes fell on the Veyron's speedometer, already registering seventy-five kilometers. The red pointer of the instrument jumped to eighty, as the Prince kept going faster and faster. Justin coughed to get the attention of the Prince, but he kept his gaze on the road. Trees, electric poles and streetlights all became a big blur.

A Peugeot appeared in the other direction and the Prince eased on the gas pedal. As the two cars passed each other, Justin noticed the wide eyes and the dropped jaw of the Peugeot driver.

The Prince grinned smugly. "It's a good ride. Sticks to the road."

He touched the throttle and shifted gears. Then he slammed on the accelerator. The Veyron's engine thundered and the supercar slid around another sharp turn, following its trajectory to perfection. Still, it came within inches from a concrete retaining wall of one of the houses. Justin saw pieces of mulch flying around and a cluster of flowers bending very close to their breaking point.

"I think you're going a bit too fast," he said finally in a low voice. "Can you please slow down?"

The Prince did not look at Justin and gave no reply. Instead, he kept the same crazy speed, now holding the top center of the steering wheel with only his right hand.

"Why? What's the problem? You're afraid we'll scratch Mr. Romanov's car?"

Before Justin could react to his blown cover, he noticed the muzzle of a small SIG-Sauer jutting out from underneath the Prince's robe. Without a word, Justin placed his hands on the dashboard.

"You look surprised." The Prince stepped on the brakes. "You're not the only one who does his homework."

Justin just stared at the Prince. A moment later, he said, "We're not the same. We don't kill in cold blood, like you."

Prince Al-Farhan grinned. "You should have taken my offer and left Tripoli when you still could. But you wanted to set up this trap." He shook his head. "And your best plan was this pathetic used car."

A quick glance at the side mirror confirmed Justin's fear that Carrie and Abdul were also captured, since their Mercedes was not following behind the Veyron. If Justin were to get out of this situation alive, he could not count on any outside help.

"You should have known it's not very difficult to find the true owners of Veyrons, especially of this limited edition series." The Prince's pistol was trained on Justin. "It was even easier to determine which of the owners would actually bargain with a secret agent."

Justin frowned. He was mad at himself for underestimating the Prince.

"You see, the bait was not the car, Justin. You and your accomplices were the true bait. You thought you were setting up this trap to get to me. Instead, this was my chance to get rid of you."

Justin's head sank between his shoulders. But his mind and his senses were very much alert. *If I appear defeated, maybe he'll let his guard down. All I need is a second.*

They were now meandering through a small forest, and soon after they began climbing the next hill. Mansions here were even bigger than the ones they had seen earlier. Their tall walls resembled those of castles.

"Where are we going?" Justin asked in a low voice.

"You'll see."

Wherever it is, I need to get out of this car before we get there.

"So, you're behind the Prime Minister's assassination?"

"No. I consider myself a powerful man, but even I would not attempt to overthrow single-handedly the head of a state. I have help. A lot of inside help."

Justin's eyes caught those of the Prince, who was staring down at him.

"And neither you, nor the CIA will be able to stop me."

"The CIA?"

"Don't even try to pretend you're not working with them. You Canadians never do anything without America's blessing."

Justin produced a tiny smile. "I'm afraid you're mistaken."

"I know you're not fool enough to try to derail my plan with just another man and a woman. If you don't want to spill out your accomplices, that's fine. Once we reach our destination, oh, I'm sure you'll spill more than your guts."

The Prince added a fierce frown to his threat. Justin responded with a sigh of surrender and a desperate headshake.

The supercar zigzagged through another set of curves. Now, they stood at the top of the hill. In the distance, over the plains separating the rows of twin hills, Justin spotted a black helicopter landing behind one of the large mansions. A second later, he saw a malicious glint in the Prince's eyes as he also noticed the helicopter.

So, that's where you're taking me, eh? I've got to make my move. Now!

As they came to a hidden driveway, leading to one of the hillside houses, Justin shouted, "Watch out," and lowered his head.

The Prince slammed on the brakes and looked to his left, expecting a car driving out of the driveway. Instead, he felt Justin's strong hands reaching for his pistol. The Prince squeezed the trigger. The SIG-Sauer fired a round and the passenger's window shattered right above Justin's head. He thrust his shoulder into the Prince, as they wrestled for the pistol.

"Give me the gun." Justin let out a deep growl.

"Never," the Prince growled back.

He hit Justin at the side of the head with his right fist, letting go of the steering wheel. The Bugatti veered off the road and into the hedge of the next house. Justin latched on to the Prince's left hand still holding the pistol, trying to unhook his fingers from the handle. Another round went off. The bullet wheezed inches away from Justin's face. It hit the windshield, smashing it to pieces. The Prince threw another punch at Justin's head, before grabbing the steering wheel. At the last possible second, he drove the Veyron away from the walled garden, but not soon enough. The right side of the hood smashed into a sandstone pillar. The impact pushed the Veyron to the wrong side of the road.

"Stop the car before we both die!" Justin shouted.

"Let go of the gun," the Prince cried out.

He struggled to control the Veyron, before other cars came from the opposite direction. He steered it slowly around the curve, and then Justin's left fist caught him under the chin. The Prince's head jerked upwards and he let go of the steering wheel. Feeling that Justin had almost yanked the gun out of his hand, the Prince pulled the trigger again. This time, the round hit the dashboard and ricocheted onto the floor. The Prince lashed at Justin's head and face, this time using both fists. A series of blows landed on Justin's left ear. He felt the warm blood seeping out of his torn skin. Enduring the pain, a moment later he was able to pry the gun out of the Prince's fingers. Jamming it into the Prince's ribcage, Justin shouted, "Stop the car! Now!"

The Prince grasped the steering wheel. Justin looked up in time to see his side of the Veyron scrape against a black chain link fence. Then, the right front tire climbed over a low brick wall in front of the next house. The Veyron began to tip over. Before Justin could do anything, the car rolled over to its driver's side. Then, it rested on its roof in the middle of the road.

"Oh," Justin groaned.

Despite the seatbelt, he was thrown around in the cockpit, his head banging against the dashboard and the roof. He looked around, trying to the shake off the sudden dizziness, and noticed the Prince had already unfastened his seatbelt and was pushing on the mangled door. Justin reached for his seatbelt buckle, when he heard screeching tires. A second later, he felt the approaching vehicle ram into the back of the rolled over Veyron. Everything began to spin around, and that blurry picture was the last thing he saw before blacking out.

CHAPTER 26

Somewhere over Tripoli, Libya
May 17, 4:45 p.m. local time

Justin blinked a few times, but his attempts did not clear up the fog in front of his eyes. He tried to lift his right hand to his face but noticed his wrists were fastened together with some kind of metal clasp. *Handcuffs. I'm handcuffed.* The second time he lifted both arms and rubbed his eyes with the tips of his fingers. Slowly, he regained his clear vision. At the same time, he felt jolts of pain erupting from his elbows and his shoulders. He realized someone had taken off his jacket. He counted a dozen scrapes and cuts on his arms, a few of which had been treated with butterfly bandages. He felt a few bumps on the side of his head and more scratches on his face. The fighting scene in the Bugatti replayed vividly in is mind. *The Prince! Where is the Prince? Where am I?*

He began to take in his surroundings. He was sitting in the corner of a small room. *This is a washroom.* His eyes rested on the shower glass door with a silver trim. Then, he stared at the white porcelain sink, its vanity and the large mirror of a semicircle shape. *What is this noise?* His ears felt plugged but still rang with a constant hum. He checked his ears with his hands, just as the entire bathroom shook sideways. *I'm in a plane,* he realized and swallowed hard, breathing in deep and pinching his nose. After a few tries, Justin heard a low popping sound in his ears, soon replaced by the same hum, this time much louder.

OK, the Prince has tied me up. Is this his plane? Is he here?

He found the small rectangular door and got up to his feet. He ignored the stabbing pain shooting up from his left knee and turned the round handle. The door was locked. He tried again, harder this time, shoving the door with his shoulder, wincing as the pain went through his entire body. Realizing he could not break through, Justin began to knock hard on the door, using the edge of his handcuffs.

A few seconds later, he heard the rattling of keys. The door opened slowly and Justin was greeted by the muzzle of a mini Uzi. He looked up at the gunman and frowned, recognizing the face. He was one of the two young men following him in the streets of Cairo four days ago, when he was going to the Castle, to meet with Carrie. *Where is she? Where is Abdul?*

With a quick flick of the gun, the gunman gestured to Justin to step out. He walked the four steps separating the airplane's bathroom from a set of glass doors, covered by orange drapes.

"Welcome back, Justin," he heard the voice of the Prince, as he entered what resembled a small lounge.

Prince Al-Farhan was lying in a white, L-shaped sofa. He was dressed in a golden robe, with a white headdress. A small cut was visible above his left eyebrow. Another man Justin had not seen before was sitting next to the Prince. He was probably in his forties, with a two days growth of stubble, black shoulder-length hair, and was dressed in a navy blue suit. The Prince's aide, Zakir, who Justin recognized from pictures he had seen, had taken a seat across a glass top table, separating him from the other two men. He was typing on a laptop balanced on his knees. Two gunmen, in dark suits and matching pants, armed with Heckler & Koch MP5 submachine guns, stood behind the Prince. Another dark suit was sitting by the other glass door leading to the rest of the private jet. A fourth guard rested against the door from which Justin came into the lounge.

"Sit down." The Prince pointed at an empty seat on a couch next to Zakir.

Justin followed his order. The man from Cairo came in and stood guard behind him.

"We thought you wouldn't join us until we completed our descent, but you keep surprising us, doesn't he, General?"

The stubbled man nodded then showed his white teeth in a big, wicked grin. "He always does," he replied in Arabic.

"So, you're his dog, doing his dirty job?" Justin asked in Arabic as well, arching his right eyebrow.

The general was taken aback by the insult in his mother tongue. Before he could respond, the gunman behind Justin slammed the metallic stock of his mini Uzi at the back of Justin's head.

"The general is a dear friend," the Prince said, once Justin had regained his composure from the blow. He picked up a wine glass from the table and took a small sip of the red wine. "You will show him respect."

Justin nodded slowly. "Sure, just help me understand this: The general here and you are going to kill Libya's Prime Minister today. You're giving him money, and he's organizing the military."

The Prince nodded. "Yes, you're right. You can say I'm the brain and he's the muscle."

"I was thinking more in terms of beauty and the beast, but I only see two beasts here."

The gunman behind him reacted to Justin's words, but Justin was quick to move out of the way and avoid the blow. The mini Uzi stock missed his head by a couple of inches.

"Enough already," the Prince shouted when the gunman tried again to hit Justin. "Your sarcasm, Mr. Hall, is not going to save the Prime Minister. Your CIA friends are not going to save him either."

"You sit and watch. Nothing will happen to the Prime Minister. Your plan has already failed. We know there's no assassination attempt against the American President. You were using her as a decoy, but your true target is the Prime Minister of Libya."

"You're right, Mr. Hall. Why bother with a puppet that will disappear from public life in four to eight years? If Libya's history teaches us anything, is that this Prime Minister will stay in power for a long, long time, like the previously toppled Colonel Qaddafi."

"But why do *you* want to kill him?"

The Prince sat back on the sofa. "We have a saying, Mr. Hall, which goes like this: It is better to die in revenge than to live on in shame. The Prime Minister has dishonored the House of Saud, my own family. Now, it's time for him to pay for his shameful acts."

"I see," Justin said. *I'm sure the fact that Libya has the ninth largest oil reserve in the world and pumps more than three million barrels of oil per day has nothing to do with your plans. But, OK, you have confirmed what I needed to know. Now, give me the details.* "The motorcade. You're attacking the Prime Minister's motorcade?"

The Prince responded with a surprised look. "You think so? That's how you would do it?"

The Prince's voice was flat, giving no hints about the attack. Justin decided to change tactics.

"Look, I've failed to stop you." He showed his cuffed hands. Then, he gestured toward the guards. "And I'm not going anywhere. At least, do me the courtesy of telling me."

The general leaned forward and seemed to be getting ready to speak, when the Prince silenced him with a headshake.

"You'll be there to watch with your own eyes, Justin," the Prince said, "but I can tell you one who's supposed to help the Prime Minister may actually end up killing him."

Justin pondered on his words. *The assassin is one of the Prime Minister's bodyguards? One of his drivers? One of his closest aides?*

The voice of the captain was heard over the public address system of the airplane.

"We have begun our descent over Tripoli, and we should land within the next fifteen minutes."

The airplane trembled slightly and Justin felt it beginning its descent. *Once we're on the ground, it's all over. If I'm to escape, I have to do it before we land.*

"What's on your mind?" the Prince reached for the wine bottle on the table and refilled his glass. "You're going to tell us where the CIA men are hiding?"

"Sure, once you tell me where and how you're planning to kill the Prime Minister."

"Mr. Hall, I don't think you're in a bargaining position."

"Think again."

Prince Al-Farhan frowned and placed his wine glass back on the table without a sip. The gunman behind Justin moved closer. Justin felt him breathing on his neck.

"The CIA's waiting for you," Justin said. "As soon as you land, you're their target." *Maybe I can convince him to call off the assassination.*

"That's impossible," the general replied. "My men control the airport. You're bluffing."

Justin opened his mouth to reject the general's claim, when the corner of his right eye caught a quick movement in between the orange drapes. It came from behind the dark suit guarding the right side entrance to the lounge. It lasted less than half a second, but he saw Carrie's eyes taking in every detail of the lounge. She was about the storm in.

"I'm not bluffing, you bastard," Justin blurted.

The gunman behind him growled, but Justin was expecting his move. As the gunman lashed with his gun stock, Justin leaned to the right, turning around in his seat. He grabbed the shoulder stock of the mini Uzi with both his handcuffed hands and pulled it hard toward him. The submachine gun slid from between the fingers of the gunman. Once his hands reached the trigger, Justin jabbed the muzzle of the weapon at the gunman's chest.

"Drop your guns," he shouted at the two gunmen guarding the Prince.

One of them began to lower his gun. The other pointed his at Justin.

"No, you moron," the Prince yelled at the defiant guard. "Put it down!"

"Drop the gun," Justin said.

"No way," the defiant guard replied.

Justin began to climb up to his feet, when his left knee jerked, hitting the glass table. The bump knocked over the wine bottle with a loud crack. At the same time, a spray of gunfire poured out of the defiant guard's submachine gun. Bullets hit the aircraft's walls, ricocheting around the lounge. One of them pierced through the man Justin had disarmed, killing him instantly. Justin was able to slip behind the couch, clenching the mini Uzi in his hands.

"No, no, stop," the Prince shouted in between shots as he fell to the floor.

His shouts were stifled by more gunfire, coming from the other gunman who had begun lowering his gun. Justin replied with a single shot, through the back of the couch, which struck the gunman. A second later, another single shot came from the other section of the plane. The dark suit guarding the right entrance to the lounge collapsed, as Carrie fired at him through the glass door. She stormed the lounge. Without a word, she planted a bullet in the second gunman's head and another one in the general's chest. The last gunman, who was standing by the left entrance, responded with a short burst. Carrie rolled on the floor toward Justin.

"You're hit?" he asked.

Carrie shook her head. "You are," she added, glancing at his bloodied arm.

"That's not mine."

A barrage ripped through the couch over their heads, just as the airplane leaned to the left. They heard the empty click of the last gunman's weapon.

"Now," Justin whispered.

He peeked through the holes in the couch and shoved the short barrel of the mini Uzi in one of them. Then, he squeezed off two rounds. The last gunman let out a muffled scream and fell over the table, his head crashing through the glass top.

"The Prince," Carrie shouted.

Justin knelt by the Prince, who was whimpering on the floor, lying on his back. Blood was gushing from a large wound in his chest. His golden tunic had turned crimson.

"No, don't, don't move," Justin said, as the Prince tried to lift his head.

The man's face was losing its color. He tried to speak but was only able to gurgle a bloody cough, followed by a raspy sigh.

"Shhh, shhh, shhh." Justin reached for a cushion from the sofa. As he tucked the cushion under the Prince's neck, he noticed the Prince's right hand twitching. His eyes were glassy and dim; his breathing barely noticeable.

"Zakir's gone," Carrie said, before kneeling next to Justin, "You think he'll make it?"

"No, he won't."

Carrie placed her hand on the right side of the Prince's neck, checking for his carotid pulse. She found it irregular and slow.

"Any last words?" She leaned over the Prince, almost whispering in his ear. "Where's the attack taking place?"

The Prince seemed to shake his head, but Justin thought it was the airplane shaking as if going through turbulence.

"Tell us," Justin said, "where's the ambush?"

"Sa… Sameer… Please don't hurt… don't hurt Sameer…" The Prince gasped, his eyes blinking rapidly. He swallowed and a mouthful of blood bubbled in this throat. A second later, his eyes stopped moving, and his head fell to his left side.

"He's gone," Justin said.

"And we still don't know any more about the attack."

The sound of running startled them, and they pointed their weapons at the right side entrance.

"Don't shoot, don't shoot, it's me," Abdul shouted, before entering the lounge.

"Abdul, I'm glad to see you." Justin climbed to his feet.

Abdul shook his head as he observed the carnage. His lips were moving rapidly but made no sound. Finally, he said to Carrie, who was still clenching her pistol, "You killed the Prince."

"You wish," she replied. "How's the kid?"

"What kid?" Justin asked.

"Sameer, the Prince's son. He's in the other lounge," Abdul replied.

"Oh, that's what the Prince was worried about. Us hurting his son," Justin said, making sense of the Prince's last words.

He began to walk toward the next lounge, which was smaller than the first one. Four guards were sprawled against the walls.

"They're all dead, in case you're wondering." Carrie followed one step behind.

"I had no doubt. How were you freed?"

"They made a mistake."

"Turned their back for a second?"

"Half a second."

"Where's Sameer?" Justin looked behind the couches.

"I told you, he's in the other lounge." Abdul had caught up to them.

"How many lounges are here?"

"Three. This is the private jet of a Saudi prince, remember?"

Justin looked over his shoulder at Abdul's grinning face. "Yes, I remember."

"He's playing videogames," Carrie said. "I bet you he didn't hear a thing."

Justin looked through a small crack between the drapes. He saw a little boy lying on the floor, in front of a large television screen, frantically handling a controller. Large wraparound headphones rested on his head. The screen erupted in a series of explosions and the boy nodded in satisfaction.

"An eight-year-old is playing Halo?" Justin asked.

Carrie shrugged. "I'm not his mother."

"Let's go in." Justin placed his hand on the door handle.

The voice of the captain coming from overhead stopped him.

"We're, hmm, we're experiencing some trouble with one of our engines, but…"

"Trouble? What trouble? Why did he stop talking?" asked Justin.

Carrie turned around, heading for the cockpit. "I'll check."

"Go with her. I'll talk to the boy," Abdul said.

Justin nodded. "Be gentle with him."

"Of course, Justin. I have a son of my own."

They walked back through the two lounges, making their way to the cockpit. Carrie threw open the door, and Justin pointed his mini Uzi at the startled faces of the captain and his co-pilot.

"Who the hell are you?" asked the captain.

"I'm the one giving you orders," replied Justin. "What's wrong with the plane?"

"I'm not sure." The captain eyes bounced between the airplane's control panel and Justin's submachine gun. "Two of our engines are not responding. There a slight loss of cabin pressure coming from the Prince's lounge."

"The hydraulics system is failing too," the co-pilot added.

"The shooting," Carrie murmured.

"What?" the captain asked.

"Nothing," Justin replied. "How far is the airport?"

"Five miles," the co-pilot said. "We're approaching from the north."

He was a bit calmer than the captain and still manning the tens of gadgets of the control system.

"What's our altitude?" Carrie asked.

The glass cockpit was wrapped in a thick curtain of gray clouds.

"Almost six thousand feet," the captain replied after reading the altimeter.

"Can we make it?" Justin asked.

The captain hesitated for a second. A loud bang came from the left side of the airplane. Carrie looked through a side window and saw a column of smoke pouring out of the engine.

"That was one of our working engines," the captain cried.

"We're losing power fast." The co-pilot fumbled with the switches. A second later, he heaved a great sigh of resignation.

"We're screwed," the captain said.

"We're crash-landing?" asked Justin.

"May Allah help us." The captain turned his complete attention to the control panel.

"Let's get ready." Carrie led the way out of the cockpit.

"I'll tell Abdul," Justin replied.

He ran to the back of the airplane. Carrie stayed in the smaller lounge, since it was the closest to a set of exit doors. She dragged the guards outside the lounge and threw away every object unfastened to the floor or the walls. Then, she began gathering all cushions and blankets next to the large sofa, in order to make a soft protective pad.

"Bring cushions from the rest of the plane," she said, as Abdul and Justin walked in. Sameer was following them, still holding his videogame controller. His face was pale and his lips were pursed.

"It's going to be OK," Carrie said to him, extending her hand. "My name is Carrie. What's *your* name?"

"Sameer." The boy shook her hand very gently. He sat next to her, on one of the cushions, following her lead. "Are we going to die too, like daddy?"

"No, we're not." Carrie rested her arm on his trembling shoulders, bringing him closer to her. "I've got you and I'm not letting you go."

Sameer smiled and tucked his head on her chest.

"I found this." Justin held Zakir's laptop in his left hand and a bundle of cushions under his right arm. "We may find some good intel in it once on the ground."

"You found the handcuffs key as well," Carrie said.

"Yeah, one of the guards had them in his pocket."

Abdul came in with a stack of bath towels and blankets.

"Spread them here." Carrie pointed around them. "The softer the landing, the greater our chances of survival."

"I'll take the suits of the guards," Abdul said.

"Hurry up," Carrie said. "I saw a safe in the third lounge," she added, this time talking to Justin.

He shook his head. "No time for that. Whatever secret it holds, it'll have to wait until we land."

If we're still alive, he wanted to add, but did not want to frighten Sameer any more, if that was even possible. The boy was curled up into Carrie's chest, sobbing quietly. Carrie was gently stroking his hair.

The airplane shook violently then took a nosedive. A great rattle came from the only working engine. Justin tightened the grip of his hands around the sofa legs bolted to the airplane's floor.

"Abdul," Justin called. "Quick."

Abdul appeared in the doorway, struggling to stay on his feet. Four black suits were wrapped around his arms.

"What's happening?" Sameer asked in a whimpering voice.

"The plane is broken. The pilots are trying to fix it and land us safely," Carrie explained.

"Will they do it?"

"Yes, they will," she said. "I hope they do," she added under her breath.

The rattle grew louder. The airplane continued to shake greatly as if going through severe turbulence. They huddled around each other, holding onto each other and the sofa, bracing for the crash-landing. Abdul was muttering a prayer. His eyes were closed, his lips moving faster and faster, as the airplane came closer and closer to the point of impact. Justin had wrapped his arms around Carrie.

"When will it be?" Carrie asked.

"Anytime," Justin replied.

The airplane's rattle subsided. The captain was decelerating for landing. He was dumping the leftover fuel from the airplane's tanks, to lower the risk of a fireball explosion on impact. He found a flat, open field and realigned the airplane's flying course. The airplane began to lose both altitude and speed at a swift pace. Its vibrations returned to a somewhat normal level. Almost a minute passed. Nothing seemed to be out of the ordinary, other than the repetitious cough of the engine.

Then the airplane crashed belly first on the ground.

The impact threw Justin against one of the airplane's walls. He shouted in pain as he rolled on the floor. Abdul's hand slipped off the sofa's legs. He slid backwards and went through the glass door, screaming in agony. Carrie kept her left arm hooked around the sofa's leg. Her right hand was embracing Sameer's body. The little boy kept sobbing.

The captain fought with the reverse thrust of the engine. He applied the brakes, which were still working. The airplane ploughed through the brush and olives and palms of the field. One of the engines broke off. The airplane veered to the left. It continued to rip through the field, albeit at a slower speed. A moment later, its wingtip fell off. Within a few seconds, the entire tail split from the fuselage, causing a large opening. Strong wind gusts went sweeping through the airplane. A fire erupted in the cockpit, and a burning odor entered the lounge. One of the wings collapsed with a large bang, but the fuselage kept sliding for a few more yards. It came to a slow stop near a row of wooden shacks.

"Out, out, out, quick, quick," Justin shouted, as soon as the airplane stopped sliding.

He checked on Carrie and Sameer and collected his gun and his laptop. He cast a glance toward the burning cockpit, realizing it was already too late for the pilots. Abdul got to his feet and began wrestling with the mangled exit door.

"It's jammed," he said after a few failed attempts.

"Move back." Justin raised his mini Uzi.

He fired an entire magazine at the door, stitching up a circle around the handle. Then, he kicked open the door.

"Let's go, before the fuel catches fire." He jumped to the ground, eight feet below.

Carrie lowered Sameer into Justin's arms. Then, she gave him the laptop. Abdul looked at the flames leaping at the entrance door of the first lounge. A wind gust blew the smell of burning plastic into his face. He began to cough.

"It's time to go," Carrie said to Abdul.

Thirty seconds later, while they were still running away from the crash site, a fierce explosion threw them to the ground. Scorched debris and metal shreds rained all around them, as the airplane wreckage turned into a burning hulk.

"Everyone's OK?" Justin asked when the fiery hail stopped.

"Yeah, we're fine," Carrie replied.

She had shielded Sameer underneath her body.

"Abdul?" Justin asked.

"Welcome back to Tripoli," Abdul replied. He lay on his back, cleaning dirt and ashes off his face.

Justin was the first one to get to his feet. He looked around to gather his bearings, and noticed an air traffic control tower to the south.

"The airport's that way. We have to get to the Prime Minister's motorcade before they reach the airport." Justin stared to his right, toward the Airport Highway connecting Tripoli International Airport to the Libyan capital.

"Let's hope we're not too late." Carrie caressed Sameer's wavy hair.

He looked up at her and gave her a shy smile. Streaks of tears were still visible on his face.

"The Prime Minister is supposed to meet the American President at the airport," Justin said. "She was landing at 5:30."

"What time is it now?" Abdul asked.

"No idea," Justin replied. He glanced at his wrist. "Somebody stole my Rolex."

"Yeah. They cleaned me out of my jewelry too," Carrie said.

Justin looked toward the highway about a mile away and squinted. He raised his hand to deflect the bright sunrays hitting his eyes, and noticed a military jeep, then a police car, followed by another military jeep. "It's the motorcade."

"Let's hurry," Carrie said.

She began to walk, but Sameer locked his arms around her waist.

"Don't leave me," he mumbled with a quiet sob.

Carrie crouched down so she could be at Sameer's eye level. "I will not leave you. Uncle Abdul will find you a safe place, a home, where you can stay until I come back. I will come back to get you. OK?"

Sameer nodded.

"Those houses," Justin said, looking at a few men running toward them from that direction. The airplane crash and the explosion had aroused their curiosity. "Let's take Sameer there and borrow a car, so we can get to the motorcade."

Abdul nodded.

"Still wanna do this?" Carrie touched Justin's arm.

He held her eyes for a second, before answering, "Of course, I want too. We've come so far; we can't stop now. The Prime Minister is not perfect, but the devil we know is better than the devils we don't."

CHAPTER 27

Tripoli, Libya
May 17, 5:10 p.m. local time

Justin drove over the rough ground and cut through a patch of scraggly shrubs. The borrowed BMW, a model of the 90s, bounced over a shallow irrigation ditch and landed with a loud bang on the Airport Highway. It fishtailed as Justin jacked the steering wheel.

"We need to get their attention," Abdul shouted from the back seat. "Before the Prime Minister arrives at the airport and before you kill us all."

"I'm sure they've seen the plane crash," Justin replied, "or the smoke from the explosion. If not, they'll see us coming."

Abdul said, "I know they'll see us. I just hope they don't shoot on sight."

"Well, here's where we need our man in the mukhabarat." Justin stepped on the accelerator.

"Wow." Carrie's hands gripped Zakir's laptop. She was in the passenger's seat, going through his files, looking for any specifics about the assassination. "Almost flew out of my hands."

"Sorry. Anything useful yet?"

"No. Lots of names and faces but no details. Not yet."

Justin swerved around a couple of cars and stared in the distance.

The last police truck of the Prime Minister's convoy came into view, about five hundred yards away. Earlier, he had counted about thirty vehicles, including the Prime Minister's white stretch Mercedes limousine.

"All right, Abdul," Justin said, "we need the chief of security. Get someone to radio him."

"I know, I know," Abdul replied, his voice shaky and tense.

He wiped large drops of sweat from his brows and his eyes. Then, he ran his hands through his hair. *At least my face will not scare them into shooting me.* He pulled out a white handkerchief from one of his shirt pockets. The flag of surrender.

Justin kept getting closer to the last vehicle in the convoy, as they were going through a straight section of the Airport Highway. Large arable fields stretched on both sides. Occasional one-story houses dotted the landscape.

"Now! Go, go, go," Justin said, when they were about fifty yards away.

Abdul sighed and stuck his head and his upper body through BMW's sunroof.

"Hey, guards, guards, hey, hey, guards," he shouted at the two guards in the back seats of the Toyota truck. He waved his hands, the right one holding the white handkerchief. "Guards, guards. Listen up."

The noise of the truck's engine drowned out his shouts.

Justin waited until Abdul paused to catch his breath and punched the car's horn. Three quick, short honks, followed by a long blare.

His alarm drew the guards' attention. The one on the right stuck his head out of the back window. The second guard pointed his AK-47 rifle at the BMW.

"Don't shoot, don't shoot," Abdul shouted, "I got to tell you something. Something important. I got a message."

The second guard fired off a warning shot. Abdul flinched and ducked, even though the shot rang out high above his head.

"Don't shoot, we're not a threat," Abdul continued his plea even louder, "I got a message. Listen to me. I need the chief of security."

The second guard lowered his rifle, leveling it to Abdul's head.

"No, no, no," Abdul shouted, closing his eyes, waving his arms even faster. "Don't shoot. Don't shoot."

Justin readied for a sharp turn, but noticed the first guard elbowing the second. He was saying something to him, which made the second guard lower his weapon.

"I think we got through to them," Justin said. The first guard was shouting at them and gesturing for the BMW to drive to the left of the Toyota.

"I would still be careful." Carrie set aside the laptop and reached for the mini-Uzi by her feet.

"Abdul, you've got to convince them," Justin said. "We've got only one chance."

Abdul replied with a cold sigh. Justin drove parallel to the police truck. Carrie hid her gun under the laptop and looked at the Toyota.

"I know you," the first guard said, "you're with the Counter Terrorism Branch. What do you want?"

"The Prime Minister's in danger. His life is in great danger," Abdul spat out his words as fast as he could, before the AK-47 was pointed at him again. "Someone's trying to kill him. Take me to the chief of security."

"Who's trying to kill the Prime Minister?"

"A Saudi prince."

"What? Who?" the guard asked over the loud noise of the truck's engine.

"A Saudi prince seeking revenge. The convoy will fall into an ambush."

"No, I can't believe this."

"Trust me, neither could I, at first. But we've got proof. Let me talk to—"

"When is this ambush happening?" the guard interrupted Abdul.

"Hmm... I'm not quite sure," Abdul said, "we... eh... we don't know that."

The guard groaned. "So, what am I to say to the chief?"

This is not good, this is not good. Justin shook his head, glancing ahead at the motorcade making a wide turn, as it reached the entrance to the airport complex. He had a clear view of the Prime Minister's stretch limousine.

"Shit, shit, shit, it's a landmine, it's a fucking landmine," Carrie shouted. She tapped the laptop screen, staring at the assassination plan she had just found. "Abdul there's a landmine right by the—"

Her words were interrupted by a loud explosion. The ground shook as if an earthquake ripped through its surface. The top layer of the highway was peeled back, throwing large chunks of concrete against the convoy's vehicles. Thick palm trees along the side of the road were blown away like matchsticks. Two trucks burst into huge fireballs. The Prime Minister's limousine flipped over to its passenger's side. The shockwave rippled through the convoy, smashing windows of other vehicles. A second later, the front of the convoy was swallowed up in dark gray smoke.

"Go, go, go, quick, quick," Abdul shouted at the guards. "We've got to help the Prime Minister."

The guards talked to the driver and the Toyota swerved hard to the right. It drove into the highway shoulder, the driver and the guards shouting at the people in the other cars. Justin followed right behind. Other vehicles rushed toward the Prime Minister's limousine. Many guards, men and women, in police and military uniforms, poured out of the cars. Justin had to slam on his brakes more than once, to avoid crushing into people scurrying in front of his car.

Just as they were entering the smoke cloud, Justin saw one of the police officers collapse to the ground. At first, Justin thought it was from smoke inhalation. Then, he saw the arm of a man in a military uniform explode with a blood gush.

"Someone's shooting," Justin said, slamming again on the brakes and putting the BMW on reverse.

"Stay back, stay back," Abdul shouted at a group of female bodyguards running next to their car, "there's a shooter."

More chaotic gunfire followed, this time from the police officers and the Prime Minister's bodyguards.

"Actually, there are four shooters." Carrie tapped the laptop screen. "The ambush is in two stages. Snipers are positioned on the second story of the airport's towers and the terminal rooftop."

"The general's men." Justin frowned.

"Yes. According to Zakir's notes, their plan is to kill the Prime Minister if he's pulled out of the car alive."

"In case the landmine didn't kill him," Abdul said. "It's so clever."

A few high caliber rounds scrapped the asphalt in front of the BMW and Justin began to back up slowly.

"We've got to tell them," Justin said, "otherwise the Prime Minister will die, if he's not dead already."

He opened the driver's door.

"I'm coming with you," Carrie said, before Justin could step outside.

Justin shook his head. "No. Talk to Johnson. She can call in help."

"What help? We don't even have a station in Tripoli."

"The Americans do. They have clout in this place. This plan may have other stages, assassinations of other government officials."

"I've got his back," Abdul said.

Carrie nodded. "If the two of you get shot, I'm gonna kill you." She handed the mini-Uzi to Justin.

Justin and Abdul doubled over as they snuck out of the car. The guard who recognized Abdul joined their group. He brought an extra AK-47 for Abdul.

"Let's get these people," he shouted, as they huddled behind an armored truck. Sporadic gunshots and gasps of pain pierced the thick cloud of smoke and dirt hanging just above the convoy.

"First, we need to eliminate the snipers," Justin said.

"You know where the snipers are?" asked the guard.

"Yes, second story of the control tower and the terminal rooftop," Justin said. "We need to tell the security chief, so that all firepower is hitting those targets."

"The Prime Minister's limo is bulletproof, but the landmine has damaged it," Abdul said. "I wonder if the Prime Minister is still alive."

"We can't extract him until all snipers are gone," Justin said.

"I agree," the guard said.

They ran along the stopped cars, the guard leading the way. Occasionally, he gestured at police and military officers, all of them positioned around their vehicles, to explain that the two civilians with him were on their side. The smoke thickened as they came near the middle of the convoy. Justin coughed and squinted, in order to see his footsteps.

Gunfire erupted to his left. He hit the ground. A heavy machine gun drummed from atop one of the military trucks. A handful of spent cartridges bounced around his feet. Justin, Abdul and the guard pressed forward and stopped when they were three cars away from the limousine. Bodyguards and police officers had formed a barricade, using two of their trucks. A few men were lying in the ditch along the road. A large man in a gray suit was shouting orders at everyone.

"That's the chief," the guard said timidly.

The chief noticed them out of the corner of his eyes. "Who are you? What do you want?" he shouted at them.

The guard relayed the information to the chief, who listened for a few seconds.

He doesn't believe us, Justin thought, as the chief turned his back to them.

The chief took a pair of binoculars from one of the jeeps and walked to the edge of the road. He took a few steps in the open field, away from the curtain of smoke. Then, he scouted the areas pointed out as the snipers' positions. Once he made out the two silhouettes shooting from the control tower, he yelled at two of the bodyguards carrying light machine guns to raze down the entire tower. Moments later, more PKM machine gun fire began hammering the control tower and the terminal rooftop. After a couple of minutes, the chief ordered everyone to cease fire.

"I think all shooters are dead." Abdul listened for any gunshots.

Justin found a pair of binoculars and surveyed the targets. All windows of the control tower were shattered. The terminal rooftop was shredded to pieces.

"I think you're right," Justin said slowly, "but I still have a feeling this is not over."

A loud, sharp siren pierced Justin's eardrums. He gazed at an approaching ambulance. It screeched to a halt a few feet away from the Prime Minister's limousine.

"Where did that come from?" Justin asked.

"There's a medical center at the airport," one of the guards replied. "Someone must have called them. Or they noticed the explosion and the fighting."

A dozen or so bodyguards rushed toward the white limousine. Two of them jammed their rifles into the twisted doors, using them as crowbars, to release the doors from their hinges. Finally, the driver was dragged out of the limousine. Then, four bodyguards escorted the shaken, but alive, Prime Minister into the ambulance. A man in a white paramedic uniform was standing by its back doors. He was glancing around nervously and looked away as Justin's gaze caught his eyes. Turning around, he closed the ambulance doors, although the bodyguards were hardly out of the way.

"Where are they taking the Prime Minister in such a hurry?" Justin asked.

"Downtown, to a hospital," one of the guards ventured a guess.

"They're supposed to hurry, since the Prime Minister is probably wounded." Abdul noticed Justin's uneasiness. "They're just trying to help."

The paramedic climbed into the driver's seat and began backing up the ambulance.

Justin turned his complete attention to Abdul. "What did you just say?"

"I said they're trying to help the Prime Minister."

Justin's face turned pale. He swallowed hard as his stomach turned. "That's what the Prince said. Those supposed to help the Prime Minister will kill him." He looked around and shouted at one of the guards, "Give me that gun."

Before the guard could reply, Justin had snatched the AK-47 from his hands.

"What are you doing?" the guard asked.

"Justin, what's going on?" Abdul said.

Justin shouldered the rifle and pointed it at the ambulance, which was rounding one of the trucks in the barricade. It drove into the shoulder of the highway, and it began to come toward Justin. As the sunlight fell on the ambulance, Justin recognized the face of the second paramedic sitting in the passenger's seat. He was the man who shot Nour.

"They're not medics," Justin shouted. "They're going to kill the Prime Minister."

"Don't shoot, don't shoot," Abdul shouted at a few bodyguards and police officers aiming their weapons at Justin.

His words were followed by a quick burst of automatic gunfire. The passenger was shooting at Justin through the ambulance windshield. One of the bullets pierced the side of Justin's left thigh. Others whizzed past his head.

"Ah," he cried, maintaining his shooting position. He pulled the trigger. His single shot went through the neck of the shooter.

Justin moved his rifle sight half an inch, aiming at the driver's head. The ambulance abruptly stopped. Six bodyguards stormed it.

"Make sure the driver is not lynched," Justin said to Abdul. "We need a witness." He dropped the AK-47 to the ground just as his left knee buckled underneath him.

"I got you," Abdul caught Justin by his waist and arms and lowered him to the ground. "We'll get a medic for you."

"OK, just make sure he's for real," Justin said with a grin.

CHAPTER 28

Canadian Intelligence Service Cairo Station, Egypt
May 18, 2:10 p.m. local time

Justin rested his wounded leg on the empty seat beside him. The bullet had sliced through his hamstring muscles but had missed the femoral artery and nerve. Still, he found it extremely painful to walk and was hobbling around on crutches. He glanced at Carrie, seating to his right. She smiled at him and opened her notebook. Across the square black table of the Maple Leaf Conference Room, George was fumbling with a keyboard, preparing their secure videoconference with the CIS headquarters in Ottawa.

"How are you feeling?" Carrie whispered at Justin.

"Great. You?"

"OK. You know we don't have to do this today."

"No, I want to. I want to get it over with."

Justin took a sip of his hot coffee. "Hmmm, thanks for making this."

"No problem."

"Well, we're almost ready," George said.

Justin coughed to clear his throat, waiting for Johnson to appear on the plasma screen on the wall. His BlackBerry chirped in his white shirt pocket and Justin picked it up. He frowned as he saw the caller's name displayed on the screen.

"George, I got to take this."

"Ms. Johnson is waiting for us," George replied with a headshake.

"I said I have to take this, in private," Justin shouted.

George flinched at Justin's outburst.

"Sorry, George, didn't mean to yell at you. I just… This is an important call and I find it hard to walk."

"You've got two minutes." George left the conference room, closing the door behind him.

The BlackBerry rang one more time before Justin answered it.

"Hello, Mr. Romanov, how are you?" Justin pressed the loudspeaker button and placed his BlackBerry on the desk.

"Fine, I'm doing really fine. But I hear you're not doing so well."

"You've heard it right."

Justin sighed before continuing, "I meant to call you earlier, but I had a few things to do. Hospitals to visit and such. With regard to your Bugatti Veyron, I'm afraid I owe you an apology."

"I'm listening."

"I got into an accident while in the Veyron. Unfortunately, the beauty is wrecked."

Justin hated the ensuing tense silence, which lasted for several long seconds.

"Is that it?" Romanov asked in a flat voice.

"Eh, yes. I'm very, very sorry about this and I will—"

"Don't worry too much about it. It was just a car. I'm glad you are doing well, my friend."

"Pardon?" Justin said, glancing at Carrie. Her face was filled with great wonder, just like his. Romanov was not concerned about the supercar reduced to a heap of scrap and was calling Justin 'my friend.'

"I didn't like that car very much."

"Eh, why is that?"

"The ashtray was full."

Justin and Carrie heard Romanov's loud gurgle as he laughed at his own joke. There was a moment of silence, then they heard

Romanov's voice again, "Plus, I could have never gotten two million dollars for it, like I did from your old man Carter." This time Romanov was dead serious.

Justin face froze at the mentioning of his father's name. *What has he done to me?*

Carrie leaned over the phone. "What did you just say?"

"Hey, Carrie, nice to hear from you."

"Can you repeat your last?"

"About Mr. Hall, Senior? Sure. He vouched for his son, in case something went wrong with my car."

"You're lying, you bastard."

Romanov snorted. "I'm glad to see you haven't changed a bit. You think rich people are just a bunch of pricks, corrupted by their money don't you?"

"No, I don't *think* that. People like you *show* me that."

"Well, let me *show* you something else, Carrie. Money is not that bad. It can buy you things. Like possibilities. Without Mr. Hall's guarantee, you would have not gotten my Bugatti. In turn, you would have not been able to execute your operation."

"That doesn't make you less of a slimeball."

"I'm not finished, Carrie. Sometimes money can buy information. Like classified FSB files from the Soviet era. About foreign army colonels in covert ops in the dead of winter. Around 1988. Still with me?"

Carrie slammed her fist on the table. The BlackBerry bounced, flipping over. Justin reached and turned it over.

"Don't you even dare to talk about my father, you—"

"Let me finish, Carrie. I have some information that may help you in your investigation. The personal one. I'll send it tomorrow."

"I don't want anything from you."

"Romanov, I *will* pay you back," Justin said. His voice was weak, still recovering from the early shock.

"No, I will not accept double payment."

Another ringtone sounded in the distance. Romanov began

speaking in unintelligible Russian. A few seconds later, he said, "Justin and Carrie, I have to go, but get better soon, OK?"

Justin ended the call without saying a word.

"What is he up to?" Carrie asked.

"I have no clue."

As if eavesdropping behind the door, George entered the room before Justin could even put his BlackBerry back in his pocket.

"Ms. Johnson is losing her patience," George said, wiggling a cellphone in his hands. "We should start our conference call now."

"I think you'll have to take this alone, Carrie." Justin struggled to stand up on his good foot.

Carrie helped him with his crutches. "Are you OK?"

"I will be, after I talk to him. It shouldn't take long."

"No rush. Take your time."

Limping outside, Justin crashed into one of the seats of the small waiting lounge.

"I need some privacy," he told the assistant behind her desk. "Take a coffee break or something. Those phones can wait."

The young woman nodded and left the room in silence. Justin dialed his father's direct office number. Carter answered the phone after its first ring.

"Tell me, why did you pay Romanov?" Justin barked on the phone.

"Justin, how are you?"

"I was fine until I heard you stuck your nose into my work. Again. Why do you keep doing that, eh? Why can't you just stay away?"

Carter sighed. "Because I care about you, my son."

"Stop caring about me. I'm a grown up man and I can take care of myself."

"I know you can. You could do that even when you were a child."

"Well, it's about time you learn to leave me alone. If I need your help, I'll ask you."

Another sigh, this time deeper and sadder. "I'm afraid I don't have time to learn that or anything else."

"Why? Why is that?" Justin asked gruffly.

"Justin… Last week I found out I have cancer. The prognosis is not good. A few months, a year at the most."

It was time for Justin to let out a sigh. "No, no, this can't be. You're a strong man, a very strong man."

"I used to be. Now, I'd like to ask you something. I'd like to see you one last time, before—"

"Of course, Dad. I'll be home tomorrow."

Justin had not called Carter "Dad" for over twenty-five years. He had not stepped foot inside Carter's home in Toronto in nineteen years. He knew he was breaking every promise he had made himself all these years. But he also knew his dad needed him at this moment, and he was going to be there.

"Thank you, my son."

"No, thank you… Dad."

Justin's left eye had produced a small tear. He rubbed it away quickly before the assistant or someone else saw it. He felt weak and empty and it was not because of his wounds. Justin took a few deep breaths, trying to slow down his racing heart. Then, as the assistant reappeared, he struggled to climb to his feet and limped back to the conference room.

Carrie was midway through her debrief, describing the course of events that took place in Nice. Johnson was in her office and had placed her camera on the left side of her computer monitor.

"Oh, Justin, welcome, welcome." Johnson's voice was colder and sharper than usually. "I'm glad you could join us."

Justin brushed away her sarcastic bite with a nod and perched himself on his seat.

"Carrie was telling me about the *unauthorized* Nice operation. What do you have to say?"

"Not much. The results speak for themselves. We stopped the Prince's attempt on the Prime Minister's life. Everyone is safe."

Johnson frowned. "I think you're forgetting something. You're forgetting how you endangered the lives of Carrie and Abdul, by running this clandestine operation, for which you had no authorization whatsoever. You put the lives of CIS agents at risk, and also the reputation of our entire Service, by operating illegally in a friendly, ally country. On top of that, a Saudi prince is dead and my agents are the primary suspects."

"I agree, Madam Director. I miscalculated the Prince and his reaction to our plan. I believed he was going to refrain from violence. I admit it. I was wrong."

Johnson nodded, pleased at Justin's confession.

"However, Carrie and Abdul knew what they getting into, and they went to France upon their own free will. And I was there with them, all the time. I went with them all the way. I never mislead them or held back vital intel."

"Are you accusing me of any indiscretion, Mr. Hall?"

"Yes, I am. You should have told us you gave the Mossad the location of our meeting with Sheikh Ayman and that the Mossad was active in Sudan to kill him."

"That was irrelevant to your mission."

"I disagree. The Mossad attack almost killed two CIS agents and cancelled our extraction plans."

Johnson's face came very close to the screen. "Your disagreement is duly noted," she said in a solemn tone as if rendering a final verdict.

Justin did not blink. "Providing misleading information about our Prime Minister's visit to Tripoli was even a greater offence. You put two of your agents in harm's way. Intentionally."

"At the time when I ordered you to go to Tripoli it was uncertain whether our Prime Minister was going to attend the G-20 meeting—"

"With all due respect, Madam Director, that's bullshit. The Prime Minister never planned to go to Tripoli. You knew it and you chose to lie to us."

Silence fell on the other side of the line. Johnson leaned back in her chair. She tried to maintain a certain amount of composure, but there was an almost invisible twitch at the corners of her lips. She clenched her jaws and her left hand fingers closed tightly around her coffee mug.

"Justin, you'll go on administrative leave. A few weeks of holiday would do you—"

"Listen to me, Claire," Justin said.

George shook his head. Carrie kept staring at Justin. Nobody ever dared to call the Director General of Intelligence by her first name.

"Justin, shall I remind you of protocol?"

Johnson's blazing eyes made such a reminder unnecessary.

"Claire, you have one hour to resign from all your duties with the CIS."

"What? What did you say? Are you crazy?"

"I will not allow you to endanger the lives of agents serving their country with their blood and their soul. Leave now, and you'll will leave with honor."

"Or what, Justin?" Johnson sputtered out her reply. A tiny drop of her saliva landed on the video camera. "What are you going to do?"

"If you're still around, you'll see."

Justin grabbed his crutches and began to stand up.

"Hey, where are you going? This is not over; it's not over, Justin."

"You're right. It's not over." He didn't look back. "I still have one last thing to do."

"Let me help you." Carrie was already on her feet. She whispered in Justin's ear, "I really hope you know what you're doing."

"Trust me. I know what I'm doing."

"I do trust you."

They left the room, paying no attention to Johnson shouting vile threats.

EPILOGUE

Cairo International Airport, Egypt
May 19, 8:25 a.m. local time

Justin nursed his water bottle, patiently waiting for Carrie to return from her phone call. Thomas had just called and their plane for Toronto was not leaving for another hour. If it were up to her, Carrie would talk to her boyfriend for that entire hour.

"Eh, there you are," Abdul shouted from across the departure hall. A few passengers looked up with curiously mixed with annoyance at the loud interruption.

"Hey, Chief," Justin greeted him once Abdul was a couple of feet away, "or should I say General?"

"Shhhh, don't use that word." Abdul sat next to Justin. "After the plot, the Prime Minister hates generals." His eyes darted around the hall for anyone eavesdropping on their conversation. "Conspirators were everywhere, in the Assembly, the Ministry of Defense, everywhere. However, after they learned the attempt on the Prime Minister's life failed, they mounted very little resistance. A few of the Alliance fighters were able to leave the country, though."

"So, what was your reward for all your hard work?"

"I got the position of Colonel Haydar. You're talking to the new chief of the Counter Terrorism Branch for Tripoli."

"That's great. Congrats."

"It was thanks to you."

"No. Your put your life on the line. It's the least the Prime Minister can do for you."

Abdul nodded and patted Justin on his shoulder.

"Did you find Colonel Haydar's body?" Justin asked.

"No. I don't think we'll ever find it, but we'll keep looking."

Justin nodded.

"But we found Tarek's body."

"You did?" Justin asked with excitement. "Tell me he's really dead."

"Dead and rotting. Someone obviously retrieved his body from the scene of that attack but never got around to burying it."

"I'm glad you found him."

"This morning I got an important call," Abdul said. "Guess who it was?"

"The Prime Minister?"

"No, he called yesterday. I'll give you a hint. It's a prince."

"Oh, that's really helpful."

"A Saudi prince."

"That narrows it down to about five thousand."

"Someone very close to Prince Al-Farhan."

"Now you're making it too easy. It was one of his brothers, Prince Fouad bin Al-Farhan."

Abdul peered curiously at Justin. "How did you…"

"I know because he called me too. Thanked me for saving Sameer and told me he's going to take care of the kid."

"Did he make you an offer you were tempted to accept?"

"Yeah, he offered to make a small donation to a charity of my choice."

"I was so close to saying 'yes' when he made me the ten million dollar offer."

"But I'm glad you said 'no.'"

Abdul nodded. "I don't want to be in debt to anyone," he said quietly.

"Neither do I. How is Nour doing?"

"Stable. You know, he came out of his coma yesterday."

"Yes. I saw him last night before leaving Tripoli. I also talked to Matthew, who said they found the mole in the White House admin. Remember, we were wondering how all that information about the US President's schedule got out? Some intern in human resources was working for one of the Prince's associates in the States."

"That's good."

Justin took another sip of his water. Then, he glanced at his watch and at the television screen mounted to the ceiling ten feet away. It was tuned to CNN.

"You shouldn't miss this." Justin drew Abdul's attention to the news edition, about to start in a few seconds.

"What, American politics?"

"Be quiet and listen."

The anchorwoman, a voluptuous blonde, opened up the newscast with breaking news. In a clear, solemn, yet somber tone, she read from the teleprompter. "The identity of a senior official with the Canadian Intelligence Service was revealed in today's edition of *The New York Times*." The screen switched to a picture of Johnson. "Ms. Claire Johnson, the CIS Director General of Intelligence for the Western and North Africa Division, is suspected of leaking information about covert operations to secret intelligence agencies of several countries, including the CIA. The latest of these leaks surrounds the alleged assassination attempt on the US President during her trip to attend the G-20 meeting in Tripoli, Libya."

"I can't believe you did this." Abdul's eyes almost popped out of their sockets.

"I offered Johnson an exit option. She didn't take it."

"She'll have to retire?"

"Absolutely. She's burned. She has to go away. For good."

"But won't the CIS inquiry link you to this leak?"

"The inquiry will show I had a disagreement with Johnson on how she handled certain aspects of our operations. However, this job was done by someone else."

"Who?"

Justin smiled. "Someone the CIS won't find."

Abdul did not insist. Justin wanted to tell Abdul how the Mossad had agreed to leak the information about Johnson to their trusted sources in *The New York Times.* The price Justin had to pay for this leak was not cheap. He had to confirm that Prince Al-Farhan, one of the most wanted people on the Mossad's hit list, was terminated. The laptop of Prince's aide, Zakir, contained a recording of all the events taking place aboard the Prince's Boeing 707. *The paranoid Prince and his cameras installed everywhere. I just hope that recording doesn't end up on YouTube or Wikileaks.*

"Hi, guys," Carrie said in a bubbly voice. Her face radiated with happiness. "Guess what Thomas did?"

"Really? He proposed? That's wonderful," Justin said.

"Yes, he just did. On the phone… but he did it."

She held Justin close in a tight embrace, under the gawking eyes of Abdul.

"Congratulations," he told her when she sat next to them. "When's the big day?"

"Oh, we haven't gone that far."

Her voice faded as she looked at her leather briefcase on the floor.

"There are so many things to do." Her left hand rested over the briefcase handle.

Justin understood her concern. Abdul did not. "Yes, yes," Abdul said, "a wedding has so many preparations. The dress, the place, the guest lists, the photographer…"

Carrie tuned him out. She was tempted to open her briefcase and look again at the photograph of which every detail was engraved in her memory. Last night she had received an envelope sent from Romanov. It contained a single photograph of a wooden cross placed upon a tomb. The inscription on the cross read: O'Connor. An address was scribbled on the back. Northern Grozny, Chechnya. *If this is Romanov's idea of a sick joke, I'm going to kill the bastard,* Carrie had thought more than once. But deep down she felt the photograph was real. She just hoped the tomb contained her father, the man she had searched for most of her life. *After I see mom and Susan, it's time to visit Grozny.*

"Is it time to go?" She looked at her wristwatch, in order to hide her watery eyes rather than check out the time.

"Yes, we should go," Justin said with a nod.

"When will you be back?" Abdul asked.

"Oh, I'm planning on taking a long break."

"Vacations in some place warm?"

"That too. But first I need to attend to some family affairs."

"Family affairs? I thought you said you had no family."

"I do have a family now," Justin said.

"Eventually, he'll go sailing with Anna." Carrie smiled.

"Yes, I should do that. If she finds out I went to France without her, I'll be in big trouble."

"So, everything is well now?"

"Oh, yeah. She'll be glad to finally see me."

Justin stood up and stretched his hand toward Abdul. "Goodbye, my friend."

Abdul spread his arms and hugged Justin. "Be safe." A moment later he added, "I can't believe I'm saying this, but I hope to see you soon."

"We'll miss you, Abdul," Carrie said, as Abdul embraced her as well. "Thanks for everything."

Justin pulled the handle of his suitcase. Carrie picked up her briefcase.

"Time flies," Justin said, "but it won't be long before we're back."

AUTHOR'S NOTE

I would love to hear your thoughts about this book and you can always reach me at Ethan.Jones@shaw.ca. I promise to answer all e-mails.

It will be greatly appreciated if you can take a few minutes today and post a review on Amazon and other book retailers' websites. Your opinions are really important and they can help other readers learn about this book and my style of writing.

My blog at http://ethanjonesbooks.wordpress.com is the place to learn about my future works, to enjoy exclusive book reviews and author interviews. You can also follow me on Twitter at https://twitter.com/EthanJonesBooks or find me on Facebook page at http://www.facebook.com/pages/Ethan-Jones/329693267050697

BONUS CONTENT FROM FOG OF WAR

Please enjoy the prologue and Chapter One of Fog of War, the third novel in the Justin Hall series.

When an Iranian nuclear scientist wants to defect, the Canadian Intelligence Service sends in its best agent, Justin Hall. After his mission is compromised and Justin barely escapes northern Iran with his life, he sets out to discover who has put him and the Service in grave danger.

CIA information about a traitor in the Service sends Justin into violence-soaked Somalia, where he quickly becomes ensnared in a web of lies and deceit. He's left with no choice but to go rogue and form an alliance with Romanov, a sinister Russian oil baron.

Cut off from the Service, Justin is forced to navigate through ever-shifting alliances and survive deep inside a Yemeni terrorist stronghold. All the while, he's being hunted by a traitor.

This tour-de-force spy thriller is the hottest page-turner of the summer. New and old fans alike will love this new suspenseful novel in the Justin Hall series.

PRAISE FOR FOG OF WAR

"I've enjoyed all the Justin Hall thrillers, but I have to say, they just keep getting better." -- Marc Cameron, author of the bestselling Jericho Quinn spy thriller series

"It read authentic, real and compelling . . . a story that was both hardboiled yet believable." -- Andrew Kaplan, author of the bestselling Scorpion spy thriller series

PROLOGUE

Afmadow, southern Somalia
September 20, 3:30 a.m. local time

Bullets hammered the MH-60 Black Hawk. The Navy SEALs squad leader Alex Roberts glanced at the control panel in front of him. The last mud-brick shacks of the village were falling behind, but the hail of bullets was relentless. It seemed like everyone on the ground was taking aim at their helicopter. People were shooting from the streets, from the trucks, from the rooftops of this stronghold of al-Shabaab, al-Qaeda's branch in southern Somalia. Rocket-propelled grenades ripped through the night sky with their amber streaks, missing their target by sheer luck. The Black Hawk could withstand small-arms fire, but not RPGs. Their warheads could disable the helicopter's rotors and force a crash landing.

Roberts looked at two squad members shattering the night with their M134 machine guns. The weapons were pouring forth a torrent of bullets at two thousand rounds per minute. He could not see it, but he was sure some of those bullets were shredding al-Shabaab militants engaged in the firefight.

Seconds later, the Black Hawk veered to the right, and the Islamic bastion disappeared into the darkness. The hail-like sound of bullets died down. Roberts looked back at the gunners falling in their seats and then at the other five members of his squad, who were securing their "cargo," the targets of this operation, in the back of the helicopter. Two high-ranking al-Shabaab leaders lay tied, gagged, and blindfolded on the cabin floor.

"What's our status?" Robert asked.

"We're clean. All systems seem functional," the pilot replied, glancing at Roberts in the co-pilot's seat.

Roberts nodded. "You all did well down there. In and out in fifteen."

The snatch-and-grab operation was executed with the assistance of Joint Task Force Two, the elite Canadian counter-terrorism unit of the Special Operations Forces. Canadian Intelligence Service had obtained actionable intelligence on the target, and CIA had engaged one of their local assets. Their man on the ground had confirmed the target's location thirty minutes before the start of the operation.

The SEALs dropped into Afmadow's outskirts, neutralized the guards, and plucked the two militant leaders out of their safe house. The SEALs actions had drawn the terrorists' fury, but their backlash was weak and easily counteracted. Hellfire missiles and machine gun fire had kept them at bay. The SEALs were now on their way to extract CIA's man, Mussad Weydow. Their meeting point was another village twenty miles to the west. Then the squad was to proceed to the safety of Dhobley, a village close to the border with Kenya, in the hands of African Union peacekeepers.

"Will we be late?" asked Roberts.

"Negative," replied the pilot. "We'll make up the lost time."

One of the militants jerked, kicked up his feet, and rolled against the cabin door. Walker, one of the gunners, leaned over and lifted the man's blindfold. "We said don't move, so don't you dare to move," he shouted in Arabic.

The militant's gray eyes burned against his dark face. He mumbled something, but the rag stuffed deep into his mouth made his words inaudible.

Walker pulled down the blindfold and pushed the man back to his place next to the other detainee. "What a prick," Walker spat out his words, "luring kids into this kind of a shithole life."

"Chill out, man," said Green, the other gunner. "They'll pay for it soon enough."

"Yeah, but how many innocents have they brainwashed so far?"

Green nodded with a sigh. Al-Shabaab had recently stepped up its aggressive recruitment campaign. US- and Canadian-born Somalis joined it in droves. The name al-Shabaab meant "the boys" in Arabic, and they lived up to it. The terrorist network kidnapped children as young as ten from all over Somalia and forced them to fight. Many foreign fighters from Afghanistan, Iran, Lebanon, Yemen, and Syria had also joined al-Shabaab's army, which claimed around fifteen thousand fighters.

"Green, is our contact in place?" Roberts asked.

"He should be. Last time I checked, he was two miles away from the exfil point. That was five minutes ago, give or take. I'll call him to confirm his current position."

Green dialed Weydow's number on his satellite phone. He talked for a few seconds then hung up. "Weydow's waiting at the abandoned warehouse, a mile east of the village. Everything's going according to plan."

"We'll be there in five," the pilot said.

* * *

The warehouse was a one-story cinder block building smaller than a school bus. It had a tin roof and was surrounded by a thatched fence with large holes and an open metal gate. Green switched on his night-vision goggles and looked down from the helicopter. Everything took a greenish tinge with a grainy feel. He spotted a small acacia tree behind the warehouse, the hulk of a large truck, and other debris scattered around in the yard. Weydow's white van was nowhere in sight. "Where is Weydow?"

"Don't see him," Walker replied. He was also scanning the

warehouse and its surroundings.

"Maybe he's inside," Green said.

Roberts pondered their options. At the relatively safe altitude of one thousand and five hundred feet, he could not observe the situation on the ground with accuracy. But he did not want to land until they had a visual on CIA's man. On the ground, the helicopter was a sitting duck. They had carried out their operation so far with barely a scratch. He did not want to put his men needlessly in harm's way.

"Call him again," he ordered Green.

Green dialed Weydow's number. No signal. He tried again. Again no signal.

"He's not answering. Must have turned off his satphone."

"What? Why?" Roberts asked.

"No idea."

"He's afraid someone will trace him?" Walker said.

"Who? Al-Shabaab? It doesn't have that kind of gear," Green said.

Roberts shrugged. "You never know. Weydow didn't last this long in this hell of a place by being careless."

"We're landing?" Walker asked.

Before Roberts could reply, the warehouse's metal doors swung open.

"Wait. There's movement," he said.

A white van zoomed outside the warehouse. The driver swerved around the acacia tree and headed toward the gate. Something resembling a spare tire was strapped to the front of the van.

"What? Where's he going?" Roberts asked.

"I'm sure he can see us. He knows we're coming. What's going on?" said Walker.

An RPG warhead rushed toward them. Roberts saw it at the last moment, too late to do anything to avoid it. The warhead flew past them. It missed the Black Hawk's main rotor by about three feet. A plume of gray smoke engulfed the helicopter.

"Ambush!" Walker shouted.

The pilot tilted the helicopter to the left, dropping out of the smoke cloud. Another RPG tore up the dark sky. This one widely missed its mark.

Walker pushed the cabin door to the side and rushed into position behind his M134 machine gun. Muzzle flashes lit up the left side of the warehouse. He focused his firepower at that target and kept his finger on the trigger. The bullets tore chunks out of the cinder block walls.

The pilot turned the helicopter around. Two shooters came into Green's line of fire, and their muzzle flashes soon died. "Got the shooters by the acacia."

"Nailed the three on the left," Walker replied.

Roberts looked at the white van. It was quickly disappearing in the distance. He made a swift decision. "We're going after them. Green, advise the command. Tell them we'll be late."

"Right away, sir."

Green got through to the command center in Nairobi, Kenya and updated them on their status.

"How did they know we were coming?" asked one of the SEALs from the back.

"They've gotten to Weydow and made him talk," Roberts said in a tense voice.

"You think he's in the van?" asked Walker.

"Not sure—"

A loud bang rattled the back of the helicopter, almost jolting Roberts out of his seat. A moment later, the control panel beeped a sharp sound of alarm.

"We're hit," the pilot said. He studied the screens in front of him. "An RPG clipped our rear rotor."

"We're going down?" Roberts asked.

"Yeah, we're going down," the pilot replied.

The Black Hawk overtook the white van. Roberts squinted but could not make out the driver. The ground sped toward them fast and hard. The pilot slowed down. He tried to seal the helicopter's fuel lines to avoid an explosion on impact. Roberts braced for the crash landing, a sick feeling forming in the pit of his stomach. His team was going down on his watch. He muttered a short prayer.

The helicopter swerved in a large circle. It tilted to the left and began another turn. The pilot struggled with the system controls. He tried to level the helicopter and execute a somewhat controlled crash landing. The main rotor stopped turning. The Black Hawk fell into gravity's clutches. It completed another 360-degree turn.

Then it crashed on its starboard side.

The impact rolled the helicopter over. The main rotor blades crumpled as if made of tinfoil, the metal crunching and the glass shattering all around them. The cabin walls closed in. Everything not fastened to the Black Hawk's airframe was hurled around the cabin like balls in a bingo blower. The pilot's crashworthy seat protected him from the direct impact, but the windshield folded in as it hit the ground, killing the pilot and Roberts instantly.

The Black Hawk exploded into a million fiery fragments.

CHAPTER 1

Twenty miles east of Khan Giran, northeast Iran
September 20, 11:15 a.m. local time

Justin Hall glanced through his binoculars at the dirt road down in the valley, expecting to see the silver Toyota of the Iranian defector. His eyes took in the vast semi-desert, the scrub and the gas pipeline alongside the road, the hot air sizzling over the ground, but no sign of the car. He wondered if the nuclear physicist had changed his mind. Or worse. The Islamic Revolutionary Guards or one of the Iranian intelligence services had caught him.

He sighed, blowing at the sand in front of his face. He was on his stomach, observing from a vantage point atop one of the jagged hills in this remote part of northeast Iran. The sun had been baking the land for the last two hours at a constant ninety degrees. Justin wiped the sweat off his brow with his tan headscarf. He took a few sips from his canteen. The warm water did nothing to quench his parched throat.

Justin glanced at the road again, this time through the scope of his C8 carbine. Something moved on the side of the road. A flock of goats, seven, no eight, and a young boy, perhaps no older than eleven, driving them toward the road. Justin smiled as the boy looked both ways for traffic before taking the livelihood of his family to the other side. One of the stubborn goats decided to relieve itself in the middle of the road. The boy ran and shooed it away, back to the flock.

There had been no sighting of a car, not even a motorcycle or a bicycle, for more than an hour. Along with Nathan Smyth, his partner in this clandestine rescue operation of the Canadian Intelligence Service, Justin had travelled early in the morning from Turkmenistan up north. The team had crossed through the porous border with the help of two Turkmen drug runners familiar with the broken terrain. This area had been a theater of war during most of its five thousand years of history. It remained a lawless haven and a preferred route for traffickers smuggling Afghan opium to Russian and European markets. Persians, Pashtuns, Uzbeks, Turkmens, and Arabs lived in a state of a delicate balance of power shared among tribal leaders and clansmen.

"What are we going to do?" asked Nathan, stretched next to Justin. He leaned back against a large boulder, seeking shelter from the scorching sun.

"We'll wait," Justin replied.

"Our guides are growing restless."

"They'll have to wait, like we do."

Justin hung his binoculars around his neck and crawled back. Once he was behind the boulder, he got to his feet and shook the dirt off his desert camouflage fatigues. He took another sip of warm water and used it to wash his dried mouth. He headed toward the battered Nissan Pathfinder of the drug runners. They were supposed to keep watch on the other side of the hill overlooking the steep path leading to the top. Justin found them sheltered away from the heat, enjoying the air conditioning in their cabin, glancing occasionally at the path through the windshield.

One of the guides, the younger one sitting in the driver's seat, rolled down the window. "Your man is not coming," he said in English with a heavy accent. "We should go back."

Justin shook his head. "No. He'll come. We'll wait."

Ruslan, the older guide, rolled down his window. He gave Justin a deep frown and a stern headshake. "This is not the deal we had. We brought you here two hours ago. You were meeting someone at ten. It's now eleven thirty. We must go back," he said in Arabic.

Justin stepped closer to Ruslan and locked eyes with him. He replied to him in Arabic, "I made no deal with you. You have a deal with Colonel Garryev. Your deal with him is to bring us here and take us back once we've finished our job. As you can see, we haven't."

Ruslan seemed unfazed by Justin's words. "Every minute we stay here we risk being discovered. I know government troops patrol this area. You know they hang drug traffickers in this country, do you?" He rubbed his thick neck as if to emphasize his point.

And you know what they do to foreign secret agents derailing their nuclear program?

The thought brought back bitter memories. Five years ago. The deepest, darkest cells of Tehran's Evin Prison. He spent a long week in solitary confinement. The jailers fed him moldy bread and foul water but put him on a healthy diet of daily beatings. It took the intervention of Canada's Prime Minister, complicated negotiations, and an exchange of favors before Justin was allowed to go home.

Justin nodded. "I know what they do. You're not going to lose your necks. Another day perhaps, but not today."

Ruslan grinned. "Another thirty minutes. If he's not here, we're driving back, with or without you."

Justin shrugged and walked to the edge of the path. A light breeze toyed with the loose flap of his headscarf. He took a deep breath, enjoying the temporary relief from the dry air. He lifted the binoculars to his eyes and searched the bottom of the hill and the surrounding area. No sign of human or animal life. Just patches of scraggly brush, rock boulders, and sand. A lot of sand.

He turned around.

Ruslan gave him a frown and tapped the gold Rolex on his wrist. "Another thirty minutes, Mohammed," he said.

Colonel Garryev from Turkmenistan's Ministry of National Security had introduced the two agents to Ruslan as Mohammed and Mehmet—Nathan's idea, since he loved M&M's chocolates. They were liaison officers of the Kurdistan Workers' Party, better known as the PKK, a terrorist group waging war against Turkey and seeking the creation of an independent Kurdistan. The two officers were to obtain information from a reliable source about operations of the Islamic Revolutionary Guards. One of the PKK's largest bases in northern Iraq had been attacked by a joint Turkish and Iranian force, giving credibility to the Canadian secret agents' cover story. Colonel Garryev knew the true identities of Justin and Nathan, but he was in the dark about the nature of their operation in Iran.

Nuclear physicist Massoud Safavi had made his first contact with the Canadian Intelligence Service three months ago. He had promised the CIS his vast knowledge of Iran's uranium enrichment program and its plans to build a nuclear bomb. In exchange, Safavi wanted a new life in the Western world.

The CIS had checked, double-checked, and triple-checked Safavi's credentials and his story, his motives, and his reasons for this defection. He worked as a chief physicist at the secret, heavily fortified Fordo Plant near Qom, in northern Iran. He was not married and had very few friends. He lived with his elderly mother and a younger brother but was almost always away because of work. Safavi was a devoted Muslim, but moderate in his beliefs. Afraid of the new wave of killings of nuclear scientists all over Iran—the most recent a month ago in the heart of the capital, Tehran—Safavi had decided to get out while he still could.

A defection scenario was one of the most difficult and dreaded operations by all secret agents. It was a ticking bomb waiting to explode at any second. No matter how hard one tried to cover all the angles, there were too many variables that could not be identified, let alone controlled. Was Safavi really defecting or simply luring the agents into an ambush? Was his intelligence going to be any good? Useful? Actionable? Was he a double agent, sent by the Iranians to spy on the CIS and their partner agencies and give them bogus information?

These and many other questions ran through Justin's mind. He had no answers to most of them. The potential of securing a highly valued defector and top secret intelligence had convinced him to set foot again on Iranian soil. He had picked this remote meeting point—fifteen miles south of the Turkmenistan-Iran border—and had set up every detail of the operation. And now here they were, a mile away from their meeting point, almost two hours past their appointed time, and the defector was nowhere to be seen.

"Anything new?" Justin asked Nathan, who was keeping an eye on the road.

"No, nothing. What did Ruslan say?"

"He threatened to leave us here. He's not gonna do it."

Justin looked at Nathan's calm face. He was twenty-seven, ten years his junior, but already a great field agent. In the absence of his regular partner Carrie O'Connor—who was searching for her father's grave in Grozny, Chechnya—Justin and Nathan had previously worked together in a reconnaissance mission in Mali. Nathan's orienteering skills had saved their lives after their local contacts were shot dead. Even if the drug runners left them behind, Nathan would be able to find his way through the dry river beds and over the hills and back to Turkmenistan.

Nathan raised his binoculars. "I see some movement. A silver Toyota."

Justin fell to the ground and stared at the road through his binoculars. The Toyota was travelling very fast for the dirt road, bouncing over natural speed bumps and dipping into shallow potholes. A long tail of gray dust clouded the view behind the car.

"That's our man?" Nathan asked.

"Not sure. The Toyota matches the description, but I can't make out his face."

"Can't tell if he's being followed."

"We stay put until we have a visual."

Justin crawled forward and followed the car through his carbine scope. It would be practically impossible for the driver and any passengers in the Toyota to spot Justin's and Nathan's position from that distance. Even if the car stopped and someone searched the hilltop, the chances of finding the carbine muzzle were extremely slim. Justin had picked their vantage point keeping in mind counter-surveillance tactics. A few shrubs, some rocks jutting out of the ground, and two heaps of sand formed a natural cover in front of their position.

The Toyota followed the curved road, slowed down, then stopped. Justin had given Safavi the GPS coordinates of their meeting point, and the car was right on the designated spot. The driver rolled down his window, as per Justin's instructions.

"That's Safavi," Justin said.

His features matched those of the pictures Justin had seen, except for the curtain of sweat flowing down the man's black and gray beard. Safavi's eyes had dark circles around them. He ran his hands through his receding hair and fixed his black-rimmed glasses. Then he looked out the window.

Justin moved the sight of his scope to the back seats. It seemed there was no one else in the Toyota, but he had no way of being completely sure. He reached for his satellite phone and dialed Safavi's number.

"You're late," Justin said in English. "What happened?"

"Traffic, I ran into heavy traffic." Safavi's voice was weak, and he was huffing as if trying to catch his breath. Justin looked through the carbine's scope. Safavi's hands were shaking, and he almost dropped his cellphone. "There was also an accident. Not me. A truck."

"Anyone else with you in the car?" he asked.

"No. I'm alone."

"Anyone follow you?"

"No. I don't think so."

"You're not sure?"

"I didn't see anyone following me."

The cloud of dust had started to thin out. Justin surveyed the road for the next five, six, then seven miles behind Safavi's car. No trace of a tail. He raised his scope and scanned the horizon. No sign of any helicopter or airplane. It seemed everything was going according to the plan.

"You see anything strange?" he asked Nathan, who had been mimicking Justin's reconnaissance actions.

"No, but that's doesn't mean it's not there."

"Uh-huh." Justin grunted. He spoke to Safavi over the phone, "Turn off the car, but leave the key in. Take everything you need and step out."

Safavi followed Justin's orders. A briefcase hung from his left hand. "Where are you?"

"We'll meet you soon. Start walking toward the north. Stay on the road. Stop once five minutes have passed."

"In the sun?"

Justin sighed. "Yes, in the sun. I'll call you in five."

"All right."

Safavi began to walk slowly. He was wearing dress shoes, almost useless for the hike he had just started. The briefcase was not heavy. It was swinging back and forth as he took small steps.

"Keep an eye on him and on the car. I'm going to meet him. I'll tell you when I know he's clean." Justin tapped his throat mike, while looking at Nathan.

Nathan nodded. He placed his eye on his C8 carbine's scope. His index finger caressed the trigger.

Justin crawled backwards until he reached the boulder then jumped to his feet. "Our contact's here," he told Ruslan when he got to the Nissan. "I'm going to meet with him. Mehmet will let you know when I've gotten what I need. At that time, bring the car around. Meet me down at the road, and we'll get out of here. Is that clear?"

Ruslan nodded and showed Justin his crooked teeth. "Yes," he muttered and lit up a cigar.

* * *

Justin skirted around the hill, watching his step for loose rocks. His feet sank ankle deep into the sand as he slithered downhill, hidden from Safavi's line of sight. He advanced fast, moving toward the next hill to his right, always keeping Safavi's car in his peripheral vision. At the same time, he checked farther away on both sides of the road, as well as the peaks of surrounding hills and the horizon. The operation seemed to be running without a glitch.

He popped out in the open at the bottom of the hill, about half a mile away from Safavi, who saw him right away. Safavi stopped and switched the briefcase from one hand to the other. Justin gestured for him to keep walking and come closer. At the same time, Justin pulled out his H&K P30 pistol from the knapsack on his shoulders and pointed it at Safavi.

Safavi continued to walk with unsteady steps, glancing at the hillside from where Justin had appeared. He seemed to have quickened his pace. At some point, he raised his hand to protect his face and his head from the sun. Once he was close enough to notice the gun, he shrugged and shook his head.

"Stop, stop," Justin called out to him. "Put the briefcase on the ground and open it slowly."

"Why? Is this necessary?"

"Yes. I explained to you it's our standard procedure."

"But I don't understand."

"You don't have to. Just do it."

Safavi opened the briefcase.

"Leave it there and keep walking toward me for another fifty yards."

Safavi shook his head again but followed Justin's order.

"Now what?" he asked when he reached the spot.

"Get on your knees facing me, lock your hands behind your head, and do not, *I repeat,* do not look behind you. Got it?"

"Do we have to do this?"

"You agreed to these terms. Now keep your side of the deal." Justin gestured with his gun at a point on the side of the road. "Right there."

Safavi shuffled his feet and followed Justin's orders to the dot. "Satisfied now?"

"Delighted. Don't move."

"This is too much. I'm here because I want to be here, not to kill you."

Justin ignored his words and advanced carefully, keeping his gun trained on Safavi at all times. Once he reached the man, he circled around him. Safavi's jacket was open. He was wearing no suicide bomber vest or belt. Justin pulled out a pair of plastic handcuffs and snapped them on Safavi's wrists. He offered no resistance. Justin patted him down and removed Safavi's cellphone from one of his pants pockets. Once he was convinced the defector was clean, Justin spoke to Nathan, telling him to come out and meet them.

"Get up." Justin helped Safavi to his feet. "We're good. That was for your protection and for mine. Don't turn around."

"Do you not trust me?"

"I don't trust anyone."

Justin walked over to the briefcase. It contained only a thick folder with documents, pictures, sketches, and diagrams. He flipped through the pages. They were mostly in Farsi, but a few were in English. Justin recognized some formulas and sketches he was trained to look for and the universal chemical symbols Pu and U of Plutonium and Uranium, two elements used to make a nuclear bomb. He picked up the folder and returned to Safavi.

Nathan was heading toward the Toyota. He inspected it from a distance, looking for any signs it might be explosive-rigged. Keeping his carbine in a two-handed position ready to fire, he stepped closer to the car. He looked through the windows then opened the doors. He searched the seats and underneath them, and popped the trunk. Once his search was complete, he flashed Justin the OK sign with his arm raised up. "It's all good here. The car's clean."

"You can turn around now," Justin said.

Safavi's face was covered in sweat. He was panting. He did a double take when he saw a man in military fatigues with an assault rifle in his hand coming toward them from the direction of his car.

Justin removed Safavi's handcuffs. "Don't worry. He's Mehmet, my partner."

"OK, and you're Mohammed, right?"

Civilians. "Yes, I am."

Justin showed Safavi his cellphone. "You won't need this anymore." He removed the SIM card and the battery. He broke the SIM card in half and threw the pieces on the ground, along with the battery. "You won't need the Toyota either."

"How are we getting away?" Safavi's voice carried a hint of concern.

"We've got our own transport."

"What will happen to the car?"

"One of the locals will snatch it. Authorities will never find it."

"And my friend?"

"What about him?"

"It's his car."

"I hope he has insurance."

Justin had worked out Safavi's disappearance. He was to borrow a friend's car for a short vacation in Rasht—an Iranian city on the Caspian Sea—to escape the stress of work. After being seen by many witnesses walking along the seashore, acting illogically, and rambling to himself, he was to get into the water with his clothes on and be seen no more. Then, he was to change into a different outfit and drive to their meeting point.

"You followed our plan to the letter, did you?" Justin asked.

"Yes, I did."

"And no one followed you?"

"I saw no one."

Nathan was a few feet away when the Nissan appeared on the side of the road. Ruslan had taken the scenic route.

"That's our transport. Let's go," Justin said.

When they reached the car, Ruslan asked, "Who is this?"

"Our contact," Justin replied.

"He gave you the information?"

Justin raised the folder. "He did."

"So he's not coming with us."

"Of course he is."

"Our deal was not to—"

"Listen, I don't have time for this bullshit." Justin stood an inch away from Ruslan's face. "He comes with us. You have a problem with that, talk to Colonel Garryev."

Ruslan cursed through his teeth. "What are you looking at?" he barked at the driver. "Start the car."

Justin sat behind the driver, Safavi behind Ruslan. Nathan threw their C8 carbines and knapsacks in the trunk and slid in the third row of seats. The driver started the car, and they continued along the dirt road.

Safavi was perched on the edge of the seat, his hands trembling.

Justin offered him his canteen. "You made it," he said, resting his hand on Safavi's shoulder. "There's nothing to fear now. We'll be across the border in a few minutes."

Safavi nodded but did not take a drink.

Justin passed the folder with Safavi's intelligence to Nathan. He shuffled through the documents. "Is this all?"

"Yes. It's plenty to convince any scientists that Iran is very, very close to having a nuclear weapon. The rest of the evidence is here, in my mind." Safavi tapped his left temple. "I will tell you everything I know once—"

The explosion of the window glass and the bullet striking his head ended his sentence. Blood and brain matter sprayed Justin's face. Safavi's head slammed again his shoulder.

"What the hell was that?" Ruslan shouted.

The driver panicked. He drove the Nissan toward a pile of rocks at the side of the road. Ruslan slapped him on the back of his head and reached to grab a hold of the steering wheel. Justin snapped his head to the side to look out the window for the shooter. He took in the entire landscape in a quick sweep. Everything was as peaceful as a moment ago. But the defector was dead, blood spurting from the bullet hole in his head.

"See anything?" Justin shouted at Nathan.

"No. Nothing. No shooter."

"What the hell was that?" Ruslan asked again.

The side window shattered, and Ruslan's head exploded. His blood spattered the driver and the car's interior.

"Who's shooting? Who's killing us?" shouted the driver. He stared at Ruslan's blank eyes.

"Sniper at nine o'clock. Four, five hundred yards," Justin shouted, suppressing the anger rising in his voice. He had followed the angle of the shot and had discovered the shooter. He pointed to a tall ridge overlooking the road with a sweaty, shaky hand. They had searched that area earlier but had seen no traces of a sniper's nest. He swore under his breath.

"I see no movement, but it looks like a perfect place," Nathan said. He recalibrated his binoculars. "Yes, he's there. I see him."

The Nissan veered off and headed for a ditch, the driver still staring at Ruslan. Another round slammed the side of the car.

"Watch the ditch! The ditch!" Justin yelled.

The driver snapped out of his trance and steered the car back to the road. It fell into a deep pothole that almost broke its shock absorbers. The driver pressed the gas pedal, and the Nissan bounced back onto the dirt road.

"Turn, turn, left, then right!" Justin ordered the driver. "Make it harder for the shooter. And get us out of this road!"

Nathan reached for their carbines. He handed Justin his, then swung his own carbine over his shoulder, rammed the barrel through the window glass and began hammering away at the sniper's nest.

Justin did the same. He blasted round after round. A hollow click signaled an empty chamber. He reloaded in a flash. He had little hope their shots were going to hit the sniper. Their enemy's nest was within their carbines' maximum fire range, but well beyond their effective range of three hundred yards. They were in a moving vehicle, and its driver was taking sharp turns. Their suppressive fire was intended to keep the sniper down or reduce his efficiency. At least for a few more seconds.

The driver found a flat patch of barren land, clear of any large boulders, and turned the steering wheel in that direction. He misjudged the distance, and the Nissan's front tire hit a large rock. The car tilted to its right side as it climbed over the obstacle, then sank at the edge of a sand bank. The driver hit the gas pedal. The Nissan groaned and jerked forward, but went nowhere. A bullet pierced the back window.

Nathan let off a long barrage, a full thirty-round magazine.

The driver swore and shifted gears. He gave the gas pedal a light touch. The tires spun. He steered to the left, toward the hard ground. The car inched forward with a rattle. He pressed the gas pedal again. The car responded, and they slid downhill. They took two more turns, rounded the hill and were finally out of the line of fire.

Justin pressed his pistol against the driver's head. "Stop the car."

"What? What are you doing? Why?"

"Stop the car. Last time."

The driver slammed the brakes. The car came to an abrupt halt. He raised his hands up.

"How did they learn about us?" Justin asked. "Whom did you call? Whom did Ruslan call?"

"I don't . . . I don't know. Don't kill me. I called . . . called nobody."

"Did *he* call anyone?"

"No, no, he didn't."

Justin shoved his gun deeper into the back of the driver's head. "Don't lie to me."

"I'm not lying. Check my phone and Ruslan's phone. We had no idea where we were going. Remember, you only told us it was somewhere in Iran. You gave us directions as we drove. Don't kill me. We didn't betray you."

"But who did? Who did this?" He nodded toward the dead bodies.

Nathan got out of the car and searched Ruslan for his cellphone. He reached into the driver's jacket and got his as well. He scanned quickly through their call logs.

"Get out of the car," Justin said. He kept his gun pointed at the driver, as they both climbed out of the Nissan.

Nathan frowned. "He's telling the truth. No phone calls since this morning, before we left." He handed the driver back his cellphone.

Justin sighed.

"OK, so how the hell did they know? They were waiting for us."

Nathan glanced at the dead defector then at Justin.

Justin narrowed his eyes. "No, it can't be him. I gave him general directions and told him the exact coordinates only this morning. And a sniper doesn't just happen. Not such a good sniper."

Nathan took Justin to the side, away from the driver. He couldn't hear their words, but they could still keep an eye on him.

"What if the defector was a double agent? Entices us with his story, then tells the Revolutionary Guards about our position," Nathan said.

"But they killed him."

"Perhaps that bullet wasn't meant for him."

"It was easier to target us when we were walking toward him. Why wait until we're in the car?"

Nathan shrugged then looked over Justin's shoulder at the driver, who was trying to light a cigarette. Justin turned around and saw the driver's hands shaking so much he succeeded only on his fourth try.

"Maybe he wasn't in position yet. Too little time to prepare."

Justin shook his head. "No, it doesn't make sense. The Guards—or whoever the sniper is—wouldn't just send a man or two. They would send an army and attempt to take us alive."

Nathan nodded.

Justin glanced around the area. "Something doesn't fit quite right. But I can't tell what it is."

"That sniper is a great marksman. Maybe he thought a clear shot was too easy. He wanted to make the game interesting, challenging. That's why he waited until we got into the car."

Justin wiped some of Safavi's blood from his forehead. "Whatever it is, we don't have to figure it out now. Take the folder and everything else we need out of the car. I'll call for an exfil."

"Got it."

They returned to the car at a fast pace.

"Are we leaving now?" the driver asked.

"Yes. On foot. You're welcome to join us."

The driver frowned, looking down at his belly. He was in no shape to hike the rugged hills. "Why not take the car?"

"Because it has a bull's-eye painted on the back. The sniper will call for reinforcements. If they dispatch a helicopter, the Nissan will be your coffin. We have a better chance of survival if we ditch the car."

The driver seemed to mull over Justin's words. Justin loaded his knapsack on his shoulders then picked up his carbine. He walked over to Safavi and gave him a last glance. "I wish I could give you a proper burial," he muttered, "especially if you had nothing to do with this."

Nathan was ready, waiting for Justin.

"Are you coming?" Justin asked the driver.

He shook his head.

"Fine. If you make it, I'll call you. We need to meet and figure out what exactly happened here and why."

The driver nodded after a brief pause.

Nathan took a step forward. "This way," he said, pointing toward a steep path winding around the hill. "We'll be safe soon enough." He began marching.

Justin raised his satellite phone to his ear and followed him. "Let's hope the Guards' choppers don't find us before our exfiltration team.

6769823R00176

Made in the USA
San Bernardino, CA
15 December 2013